Bonnie Prince Charlie : a Tale of Fontenoy and Culloden

by G. A. Henty

Copyright © 7/23/2015
Jefferson Publication

ISBN-13: 978-1515204527

Printed in the United States of America

All rights reserved. No part of this book may be reprinted or reproduced or utilized in any form or by any electronic, mechanical, or other means, now known or hereafter invented, including photocopying and recording, or in any form of storage or retrieval system, without prior permission in writing from the publisher.'

Contents

CHAPTER I: The Return of a Prodigal. 3
CHAPTER II: The Jacobite Agent. 8
CHAPTER III: Free. 13
CHAPTER IV: In France. 17
CHAPTER V: Dettingen. 22
CHAPTER VI: The Convent of Our Lady. 26
CHAPTER VII: Mother! 31
CHAPTER VIII: Hidden Foes. 36
CHAPTER IX: Fontenoy. 39
CHAPTER X: A Perilous Journey. 43
CHAPTER XI: Free. 48
CHAPTER XII: The End of the Quarrel. 53
CHAPTER XIII: Prince Charles. 58
CHAPTER XIV: Prestonpans. 63
CHAPTER XV: A Mission. 67
CHAPTER XVI: The March to Derby. 71
CHAPTER XVII: A Baffled Plot. 76
CHAPTER XVIII: Culloden. 80
CHAPTER XIX: Fugitives. 84
CHAPTER XX: Happy Days. 89

CHAPTER I: The Return of a Prodigal.

It was a dull evening in the month of September, 1728. The apprentices had closed and barred the shutters and the day's work was over. Supper was laid in the long room over the shop, the viands were on the table, and round it were standing Bailie Anderson and his wife, his foreman John Gillespie, and his two apprentices. The latter were furtively eying the eatables, and wondering how much longer the grace which their master was delivering would be. Suddenly there was a knock at the door below. No one stirred until the bailie had finished his grace, before which time the knock had been twice repeated.

"Elspeth, woman," the bailie said when he had brought the grace to an end, "go down below and see who knocks so impatiently; look through the grille before you open the door; these are nor times when one opens to the first stranger who knocks."

The old servant, who had been standing behind her mistress, went downstairs. The door was opened, and they heard an exclamation of surprise at the answer to her question, "Who is it that's knocking as if the house belonged to him?"

Those gathered up stairs heard the bolts withdrawn. There was a confused sound of talking and then a heavy step was heard ascending the stairs, and without introduction a tall man, wrapped in a cloak and carrying a child of some two years old, strode into the room. He threw his hat on to a settle and advanced straight towards the bailie, who looked in surprise at this unceremonious entry.

"Don't you know me, Andrew?"

"Heaven preserve us," the bailie exclaimed, "why it's Malcolm!"

"Malcolm himself," the visitor repeated, "sound in wind and limb."

"The Lord be praised!" the bailie exclaimed as he grasped the other's hand and wrung it warmly. "I had thought you dead years and years ago. Janet, this is my brother Malcolm of whom you have often heard me speak."

"And of whom you can have heard little good, mistress, if my brother has spoken the truth concerning me. I was ever a ne'er do well, while Andrew struck hard and fast to our father's trade."

"My husband has ever spoken with affection of you," Janet Anderson said. "The bailie is not given to speak ill of any, much less of his own flesh and blood."

"And now sit down, Malcolm. Supper is waiting, and you are, I doubt not, ready for it. It is ill talking to a fasting man. When you have done you shall tell me what you have been doing for the last fifteen years, and how it comes that you thus suddenly come back among us with your boy."

"He is no boy of mine," Malcolm said; "but I will tell you all about it presently. First let me lay him down on that settle, for the poor little chap is fast asleep and dead tired out. Elspeth, roll up my cloak and make a pillow for him. That's right, he will do nicely now. You are changed less than any of us, Elspeth. Just as hard to look at, and, I doubt not, just as soft at heart as you used to be when you tried to shield me when I got into scrapes. And now to supper."

Little was said during the meal; fortunately the table was bounteously spread, for the newcomer's appetite was prodigious; but at last he was satisfied, and after a long drink at the horn beside him, which Elspeth had kept filled with ale, he said:

"There's nothing like a Scottish meal after all, Andrew. French living is well enough for a time, but one tires of it; and many a time when I have been lying down supperless on the sod, after marching and fighting the whole day, I have longed for a bowl of porridge and a platter well filled with oatmeal cakes."

Supper over, John and the apprentices retired. Elspeth went off to prepare the guest's chamber and to make up a little bed for the child.

"Now, brother, let us hear your story; but, first of all, perhaps you want to light your pipe?"

"That do I," Malcolm replied, "if Mistress Janet has no objection thereto."

"She is accustomed to it," the bailie said, answering for her. "I smoke myself; I deem that tobacco, like other things, was given for our use, and methinks that with a pipe between the lips men's brains work more easily and that it leadeth to pleasant converse."

Janet went to a cupboard, brought out two long pipes and a jar of tobacco, placed two tumblers, a flat bottle, and a jug of water on the table.

"That is right," the bailie said. "I do not often touch strong waters. The habit, as I see too plainly, is a harmful one, and in this good city of Glasgow there are many, even of those so placed that they should be an example to their fellows, who are given nightly to drink more than is good for them; but on an occasion like the present I deem it no harm to take a glass."

"I should think not," Malcolm said heartily; "it is long since I tasted a glass of real Scotch spirit, and I never need an excuse for taking a glass of whatever it be that comes in my way. Not, Mistress Janet, that I am a toper. I don't say that at the sack of a town, or at times when liquor is running, so to speak, to waste, I am more backward than the rest; but my hand wouldn't be as steady as it is if I had been one of those who are never so happy as when they are filling themselves with liquor. And now, Andrew, to my story. You know that when I saw you last--just when the troubles in '15 began--in spite of all your warnings to the contrary, I must needs throw myself into the thick of them. You, like a wise man, stuck to your shop, and here you are now a bailie of Glasgow; while I, who have been wandering over the face of the earth fighting for the cause of France and risking my life a thousand times in a matter which concerned me in no way, have returned just as penniless as I set out."

"It is said, brother Malcolm," Janet said mildly, "that a rolling stone gathers no moss."

"That is true enough," Malcolm assented; "and yet do you know there are few rolling stones who, if their time were to come over again, would remain fixed in their bed. Of course we have not the pleasures of home, of wives and children; but the life of adventure has its own joys, which I, for one, would not change for the others. However, brother, as you know, I threw myself heart and soul into that business.

"The last time I saw you was just as I was starting with a score of others to make our way to join the Earl of Mar's army at Perth. I have seen many an army since, but never did I see sixteen thousand finer fighting men than were there assembled. The Laird of Mackintosh brought five hundred clansmen from Inverness shire, the Marquis of Huntly had five hundred horse and two thousand foot, and the Earl Marischal had a thousand men. The Laird of Glenlyon brought five hundred Campbells, and the Marquis of Tullibardine fourteen hundred, and a score of other chiefs of less power were there with their clansmen. There were enough men there to have done anything had they been properly armed and led; but though arms and ammunition had been promised from France, none came, and the Earl of Mar had so little decision that he would have wrecked the finest army that ever marched.

"The army lay doing nothing for weeks, and just before we were expecting a movement, the company I belonged to was sent with a force of Highlanders under Mackintosh to join the army under the Lords Derwentwater, Kenmure, and Nithsdale. Lord Derwentwater had risen with a number of other gentlemen, and with their attendants and friends had marched against Newcastle. They had done nothing there but remained idle near Hexham till, joined by a force raised in the Lowlands of Scotland by the Earls of Nithsdale, Carnwath, and Wintoun, the united army marched north again to Kelso, where we joined them.

"We Scots soon saw that we had gained nothing by the change of commanders. Lord Derwentwater was ignorant of military affairs, and he was greatly swayed by a Mr. Forster, who was somehow at the head of the business, and who was not only incompetent, but proved to be a coward, if not, as most folks believed, a traitor. So dissension soon broke out, and four hundred Highlanders marched away north. After a long delay it was resolved to move south, where, it was said, we should be joined by great numbers in Lancashire; but by this time all had greatly lost spirit and hope in the enterprise. We crossed the border and marched down through Penrith, Appleby, and Kendal to Lancaster, and then on to Preston.

"I was little more than a lad, Andrew, but even to me it seemed madness thus to march into England with only two thousand men. Of these twelve hundred were foot, commanded by Brigadier Mackintosh; the others were horse. There were two troops of Stanhope's dragoons quartered in Preston, but these retired when we neared the town, and we entered without opposition. Next day, which was, I remember, the 10th of November, the Chevalier was proclaimed king, and some country gentlemen with their tenants came in and joined us.

"I suppose it would have come to the same thing in the end, but never were things so badly managed as they were by Mr. Forster.

"Preston was a strong natural position; an enemy coming from the south could only reach it by crossing a narrow bridge over the river Ribble a mile and a half away, and this could have been held by a company against an army. From the bridge to the town the road was so narrow that in several places two men could not ride abreast. It ran between two high and steep banks, and it was here that Cromwell was nearly killed when he attacked Charles's troops.

"Well, all these places, where we might certainly have defended ourselves, were neglected, and we were all kept in the town, where we formed four main posts. One was in the churchyard, and this was commanded by Brigadier Mackintosh. In support of this was the volunteer horse under Derwentwater and the three other lords. Lord Charles Murray was in command at a barricade at a little distance from the churchyard. Colonel Mackintosh had charge of a post at a windmill; and the fourth was in the centre of the town.

"Lord Derwentwater was a poor general, but he was a brave man. He and his two brothers, the Ratcliffs, rode about everywhere, setting an example of coolness, animating the soldiers, and seeing to the work on the barriers. Two days after we reached the town we heard that General Wilde was approaching. Colonel Farquharson was sent forward with a portion of Mackintosh's battalion to hold the bridge and the pass; but Mr. Forster, who went out on horseback, no sooner saw the enemy approaching than he gave orders to Farquharson and his men to retreat to the town. If I had been in Farquharson's place I would have put a bullet through the coward's head, and would have defended the bridge till the last.

"After that everything was confusion; the Highlanders came back into the town furious and disheartened. The garrison prepared to receive the enemy. Mr. Forster was seen no more, and in fact he went straight back to the house where he was lodging and took his bed, where he remained till all was over. The enemy came on slowly. They could not understand why strong posts should be left undefended, and feared falling in an ambuscade. I was at the post commanded by Brigadier Mackintosh. I had joined a company commanded by Leslie of Glenlyon, who had brought with him some twenty men, and had made up his company with men who, like myself, came up without a leader. His company was attached to Mackintosh's regiment.

"Presently the English came in sight, and as soon as they ascertained that we were still there, which they had begun to doubt, they attacked us. We beat them back handsomely, and Derwentwater with his cavalry charged their dragoons so fiercely that he drove them out of the town. It was late in the afternoon when the fight began, and all night the struggle went on. At each of our posts we beat them back over and over again. The town was on fire in half a dozen places, but luckily the night was still and the flames did not spread. We knew that it was a hopeless fight we were making; for, from some prisoners, we learned that three regiments of dragoons were also coming up against us, and had already arrived at Clitheroe. From some inhabitants, I suppose, the enemy learned that the street leading to Wigan had not been barricaded, and Lord Forrester brought up Preston's regiment by this way, and suddenly fell on the flank of our barrier. It was a tough fight, but we held our own till the news came that Forster had agreed to capitulate.

"I don't say that our case wasn't hopeless. We were outnumbered and had no leader; sooner or later we must have been overpowered. Still, no capitulation should have been made except on the terms of mercy to all concerned. But Forster no doubt felt safe about himself, and that was all he cared for; and the end showed that he knew what he was about, for while all the brave young noblemen, and numbers of others, were either executed or punished in other ways, Forster, who had been the leading spirit who had persuaded them to rise, and led them into this strait, was after a short imprisonment suffered to go free. I tell you, brother Andrew, if I were to meet him now, even if it were in a church, I would drive my dagger into his heart.

"However, there we were. So furious were we that it was with difficulty the officers could prevent us from sallying out sword in hand and trying to cut our way through the enemy. As to Forster, if he had appeared in the streets he would have been hewn to pieces. However, it was useless to resist now; the English troops marched in and we laid down our arms, and our battalions marched into a church and were guarded as prisoners. It was not a great army they had taken, for there were but one thousand four hundred and ninety captured, including noblemen, gentlemen, and officers.

"Many of us were wounded more or less. I had got a slice on the shoulder from a dragoon's sword. This I gained when rushing out to rescue Leslie, who had been knocked down, and would have been slain by three dragoons had I not stood over him till some of our men rushed out and carried him in. He was not badly hurt, the sword having turned as it cut through his bonnet. My action won his regard, and from that time until a month since we have never been separated. Under a strong escort of soldiers we were marched south. In most places the country people mocked us as we passed; but here and there we saw among the crowds who gathered in the streets of the towns through which we passed, faces which we passed, faces which expressed pity and sympathy

"We were not badly treated on the march by our guard, and had little to complain of. When we reached Barnet we fell out as usual when the march was over, and I went up to the door of a house and asked a woman, who looked pityingly at us, for a drink of water. She brought me some, and while I drank she said:

"'We are Catholics and well wishers of the Chevalier; if you can manage to slip in here after it is dark we will furnish you with a disguise, and will direct you to friends who will pass you on until you can escape.'

"'Can you give me disguises for two?' I asked. 'I will not go without my captain.'

"'Yes,' she said, 'for two, but no more.'

"'I will steal away after dark,' I said as I gave her back the jug.

"I told Leslie what had happened, and he agreed to join me in time to escape, for there was no saying what fate might befall us in London; and, indeed, the very next morning severities commenced, the whole of the troops being obliged to suffer the indignity of having their arms tied behind them, and so being marched into London.

"After it was dark Leslie and I managed to steal away from our guards, who were not very watchful, for our uniform would at once have betrayed us, and the country people would have seized and handed us over. The woman was on the watch, and as soon as we neared the door she opened it. Her husband was with her and received us kindly. He at once furnished us with the attire of two countrymen, and, letting us out by a back way, started with us across the country.

"After walking twenty miles he brought us to the house of another adherent of the Chevalier, where we remained all day. So we were passed on until we reached the coast, where we lay hid for some days until an arrangement was made with the captain of a fishing boat to take us to sea, and either to land us at Calais or to put us on board a French fishing boat. So we got over without trouble.

"Long before that, as you know, the business had virtually come to an end here. The Earl of Mar's army lay week after week at Perth, till at last it met the enemy under Argyle at Sheriffmuir.

"You know how that went. The Highland clans in the right and centre carried all before them, and drove the enemy from the field, but on the left they beat us badly. So both parties claimed the victory. But, victory or defeat, it was fatal to the cause of the Chevalier. Half the Highland clans went off to their homes that night, and Mar had to fall back to Perth.

"Well, that was really the end of it. The Chevalier landed, and for a while our hopes rose. He did nothing, and our hopes fell. At last he took ship and went away, and the affair was over, except for the hangings and slaughterings.

"Leslie, like most of the Scottish gentlemen who succeeded in reaching France, took service with the French king, and, of course, I did the same. It would have done your heart good to see how the Scottish regiments fought on many a field; the very best troops of France were never before us, and many a tough field was decided by our charge. Leslie was a cornet. He was about my age; and you know I was but twenty when Sheriffmuir was fought. He rose to be a colonel, and would have given me a pair of colours over and over again if I would have taken them; but I felt more comfortable among our troopers than I should have done among the officers, who were almost all men of good Highland family; so I remained Leslie's right hand.

"A braver soldier never swung a leg over saddle; but he was always in some love affair or another. Why he didn't marry I couldn't make out. I suppose he could never stick long enough to one woman. However, some four years ago he got into an affair more serious than any he had been in before, and this time he stuck to it in right earnest. Of course she was precisely one of the women he oughtn't to have fallen in love with, though I for one couldn't blame him, for a prettier creature wasn't to be found in France. Unfortunately she was the only daughter of the Marquis de Recambours, one of the wealthiest and most powerful of French nobles, and there was no more chance of his giving his consent to her throwing herself away upon a Scottish soldier of fortune than to her going into a nunnery; less, in fact. However, she was as much in love with Leslie as he was with her, and so they got secretly married. Two years ago this child was born, but she managed somehow to keep it from her father, who was all this time urging her to marry the Duke de Chateaurouge.

"At last, as ill luck would have it, he shut her up in a convent just a week before she had arranged to fly with Leslie to Germany, where he intended to take service until her father came round. Leslie would have got her out somehow; but his regiment was ordered to the frontier, and it was eighteen months before we returned to Paris, where the child had been in keeping with some people with whom he had placed it. The very evening of his return I was cleaning his arms when he rushed into the room.

"'All is discovered,' he said; 'here is my signet ring, go at once and get the child, and make your way with it to Scotland; take all the money in the escritoire, quick!'

"I heard feet approaching, and dashed to the bureau, and transferred the bag of louis there to my pocket. An official with two followers entered.

"'Colonel Leslie,' he said, 'it is my duty to arrest you by order of his gracious majesty;' and he held out an order signed by the king.

"'I am unconscious of having done any wrong, sir, to his majesty, whom I have served for the last sixteen years. However, it is not for me to dispute his orders;' thereupon he unbuckled his sword and handed it to the officers. 'You will look after the things till I return, Malcolm. As I am sure I can clear myself of any charge that may be brought against me, I trust to be speedily back again.

"'Your trooper need not trouble himself,' the officer said; 'the official with me will take charge of everything, and will at once affix my seal to all your effects.'

"I went down stairs and saw the colonel enter a carriage with the two officials, then I went straight to the major. 'Colonel Leslie has been arrested, sir, on what charge I know not. He has intrusted a commission to me. Therefore, if you find I am absent from parade in the morning you will understand I am carrying out his orders.'

"The major was thunderstruck at the news, but told me to do as the colonel had ordered me, whatever it might be. I mounted the colonel's horse at once and rode to the house where the child was in keeping. The people knew me well, as I had often been there with messages from the colonel. When I showed them the signet ring, and told them that I had orders to take the child to his father, they made no opposition. I said I would return for him as soon as it was dusk. I then went and purchased a suit of civilian clothes, and returning to the house attired myself in these, and taking the child on the saddle before me, rode for the frontier.

"Following unfrequented roads, travelling only at night, and passing a day in a wood, I passed the frontier unmolested, and made my way to Ostend, where I sold the horse and took passage in the first ship sailing for Leith. I arrived there two days ago, and have walked here, with an occasional lift in a cart; and here I am, brother Andrew, to ask you for hospitality for a while for myself and Leslie's boy. I have a hundred louis, but these, of course, belong to the child. As for myself, I confess I have nothing; saving has never been in my line."

"You are heartily welcome, Malcolm, as long as you choose to stop; but I trust that ere long you will hear of Colonel Leslie."

"I trust so," Malcolm said; "but if you knew the court of France as well as I do you would not feel very sanguine about it. It is easier to get into a prison than out of one."

"But the colonel has committed no crime!" the bailie said.

"His chance would be a great deal better if he had," Malcolm laughed. "A colonel of one of his majesty's Scottish regiments can do a good deal in the way of crime without much harm befalling him; but when it comes to marrying the daughter of a nobleman who is a great personage at court, without his consent, it is a different affair altogether, I can tell you. Leslie has powerful friends, and his brother officers will do what they can for him; but I can tell you services at the court of France go for very little. Influence is everything, and as the nobleman the marquis intended to be the husband of his daughter is also a great personage at court and a friend of Louis's, there is no saying how serious a matter they may make of it. Men have been kept prisoners for life for a far less serious business than this."

"But supposing he is released, does he know where to communicate with you?"

"I am afraid he doesn't," Malcolm said ruefully. "He knows that I come from Glasgow, but that is all. Still, when he is freed, no doubt he will come over himself to look for his son, and I am sure to hear of his being here."

"You might do, and you might not," the bailie said. "Still, we must hope for the best, Malcolm. At any rate I am in no haste for the colonel to come. Now I have got you home again after all these years, I do not wish to lose you again in a hurry."

Malcolm only remained for a few weeks at his brother's house. The restraint of life at the bailie's was too much for him. Andrew's was a well ordered household. The bailie was methodical and regular, a leading figure in the kirk, far stricter than were most men of his time as to undue consumption of liquor, strong in exhortation in season and out of season. His wife was kindly but precise, and as outspoken as Andrew himself. For the first day or two the real affection which Andrew had for his younger brother, and the pleasure he felt at his return, shielded Malcolm from comment or rebuke; but after the very first day the bailie's wife had declared to herself that it was impossible that Malcolm could long remain an inmate of the house. She was not inhospitable, and would have made great sacrifices in some directions for the long missing brother of her husband; but his conduct outraged all the best feelings of a good Scotch housewife.

Even on that first day he did not come punctually to his meals. He was away about the town looking up old acquaintance, came in at dinner and again at supper after the meal had already begun, and dropped into his place and began to eat without saying a word of grace. He stamped about the house as if he had cavalry spurs still on his heels; talked in a voice that could be heard from attic to basement; used French and Flemish oaths which horrified the good lady, although she did not understand them; smoked at all hours of the day, whereas Andrew always confined himself to his after supper pipe, and, in spite of his assertions on the previous evening, consumed an amount of liquor which horrified the good woman.

At his meals he talked loudly, kept the two apprentices in a titter with his stories of campaigning, spoke slightingly of the city authorities, and joked the bailie with a freedom and roughness which scandalized her. Andrew was slow to notice the incongruity of his brother's demeanour and bearing with the atmosphere of the house, although he soon became dimly conscious that there was a jarring element in the air. At the end of a week Malcolm broached the subject to him.

"Andrew," he said, "you are a good fellow, though you are a bailie and an elder of the kirk, and I thank you for the hearty welcome you have given me, and for your invitation to stay for a long time with you; but it will not do. Janet is a good woman and a kindly, but I can see that I keep her perpetually on thorns. In good truth, fifteen years of campaigning are but an indifferent preparation for a man as an inmate of a respectable household. I did not quite know myself how thoroughly I had become a devil may care trooper until I came back to my old life here. The ways of your house would soon be as intolerable to me as my ways are to your good wife, and therefore it is better by far that before any words have passed between you and me, and while we are as good friends as on the evening when I returned, I should get out of this. I met an old friend today, one of the lads who went with me from Glasgow to join the Earl of Mar at Perth. He is well to do now, and trades in cattle, taking them in droves down into England. For the sake of old times he has offered me employment, and methinks it will suit me as well as any other."

"But you cannot surely be going as a drover, Malcolm!"

"Why not? The life is as good as any other. I would not sit down, after these years of roving, to an indoor life. I must either do that or cross the water again and take service abroad. I am only six and thirty yet, and am good for another fifteen years of soldiering, and right gladly would I go back if Leslie were again at the head of his regiment, but I have been spoiled by him. He ever treated me as a companion and as a friend rather than as a trooper in his regiment, and I should miss him sorely did I enter any other service. Then, too, I would fain be here to be ready to join him again if he sends for me or comes, and I should wish to keep an eye always on his boy. You will continue to take charge of him, won't you, Andrew? He is still a little strange, but he takes to Elspeth, and will give little trouble when he once learns the language."

"I don't like it at all, Malcolm," the bailie said.

"No, Andrew, but you must feel it is best. I doubt not that ere this your wife has told you her troubles concerning me."

As the bailie on the preceding night had listened to a long string of complaints and remonstrances on the part of his wife as to his brother's general conduct he could not deny the truth of Malcolm's supposition.

"Just so, Andrew," Malcolm went on; "I knew that it must be so. Mistress Janet has kept her lips closed firm to me, but I could see how difficult it was for her sometimes to do so. It could not be otherwise. I am as much out of place here as a wolf in a sheepfold. As to the droving, I shall not mention to all I meet that I am brother to one of the bailies of Glasgow. I shall like the life. The rough pony I shall ride will differ in his paces from my old charger, but at least it will be life in the saddle. I shall be earning an honest living; if I take more than is good for me I may get a broken head and none be the wiser, whereas if I remain here and fall foul of the city watch it would be grief and pain for you."

The bailie was silenced. He had already begun to perceive that Malcolm's ways and manners were incompatible with the peace and quiet of a respectable household, and that Janet's complaints were not altogether unreasonable. He had seen many of his acquaintances lift their eyebrows in disapprobation at the roystering talk of his brother, and had foreseen that it was probable trouble would come.

At the same rime he felt a repugnance to the thought that after so many years of absence his brother should so soon quit his house. It seemed a reflection alike on his affection and hospitality.

"You will take charge of the child, won't you?" Malcolm pleaded. "There is a purse of a hundred louis, which will, I should say, pay for any expense to which he may put you for some years."

"As if I would take the bairn's money!" Andrew exclaimed angrily. "What do you take me for, Malcolm? Assuredly I will take the child. Janet and I have no bairn of our own, and it's good for a house to have a child in it. I look upon it as if it were yours, for it is like enough you will never hear of its father again. It will have a hearty welcome. It is a bright little fellow, and in time I doubt not that Janet will take greatly to it. The charge of a child is a serious matter, and we cannot hope that we shall not have trouble with it, but there is trouble in all things. At any rate, Malcolm, we will do our best, and if at the end of a year I find that Janet has not taken to it we will see about some other arrangement. And, Malcolm, I do trust that you will stay with us for another week or two. It would seem to me as if I had turned you out of my house were you to leave me so soon."

So Malcolm made a three weeks' stay at his brother's, and then started upon his new occupation of driving Highland cattle down into Lancashire. Once every two or three months he came to Glasgow for a week or two between his trips. In spite of Andrew's entreaties he refused on these occasions to take up his abode with him, but took a lodging not far off, coming in the evening for an hour to smoke a pipe with his brother, and never failing of a morning to come in and take the child for a long walk with him, carrying him upon his shoulder, and keeping up a steady talk with him in his native French, which he was anxious that the boy should nor forget, as at some time or other he might again return to France.

Some weeks after Malcolm's return to Scotland, he wrote to Colonel Leslie, briefly giving his address at Glasgow; but making no allusion to the child, as, if the colonel were still in prison, the letter would be sure to be opened by the authorities. He also wrote to the major, giving him his address, and begging him to communicate it to Colonel Leslie whenever he should see him; that done, there was nothing for it but to wait quietly. The post was so uncertain in those days that he had but slight hope that either of his letters would ever reach their destination. No answer came to either of his letters.

Four years later Malcolm went over to Paris, and cautiously made inquiries; but no one had heard anything of Colonel Leslie from the day he had been arrested. The regiment was away fighting in the Low Countries, and the only thing Malcolm could do was to call upon the people who had had charge of the child, to give them his address in case the colonel should ever appear to inquire of them. He found, however, the house tenanted by other people. He learned that the last occupants had left years before. The neighbors remembered that one morning early some officers of the law had come to the house, and the man had been seized and carried away. He had been released some months later, only to find that his wife had died of grief and anxiety, and he had then sold off his goods and gone no one knew whither. Malcolm, therefore, returned to Glasgow, with the feeling that he had gained nothing by his journey.

CHAPTER II: The Jacobite Agent.

So twelve years passed. Ronald Leslie grew up a sturdy lad, full of fun and mischief in spite of the sober atmosphere of the bailie's house; and neither flogging at school nor lecturing at home appeared to have the slightest effect in reducing him to that state of sober tranquillity which was in Mrs. Anderson's eyes the thing to be most desired in boys. Andrew was less deeply shocked than his wife at the discovery of Ronald's various delinquencies, but his sense of order and punctuality was constantly outraged. He was, however, really fond of the lad; and even Mrs. Anderson, greatly as the boy's ways constantly disturbed and ruffled her, was at heart as fond of him as was her husband. She considered, and not altogether wrongly, that his wilderness, as she called it, was in no slight degree due to his association with her husband's brother.

Ronald looked forward to the periodical visits of the drover with intense longing. He was sure of a sympathetic listener in Malcolm, who listened with approval to the tales of the various scrapes into which he had got since his last visit; of how, instead of going to school, he had played truant and with another boy his own age had embarked in a fisherman's boat and gone down the river and had not been able to get back until next day; how he had played tricks upon his dominie, and had conquered in single combat the son of Councillor Duff, the butcher, who had spoken scoffing words at the Stuarts. Malcolm was, in fact, delighted to find, that in spite of repression and lectures his young charge was growing up a lad of spirit. He still hoped that some day Leslie might return, and he knew how horrified he would be were he to find that his son was becoming a smug and well conducted citizen. No small portion of his time on each of his visits to Glasgow Malcolm spent in training the boy in the use of arms.

"Your father was a gentleman," he would say to him, "and it is fitting that you should know how to handle a gentleman's arms. Clubs are well enough for citizens' apprentices, but I would have you handle rapier and broadsword as well as any of the young lairds. When you get old enough, Ronald, you and I will cross the seas, and together we will try and get to the bottom of the mystery of your father's fate, and if we find that the worst has come to the worst, we will seek our your mother. She will most likely have married again. They will be sure to have forced her into it; but even if she dare not acknowledge you as her son, her influence may obtain for you a commission in one of the king's regiments, and even if they think I'm too old for a trooper I will go as your follower. There are plenty of occasions at the court of France when a sharp sword and a stout arm, even if it be somewhat stiffened by age, can do good service."

The lessons began as soon as Ronald was old enough to hold a light blade, and as between the pauses of exercise Malcolm was always ready to tell stories of his adventures in the wars of France, the days were full of delight to Ronald. When the latter reached the age of fourteen Malcolm was not satisfied with the amount of proficiency which the lad was able to gain during his occasional visits, and therefore took him for further instruction to a comrade who had, like himself, served in France, and had returned and settled down in Glasgow, where he opened a fencing school, having been a maitre d'armes among the Scotch regiments.

The arrangement was, however, kept a profound secret from Andrew and his wife; but on half holidays, and on any other days when he could manage to slip away for an hour, Ronald went to his instructor and worked hard and steadily with the rapier. Had Mrs. Anderson had an idea of the manner in which he spent his time she would have been horrified, and would certainly have spared her encomiums on his improved conduct and the absence of the unsatisfactory reports which had before been so common.

The cloud of uncertainty which hung over his father's fate could not but have an influence upon the boy's character, and the happy carelessness and gaiety which were its natural characteristics were modified by the thought that his father might be languishing in a dungeon. Sometimes he would refuse to accompany his school fellows on their rambles or fishing expeditions, and would sit for hours thinking over all sorts of wild plans by which he might penetrate to him and aid him to escape. He was never tired of questioning Malcolm Anderson as to the prisons in which, if still alive, his father would be likely to be confined. He would ask as to their appearance, the height of their walls, whether they were moated or not, and whether other houses abutted closely upon them. One day Malcolm asked him the reason of these questions, and he replied, "Of course I want to see how it will be possible to get my father out." And although Malcolm tried to impress upon him that it would be an almost impossible task even to discover in which prison his father was kept, he would not allow himself to be discouraged.

"There must be some way of finding out, Malcolm. You tell me that prisoners are not even known by their name to the warders, but only under a number. Still someone must know--there must be lists kept of those in prison, and I shall trust to my mother to find out for me. A great lady as she is must be able to get at people if she sets about it, and as certainly she must have loved my father very very much, or she never would have married him secretly, and got into such trouble for it. I am sure she will do her best when she finds that you and I have come over to get him out. When we know that, I think we ought to be able to manage. You could get employment as a warder, or I could go disguised as a woman, or as a priest, or somehow. I feel sure we shall succeed if we do but find out that he is alive and where he is."

Malcolm knew too much about the strong and well guarded prisons of France to share in the boy's sanguine hopes, but he did not try to discourage him. He thought that with such an object in life before him the boy would devote himself all the more eagerly to exercises which would strengthen his arm, increase his skill with weapons, and render him a brave and gallant officer, and in this he was right. As the time went on Ronald became more and more serious. He took no part whatever in the school boy games and frolics in which he had been once a leader. He worked hard at his school tasks the sooner to be done with them, and above all devoted himself to acquiring a mastery of the sword with a perseverance and enthusiasm which quite surprised his instructor.

"I tell you, Malcolm, man," he said one day to his old comrade, after Ronald had been for upwards of two years his pupil, "if I had known, when you first asked me to teach the lad to handle a sword, how much of my time he was going to occupy, I should have laughed in your face, for ten times the sum you agreed to pay me would not have been enough; but, having begun it for your sake, I have gone on for the lad's. It has been a pleasure to teach him, so eager was he to learn--so ready to work heart and soul to improve. The boy's wrist is as strong as mine and his eye as quick. I have long since taught him all I know, and it is practice now, and not teaching, that we have every day. I tell you I have work to hold my own with him; he knows every trick and turn as well as I do, and is quicker with his lunge and riposte. Were it not that I have my extra length of arm in my favour I could not hold my own. As you know, I have many of the officers of the garrison among my pupils, and some of them have learned in good schools, but there is not one of them could defend himself for a minute against that boy. If it were not that the matter has to be kept secret I would set him in front of some of them, and you would see what short work he would make of them. Have you heard the rumours, Malcolm, that the young Chevalier is likely to follow the example of his father, thirty years back, and to make a landing in Scotland?"

"I have heard some such rumours," Malcolm replied, "though whether there be aught in them I know not. I hope that if he does so he will at any rate follow the example of his father no further. As you know, I hold to the Stuarts, but I must own they are but poor hands at fighting. Charles the First ruined his cause; James the Second threw away the crown of Ireland by galloping away from the battle of the Boyne; the Chevalier showed here in '15 that he was no leader of men; and unless this lad is made of very different stuff to his forefathers he had best stay in France."

"But if he should come, Malcolm, I suppose you will join him? I am afraid I shall be fool enough to do so, even with my fifty years on my head. And you?"

"I suppose I shall be a fool too," Malcolm said. "The Stuarts are Scotch, you see, and with all their faults I would rather a thousand times have a Scottish king than these Germans who govern us from London. If the English like them let them keep them, and let us have a king of our own. However, nought may come of it; it may be but a rumour. It is a card which Louis has threatened to play a score of times, whenever he wishes to annoy England. It is more than likely that it will come to nought, as it has so often done before."

"But they tell me that there are agents travelling about among the Highland clans, and that this time something is really to be done."

"They have said so over and over again, and nothing has come of it. For my part, I don't care which way it goes. After the muddle that was made of it thirty years ago it does not seem to me more likely that we shall get rid of the Hanoverians now. Besides, the hangings and slaughterings then, would, I should think, make the nobles and the heads of clans think twice ere they risked everything again."

"That is true, but when men's blood is up they do not count the cost; besides, the Highland clans are always ready to fight. If Prince Charles comes you will see there will not be much hanging back whatever the consequences may be. Well, you and I have not much to lose, except our lives."

"That is true enough, old friend; and I would rather die that way than any other. Still, to tell you the truth, I would rather keep my head on my shoulders for a few years if I can."

"Well, nothing may come of it; but if it does I shall strike a blow again for the old cause."

At home Ronald heard nothing but expressions of loyalty to the crown. The mere fact that the Highlanders espoused the cause of the Stuarts was sufficient in itself to make the Lowlanders take the opposite side. The religious feeling, which had always counted for so much in the Lowlands, and had caused Scotland to side with the Parliament against King Charles, had not lost its force. The leanings of the Stuarts were, it was known, still strongly in favour of the Catholic religion, and although Prince Charles Edward was reported to be more Protestant in feelings than the rest of his race, this was not sufficient to counterbalance the effect of the hereditary Catholic tendency. Otherwise there was no feeling of active loyalty towards the reigning king in Scotland. The first and second Georges had none of the attributes which attract loyal affection. The first could with difficulty speak the language of the people over whom he ruled. Their feelings and sympathies were Hanoverian rather than English, and all court favours were bestowed as fast as possible upon their countrymen. They had neither the bearing nor manner which men associate with royalty, nor the graces and power of attraction which distinguished the Stuarts. Commonplace and homely in manner, in figure, and in bearing, they were not men whom their fellows could look up to or respect; their very vices were coarse, and the Hanoverian men and women they gathered round them were hated by the English people.

Thus neither in England nor Scotland was there any warm feeling of loyalty for the reigning house; and though it was possible that but few would adventure life and property in the cause of the Stuarts, it was equally certain that outside the army there were still fewer who would draw sword for the Hanoverian king. Among the people of the Lowland cities of Scotland the loyalty which existed was religious rather than civil, and rested upon the fact that their forefathers had fought against the Stuarts, while the Highlanders had always supported their cause. Thus, although in the household and in kirk Ronald had heard King George prayed for regularly, he had heard no word concerning him calculated to waken a boyish feeling of loyalty, still less of enthusiasm. Upon the other hand he knew that his father had fought and suffered for the Stuarts and was an exile in their cause, and that Hanoverians had handed over the estate of which he himself would now be the heir to one of their adherents.

"It is no use talking of these matters to Andrew," Malcolm impressed upon him; "it would do no good. When he was a young man he took the side of the Hanoverians, and he won't change now; while, did Mistress Janet guess that your heart was with the Stuarts, she would say that I was ruining you, and should bring you to a gallows. She is not fond of me now, though she does her best to be civil to her husband's brother; but did she know that you had become a Jacobite, like enough she would move Andrew to put a stop to your being with me, and there would be all sorts of trouble."

"But they could nor prevent my being with you," Ronald said indignantly. "My father gave me into your charge, not into theirs."

"That's true enough, laddie; but it is they who have cared for you and brought you up. When you are a man you can no doubt go which way it pleases you; but till then you owe your duty and respect to them, and not to me, who have done nought for you but just carry you over here in my cloak."

"I know they have done everything for me," Ronald said penitently. "They have been very good and kind, and I love them both; but for all that it is only natural that my father should be first, and that my heart should be in the cause that he fought for."

"That is right enough, Ronald, and I would not have it otherwise, and I have striven to do my best to make you as he would like to see you. Did he never come back again I should be sorry indeed to see Colonel Leslie's son growing up a Glasgow tradesman, as my brother no doubt intends you to be, for I know he has long since given up any thought of hearing from your father; but in that you and I will have a say when the time comes. Until then you must treat Andrew as your natural guardian, and there is no need to anger him by letting him know that your heart is with the king over the water, any more than that you can wield a sword like a gentleman. Let us have peace as long as we can. You are getting on for sixteen now; another two years and we will think about going to Paris together. I am off again tomorrow, Ronald; it will not be a long trip this time, but maybe before I get back we shall have news from France which will set the land on fire."

A short time after this conversation, as Ronald on his return from college (for he was now entered at the university) passed through the shop, the bailie was in conversation with one of the city magistrates, and Ronald caught the words:

"He is somewhere in the city. He came down from the Highlands, where he has been going to and fro, two days since. I have a warrant out against him, and the constables are on the lookout. I hope to have him in jail before tonight. These pestilent rogues are a curse to the land, though I cannot think the clans would be fools enough to rise again, even though Charles Stuart did come."

Ronald went straight up to his room, and for a few minutes sat in thought. The man of whom they spoke was doubtless an emissary of Prince Charles, and his arrest might have serious consequences, perhaps bring ruin on all with whom he had been in communication. Who he was or what he was like Ronald knew not; but he determined at any rate to endeavour to defeat the intentions of the magistrate to lay hands on him. Accordingly a few minutes later, while the magistrate was still talking with Andrew, he again went out.

Ronald waited about outside the door till he left, and then followed him at a short distance. The magistrate spoke to several acquaintances on the way, and then went to the council chamber. Waiting outside, Ronald saw two or three of the magistrates enter. An hour later the magistrate he was watching came out; but he had gone but a few paces when a man hurrying up approached him. They talked earnestly for a minute or two. The magistrate then re-entered the building, remained there a few minutes, and then joined the man who was waiting outside. Ronald had stolen up and taken his stand close by.

"It is all arranged," the magistrate said; "as soon as night has fallen a party will go down, surround the house, and arrest him. It is better not to do it in daylight. I shall lead the party, which will come round to my house, so if the men you have left on watch bring you news that he has changed his hiding place, let me know at once.

The magistrate walked on. Ronald stood irresolute. He had obtained no clue as to the residence of the person of whom they were in search, and after a moment's thought he determined to keep an eye upon the constable, who would most likely join his comrade on the watch. This, however, he did not do immediately. He had probably been for some time at work, and now took the opportunity of going home for a meal, for he at once made his way to a quiet part of the city, and entered a small house.

It was half an hour before he came out again, and Ronald fidgeted with impatience, for it was already growing dusk. When he issued out Ronald saw that he was armed with a heavy cudgel. He walked quickly now, and Ronald, following at a distance, passed nearly across the town, and down a quiet street which terminated against the old wall running from the Castle Port to a small tower. When he got near the bottom of the street a man came out from an archway, and the two spoke together. From their gestures Ronald felt sure that it was the last house on the left hand side of the street that was being watched. He had not ventured to follow far down the street, for as there was no thoroughfare he would at once be regarded with suspicion. The question now was how to warn the man of his danger. He knew several men were on the watch, and as only one was in the street, doubtless the others were behind the house. If anything was to be done there was no time to be lost, for the darkness was fast closing in.

After a minute's thought he went quickly up the street, and then started at a run, and then came down upon a place where he could ascend the wall, which was at many points in bad repair. With some difficulty he climbed up, and found that he was exactly opposite the house he wished to reach. It was dark now. Even in the principal streets the town was only lit by oil lamps here and there, and there was no attempt at illumination in the quiet quarters, persons who went abroad after nightfall always carrying a lantern with them. There was still sufficient light to show Ronald that the house stood at a distance of some fourteen feet from the wall. The roof sloped too steeply for him to maintain his holding upon it; but halfway along the house was a dormer window about three feet above the gutter. It was unglazed, and doubtless gave light to a granary or store room.

Ronald saw that his only chance was to alight on the roof close enough to this window to be able to grasp the woodwork. At any other moment he would have hesitated before attempting such a leap. The wall was only a few feet wide, and he could therefore get but little run for a spring. His blood was, however, up, and having taken his resolution he did not hesitate. Drawing back as far as he could he took three steps, and then sprang for the window. Its sill was some three feet higher than the edge of the wall from which he sprang.

The leap was successful; his feet struck just upon the gutter, and the impetus threw forward his body, and his hands grasped the woodwork of the window. In a moment he had dragged himself inside. It was quite dark within the room. He moved carefully, for the floor was piled with disused furniture, boxes, sacking, and rubbish. He was some time finding the door, but although he moved as carefully as he could he knocked over a heavy chest which was placed on a rickety chair, the two falling with a crash on the floor. At last he found the door and opened it. As he did so a light met his eyes, and he saw ascending the staircase a man with a drawn sword, and a woman holding a light above her head following closely. The man uttered an exclamation on seeing Ronald appear.

"A thief!" he said. "Surrender, or I will run you through at once."

"I am no thief," Ronald replied. "My name is Ronald Leslie, and I am a student at the university. I have come here to warn someone, whom I know not, in this house that it is watched, and that in a few minutes at the outside a band of the city watch will be here to capture him."

The man dropped the point of his sword, and taking the light from the woman held it closer to Ronald's face.

"How came you here?" he asked. "How did you learn this news?"

"The house is watched both sides below," Ronald said, "and I leapt from the wall through the dormer window. I heard a magistrate arranging with one of the constables for a capture, and gathered that he of whom they were in search was a Jacobite, and as I come of a stock which has always been faithful to the Stuarts, I hastened to warn him."

The woman uttered a cry of alarm.

"I thank you with all my heart, young sir. I am he for whom they are in search, and if I get free you will render a service indeed to our cause; but there is no time to talk now, if what you tell me be true. You say the house is watched from both sides?"

"Yes; there are two men in the lane below, one or more, I know not how many, behind."

"There is no escape behind," the man said; "the walls are high, and other houses abut upon them. I will sally out and fight through the men in front."

"I can handle the sword," Ronald put in; "and if you will provide me with a weapon I will do my best by your side."

"You are a brave lad," the man said, "and I accept your aid."

He led the way down stairs and entered a room, took down a sword from over the fireplace, and gave it to Ronald.

As he took it in his hand there was a loud knocking at the door.

"Too late!" the man exclaimed. "Quick, the light, Mary! At any rate I must burn my papers."

He drew some letters from his pocket, lit them at the lamp, and threw them on the hearth; then opening a cabinet he drew forth a number of other papers and crumpling them up added them to the blaze.

"Thank God that is safe!" he said; "the worst evil is averted."

"Can you not escape by the way by which I came hither?" Ronald said. "The distance is too great to leap; but if you have got a plank, or can pull up a board from the floor, you could put it across to the wall and make your escape that way. I will try to hold the stairs till you are away."

"I will try at least," the man said. "Mary, bring the light, and aid me while our brave friend does his best to give us time."

So saying he sprang upstairs, while Ronald made his way down to the door.

"Who is making such a noise at the door of a quiet house at this time of night?" he shouted.

"Open in the king's name," was the reply; "we have a warrant to arrest one who is concealed here."

"There is no one concealed here," Ronald replied, "and I doubt that you are, as you say, officers of the peace; but if so, pass your warrant through the grill, and if it be signed and in due form I will open to you."

"I will show my warrant when need be," the voice answered. "Once more, open the door or we will break it in."

"Do it at your peril," Ronald replied. "How can I tell you are not thieves who seek to ransack the house, and that your warrant is a pretence? I warn you that the first who enters I will run him through the body."

The reply was a shower of blows on the door, and a similar attack was begun by a party behind the house. The door was strong, and after a minute or two the hammering ceased, and then there was a creaking, straining noise, and Ronald knew they were applying a crowbar to force it open. He retreated to a landing halfway up the stairs, placed a lamp behind him so that it would show its light full on the faces of those ascending the stairs, and waited. A minute later there was a crash; the lock had yielded, but the bar still held the door in its place. Then the blows redoubled, mingled with the crashing of wood; then there was the sound of a heavy fall, and a body of men burst in.

There was a rush at the stairs, but the foremost halted at the sight of Ronald with his drawn sword.

"Keep back," he shouted, "or beware! The watch will be here in a few minutes, and then you will all be laid by the heels."

"Fools! We are the watch," one of the men exclaimed, and, dashing up the stairs, aimed a blow at Ronald. He guarded it and ran the man through the shoulder. He dropped his sword and fell back with a curse.

At this moment the woman ran down stairs from above and nodded to Ronald to signify that the fugitive had escaped.

"You see I hold to my word," Ronald said in a loud voice. "If ye be the watch, which I doubt, show me the warrant, or if ye have one in authority with you let him proclaim himself."

"Here is the warrant, and here am I, James M'Whirtle, a magistrate of this city."

"Why did you not say so before?" Ronald exclaimed, lowering his sword. "If it be truly the worshipful Mr. M'Whirtle let him show himself, for surely I know him well, having seen him often in the house of my guardian, Bailie Anderson."

Mr. M'Whirtle, who had been keeping well in the rear, now came forward.

"It is himself." Ronald said. "Why did you not say you were here at once, Mr. M'Whirtle, instead of setting your men to break down the door, as if they were Highland caterans on a foray?"

"We bade you open in the king's name," the magistrate said, "and you withstood us, and it will be hanging matter for you, for you have aided the king's enemies."

"The king's enemies!" Ronald said in a tone of surprise. "How can there be any enemies of the king here, seeing there are only myself and the good woman up stairs? You will find no others."

"Search the house," the magistrate said furiously, "and take this malapert lad into custody on the charge of assisting the king's enemies, of impeding the course of justice, of withstanding by force of arms the issue of a lawful writ, and with grievously wounding one of the city watch."

Ronald laughed.

"It is a grievous list, worshipful sir; but mark you, as soon as you showed your warrant and declared yourself I gave way to you. I only resisted so long as it seemed to me you were evildoers breaking into a peaceful house."

Two of the watch remained as guard over Ronald; one of the others searched the house from top to bottom. No signs of the fugitive were discovered.

"He must be here somewhere," the magistrate said, "since he was seen to enter, and the house has been closely watched ever since. See, there are a pile of ashes on the hearth as if papers had been recently burned. Sound the floors and the walls."

The investigation was particularly sharp in the attic, for a board was here found to be loose, and there were signs of its being recently wrenched out of its place, but as the room below was unceiled this discovery led to nothing. At last the magistrate was convinced that the fugitive was not concealed in the house, and, after placing his seals on the doors of all the rooms and leaving four men in charge, he left the place, Ronald, under the charge of four men, accompanying him.

On the arrival at the city Tolbooth Ronald was thrust into a cell and there left until morning. He was then brought before Mr. M'Whirtle and two other of the city magistrates. Andrew Anderson was in attendance, having been notified the night before of what had befallen Ronald. The bailie and his wife had at first been unable to credit the news, and were convinced that some mistake had been made. Andrew had tried to obtain his release on his promise to bring him up in the morning, but Mr. M'Whirtle and his colleagues, who had been hastily summoned together, would not hear of it.

"It's a case of treason, man. Treason against his gracious majesty; aiding and abetting one of the king's enemies, to say nought of brawling and assaulting the city watch."

The woman found in the house had also been brought up, but no precise charge was made against her. The court was crowded, for Andrew, in his wrath at being unable to obtain Ronald's release, had not been backward in publishing his grievance, and many of his neighbours were present to hear this strange charge against Ronald Leslie.

The wounded constable and another first gave their evidence.

"I myself can confirm what has been said," Mr. M'Whirtle remarked, "seeing that I was present with the watch to see the arrest of a person against whom a warrant had been issued."

"Who is that person?" Ronald asked. "Seeing that I am charged with aiding and abetting his escape it seems to me that I have a right to know who he is."

The magistrates looked astounded at the effrontery of the question, but after a moment's consultation together Mr. M'Whirtle said that in the interest of justice it was unadvisable at the present moment to state the name of the person concerned.

"What have you to say, prisoner, to the charge made against you? In consideration of our good friend Bailie Anderson, known to be a worthy citizen and loyal subject of his majesty, we would be glad to hear what you have to say anent this charge."

"I have nothing to say," Ronald replied quietly. "Being in the house when it was attacked, with as much noise as if a band of Border ruffians were at the gate, I stood on the defence. I demanded to see what warrant they had for forcing an entry, and as they would show me none, I did my best to protect the house; but the moment Mr. M'Whirtle proclaimed who he was I lowered my sword and gave them passage."

There was a smile in the court at the boy's coolness.

"But how came ye there, young sir? How came ye to be in the house at all, if ye were there for a good motive?"

"That I decline to say," Ronald answered. "It seems to me that any one may be in a house by the consent of its owners, without having to give his reasons therefor."

"It will be the worse for you if you defy the court. I ask you again how came you there?"

"I have no objection to tell you how I came there," Ronald said. "I was walking on the old wall, which, as you know, runs close by the house, when I saw an ill looking loon hiding himself as if watching the house, looking behind I saw another ruffianly looking man there." Two gasps of indignation were heard from the porch at the back of the court. "Thinking that there was mischief on hand I leapt from the wall to the dormer window to warn the people of the house that there were ill doers who had designs upon the place, and then remained to see what came of it. That is the simple fact."

There was an exclamation of incredulity from the magistrates.

"If you doubt me," Ronald said, "you can send a man to the wall. I felt my feet loosen a tile and it slid down into the gutter."

One of the magistrates gave an order, and two of the watch left the court.

"And who did you find in the house?"

"I found this good woman, and sorely frightened she was when I told her what kind of folk were lurking outside."

"And was there anyone else there?"

"There was a man there," Ronald said quietly, "and he seemed alarmed too."

"What became of him?"

"I cannot say for certain," Ronald replied; "but if you ask my opinion I should say, that having no stomach for meeting people outside, he just went out the way I came in, especially as I heard the worshipful magistrate say that a board in the attic had been lifted."

The magistrates looked at each other in astonishment; the mode of escape had not occurred to any, and the disappearance of the fugitive was now explained.

"I never heard such a tale," one of the magistrates said after a pause. "It passes belief that a lad, belonging to the family of a worthy and respectable citizen, a bailie of the city and one who stands well with his fellow townsmen, should take a desperate leap from the wall through a window of a house where a traitor was in hiding, warn him that the house was watched, and give him time to escape while he defended the stairs. Such a tale, sure, was never told in a court. What say you, bailie?"

"I can say nought," Andrew said. "The boy is a good boy and a quiet one; given to mischief like other boys of his age, doubtless, but always amenable. What can have possessed him to behave in such a wild manner I cannot conceive, but it seems to me that it was but a boy's freak."

"It was no freak when he ran his sword through Peter Muir's shoulder," Mr. M'Whirtle said. "Ye will allow that, neighbour Anderson."

"The man must have run against the sword," the bailie said, "seeing the boy scarce knows one end of a weapon from another."

"You are wrong there, bailie," one of the constables said; "for I have seen him many a time going into the school of James Macklewain, and I have heard a comrade say, who knows James, that the lad can handle a sword with the best of them."

"I will admit at once," Ronald said, "that I have gone to Macklewain's school and learned fencing of him. My father, Colonel Leslie of Glenlyon, was a gentleman, and it was right that I should wield a sword, and James Macklewain, who had fought in the French wars and knew my father, was good enough to teach me. I may say that my guardian knew nothing of this."

"No, indeed," Andrew said. "I never so much as dreamt of it. If I had done so he and I would have talked together to a purpose."

"Leslie of Glenlyon was concerned in the '15, was he not?" Mr. M'Whirtle said; "and had to fly the country; and his son seems to be treading in his steps, bailie. I doubt ye have been nourishing a viper in your bosom."

At this moment the two constables returned, and reported that certainly a tile was loose as the prisoner had described, and there were scratches as if of the feet of someone entering the window, but the leap was one that very few men would undertake.

"Your story is so far confirmed, prisoner; but it does not seem to us that even had you seen two men watching a house it would be reasonable that you would risk your neck in this way without cause. Clearly you have aided and abetted a traitor to escape justice, and you will be remanded. I hope, before you are brought before us again, you will make up your mind to make a clean breast of it, and throw yourself on the king's mercy."

Ronald was accordingly led back to the cell, the bailie being too much overwhelmed with surprise at what he had heard to utter any remonstrance.

CHAPTER III: Free.

After Ronald had been removed from the court the woman was questioned. She asserted that her master was away, and was, she believed, in France, and that in his absence she often let lodgings to strangers. That two days before, a man whom she knew not came and hired a room for a few days. That on the evening before, hearing a noise in the attic, she went up with him, and met Ronald coming down stairs. That when Ronald said there were strange men outside the house, and when immediately afterwards there was a great knocking at the door, the man drew his sword and ordered her to come up stairs with him. That he then made her assist him to pull up a plank, and thrust it from the attic to the wall, and ordered her to replace it when he had gone. She supposed he was a thief flying from justice, but was afraid to refuse to do his bidding.

"And why did you not tell us all this, woman, when we came in?" Mr. M'Whirtle asked sternly. "Had ye told us we might have overtaken him."

"I was too much frightened," the woman answered. "There were swords out and blood running, and men using words contrary both to the law and Scripture. I was frighted enough before, and I just put my apron over my head and sat down till the hubbub was over. And then as no one asked me any questions, and I feared I might have done wrong in aiding a thief to escape, I just held my tongue."

No cross questioning could elicit anything further from the woman, who indeed seemed frightened almost out of her senses, and the magistrate at last ordered her to return to the house and remain there under the supervision of the constable until again sent for.

Andrew Anderson returned home sorely disturbed in his mind. Hitherto he had told none, even of his intimates, that the boy living in his house was the son of Colonel Leslie, but had spoken of him as the child of an old acquaintance who had left him to his care. The open announcement of Ronald that he was the son of one of the leaders in the last rebellion, coming just as it did when the air was thick with rumours of another rising, troubled him greatly; and there was the fact that the boy had, unknown to him, been learning fencing; and lastly this interference, which had enabled a notorious emissary of the Pretender to escape arrest.

"The boy's story may be true as far as it goes," he said to his wife when relating to her the circumstances, "for I have never known him to tell a lie; but I cannot think it was all the truth. A boy does not take such a dreadful leap as that, and risk breaking his neck, simply because he sees two men near the house. He must somehow have known that man was there, and went to give him warning. Now I think of it, he passed through the shop when Peter M'Whirtle was talking to me about it, though, indeed, he did not know then where the loon was in hiding. The boy went out soon afterwards, and must somehow have learned, if indeed he did not know before. Janet, I fear that you and I have been like two blind owls with regard to the boy, and I dread sorely that my brother Malcolm is at the bottom of all this mischief."

This Mrs. Anderson was ready enough to credit, but she was too much bewildered and horrified to do more than to shake her head and weep.

"Will they cut off his head, Andrew?" she asked at last.

"No, there's no fear of that; but they may imprison him for a bit, and perhaps give him a good flogging--the young rascal. But there, don't fret over it, Janet. I will do all I can for him. And in truth I think Malcolm is more to blame than he is; and we have been to blame too for letting the lad be so much with him, seeing that we might be sure he would put all sorts of notions in the boy's head."

"But what is to be done, Andrew? We cannot let the poor lad remain in prison."

"We have no choice in the matter, Janet. In prison he is, and in prison he has to remain until he is let out, and I see no chance of that. If it had only been a brawl with the watch it could have been got over easily enough; but this is an affair of high treason--aiding and abetting the king's enemies, and the rest of it. If it were in the old times they would put the thumb screws on him to find out all he knew about it, for they will never believe he risked his life in the plot; and the fact that his father before him was in arms for the Chevalier tells that way. I should not be surprised if an order comes for him to be sent to London to be examined by the king's councillors; but I will go round now and ask the justices what they think of the matter."

His tidings when he returned were not encouraging; the general opinion of the magistrates being that Ronald was certainly mixed up in the Jacobite plot, that the matter was altogether too serious to be disposed of by them, being of the nature of high treason, and that nothing could be done until instructions were received from London. No clue had been obtained as to the whereabouts of the man who had escaped, and it was thought probable that he had at once dropped beyond the walls and made for the west.

Malcolm arrived ten days later from a journey in Lancashire, and there was a serious quarrel between him and Andrew on his presenting himself at the house.

"It is not only that you led the lad into mischief, Malcolm, but that you taught him to do it behind my back."

"You may look at it in that way if you will, Andrew, and it's natural enough from your point of view; but I take no blame to myself. You treated the boy as if he had been your son, and I thank you with all my heart for your kindness to him; but I could not forget Leslie of Glenlyon, and I do not blame myself that I have kept the same alive in his mind also. It was my duty to see that the young eagle was not turned into a barn door fowl; but I never thought he was going to use his beak and his claws so soon."

"A nice thing you will have to tell his father, that owing to your teachings his son is a prisoner in the Tower, maybe for life. But there-- there's no fear of that. You will never have to render that account, for there's no more chance of your ever hearing more of him than there is of my becoming king of Scotland. It's bad enough that you have always been a ne'er do well yourself without training that unfortunate boy to his ruin."

"Well, well, Andrew, I will not argue with you, and I don't blame you at being sore and angry over the matter; nor do I deny what you have said about myself; it's true enough, and you might say worse things against me without my quarreling with ye over it. However, the less said the better. I will take myself off and think over what's to be done."

"You had better come up and have your supper with us," Andrew said, mollified by his brother's humility.

"Not for twenty golden guineas, Andrew, would I face Mistress Janet. She has borne with me well, though I know in her heart she disapproves of me altogether; but after this scrape into which I have got the boy I daren't face her. She might not say much, but to eat with her eye upon me would choke me."

Malcolm proceeded at once to the establishment of his friend Macklewain.

"This is a nice kettle of fish, Malcolm, about young Leslie. I have had the justices down here, asking me all sorts of questions, and they have got into their minds that I taught him not only swordplay but treason, and they have been threatening to put me in the stocks as a vagabond; but I snapped my fingers in their faces, saying I earned my money as honestly as they did, and that I concern myself in no way in politics, but teach English officers and the sons of Glasgow tradesmen as well as those of Highland gentlemen. They were nicely put out, I can tell you; but I didn't care for that, for I knew I was in the right of it. But what on earth made the young cock meddle in this matter? How came he to be mixed up in a Jacobite plot? Have you got your finger in it?"

"Not I, James; and how it happens that he is concerned in it is more than I can guess. I know, of course, his heart is with the king over the water; but how he came to get his hand into the pie is altogether beyond me."

"The people here are well nigh mad about it. I know not who the gallant who has escaped is; but it is certain that his capture was considered a very important one, and that the justices here expected to have gained no small credit by his arrest, whereas now they will be regarded as fools for letting him slip through their fingers."

"I cannot for the life of me make out how he came to be mixed up in such a matter. No one but you and I could have known that he was a lad of mettle, who might be trusted in such a business. It can hardly be that they would have confided any secrets to him; still, the fact that he was in the house with the man they are in search of, and that he drew and risked his life and certain imprisonment to secure his escape, shows that he must have been heart and soul in the plot."

"And what do you think of doing, Malcolm?"

"I shall get him out somehow. I can lay hands on a score or two or more of our old comrades here in Glasgow, and I doubt not that they will all strike a blow with me for Leslie's son, to say nothing of his being a follower of the Stuarts."

"You are not thinking, man, of attacking the jail! That would be a serious matter. The doors are strong, and you would have the soldiers, to say nought of the town guard and the citizens, upon you before you had reached him."

"No, no, James, I am thinking of no such foolishness. I guess that they will not be trying him for withstanding the watch, that's but a small matter; they will be sending him south for the king's ministers to get out of him what he knows about the Jacobite plot and the names of all concerned, and it's upon the road that we must get him out of their hands. Like enough they will only send four troopers with him, and we can easily master them somewhere in the dales."

"It's more like, Malcolm, they will send him by ship. They will know well enough that if the lad knows aught there will be plenty whose interest it is to get him out of their hands. I think they will take the safer way of putting him on board ship."

"Like enough they will," Malcolm agreed, "and in that case it will be a harder job than I deemed it. But at any rate I mean to try. Ronald's not the lad to turn traitor; he will say nothing whatever they do to him, you may be sure, and he may lie for years in an English prison if we do not get him out of their hands before he gets there. At any rate what we have got to do now is to mark every ship in the port sailing for London, and to find out whether passages are taken for a prisoner and his guard in any of them. I will make that my business, and between times get a score of trusty fellows together in readiness to start if they should send him by land; but I doubt not that you are right, and that he will be taken off by ship."

The days of waiting passed slowly to Ronald, and Andrew Anderson once or twice obtained permission to see him. The bailie wisely abstained from any reproaches, and sought only to persuade him to make a clean breast of the business, and to tell all he knew about a plot which could but end in failure and ruin to all concerned. Although his belief in Ronald's truthfulness was great he could not credit that the story which he had told contained all the facts of the matter. To the bailie it seemed incredible that merely from an abstract feeling in favour of the Stuarts Ronald would have risked his life and liberty in aiding the escape of a Jacobite agent, unless he was in some way deeply involved in the plot; and he regarded Ronald's assurances to the contrary as the outcome of what he considered an entirely mistaken sense of loyalty to the Stuart cause.

"It's all very well, Ronald," he said, shaking his head sadly; "but when they get you to London they will find means to make you open your mouth. They have done away with the thumb screws and the rack, but there are other ways of making a prisoner speak, and it would be far better for you to make a clean breast of it at once. Janet is grieving for you as if you were her own son, and I cannot myself attend to my business. Who would have thought that so young a lad should have got himself mixed up in such sair trouble!"

"I have really told you all, bailie, though you will not believe me, and I am sorry indeed for the trouble I have brought upon you and my aunt"--for Ronald had from the first been taught to address the bailie and his wife as if Malcolm Anderson had been his real father; "anyhow I wish they would settle it. I would rather know the worst than go on from day to day expecting something that never happens."

"You have to wait, Ronald, till word comes from London. If they write from there that your case can be dealt with merely for the assault upon the watch I can promise you that a few weeks in jail are all that you are like to have; but I fear that there is little chance of that. They are sure to send for you to London, and whether you will ever come back alive the gude Lord only knows. We know what came of treason thirty years ago, and like enough they will be even more severe now, seeing that they will hold that folks have all the less right to try and disturb matters so long settled."

"Have you seen Malcolm?" Ronald asked, to change the conversation.

"Ay, lad, I have seen him, and the meeting was not altogether a pleasant one for either of us."

"I hope you have not quarrelled with him on my account!" Ronald said eagerly.

"We have not exactly quarrelled, but we have had words. I could not but tell him my opinion as to his learning you to take such courses, but we parted friends; but I doubt it will be long before Janet can see him with patience."

The jailer, who was present at the interview, here notified that the bailie's time was up.

"I shall see you again, Ronald, before they take you south. I would that I could do more to help you besides just coming to see you."

"I know you cannot, uncle. I have got into the scrape and must take the consequences; but if I were placed in the same position I should do it again."

A few days afterwards, as he was eating his ration of prison bread, Ronald found in it a small pellet of paper, and on opening it read the words: "Keep up your courage, friends are at work for you. You will hear more yet of M. A."

Ronald was glad to know that his old friend was thinking of him, but, knowing how strong was the prison, he had little hopes that Malcolm would be able to effect anything to help him. Still the note gave him comfort.

Three days later Andrew called again to bid him goodbye, telling him that orders had been received from London that he was to be sent thither by ship.

"I should like to have seen Malcolm before I went, if I could," Ronald said.

"I have not seen him for several days," the bailie said. "I have sent down several times to the house where he lodges, but he is always away; but, whether or no, there would be no chance of your seeing him. I myself had difficulty in getting leave to see you, though a bailie and known to be a loyal citizen. But Malcolm knows that there would be no chance of one with such a character as his getting to see you, and that it would draw attention to him even to ask such a thing, which, if he has a hand in this mad brain plot, he would not wish."

"Malcolm would not mind a straw whether they kept a watch on him or not," Ronald said. "Will you tell him, when you see him next, that I got his message?"

"What message? I have given you no message that I know of."

"He will know what I mean. Tell him, whether aught comes of it or not I thank him, and for all his kindness to me, as I do you and Aunt Janet."

At the same time with the order that Ronald should be sent to London the authorities of Glasgow received an intimation that the ministers felt great surprise at the lukewarmness which had been shown in allowing so notorious and important an enemy of his majesty to escape, and that the king himself had expressed marked displeasure at the conduct of the city authorities in the matter. Greatly mortified at the upshot of an affair from which they had hoped to obtain much credit from government, and believing it certain that there were many greatly interested in getting Ronald out of the hands of his captors, the authorities took every precaution to prevent it. He was taken down to the river side under a strong escort, and in addition to the four warders who were to be in charge of the prisoner as far as London, they put on board twelve men of the city guard. These were to remain with the ship until she was well out at sea, and then to return in a boat which the vessel was to tow behind her.

Ronald could not but smile when he saw all these formidable preparations for his safety. At the same time he felt that any hope he had entertained that Malcolm might, as the message hinted, make an attempt at rescue were blighted. The vessel dropped down with the tide. The orders of the justices had been so strict and urgent that the whole of the men placed on board kept a vigilant watch.

Just as they were abreast of Dumbarton the sound of oars was heard, and presently a boat was seen approaching. As it got nearer two men were seen to be rowing, and two others seated in the stern; but as the craft was a large one there was room for others to be lying in the bottom. The constable in charge shouted to the boat to keep them off.

"Stop rowing," he cried, "and come no nearer. If you do we fire, and as I don't want to shed your blood I warn you that I have sixteen armed men here."

As his words were emphasized by the row of men, who with levelled muskets ranged themselves along at the side of the ship, the boat ceased rowing.

"What are you afraid of?" one of the men in the stern shouted. "Cannot a fisherman's boat row out without being threatened with shooting? What are you and your sixteen armed men doing on board? Are you expecting a French fleet off the coast? And do you think you will beat them off if they board you? How long have the Glasgow traders taken to man their ships with fighting men?"

Ronald was in the cabin under the poop; it opened on to the waist, and received its light from an opening in the door, at which two armed men had stationed themselves when the boat was heard approaching. Had the cabin possessed a porthole through which he could have squeezed himself he would long before have jumped overboard and tried to make his escape by swimming under cover of the darkness. He now strove to force the door open, for he recognized Malcolm's voice, and doubted not that his friend had spoken in order to let him know that he was there, that he might if possible leap over and swim to the boat; but it was fastened strongly without, and the guards outside shouted that they would fire unless he remained quiet.

No reply was made to the taunts of the man in the boat, and slowly, for the wind was but just filling her sails, the vessel dropped down the river, and the boat was presently lost sight of.

In the morning the breeze freshened. It was not till the ship was eight miles beyond the mouth of the river that the boat was pulled up alongside, and the guard, taking their places on board, hoisted sail and started on their return to Glasgow.

Once fairly at sea Ronald was allowed to leave his cabin. Now that he was enjoying the fresh air his spirits soon recovered the tone which they had lost somewhat during his three weeks' confinement in prison, and he thoroughly enjoyed his voyage. The man who was in charge of the guard had at first wished to place some restriction on his going about on board as he chose; but the crew sided with the young prisoner, and threw such ridicule on the idea that four warders and a head constable were afraid, even for a moment, to lose sight of a boy on board a ship at sea, that he gave way, and allowed Ronald free liberty of action, although he warned his subordinates that they must nor relax their caution for a moment.

"The crew are all with him. They think it a shame that a lad like this should be hauled to London as a prisoner charged with treasonable practices; and sailors, when they once get an idea into their head, are as obstinate as Highland cattle. I have told them that he drew a sword and held the staircase against us all while a noted traitor made his escape, and that he ran one of us through the shoulder, and they only shouted with laughter, and said he was a brave young cock. Like as not, if they had a chance, these men would aid him to escape, and then we should have to answer for it, and heavily too; loss of place and imprisonment would be the least of what we might expect; so though, while at sea and in full daylight he can do as he pleases, we must be doubly vigilant at night, or in port if the vessel should have to put in."

Accordingly, to the great disgust of the sailors the watch by turns stood sentry outside Ronald's door at night, thereby defeating a plan which the sailors had formed of lowering a boat the first night they passed near land, and letting Ronald make his escape to shore.

The wind was favourable until the vessel rounded the Land's End. After that it became baffling and fickle, and it was more than three weeks after the date of her sailing from Glasgow that the vessel entered the mouth of the Thames. By this time Ronald's boyish spirits had allayed all suspicion on the part of his guards. He joked with the sailors, climbed about the rigging like a cat, and was so little affected by his position that the guards were convinced that he was free from the burden of any state secret, and that no apprehension of any serious consequence to himself was weighing upon him.

"Poor lad!" the head warder said; "he will need all his spirits. He will have hard work to make the king's council believe that he interfered in such a matter as this from pure love of adventure. He will have many a weary month to pass in prison before they free him, I reckon. It goes against my heart to hand over such a mere laddie as a prisoner; still it is no matter of mine. I have my duty to do, and it's not for me to question the orders I have received, or to argue whether a prisoner is innocent or guilty."

As the vessel anchored off Gravesend to wait for the turn of the tide to take her up, a boat rowed by a waterman, and with a man sitting in the stern, passed close by the ship. The head warder had now redoubled his vigilance, and one of the guards with loaded musket was standing on the deck not far from Ronald, who was standing on the taffrail. As the boat passed some twenty yards astern of the ship the man who was not rowing turned round for a moment and looked up at Ronald. It was but a momentary glance that the lad caught of his face, and he suppressed with difficulty a cry of surprise, for he recognized Malcolm Anderson. The rower continued steadily to ply his oars, and continued his course towards another ship anchored lower down the river. Ronald stood watching the boat, and saw that after making a wide sweep it was rowed back again to Gravesend.

Ronald had no doubt that Malcolm had come south in hopes of effecting his escape, and guessed that he had taken up his post at Gravesend with the intention of examining every ship as she passed up until the one in which he knew he had sailed made its appearance. What his next step would be he could not tell; but he determined to keep a vigilant lookout, and to avail himself instantly of any opportunity which might offer.

As the captain did nor care about proceeding up the river after dark it was not until the tide turned, just as morning broke, that the anchor was weighed. There was a light breeze which just sufficed to give the vessel steerage way, and a mist hung on the water. Ronald took his favourite seat on the taffrail, and kept a vigilant watch upon every craft which seemed likely to come near the vessel.

Greenwich was passed, and the vessel presently approached the crowded part of the Pool. It was near high tide now, and the captain was congratulating himself that he should just reach a berth opposite the Tower before it turned. Presently a boat with two rowers shot out from behind a tier of vessels and passed close under the stern of the Glasgow Lass. A man was steering whom Ronald instantly recognized.

"Jump!" he cried, and Ronald without a moment's hesitation leaped from the taffrail.

He came up close to the boat, and was instantly hauled on board by Malcolm. Just at that moment the guard, who had stood stupefied by Ronald's sudden action, gave a shout of alarm and discharged his piece. The ball struck the boat close to Ronald. It was already in motion; the men bent to their oars, and the boat glided towards the Surrey side of the river. Loud shouts arose from on board the vessel, and four bullets cut the water round the boat; but before the muskets could be reloaded Malcolm had steered the boat through a tier of vessels, whose crews, attracted by the firing, cheered the fugitives lustily.

A minute later they had reached some landing steps. Malcolm tossed some money to the rowers, and then sprang ashore with Ronald, and handed the latter a long coat which would reach to his heels and conceal the drenched state of his clothing from notice.

"We have tricked them nicely, dear boy," he said; "we are safe now. Long before they can lower a boat and get here we shall be safe in shelter, and our five Glasgow bodies will have something to do to look for us here."

Moderating his pace so as to avoid attracting attention, Malcolm proceeded along several streets and lanes, and presently stopped at the door of a little shop.

"I am lodging here," he said, "and have told the people of the house that I am expecting a nephew back from a cruise in the Mediterranean."

As he passed through the shop he said to the woman behind the counter:

"Here he is safe and sound. He's been some days longer than I expected, but I was nor so very far wrong in my calculations. The young scamp has had enough of the sea, and has agreed to go back again with me to his own people."

"That's right," the woman said. "My own boy ran away two years ago, and I hope he will have come to his senses by the time he gets back again."

When they were together in their room up stairs Malcolm threw his arms round Ronald's neck.

"Thank God, my dear boy, I have got you out of the clutches of the law! You do not know how I have been fretting since I heard you were caught, and thought that if ill came to you it would be all my fault. And now tell me how you got into this scrape, for it has been puzzling me ever since I heard it. Surely when I saw you last you knew nothing about any Jacobite goings on?"

Ronald related the whole particulars of his adventure, and said that even now he was absolutely ignorant who was the man whom he had aided to escape.

"I know no more than you do, Ronald, but they must have thought his capture an important one by the fuss they made over his escape. And now, to think that you have slipped out of their hands too!" and Malcolm broke into a loud laugh. "I would give a month's earnings to see the faces of the guard as they make their report that they have arrived empty handed. I was right glad when I saw you. I was afraid you might have given them the slip on the way, and then there would have been no saying when we might have found each other again."

"The sailors would have lowered a boat at night and let me make for the land," Ronald said, "but there was a good guard kept over me. The door was locked and a sentry always on watch, and I had quite given up all hope until I saw you at Gravesend. And now, what do you intend to do? Make our way back to Scotland?"

"No, no, lad, that would never do. There will be a hue and cry after you, and all the northern routes will be watched. No, I shall make a bargain with some Dutch skipper to take us across the water, and then we will make our way to Paris."

"But have you got money, Malcolm?"

"I have got your purse, lad. I went to Andrew and said that I wanted it for you, but that he was to ask no questions, so that whatever came of it he could say that he knew nothing. He gave it me at once, saying only:

"'Remember, Malcolm, you have done the boy some harm already with your teaching, see that you do him no further harm. I guess you are bent on some hare brained plan, but whatever it be I wish you success.'"

CHAPTER IV: In France.

The next day Malcolm went out alone, and on his return told Ronald that there were placards on the walls offering a reward of a hundred pounds for his apprehension.

"You don't think the people below have any suspicion, Malcolm?"

"Not they," Malcolm replied. "I was telling them last night after you had gone to bed all about the places you have been voyaging to, and how anxious your father, a snug farmer near Newcastle, was to have you back again. I had spoken to them before so as to prepare them for your coming, and the old woman takes quite an interest in you, because her son at sea is a lad just about your age. I have brought you in a suit of sailor clothes; we will go down and have a chat with them after the shop is closed of a night. You will remember Newcastle and the farm, and can tell them of your escape from Greek pirates, and how nearly you were taken by a French frigate near the straits."

The consternation of the watch at Ronald's escape was extreme. The shot which the man on guard had fired was their first intimation of the event, and seizing their muskets they had hastily discharged them in the direction of the fugitive, and had then shouted for a boat to be lowered. But never was a boat longer getting into the water than was that of the Glasgow Lass upon this occasion. The captain gave his orders in a leisurely way, and the crew were even slower in executing them. Then somehow the fall stuck and the boat wouldn't lower. When at last she was in the water it was found that the thole pins were missing; these being found she was rowed across the river, the five constables undergoing a running fire of jokes and hilarity from the sailors of the ships they passed near. In answer to their inquiries where the fugitives landed, some of the sailors shouted that she had pulled up the river behind the tier of vessels, others insisted that she had sunk with all hands close by.

Completely bewildered, the chief of the party told the sailors to put them ashore at the first landing. When the party gained the streets they inquired eagerly of all they met whether they had seen aught of the fugitives. Few of those they questioned understood the broad Scotch in which the question was asked, others laughed in their faces and asked how they were to know the man and boy they wanted from any others; and after vainly looking about for some time they returned to the stairs, only to find that the boat had returned to the ship.

A waterman's boat was now hired, and the rower, who had heard what had happened, demanded a sum for putting them on board which horrified them; but at last, after much bargaining, they were conveyed back to the ship. An hour later the chief of the party went ashore, and repairing to the Tower, where he had been ordered to conduct the prisoner, reported his escape. He was at once taken into custody on the charge of permitting the escape of his prisoner, and it was not until three days later, upon the evidence of his men and of the captain and officers of the ship, that he was released.

His four men were put on board a ship returning to Glasgow next day, while he himself was kept to identify the fugitive should he be caught.

A week later Malcolm told Ronald that he had made arrangements with the captain of a Dutch vessel to take them over to Holland.

"We are to go on board at Gravesend," he said, "for they are searching all ships bound for foreign ports. It is not for you especially, but there are supposed to be many Jacobites going to and fro, and they will lay hands on anyone who cannot give a satisfactory account of himself. So it is just as well for us to avoid questioning."

Accordingly the next day they walked down to Gravesend, and taking boat there boarded the Dutch vessel when she came along on the following day. The Dutch captain received them civilly; he had been told by Malcolm that they wished to leave the country privately, and guessed that they were in some way fugitives from the law, but as he was to be well paid this gave him no concern. There were no other passengers, and a roomy cabin was placed at their disposal. They passed down the river without impediment, and anchored that night off Sheerness.

"These Dutch traders are but slow craft," Malcolm said as he walked impatiently up and down the deck next morning, watching the slow progress which they made past the shore. "I wish we could have got a passage direct to France, but of course that is impossible now the two nations are at war."

"What is the war about, Malcolm? I heard at home that they were fighting, but yet that somehow the two countries were not at war."

"No, I don't know how that comes about," Malcolm said. "England has a minister still at Paris; but for all that King George is at the head of a number of British troops in Germany fighting against the French there."

"But what is it about, Malcolm?"

"Well, it is a matter which concerns Hanover more than England; in fact England has no interest in the matter at all as far as I can see, except that as France takes one side she takes the other, because she is afraid of France getting too strong. However, it is a German business, and England is mixed up in it only because her present king is a Hanoverian and not an Englishman. This is the matter as far as I can make it out. Charles VI., Emperor of Germany, died in October, 1740. It had been arranged by a sort of general agreement called the Pragmatic Sanction--"

"What an extraordinary name, Malcolm! What does it mean?"

"I have not the least idea in the world, lad. However, that is what it is called. It was signed by a lot of powers, of whom England was one, and by it all parties agreed that Charles's daughter Maria Theresa was to become Empress of Austria. However, when the emperor was dead the Elector of Bavaria claimed to be emperor, and he was supported by France, by Spain, and by Frederick of Prussia, and they marched to Vienna, enthroned the elector as Duke of Austria, and drove Maria Theresa to take refuge in Hungary, where she was warmly supported.

"The English parliament voted a large sum to enable the empress to carry on the war, and last year sixteen thousand men under the Earl of Stair crossed the seas to cooperate with the Dutch, who were warm supporters of the empress, and were joined by six thousand Hessians and sixteen thousand Hanoverians in British pay; but after all nothing was done last year, for as in the last war the Dutch were not ready to begin, and the English army were in consequence kept idle."

"Then it seems that everyone was against the empress except England and these three little states."

"That is pretty nearly so," Malcolm said; "but at present the empress has bought off the Prussians, whose king joined in the affair solely for his own advantage, by giving him the province of Silesia, so that in fact at present it is England and Hanover, which is all the same thing, with the Dutch and Hessians, against France and Bavaria, for I don't think that at present Spain has sent any troops."

"Well, it seems to me a downright shame," Ronald said indignantly; "and though I have no great love for the English, and hate their Hanoverian George and his people, I shouldn't like to fight with one of the Scotch regiments in the French service in such a quarrel."

Malcolm laughed.

"My dear lad, if every soldier were to discuss the merits of the quarrel in which he is ordered to fight there would be an end of all discipline."

"Yes, I see that," Ronald agreed; "if one is once a soldier he has only to obey orders. But one need not become a soldier just at the time when he would be called upon to fight for a cause which he considers unjust."

"That is so, Ronald, and it's fortunate, if your feelings are in favour of Maria Theresa, that we are not thinking of enlisting just at present, for you would be puzzled which side to take. If you fought for her you would have to fight under the Hanoverian; if you fight against the Hanoverian you are fighting against Maria Theresa."

"Well, we don't want to fight at all," Ronald said. "What we want to do is to find out something about my father. I wish the voyage was at an end, and that we had our faces towards Paris."

"It will not be so easy to cross from Holland into France," Malcolm said. "I wish our voyage was at an end for another reason, for unless I mistake there is a storm brewing up."

Malcolm's prediction as to the weather was speedily verified. The wind rose rapidly, ragged clouds hurried across the sky, and the waves got up fast, and by nightfall the sea had become really heavy, dashing in sheets high in the air every time the bluff bowed craft plunged into it. Long before this Ronald had gone below prostrate with seasickness.

"It's just like the obstinacy of these Dutchmen," Malcolm muttered to himself as he held on by a shroud and watched the labouring ship. "It must have been clear to anyone before we were well out of the river that we were going to have a gale, and as the wind then was nearly due south, we could have run back again and anchored in shelter till it was over. Now it has backed round nearly into our teeth, with every sign of its getting into the north, and then we shall have the French coast on our lee. It's not very serious yet, but if the wind goes on rising as it has done for the last four or five hours we shall have a gale to remember before the morning."

Before the daylight, indeed, a tremendous sea was running, and the wind was blowing with terrible force from the north. Although under but a rag of canvas the brig was pressed down gunwale deep, and each wave as it struck her broadside seemed to heave her bodily to leeward. Malcolm on coming on deck made his way aft and glanced at the compass, and then took a long look over the foaming water towards where he knew the French coast must lie. The wind was two or three points east of north, and as the clumsy craft would not sail within several points of the wind she was heading nearly east.

"She is making a foot to leeward for every one she forges ahead," he said to himself. "If she has been at this work all night we cannot be far from the coast."

So the Dutch skipper appeared to think, for a few minutes afterwards he gave orders to bring her about on the other tack. Three times they tried and failed; each time the vessel slowly came up into the wind, but the heavy waves forced her head off again before the headsails filled. Then the skipper gave orders to wear her. Her head payed off to the wind until she was nearly before it. Two or three great seas struck her stern and buried her head deeply, but at last the boom swung over and her head came up on the other tack. During the course of these manoeuvres she had made fully two miles leeway, and when she was fairly under sail with her head to the west Malcolm took another long look towards the south.

"Just as I thought," he said. "There is white water there and a dark line behind it. That is the French coast, sure enough."

It would have been useless to speak, but he touched the arm of the skipper and pointed to leeward. The skipper looked in this direction for a minute and then gave the order for more sail to be put on the ship, to endeavour to beat out in the teeth of the gale. But even when pressed to the utmost it was evident to Malcolm that the force of the waves was driving her faster towards the coast than she could make off it, and he went below and told Ronald to come on deck.

"I would rather lie here," Ronald said.

"Nonsense, lad! The wind and spray will soon knock the sickness out of you; and you will want all your wits about you, for it won't be many hours before we are bumping on the sands, and stoutly built as the craft is she won't hold together long in such a sea as this."

"Do you really mean it, Malcolm, or are you only trying to get me on deck?"

"I mean it, lad. We are drifting fast upon the French coast, and there is no hope of her clawing off in the teeth of such a gale as this."

The news aroused Ronald effectually. He had not suffered at all on the voyage down from Glasgow, and he was already beginning to feel better when Malcolm went down to call him. He was soon on deck holding on by the bulwark.

"There it is, that long low black line; it looks a long way off because the air is full of spray and the coast is low, but it's not more than three or four miles; look at that broad belt of foam."

For some hours the Dutch skipper did his best to beat to windward, but in vain, the vessel drove nearer and nearer towards the shore; the anchors were got in readiness, and when within a quarter of a mile of the line of breakers the vessel's head was brought up into the wind, and the lashings of the two anchors cut simultaneously.

"Will they hold her, do you think?" Ronald asked.

"Not a chance of it, Ronald. Of course the captain is right to try; but no cables were ever made would hold such a bluff bowed craft as this in the teeth of such a wind and sea."

The cables ran out to the bitts. Just as they tightened a great sea rolled in on the bow. Two dull reports were heard, and then her head payed off. The jib was run up instantly to help her round, and under this sail the brig was headed directly towards the shore. The sea was breaking round them now; but the brig was almost flat bottomed and drew but little water. All on board hung on to the shrouds and bulwarks, momentarily expecting a crash, but she drove on through the surf until within a hundred yards of the shore. Then as she went down in the trough of a wave there was a mighty crash. The next wave swept her forward her own length.

Then there was another crash even more tremendous than the first, and her masts simultaneously went over the side. The next wave moved her but a few feet; the one which followed, finding her immovable, piled itself higher over her, and swept in a cataract down her sloping deck. Her stern had swung round after the first shot, and she now lay broadside to the waves. The Dutch skipper and his crew behaved with the greatest calmness; the ship lay over at such an angle that it was impossible to stand on the deck; but the captain managed to get on the upper rail, and although frequently almost washed off by the seas, contrived to cut the shrouds and ropes that still attached the masts to the ship there. Then he joined the crew, who were standing breast high in the water on the lee side, the floating masts were pulled in until within a few yards of the vessel, and such of the crew as could swim made towards them.

The skipper cut the last rope that bound them, and then plunged in and joined his men. The distance was little over fifty yards to the shore, and the wreck formed a partial shelter. A crowd of people were assembled at the edge of the beach with ropes in readiness to give any assistance in their power. Malcolm and Ronald were among those who had swum to the masts, but when within a short distance of the shore the former shouted in the latter's ear:

"Swim off, lad, the masts might crush us."

As soon as they neared the shore a number of ropes were thrown. Most of the sailors, seeing the danger of being crushed, followed the example of Malcolm, and left the masts. Malcolm and Ronald swam just outside the point where the waves broke until a line fell in the water close to them. They grasped it at once.

"Give it a twist round your arm," Malcolm shouted, "or the backwash will tear you from it."

The sailors on shore watched their opportunity, and the instant a wave passed beneath the two swimmers ran up the beach at full speed with the rope. There was a crash. Ronald felt himself shot forward with great rapidity, then as he touched the ground with his feet they were swept from under him, and so great was the strain that he felt as if his arm was being pulled from the socket. A few seconds later he was lying at full length upon the sands, and before the next wave reached him a dozen men had rushed down and seized him and Malcolm, and carried them beyond its influence. For a minute or two Ronald felt too bruised and out of breath to move. Then he heard Malcolm's voice:

"Are you hurt, Ronald?"

"No; I think not, Malcolm," he replied, making an effort to sit up. "Are you?"

"No, lad; bruised a bit, but no worse."

One by one the sailors were brought ashore, one with both legs broken from the force with which he was dashed down by the surf, and one man who stuck to the mast was crushed to death as it was rolled over and over on to the beach. The captain and three sailors were, like Malcolm and Ronald, unhurt. There still remained four men on the wreck. Fortunately she had struck just at high tide, and so stoutly was she built that she held together in spite of the tremendous seas, and in an hour the four sailors were able to wade breast high to the shore.

They found that the spot where the vessel had struck was half a mile west of Gravelines. They were taken to the town, and were hospitably entertained. A small body of soldiers were quartered there, and the officer in command told the Dutch skipper, that as the two nations were at war he and his crew must be detained until he received orders respecting them. On learning from Malcolm that he and Ronald were passengers, and were Scotsmen making their way from England to escape imprisonment as friends of the Stuarts, and that he had for twelve years served in one of the Scotch regiments of Louis, and was now bound for Paris, the officer said that they were free to continue their journey at once.

It was two or three days before they started, for they found the next morning that they were both too severely bruised to set out at once on the journey. As Malcolm had taken care to keep the purse containing Ronald's money securely fastened to a belt under his clothes they had no lack of funds; but as time was no object they started for Paris on foot. Ronald greatly enjoyed the journey. Bright weather had set in after the storm. It was now the middle of May, all nature was bright and cheerful, the dresses of the peasantry, the style of architecture so different to that to which he was accustomed in Scotland, and everything else were new and strange to him. Malcolm spoke French as fluently as his own language, and they had therefore no difficulty or trouble on the way.

They arrived at Paris without any adventure. Malcolm went to a cabaret which had at the time when he was in the French service been much frequented by Scotch soldiers, being kept by a countryman of their own, an ex-sergeant in one of the Scottish regiments.

"Ah! Sandy Macgregor," Malcolm exclaimed as the proprietor of the place approached to take their order. "So you are still in the flesh, man! Right glad am I to see you again.

"I know your face," Sandy replied; "but I canna just say what your name might be."

"Malcolm Anderson, of Leslie's Scotch regiment. It's fourteen years since I left them now; but I was here again four years later, if you can remember, when I came over to try and find out if aught had been heard of the colonel."

"Ay, ay," Sandy said, grasping Malcolm's outstretched hand warmly. "It all comes back to me now. Right glad am I to see you. And who is the lad ye have brought with you? A Scot by his face and bearing, I will be bound, but young yet for the service if that be what he is thinking of."

"He is the colonel's son, Sandy. You will remember I told you I had carried him back to Scotland with me; but I need not tell ye that this is betwixt ourselves, for those who have so badly treated his father might well have a grudge against the son, and all the more that he is the rightful heir to many a broad acre here in France."

"I give you a hearty welcome, young sir," Sandy said. "Many a time I have seen your brave father riding at the head of his regiment, and have spoken to him too, for he and his officers would drop in here and crack a cup together in a room I keep upstairs for the quality. Well, well, and to think that you are his son! But what Malcolm said is true, and it were best that none knew who ye are, for they have an unco quick way here of putting inconvenient people out of the way."

"Have you ever heard aught of my father since?" Ronald asked eagerly.

"Not a word," Sandy replied. "I have heard it talked over scores of times by men who were in the regiment that was once his, and none doubted that if he were still alive he was lying in the Bastille, or Vincennes, or one of the other cages where they keep those whose presence the king or his favourites find inconvenient. It's just a stroke of the pen, without question or trial, and they are gone, and even their best friends darena ask a question concerning them. In most cases none know why they have been put away; but there is no doubt why Leslie was seized. Three or four of his fellow officers were in the secret of his marriage, and when he had disappeared these talked loudly about it, and there was sair grief and anger among the Scottish regiment at Leslie's seizure. But what was to be done? It was just the king's pleasure, and that is enough in France. Leslie had committed the grave offence of thwarting the wishes of two of the king's favourites, great nobles, too, with broad lands and grand connections. What were the likings of a Scottish soldier of fortune and a headstrong girl in comparison! In Scotland in the old times a gallant who had carried off a daughter of a Douglas or one of our powerful nobles would have made his wife a widow ere many weeks were over, and it is the same thing here now. It wouldna have been an easy thing for his enemies to kill Leslie with his regiment at his back, and so they got an order from the king, and as surely got rid of him as if they had taken his life."

"You have never heard whether my mother has married again?" Ronald asked.

"I have never heard her name mentioned. Her father is still at court, but his daughter has never been seen since, or I should have heard of it; but more than that I cannot say."

"That gives me hopes that my father is still alive," Ronald said. "Had he been dead they might have forced her into some other marriage."

"They might so; but she was plainly a lassie who had a will of her own and may have held out."

"But why did they not kill him instead of putting him in prison if he was in their way?"

"They might, as I said, have done it at once; but once in prison he was beyond their reach. The king may grant a lettre de cachet, as these orders are called, to a favourite; but even in France men are not put to death without some sort of trial, and even Chateaurouge and De Recambours could not ask Louis to have a man murdered in prison to gratify their private spite, especially when that man was a brave Scottish officer whose fate had already excited much discontent among his compatriots in the king's service. Then again much would depend upon who was the governor of the prison. These men differ like others. Some of them are honourable gentlemen, to whom even Louis himself would not venture to hint that he wanted a prisoner put out of the way; but there are others who, to gratify a powerful nobleman, would think nothing of telling a jailer to forget a fortnight to give food to a prisoner. So you see we cannot judge from this. And now what are you thinking of doing, Malcolm, and why are you over here?"

"In the first place we are over here because young Leslie took after his father and aided a Jacobite, whom George's men were in search of, to escape, and drew his sword on a worshipful justice of Glasgow and the city watch."

"He has begun early," Sandy said, laughing; "and how did he get away?"

"They brought him down a prisoner to London, to interrogate him as to the plot. I had a boat in the Thames and he jumped over and swam for it; so here we are. There are rumours in Scotland that King Louis is helping Prince Charlie, and that an army is soon going to sail for Scotland."

"It is talked of here, but so far nothing is settled; but as King George is interfering in Louis's affairs, and is fighting him in Germany, I think it more than likely that King Louis is going to stir up a coil in Scotland to give George something to do at home."

"Then if there's nothing to be done here I shall find out the old regiment. There will be many officers in it still who have fought under Leslie, and some of them may know more about him than you do, and will surely be able to tell me what has become of the lad's mither."

"That may well be so; but keep a quiet tongue, Malcolm, as to Leslie's son, save to those on whose discretion you can rely. I tell you, if it were known that he is alive and in France his life would not be worth a week's purchase. They would not take the trouble to get a lettre de cachet for him as they did for his father; it would be just a pistol bullet or a stab on a dark night or in a lonely place. There would be no question asked about the fate of an unknown Scotch laddie."

"I will be careful, Sandy, and silent. The first thing is to find out where the old regiment is lying."

"That I can tell you at once. It is on the frontier with the Duc de Noailles, and they say that there is like to be a great battle with English George and his army."

"Well, as we have nothing else to do we will set out and find them," Malcolm said; "but as time is not pressing we will stop a few days here in Paris and I will show the lad the sights. I suppose you can put us up."

"That can I. Times are dull at present. After '15 Paris swarmed with Scotsmen who had fled to save their heads; but of late years but few have come over, and the Scotch regiments have difficulty in keeping up their numbers. Since the last of them marched for the frontier I have been looking after empty benches, and it will be good news for me when I hear that the war is over and they are on their way back."

For some days Malcolm and Ronald wandered about the narrow streets of Paris. Ronald was somewhat disappointed in the city of which he had heard so much. The streets were ill paved and worse lighted, and were narrow and winding. In the neighbourhood of the Louvre there were signs of wealth and opulence. The rich dresses of the nobles contrasted strongly indeed with the sombre attire of the Glasgow citizens, and the appearance and uniform of the royal guards filled him with admiration; but beyond the fashionable quarter it did not appear to him that Paris possessed many advantages over Glasgow, and the poorer class were squalid and poverty stricken to a far greater degree than anything he had seen in Scotland. But the chief points of attraction to him were the prisons. The Bastille, the Chatelet, and the Temple were points to which he was continually turning; the two former especially, since, if he were in Paris, it was in one of these that his father was most probably lying.

The various plans he had so often thought over, by which, in some way or other, he might communicate with his father and aid his escape, were roughly shattered at the sight of these buildings. He had reckoned on their resembling in some respect the prison in Glasgow, and at the sight of these formidable fortresses with their lofty walls and flanking towers, their moats and vigilant sentries, his hopes fell to zero. It would, he saw at once, be absolutely impossible to open communication with a prisoner of whose whereabouts he was wholly ignorant and of whose very existence he was doubtful. The narrow slits which lighted the cell in which he was confined might look into an inner court, or the cell itself might be below the surface of the soil. The legend of the troubadour who discovered King Richard of England's place of captivity by singing without the walls had always been present in his mind, but no such plan would be practicable here. He knew no song which his father, and his father only, would recognize; and even did he know such a song, the appearance of anyone loitering in the open space outside the moat round the Bastille singing at intervals at different points would have instantly attracted the attention of the sentries on the walls. Nor, even did he discover that his father was lying a prisoner in one of the cells facing outwards in the fortress, did he see any possibility of compassing his escape. The slits were wide enough only for the passage of a ray of light or the flight of an arrow. No human being could squeeze himself through them, and even if he could do so he would need a long rope to descend into the moat.

One day Ronald talked over his ideas with Malcolm, who declared at once that they were impossible of execution.

"There is scarcely a case on record," he said, "of an escape from either the Bastille or the Chatelet, and yet there have been scores of prisoners confined in them with friends of great influence and abundant means. If these have been unable, by bribing jailers or by other strategy, to free their friends, how could a stranger, without either connection, influence, or wealth, hope to effect the escape of a captive were he certain that he was within the walls. Do not waste your thought on such fancies, Ronald. If your father is still in prison it is by influence only, and influence exerted upon the king and exceeding that of your father's enemies, that his release can be obtained.

"Such influence there is no possibility of our exerting. Your father's comrades and countrymen, his position and services, availed nothing when he was first imprisoned; and in the time which has elapsed the number of those who know him and would venture to risk the king's displeasure by pleading his cause must have lessened considerably. The only possibility, mind I say possibility, of success lies in your mother.

"So far it is clear that she has been powerless; but we know not under what circumstances she has been placed. She may all this time have been shut up a prisoner in a convent; she may be dead; but it is possible that, if she is free, she may have powerful connections on her mother's side, who might be induced to take up her cause and to plead with the king for your father's liberty. She may have been told that your father is dead. She is, no doubt, in ignorance of what has become of you, or whether you are still alive. If she believes you are both dead she would have had no motive for exerting any family influence she may have, and may be living a broken hearted woman, firm only in the resolution to accept no other husband."

"Yes, that is possible," Ronald agreed. "At any rate, Malcolm, let us lose no further time, but set out tomorrow for the frontier and try to find out from my father's old comrades what has become of my mother."

CHAPTER V: Dettingen.

After walking two or three miles Malcolm and Ronald came upon the rear of a train of waggons which had set out from Paris an hour earlier. Entering into conversation with one of the drivers they found that the convoy was bound for the frontier with ammunition and supplies for the army.

"This is fortunate," Malcolm said; "for to tell you the truth, Ronald, I have looked forward to our meeting with a good many difficulties by the way. We have no passes or permits to travel, and should be suspected of being either deserters or thieves. We came down from the north easy enough; but there they are more accustomed to the passage of travellers to or from the coast. Going east our appearance if alone would be sure to incite comment and suspicion. It is hard if among the soldiers with the convoy I do not know someone who has friends in the old regiment. At any rate we can offer to make ourselves useful in case of any of the drivers falling ill or deserting by the way."

As they walked along towards the head of the long line of waggons Malcolm closely scrutinized the troopers who formed the escort, but most of them were young soldiers, and he therefore went on without accosting them until he reached the head of the column. Here two officers were riding together, a captain and a young lieutenant. Malcolm saluted the former.

"I am an old soldier of the 2d Regiment of Scottish Calvary, and am going with my young friend here, who has relations in the regiment, to join them. Will you permit us, sir, to journey with your convoy? We are ready, if needs be, to make ourselves useful in case any of your drivers are missing, no uncommon thing, as I know, on a long journey."

The officer asked a few questions about his services, and said: "What have you been doing since you left, as you say, fourteen years ago?"

"I have been in Scotland, sir. I took this lad, who was then an infant, home to my people, having had enough of soldiering, while my brother, his father, remained with the regiment. We do not know whether he is alive or dead, but if the former the lad wants to join as a trumpeter, and when old enough to fight in the ranks."

"Very well," the officer said. "You can march along with us, and if any of these fellows desert you shall take their places, and of course draw their pay."

It was a short time indeed before Malcolm's services were called into requisition, for the very first night several of the drivers, who had been pressed into the service, managed to elude the vigilance of the guard and slipped away.

The next morning Malcolm, with Ronald as his assistant, took charge of one of the heavy waggons, loaded with ammunition, and drawn by twelve horses.

"This is better than walking after all, Ronald. In the first place it saves the legs, and in the second one is partly out of the dust."

"But I think we should get on faster walking, Malcolm."

"Yes, if we had no stoppages. But then, you see, as we have no papers we might be detained for weeks by some pig headed official in a little country town; besides, we are sure to push on as fast as we can, for they will want the ammunition before a battle is fought. And after all a few days won't make much difference to us; the weather is fine, and the journey will not be unpleasant."

In fact Ronald enjoyed the next three weeks greatly as the train of waggons made its way across the plains of Champagne, and then on through the valleys of Lorraine and Alsace until it reached Strasbourg. Malcolm had speedily made friends with some of the soldiers of the escort, and of an evening when the day's work was over he and Ronald sat with them by the fires they made by the roadside, and Malcolm told tales of the campaigns in which he had been engaged, and the soldiers sang songs and chatted over the probabilities of the events of the war. None of them had served before, having been but a few months taken from their homes in various parts of France. But although, doubtless, many had at first regretted bitterly being dragged away to the wars, they were now all reconciled to their lot, and looked forward eagerly to joining their regiment, which was at the front, when the duty of looking after the convoy would be at an end.

Little was known in Paris as to the position of the contending armies beyond the fact that Lord Stair, who commanded the English army, sixteen thousand strong, which had for the last year been lying inactive in Flanders, had marched down with his Hanoverian allies towards the Maine, and that the Duc de Noailles with sixty thousand men was lying beyond the Rhine. But at Strasbourg they learned that the French army had marched north to give battle to Lord Stair, who had at present with him but twenty-eight thousand men, and was waiting to be joined by twelve thousand Hanoverians and Hessians who were on their way.

The convoy continued its journey, pushing forward with all speed, and on the 26th of July joined the army of De Noailles. The French were on the south side of the river, but having arrived on its banks before the English they had possession of the bridges. As soon as the waggons had joined the army, Malcolm obtained from the officer commanding the escort a discharge, saying that he and Ronald had fulfilled their engagement as drivers with the waggons to the front, and were now at liberty to return to France.

"Now we are our own masters again, Ronald," Malcolm said. "I have taken part in a good many battles, but have never yet had the opportunity of looking on at one comfortably. De Noailles should lose no time in attacking, so as to destroy the English before they receive their reinforcements. As he holds the bridges he can bring on the battle when he likes, and I think that tomorrow or next day the fight will take place."

It was known in the camp that evening that the English had established their chief magazines at Hanau, and were marching up the river towards Aschaffenburg. In the early morning a portion of the French troops crossed the river at that town, and took up a strong position there. Ronald and Malcolm climbed a hill looking down upon the river from the south side, and thence commanded the view of the ground across which the English were marching. On the eastern side of the river spurs of the Spessart Mountains came down close to its bank, inclosing a narrow flat between Aschaffenburg and Dettingen. At the latter place the heights approached so closely to the river as to render it difficult for an army to pass between them. While posting a strong force at Aschaffenburg to hold the passage across a stream running into the Maine there, De Noailles marched his main force down the river; these movements were hidden by the nature of the ground from the English, who were advancing unconscious of their danger towards Dettingen.

"De Noailles will have them in a trap," Malcolm said, for from their position on the hill they could see the whole ground on the further bank, Hanau lying some seven miles beyond Dettingen, which was itself less than seven miles from Aschaffenburg.

"I am afraid so," Ronald said.

"Afraid!" Malcolm repeated. "Why, you should rejoice, Ronald."

"I can't do that," Ronald replied. "I should like to see the Stuarts instead of the Hanoverians reigning over us; but after all, Malcolm, England and Scotland are one nation."

"But there are Scotch regiments with the French army, and a brigade of Irish."

"That may be," Ronald said. "Scotchmen who have got into political trouble at home may enter the service of France, and may fight heartily against the Germans or the Flemings, or other enemies of France; but I know that I should feel very reluctant to fight against the English army, except, of course, at home for the Stuarts."

"It will benefit the Stuarts' cause if the English are defeated here," Malcolm said.

"That may be or it may not," Ronald replied. "You yourself told me that Louis cared nothing for the Stuarts, and would only aid them in order to cripple the English strength at home. Therefore, if he destroys the English army here he will have less cause to fear England and so less motive for helping the Chevalier."

"That is true enough," Malcolm agreed. "You are fast becoming a politician, Ronald. Well, I will look on as a neutral then, because, although the English are certainly more nearly my countrymen than are the French, you must remember that for twelve years I fought under the French flag. However, there can be no doubt what is going to take place. See, the dark mass of the English army are passing through the defile of Dettingen, and the French have begun to cross at Seligenstadt in their rear. See, they are throwing three or four bridges across the river there."

In utter ignorance of their danger the English marched on along the narrow plain by the river bank towards Aschaffenburg.

"Look at their cavalry scouting ahead of them," Malcolm said. "There, the French are opening fire!" And as he spoke puffs of musketry rose up from the line of the stream held by the French.

The English cavalry galloped back, but the columns of infantry still advanced until within half a mile of the French position, and were there halted, while some guns from the French lines opened fire. The bridges at Seligenstadt were now completed, and masses of troops could be seen pouring over. King George and the Duke of Cumberland had joined the Earl of Stair just as the army passed through Dettingen, and were riding at the head of the column when the French fire opened. A short time was spent in reconnoitring the position of the enemy in front. The English believed that the entire French army was there opposed to them, and that the advance of the army into Franconia, which was its main objective was therefore barred. After a short consultation it was resolved to fall back at once upon the magazines at Hanau, which, from their ignorance of the near proximity of the French, had been left but weakly guarded. Believing that as they fell back they would be hotly pursued by the French army, the king took the command of the rear as the post of danger, and the columns, facing about, marched towards Dettingen.

But the French had been beforehand with them. De Noailles had sent 23,000 men under his nephew the Duke de Grammont across the river to occupy Dettingen. He himself with his main army remained on the south side, with his artillery placed so as to fire across the river upon the flank of the English as they approached Dettingen; while he could march up and cross at Aschaffenburg should the English, after being beaten back at Dettingen, try to retreat up the river.

De Grammont's position was a very strong one behind a swamp and a deep ravine hollowed out by a stream from the hill. There seemed no possibility of escape for the English army, who were as yet absolutely in ignorance of the position of the French. As the head of the column approached Dettingen, Grammont's artillery opened upon them in front, while that of De Noailles smote them in flank. As soon as the king found that his retreat was cut off he galloped from the rear of the column to its head. His horse, alarmed by the fire of the artillery and whistling of balls, ran away with him, and was with difficulty stopped just as he reached the head of the column. He at once dismounted and announced his intention of leading his troops on foot.

There was a hasty council held between him, Lord Stair, and the Duke of Cumberland, and it was agreed that the only escape from entire destruction was by fighting their way through the force now in front of them. This would indeed have been impossible had De Grammont held his position; but when that officer saw the English troops halt he believed he had only the advanced guard in front of him, and resolving to overwhelm these before their main body arrived, he abandoned his strong position, led the troops across the swamp, and charged the English in front.

De Noailles, from the opposite bank, seeing the error his nephew had made, hurried his troops towards the bridges in order to cross the river and render him assistance; but it was too late.

The English infantry, headed by the king in person, hurled themselves upon the troops of De Grammont.

Every man felt that the only hope of escape from this trap into which they had fallen lay in cutting their way through the enemy, and so furiously did they fight that De Grammont's troops were utterly overthrown, and were soon in full flight towards the bridges in the rear, hotly pursued by the English. Before they could reach the bridges they left behind them on the field six thousand killed and wounded. King George, satisfied with his success, and knowing that the French army was still greatly superior to his own, wisely determined to get out of his dangerous position as soon as possible, and pushed on that night to Hanau.

Although Malcolm and Ronald were too far off to witness the incidents of the battle, they made out the tide of war rolling away from them, and saw the black masses of troops pressing on through Dettingen in spite of the French artillery which thundered from the opposite bank of the river.

"They have won!" Ronald said, throwing up his cap. "Hurrah, Malcolm! Where is the utter destruction of the English now? See, the plain beyond Dettingen is covered by a confused mass of flying men. The English have broken out of the trap, and instead of being crushed have won a great victory."

"It looks like it certainly," Malcolm said. "I would not have believed it if I had not seen it; their destruction seemed certain. And now let us go round to the camp again."

On their way down Malcolm said:

"I think, on the whole, Ronald, that you are perhaps right, and the French defeat will do good rather than harm to the Stuart cause. Had they conquered, Louis would have been too intent on pushing forward his own schemes to care much for the Stuarts. He has no real interest in them, and only uses them as cat's paws to injure England. If he had beaten the English and Hanoverians he would not have needed their aid. As it is, it seems likely enough that he will try to create a diversion, and keep the English busy at home by aiding the Stuarts with men and money to make a landing in Scotland."

"In that case, Malcolm, we need not grieve over the defeat today. You know my sympathies are with the brave Empress of Austria rather than with her enemies, and this defeat should go far towards seating her securely on the throne. Now, what will you do, Malcolm? Shall we try and find my father's friends at once?"

"Nor for another few days," Malcolm said. "Just after a defeat men are not in the best mood to discuss bygone matters. Let us wait and see what is done next."

The next morning a portion of the French army which had not been engaged crossed the river and collected the French and English wounded, for the latter had also been left behind. They were treated by the French with the same care and kindness that was bestowed upon their own wounded. De Noailles was about to advance against the English at Hanau, when he received the news that the French army in Bavaria had been beaten back by Prince Charles, and had crossed the Rhine into Alsace. As he would now be exposed to the whole brunt of the attack of the allies he decided to retreat at once.

The next day the retreat recommenced. Many of the drivers had fled at the first news of the defeat, and Malcolm without question assumed the post of driver of one of the abandoned teams. For another week the army retired, and then crossing the Rhine near Worms were safe from pursuit.

"Now, Ronald, I will look up the old regiment, and we will see what is to be done."

The 2d Scotch Dragoons were posted in a little village a mile distant from the main camp which had now been formed. Malcolm did nor make any formal transfer of the waggon to the authorities, thinking it by no means improbable that they would insist upon his continuing his self adopted avocation as driver; but after seeing to the horses, which were picketed with a long line of transport animals, he and Ronald walked quietly away without any ceremony of adieu.

"We must not come back again here," he said, "for some of the teamsters would recognize me as having been driving lately, and I should have hard work to prove that I was not a deserter; we must take to the old regiment now as long as we are here."

On reaching the village they found the street full of troopers, who were busy engaged in cleaning their arms, grooming their horses, and removing all signs of weather and battle. Ronald felt a thrill of pleasure at hearing his native language spoken. He had now so far improved the knowledge of French as to be able to converse without difficulty, for Malcolm had from his childhood tried to keep up his French, and had lately always spoken in that language to him, unless it was necessary to speak in English in order to make him understand.

These occasions had become more and more rare, and two months of constant conversation with Malcolm and others had enabled Ronald by this time to speak with some fluency in the French tongue. None of the soldiers paid any attention to the newcomers, whose dress differed in no way from that of Frenchmen, as after the shipwreck they had, of course, been obliged to rig themselves out afresh. Malcolm stopped before an old sergeant who was diligently polishing his sword hilt.

"And how fares it with you all these years, Angus Graeme?"

The sergeant almost dropped his sword in his surprise at being so addressed in his own tongue by one whose appearance betokened him a Frenchman.

"You don't know me, Angus," Malcolm went on with a smile; "and yet you ought to, for if it hadn't been for me the sword of the German hussar who carved that ugly scar across your cheek would have followed it up by putting an end to your soldiering altogether."

"Heart alive, but it's Malcolm Anderson! Eh, man, but I am glad to see you! I thought you were dead years ago, for I have heard nae mair of you since the day when you disappeared from among us like a spook, the same day that puir Colonel Leslie was hauled off to the Bastille. A sair day was that for us a'! And where ha' ye been all the time?"

"Back at home, Angus, at least in body, for my heart's been with the old regiment. And who, think you, is this? But you must keep a close mouth, man, for it must nor be talked of. This is Leslie's son. By his father's last order I took him off to Scotland with me to be out of reach of his foes, and now I have brought him back again to try if between us we can gain any news of his father."

"You don't say so, Malcolm! I never as much heard that the colonel had a son, though there was some talk in the regiment that he had married a great lady, and that it was for that that he had been hid away in prison. And this is Leslie's boy! Only to think, now! Well, young sir, there isn't a man in the regiment but wad do his best for your father's son, for those who have joined us since, and in truth that's the great part of us, have heard many a tale of Colonel Leslie, though they may not have served under him, and not a tale but was to his honour, for a braver officer nor a kinder one never stepped the earth. But come inside, Malcolm. I have got a room to myself and a stoup of good wine; let's talk over things fair and gentle, and when I know what it is that you want you may be sure that I will do all I can, for the sake baith of the colonel and of you, auld comrade."

The trio were soon seated in the cottage, and Malcolm then gave a short sketch of all that had taken place since he had left the regiment.

"Well, well!" the sergeant said when he had ended; "and so the lad, young as he is, has already drawn his sword for the Stuarts, and takes after his father in loyalty as well as in looks, for now that I know who he is I can see his father's face in his plain enough; and now for your plans, Malcolm."

"Our plans must be left to chance, Angus. We came hither to see whether any of the colonel's friends are still in the regiment, and to learn from them whether they have any news whatever of him; and secondly, whether they can tell us aught of his mother."

"Ay, there are six or eight officers still in the regiment who served with him. Hume is our colonel now; you will remember him, Malcolm, well, for he was captain of our troop; and Major Macpherson was a captain too. Then there are Oliphant, and Munroe, and Campbell, and Graham, all of whom were young lieutenants in your time, and are now old captains of troops."

"I will see the colonel and Macpherson," Malcolm said; "if they do not know, the younger men are not likely to. Will you go along with us, Angus, and introduce me, though Hume is like enough to remember me, seeing that I was so much with Leslie?"

"They will be dining in half an hour," the sergeant said; "we'll go after they have done the meal. It's always a good time to talk with men when they are full, and the colonel will have no business to disturb him then. Our own dinner will be ready directly; I can smell a goose that I picked up, as it might be by accident, at the place where we halted last night. There are four or five of us old soldiers who always mess together when we are not on duty with our troops, and if I mistake not, you will know every one of them, and right glad they will be to see you; but of course I shall say no word as to who the lad is, save that he is a friend of yours."

A few minutes later four other sergeants dropped in, and there was a joyful greeting between them and Malcolm as soon as they recognized his identity. The meal was a jovial one, as old jokes and old reminiscences were recalled. After an hour's sitting Angus said:

"Pass round the wine, lads, till we come back again. I am taking Anderson to the colonel, who was captain of his troop. We are not likely to be long, and when we come back we will make a night of it in honour of old times, or I am mistaken."

On leaving the cottage they waited for a while until they saw the colonel and major rise from beside the fire round which, with the other officers, they had been taking their meal, and walk to the cottage which they shared between them. Angus went up and saluted.

"What is it, Graeme?" the colonel asked.

"There's one here who would fain have a talk with you. It is Malcolm Anderson, whom you may remember as puir Colonel Leslie's servant, and as being in your own troop, and he has brought one with him concerning whom he will speak to you himself."

"Of course I remember Anderson," the colonel said. "He was devoted to Leslie. Bring him in at once. What can have brought him out here again after so many years? Been getting into some trouble at home, I suppose? He was always in some scrape or other when he was in the regiment, for, though he was a good soldier, he was as wild and reckless a blade as any in the regiment. You remember him, Macpherson?"

"Yes, I remember him well," the major said. "The colonel was very fond of him, and regarded him almost as a brother."

A minute later Angus ushered Malcolm and Ronald into the presence of the two officers, who had now taken seats in the room which served as kitchen and sitting room to the cottage, which was much the largest in the village.

"Well, Anderson, I am glad to see you again," Colonel Hume said, rising and holding out his hand. "We have often spoken of you since the day you disappeared, saying that you were going on a mission for the colonel, and have wondered what the mission was, and how it was that we never heard of you again."

"I came over to Paris four years later, colonel, but the regiment was away in Flanders, and as I found out from others what I had come to learn, there was no use in my following you. As to the colonel's mission, it was this;" and he put his hand on Ronald's shoulder.

"What do you mean, Anderson?" the colonel asked in surprise.

"This is Colonel Leslie's son, sir. He bade me fetch him straight away from the folk with whom he was living and take him off to Scotland so as to be out of reach of his foes, who would doubtless have made even shorter work with him than they did with the colonel."

"Good heavens!" the colonel exclaimed; "this is news indeed. So poor Leslie left a child and this is he! My lad," he said, taking Ronald's hand, "believe me that anything that I can do for you, whatever it be, shall be done, for the sake of your dear father, whom I loved as an elder brother."

"And I too," the major said. "There was not one of us but would have fought to the death for Leslie. And now sit down, my lad, while Anderson tells us your story."

Malcolm began at the account of the charge which Colonel Leslie had committed to him, and the manner in which he had fulfilled it. He told them how he had placed the child in the care of his brother, he himself having no fixed home of his own, and how the lad had received a solid education, while he had seen to his learning the use of his sword, so that he might be able to follow his father's career. He then told them the episode of the Jacobite agent, and the escape which had been effected in the Thames.

"You have done well, Anderson," the colonel said when he had concluded; "and if ever Leslie should come to see his son he will have cause to thank you, indeed, for the way in which you have carried out the charge he committed to you, and he may well be pleased at seeing him grown up such a manly young fellow. As to Leslie himself, we know not whether he be alive or dead. Every interest was made at the time to assuage his majesty's hostility, but the influence of the Marquis of Recambours was too strong, and the king at last peremptorily forbade Leslie's name being mentioned before him. You see, although the girl's father was, of course, at liberty to bestow her hand on whomsoever he pleased, he had, with the toadyism of a courtier, asked the king's approval of the match with Chateaurouge, which, as a matter of course, he received. His majesty, therefore, chose to consider it as a personal offence against himself that this Scottish soldier of fortune should carry off one of the richest heiresses of France, whose hand he had himself granted to one of his peers. At the same rime I cannot but think that Leslie still lives, for had he been dead we should assuredly have heard of the marriage of his widow with some one else. The duke has, of course, long since married, and report says that the pair are ill-matched; but another husband would speedily have been found for the widow."

"Since the duke has married," Ronald said, "he should no longer be so bitter against my father, and perhaps after so long an imprisonment the king might be moved to grant his release."

"As the duke's marriage is an unhappy one, I fear that you cannot count upon his hostility to your father being in any way lessened, as he would all the more regret the interference with his former plans."

"Have you any idea where my mother is, sir?"

"None," the colonel said. "But that I might find out for you. I will give you a letter to the Count de Noyes, who is on intimate terms with the Archbishop of Paris, who would, no doubt, be able to tell him in which convent the lady is residing. You must not be too sanguine, my poor boy, of seeing her, for it is possible that she has already taken the veil. Indeed, if your father has died, and she has still refused to accept any suitor whom the marquis may have found for her, you may be sure that she has been compelled to take the veil, as her estates would then revert to the nearest kinsman. This may, for aught we know, have happened years ago, without a word of it being bruited abroad, and the affair only known to those most concerned. However, we must look at the best side. We shall be able, doubtless, to learn through the archbishop whether she is still merely detained in the convent or has taken the veil, and you can then judge accordingly whether your father is likely to be alive or dead. But as to your obtaining an interview with your mother, I regard it as impossible in the one case as the other.

"At any rate it is of the highest importance that it should not be known that you are in France. If it is proved that your father is dead and your mother is secluded for life, we must then introduce you to her family, and try and get them to bring all their influence to bear to have you acknowledged openly as the legitimate heir of the marquis, and to obtain for you the succession to at least a portion of his estates--say to that of those which she brought him as her dowry. In this you may be sure that I and every Scottish gentleman in the army will give you all the aid and influence we can bring to bear."

Ronald warmly thanked Colonel Hume for his kindness, and the next day, having received the letter to the Count de Noyes, set out for Paris with Malcolm. On his arrival there he lost no time in calling upon the count, and presenting his letter of introduction.

The count read it through twice without speaking.

"My friend Colonel Hume," he said at last, "tells me that you are the son, born in lawful wedlock, of Colonel Leslie and Amelie de Recambours. I am aware of the circumstances of the case, being distantly related to the lady's family, and will do that which Colonel Hume asks me, namely, discover the convent in which she is living. But I warn you, young man, that your position here is a dangerous one, and that were it known that Colonel Leslie's son is alive and in France, I consider your life would not be worth a day's purchase. When powerful people are interested in the removal of anyone not favoured with powerful protection the matter is easily arranged. There are hundreds of knives in Paris whose use can be purchased for a few crowns, of if seclusion be deemed better than removal, a king's favourite can always obtain a lettre-de-cachet, and a man may linger a lifetime in prison without a soul outside the walls knowing of his existence there.

"You are an obstacle to the plans of a great noble, and that is in France a fatal offence. Your wisest course, young man, would be to efface yourself, to get your friend Colonel Hume to obtain for you a commission in his regiment, and to forget for ever that you are the son of Colonel Leslie and Amelie de Recambours. However, in that you will doubtless choose for yourself; but believe me my advice is good. At any rate I will do what my friend Colonel Hume asks me, and will obtain for you the name of the convent where your mother is living. I do not see that you will be any the better off when you have it, for assuredly you will nor be able to obtain permission to see her. However, that again is your affair. If you will give me the address where you are staying in Paris I will write to you as soon as I obtain the information. Do not be impatient, the archbishop himself may be in ignorance on the point; but I doubt not, that to oblige me, he will obtain the information from the right quarter."

A week later, Ronald, on returning one day to Le Soldat Ecossais, found a note awaiting him. It contained only the words:

"She has not taken the veil; she is at the convent of Our Lady at Tours."

The next morning Ronald and Malcolm set out on their journey to Tours.

CHAPTER VI: The Convent of Our Lady.

Arrived at Tours, Malcolm took a quiet lodging in a retired street. Colonel Hume had furnished him with a regular discharge, testifying that the bearer, Malcolm Anderson, had served his time in the 2d Scotch Dragoons, and was now discharged as being past service, and that he recommended him as a steady man for any employment for which he might be suited. Malcolm showed this document to his landlord in order that the latter might, as required by law, duly give notice to the police of the name and occupation of his lodger, and at the same time mentioned that the relations of his wife lived near Tours, and that he hoped through them to be able to obtain some sort of employment.

As soon as they were settled in their lodgings they went out, and after a few inquiries found themselves in front of the convent of Our Lady. It was a massive building, in a narrow street near the river, to which its grounds, surrounded by a high wall, extended. None of the windows of the building looked towards the street, upon which the massive gate, with a small wicket entrance, opened.

"What building is this?" Malcolm, in a careless tone, asked a woman who was sitting knitting at her door nearly opposite the entrance. "I am a stranger in Tours."

"That needs no telling," the woman replied, "or you would have known that that is the convent of Our Lady, one of the richest in Touraine, and they say in all France. Though what they do with their riches is more than I can tell, seeing that the rules are of the strictest, and that no one ever comes beyond the gates. They have their own grounds down to the river, and there is a walk along the wall there where they take the air of an evening when the weather is fine. Poor things, I pity them from my soul."

"But I suppose they all came willingly," Malcolm said; "so there is no need for pity."

"I don't know about willingly," the woman said. "I expect most of them took the veil rather than marry the men their fathers provided for them, or because they were in the way of someone who wanted their lands, or because their lovers had been killed in the war, just as if grief for a lover was going to last one's life. Besides, they are not all sisters. They say there's many a lady of good family shut up there till she will do her father's will. 'Well, well,' I often says to myself, 'they may have all the riches of France inside those walls, but I would rather sit knitting at my door here than have a share of them.'"

"You are a wise woman," Malcolm said. "There is nothing like freedom. Give me a crust, and a sod for my pillow, rather than gold plates inside a prison. I have been a soldier all my life, and have had my share of hard knocks; but I never grumbled so long as I was on a campaign, though I often found it dull work enough when in garrison."

"Oh, you have been a soldier! I have a brother in the regiment of Touraine. Perhaps you know him?"

"I know the regiment of Touraine," Malcolm said; "and there are no braver set of men in the king's service. What is his name?"

"Pierre Pitou. I have not heard of him for the last two years. He is a tall man, and broad, with a scar over the left eye."

"To be sure, to be sure!" Malcolm said. "Of course, Pierre Pitou is one of my best friends; and now I think of it, madam, I ought to know without asking, so great is his resemblance to you. Why, his last words to me were, 'If you go to Tours, seek out my sister, who lives in a house nearly opposite the entrance to the convent of Our Lady;' and to think I should have forgotten all about it till I saw you!"

Malcolm remained for a quarter of an hour chatting with the woman about her brother, and then, promising to call again the next day in the evening to be introduced to her husband, he rejoined Ronald, who had been waiting at the corner of the lane, and had been fidgeting with impatience at the long interview between Malcolm and the woman.

"What have you been talking about all this time, Malcolm, and what could you have to say to a stranger?"

"I have been telling her all about her brother, Pierre Pitou of the Touraine regiment, and how he distinguished himself at Dettingen, and will surely be made a sergeant, with a hope some day of getting to be a captain. I have quite won her heart."

"But who is Pierre Pitou, and when did you know him?" Ronald asked surprised.

"He is a tall man with broad shoulders and a scar over his left eye," Malcolm said laughing, and he then related the whole conversation.

"But why did you pretend to this poor woman that you knew her brother?"

"Because she may be very useful to us, Ronald; and if you can't find a friend in court, it's just as well to have one near court. She is a gossiping woman, and like enough she may know some of the lay sisters, who are, in fact, the servants of the convent, and come out to buy supplies of food and other things, and who distribute the alms among the poor. I don't know what advantage will come of it yet, Ronald; but I can see I have done a great stroke of business, and feel quite an affection for my friend Pierre Pitou."

Malcolm followed up the acquaintance he had made, and soon established himself as a friend of the family. Ronald did not accompany him on any of his visits, for as the plan of proceeding was still undecided, he and Malcolm agreed that it was better that he should not show himself until some favourable opportunity offered.

Sometimes towards evening he and Malcolm would take a boat and float down the stream past the convent walls, and Ronald would wonder which of the figures whose heads he could perceive as they walked upon the terrace, was that of his mother. It was not until Malcolm had become quite at home with Madame Vipon that he again turned the conversation towards the convent. He learned that she had often been inside the walls, for before her marriage she had worked at a farm whence the convent drew a portion of its supplies; milk, butter, and eggs, and she had often carried baskets to the convent.

"Of course I never went beyond the outer court," she said; "but Farmer Miron's daughter--it was he owned the farm--is a lay sister there. She was crossed in love, poor girl. She liked Andre, the son of a neighbouring farmer, but it was but a small place by the side of that of Miron, and her father would not hear of it, but wanted her to marry Jacques Dubois, the rich miller, who was old enough to be her father. Andre went to the wars and was killed; and instead of changing when the news came, as her father expected, and taking up with the miller, she hated him worse than ever, and said that he was the cause of Andre's death; so the long and short of it was, she came as a lay sister to the convent here. Of course she never thought of taking the vows, for to do that here one must be noble and be able to pay a heavy dowry to the convent.

"So she is just a lay sister, a sort of servant, you know, but she is a favourite and often goes to market for them, and when she does she generally drops in here for a few minutes for a talk; for though she was only a child when I was at the farm we were great friends, and she hears from me how all the people she used to know are getting on."

"I suppose she knows all the ladies who reside in the convent as well as the sisters?"

"Oh, yes, and much better than the sisters! It is on them she waits. She does not see much of the sisters, who keep to their own side of the house, and have very little to do with the visitors, or as one might call them the prisoners, for that is what most of them really are."

"Now I think of it," Malcolm said, "one of the officers I served under had a relation, a lady, whom I have heard him say, when he was talking to another officer, is shut up here, either because she wouldn't marry some one her father didn't want her to, I forget exactly what it was now. Let me see, what was her name. Elise--no, that wasn't it. Amelie--Amelie de Recambours--yes, that was it."

"Oh, yes, I know the name! I have heard Jeanne speak of her. Jeanne said it was whispered among them that she had really married somebody against her father's will. At any rate she has been there ever so many years, and they have not made her take the veil, as they do most of them if they are obstinate and won't give way. Poor thing! Jeanne says she is very pretty still, though she must be nearly forty now."

"That is very interesting," Malcolm said; "and if you will not mind, Madam Vipon, I will write to the officer of whom I spoke and tell him his cousin is alive and well. I was his servant in the regiment, and I know, from what I have heard him say, he was very much attached to her. There can be no harm in that, you know," he said, as Madam Vipon looked doubtful; "but if you would prefer it, of course I will not say how I have heard."

"Yes, that will be better," she agreed. "There is never any saying how things come round; and though there's no harm in what I have told you, still it's ill gossiping about what takes place inside convent walls."

"I quite agree with you, my dear Madam Vipon, and admire your discretion. It is singular how you take after your brother. Pierre Pitou had the reputation of being the most discreet man in the regiment of Touraine."

Ronald was very excited when he heard from Malcolm that he had actually obtained news at second hand as to his mother, and it was with difficulty that his friend persuaded him to allow matters to go on as he proposed.

"It will never do to hurry things now, Ronald; everything is turning out beyond our expectations. A fortnight ago it seemed absolutely hopeless that you should communicate with your mother; now things are in a good train for it."

Accordingly Malcolm made no further allusion to the subject to Madame Vipon until a fortnight had passed; then he said, on calling on her one day:

"Do you know, my dear Madam Vipon, I have had a letter from the gentleman of whom I was speaking to you. He is full of gratitude at the news I sent him. I did not tell him from whom I had heard the news, save that it was from one of the kindest of women, the sister of an old comrade of mine. He has sent me this"--and he took out a small box which he opened, and showed a pretty gold broach, with earrings to match--"and bid me to give it in his name to the person who had sent him this good news."

"That is beautiful," Madam Vipon said, clapping her hands; "and I have so often wished for a real gold broach! Won't my husband open his eyes when he sees them!"

"I think, if I might advise, my dear madam," Malcolm said, "I should not give him the exact history of them. He might take it into his head that you had been gossiping, although there is no woman in the world less given to gossiping than you are. Still, you know what husbands are. Therefore, if I were you I would tell him that your brother Pierre had sent them to you through me, knowing, you see, that you could not have read a letter even if he could have written one."

"Yes, perhaps that would be the best," Madam Vipon said; "but you had better write to Pierre and tell him. Otherwise when he comes home, and my husband thanks him for them, he might say he had never sent them, and there would be a nice affair."

"I will do so," Malcolm said; "but in any case I am sure your wit would have come to the rescue, and you would have said that you had in fact bought them from your savings; but that thinking your husband might grumble at your little economies you had thought it best to say that they came from your brother."

"Oh, fie, monsieur; I am afraid you are teaching me to tell stories."

"That is a very hard word, my dear madam. You know as well as I do that without a little management on both sides husbands and wives would never get on well together; but now I want to tell you more. Not only does my old master write to say how glad he is to hear of his cousin's welfare, but he has told me a great deal more about the poor lady, and knowing your kindness of heart I do not hesitate to communicate the contents of his letter to you. The Countess Amelie de Recambours was secretly married to a young officer, a great friend of my late master, and her father did not discover it until after the birth of a child--a boy. Then she was shut up here. The father got the boy safely away to Scotland, but he has now come back to France. I do not suppose the poor lady has ever heard of her little son since, and it would be an act of kindness and mercy to let her know that he is alive and well."

"Yes, indeed, poor creature," Madame Vipon said sympathetically. "Only to think of being separated from your husband, and never hearing of your child for all these years!"

"I knew your tender heart would sympathize with her," Malcolm said; "she is indeed to be pitied."

"And what became of her husband?"

"I fancy he died years ago; but my master says nothing about him. He only writes of the boy, who it seems is so delighted with the news about his mother that he is coming here to see if it is possible to have an interview with her."

"But it is not possible," Madam Vipon exclaimed. "How can he see her, shut up as she is in that convent?"

"Yes, it is difficult," Malcolm agreed; "but nothing is impossible, my dear madam, when a woman of heart like yourself takes a matter in hand; and I rely, I can tell you, greatly on your counsel; as to your goodwill, I am assured of that beforehand."

"But it is quite, quite, quite impossible, I assure you, my good Monsieur Anderson."

"Well, let us see. Now I know that you would suggest that the first measure to be taken is to open communication between mother and son, and there I heartily agree with you."

"That would be the first thing of course, monsieur; but how is that to be done?"

"Now that is where I look to you, madam. Your friend Jeanne waits upon her, you see, and I know your quick wit will already have perceived that Jeanne might deliver a message. I am sure that she would never be your friend had she not a warm heart like your own, and it will need very little persuasion on your part, when you have told her this sad story, to induce her to bring gladness to this unfortunate lady."

"Yes; but think of the consequences, Monsieur Anderson: think what would happen if it were found out."

"Yes, if there were any talk of the countess running away from the convent I would not on any condition ask you to assist in such a matter; but what is this--merely to give a message, a few harmless words."

"But you said an interview, Monsieur Anderson."

"An interview only if it is possible, my dear madam, that is quite another matter, and you know you said that it was quite impossible. All that we want now is just a little message, a message by word of mouth which not even the keenest eye can discover or prevent; there can be no harm in that."

"No, I don't think there can be much harm in that," Madam Vipon agreed; "at any rate I will talk to Jeanne. It will be her day for going to market tomorrow; I will tell her the story of the poor lady, and I think I can answer beforehand that she will do everything she can."

The following afternoon Malcolm again saw Madam Vipon, who told him that although she had not actually promised she had no doubt Jeanne would deliver the message.

"She will be out again on Saturday, monsieur, at nine in the morning, and if you will be here with the boy, if he has arrived by that time, you shall speak to her."

At the time appointed Malcolm, with Ronald, attired now as a young French gentleman, arrived at the house of Madam Vipon, who was warmly thanked by Ronald for the interest she had taken in him.

"My friend here has spoken to me in the highest terms of you, Madam Vipon, and I am sure that all that he has said is no more than the truth."

"I am sure I will do all I can," replied Madam Vipon, who was greatly taken by Ronald's appearance and manner; "it's a cruel thing separating a mother from a son so many years, and after all what I am doing is no hanging matter anyway."

A few minutes later Jeanne entered; she was a pleasant looking woman of five or six and twenty, and even her sombre attire as a lay sister failed to give a formal look to her merry face.

"So these are the gentlemen who want me to become a conspirator," she said, "and to run the risk of all sorts of punishment and penalties for meddling in their business?"

"Not so much my business as the business of my mother," Ronald said. "You who have such true heart of your own, for madam has told us something of your story, will, I am sure, feel for that poor lady shut up for fifteen years, and knowing not whether her child is dead or alive. If we could but see each other for five minutes, think what joy it would be to her, what courage her poor heart would take."

"See each other!" Jeanne repeated surprised. "You said nothing about that, Francoise; you only said take a message. How can they possibly see each other? That's a different thing altogether."

"I want you to take a message first," Ronald said. "If nothing more can be done that will be very much; but I cannot think but that you and my mother between you will be able to hit upon some plan by which we might meet."

"But how," Jeanne asked in perplexity, "how could it possibly be?"

"For example," Ronald suggested; "could I not come in as a lay sister? I am not much taller than you, and could pass very well as a girl."

Jeanne burst our laughing.

"You do not know what you are saying, monsieur; it would be altogether impossible. People do not get taken on as lay sisters in the convent of Our Lady unless they are known; besides, in other ways it would be altogether impossible, and even if it were not it might be years before you could get to speak to the countess, for there are only two or three of us who ever enter the visitors' rooms; and lastly, if you were found out I don't know what would be done to both of us. No, that would never do at all."

"Well, in the next place, I could climb on to the river terrace at night, and perhaps she could come and speak to me there."

"That is more possible," Jeanne said thoughtfully; "but all the doors are locked up at night."

"But she might get out of a window," Ronald urged; "with a rope ladder she could get down, and then return again, and none be the wiser."

Jeanne sat silent for a minute, and then she asked suddenly:

"Are you telling me all, monsieur, or are you intending that the countess shall escape with you?"

"No, indeed, on my honour!" Ronald exclaimed. "I have nowhere where I could take my mother. She would be pursued and brought back, and her position would be far worse than it is now. No; I swear to you that I only want to see her and to speak to her, and I have nothing else whatever in my mind."

"I believe you, monsieur," Jeanne said gravely. "Had it been otherwise I dare not have helped, for my punishment if I was discovered to have aided in an escape from the convent would be terrible--terrible!" she repeated with a shudder. "As to the other, I will risk it; for a gentler and kinder lady I have never met. And yet I am sure she must be very, very brave to have remained firm for so many years. At any rate I will give her your message."

Ronald took from a small leather bag, which he wore round his neck, a tiny gold chain with a little cross.

"I had this round my neck when I was taken away as a child to Scotland. No doubt she put it there, and will recognize it. Say to her only: 'He whom you have not seen since he was an infant is in Tours, longing above all things to speak to you;' that is all my message. Afterwards, if you will, you can tell her what we have said, and how I long to see her. How high is her room from the ground? Because if it is high it will be better that I should climb to her window, than that she should descend and ascend again."

Jeanne shook her head.

"That could not be," she said. "The visitors have all separate cells, but the partitions do not go up to the ceiling; and even if you entered, not a word could be spoken without being overheard. But fortunately she is on the first floor, and I am sure she is not one to shrink from so little a matter as the descent of a ladder in order to have an interview with her son."

That same afternoon as Amelie de Recambours was proceeding from the refectory to her cell, following several of her fellow captives, her attendant Jeanne came out from one of the cells. Glancing behind to see that no one was following, she put her finger on her lips and then whispered: "Make some excuse not to go into the garden with the others this evening. It is most important." Then she glided back into the room from which she had come.

The countess followed the others in a state of almost bewilderment. For sixteen years nothing had occurred to break the monotony of her existence. At first occasional angry messages reached her from her father, with orders to join an application to the pope for a divorce; but when it had been found impossible to overcome her steady refusals the messages had at last ceased, and for years no word from the outer world had reached her, although she had learned from those who from time to time came to share her captivity what was passing outside. Whether her husband was alive or dead she knew not. They had told her over and over again that he was dead; but the fact that she had never had the option given her of accepting another husband or taking the final vows kept hope alive. For she was convinced that if he was really dead, efforts would be made to compel her to marry again.

What, then, she wondered to herself, could this communication so secretly given mean? She regarded the lay sister who attended upon her as a happy looking young woman whose face was in strong contrast to most of those within the walls of the convent; but she had exchanged but few words with her, knowing that she would be but a short time about her. For the policy of the abbess was to change the attendants upon the ladies in their charge frequently, in order to prevent them from being tampered with, or persuaded into conveying communications without the walls.

"You look pale, Amelie," one of the other ladies said as they gathered in a group for a moment before proceeding to their respective apartments, where they were supposed to pass the afternoon in working, reading, and meditation.

"It is the heat," the countess said. "I have a headache."

"You look it," the latter said. "It is not often that you have anything the matter with you. You know we all say that you must have a constitution of iron and the courage of a Roland to be sixteen years here and yet to have no wrinkle on your forehead, no marks of weeping round your eyes."

The countess smiled sadly.

"I wept the first six months almost without ceasing, and then I told myself that if I would be strong and resist I must weep no more. If a bird in a cage once takes to pining he is sure not to live long. There are few of us here the news of whose death would not give pleasure to those who shut us up, and I for one resolved that I would live in spite of all."

"Well, you must not get ill now, Amelie. We should miss you terribly in the one hour of the day when we really live, the hour when we walk and talk, and laugh if we can, on the river terrace.

"I don't think I shall be able to come this evening," the countess said. "I shall lie down and keep myself quiet. Tomorrow I hope to be myself again. It is a mere passing indisposition."

The hours passed slowly as Amelie lay on her couch and wondered over the coming interview. There were so many things which she might hear--that her father was dead; that her family had hopes at last of obtaining her restoration to the world. That it could be a message from her husband she had no hope, for so long as her father lived she was sure that his release would never be granted. As to the child, she scarce gave it a thought. That it had somehow been removed and had escaped the search that had been made for it she was aware; for attempts had been made to obtain from her some clue as to where it would most likely have been taken. She was convinced that it had never been found, for if it had she would have heard of it. It would have been used as a lever to work upon her.

At last the hour when she was accustomed to go into the garden arrived, and as the convent bell struck seven she heard the doors of the other cells open, the sound of feet in the corridor, and then all became still. In a few minutes a step approached, and one of the sisters entered to inquire why she was not in the garden with the others.

She repeated that her head ached.

"You look pale," the sister said, "and your hand is hot and feverish. I will send you up some tisane. It is the heat, no doubt. I think that we are going to have thunder."

In a few minutes a step was again heard approaching, and Jeanne entered with the medicament. As she closed the door the countess started into a sitting position.

"What is it, Jeanne? What is it that you have to say to me?"

"Calm yourself, I pray you, countess," Jeanne said. "For both our sakes I pray you to hear what I have to say calmly. I expect Sister Felicia will be here directly. When she heard you were unwell she said she would come up and see what you needed. And now, I will begin my message. In the first place I was to hand you this." And she placed in Amelie's hand the little necklet and cross.

For a moment the countess looked at them wonderingly, and then there flashed across her memory a sturdy child in its nurse's arms, and a tall man looking on with a loving smile as she fastened a tiny gold chain round the child's neck. A low cry burst from her lips as she started to her feet.

"Hush, lady, hush!" Jeanne exclaimed. "This is my message: 'He whom you have not seen since he was an infant is in Tours, longing above all things to speak to you.'"

"My child! my child!" the countess cried. "Alive and here! My God, I thank thee that thou hast remembered a friendless mother at last. Have you seen him, Jeanne? What is he like? Oh, tell me everything!"

"He is a right proper young gentleman, madam. Straight and comely and tall, with brown waving hair and a bright pleasant face. A son such as any mother might be proud of."

The countess suddenly threw her arms around Jeanne's neck and burst into tears.

"You have made me so happy, Jeanne; happy as I never thought to be again. How can I thank you?"

"The best way at present, madam," Jeanne said with a smile, "will be by drinking up that tisane, and lying down quietly. Sister Felicia moves about as noiselessly as a cat, and she may pop in at any moment. Do you lie down again, and I will stand a little way off talking. Then if she comes upon us suddenly she will suspect nothing."

The countess seized the bowl of tisane and drank it off, and then threw herself on the couch.

"Go on, Jeanne, go on. Have pity on my impatience. Think how I am longing to hear of him. Did the message say he was longing to see me? But that is not possible."

"It is not quite impossible, madam; though it would be dangerous, very dangerous. Still it is not quite impossible."

"How then could it be done, Jeanne? You know what our life is here. How can I possibly see my boy?"

"What he proposes, madam, is this: that he should some night scale the river wall, and await you on the terrace, and that you should descend from your window by a rope ladder, and so return after seeing him."

"Oh, yes, that is possible!" the countess exclaimed; "I could knot my bed clothes and slide down. It matters not about getting back again, since we have no ladder."

"I can manage to bring in two light ropes," Jeanne said. "It would not do for you to be found in the garden, for it would excite suspicion, and you would never have a chance of doing it again. But it is not an easy thing to climb up a rope ladder with no one to help you, and you know I shall be at the other end of the house."

"That is nothing," the countess said. "Had I to climb ten times the height, do you think I should hesitate for a moment when it was to see my son? Oh, Jeanne, how good you are! And when will it be?"

"I will bring in the ropes next time I go out. Mind and place them in your bed. You will know that that night at eleven o'clock your son will be on the terrace awaiting you.

As Jeanne finished speaking she placed her finger on her lips, for she thought she heard a slight noise without. The countess closed her eyes and then lay down on her pillow, while Jeanne stood as if watching her. The next instant the door opened noiselessly and Sister Felicia entered. She moved with a noiseless step up to Jeanne.

"Is she asleep?" she whispered.

"Oh no!" Jeanne answered in a louder voice, guessing that the sister would have heard the murmur of voices. "She has only just closed her eyes."

The countess looked up.

"Ah! is it you, sister? I have taken the tisane Sister Angela sent up, but my hands are burning and my head aches. The heat in chapel was so great I thought I should have fainted."

"Your hands are indeed burning," the sister said, convinced, as soon as she touched them, that the countess was really indisposed. "Yes; and your pulse is beating quicker than I can count. Yes, you have a touch of fever. I will mix you a draught and bring it up to you at once. Hark! that is the first peal of thunder; we are going to have a storm. It will clear the air, and do you even more good than my medicine. I will leave you here for tonight; if you are not better tomorrow we will move you into the infirmary."

The next morning Sister Felicia found her patient much better, though she still seemed languid and weak, and was ordered to remain quietly in her apartment for a day or so, which was just what she desired, for she was so filled with her new born happiness that she feared that if she went about her daily tasks as usual she should not be able to conceal from the sharp eyes of the sisters the joyousness which was brimming over in her, while had she laughed she would have astonished the inmates of the gloomy convent.

CHAPTER VII: Mother!

When Jeanne, after accomplishing her errands the next time she went out, entered Madam Vipon's, she found Ronald and Malcolm awaiting her.

"You have told my mother?" the former asked eagerly as she entered.

"Yes, I have told her, and if I had been an angel from heaven, with a special message to her, the poor lady could not have looked more happy."

"And you have been like an angel to us!" Ronald exclaimed, taking her hand. "How can I thank you for your goodness?"

"For shame, sir!" Jeanne said, smiling and colouring as Ronald, in his delight, threw his arms round her and kissed her. "Remember I am a lay sister."

"I could not have helped it," Ronald said, "if you had been the lady superior. And now," he went on eagerly, "is all arranged? See, I have brought a ladder of silk rope, light and thin, but quite strong enough to bear her."

"You take all for granted then, sir. You know I said I would take your message, but that I would not engage to meddle further in it."

"I know you said so; but I was sure that having gone so far you would do the rest. You will, won't you, Jeanne?"

"I suppose I must," Jeanne said; "for what with the countess on one side and you on the other, I should get no peace if I said no. Well, then, it is all arranged. At eleven o'clock tonight you are to be on the terrace, and you can expect her there. If she does not come you will know that something has occurred to prevent her, and she will come the following night at the same hour."

Jeanne took the silken cords and wound them round her, under her lay sister's robe, and then, with a kindly nod at Ronald, and an injunction to be as noiseless as a mouse in climbing up the terrace, and above all not to raise his voice in speaking to his mother, she tripped away across the street to the convent.

Malcolm and Ronald sallied out from Tours before the city gates were closed at sunset, and sat down on the slope which rises from the other side of the river and waited till it was time to carry the plan into operation. Gradually the lights disappeared from the various windows and the sounds which came across the water ceased, and by ten o'clock everything was profoundly still. They had, in the course of the afternoon, hired a boat, saying they were going out for a night's fishing. This they had moored a short distance below the town, on the side of the river where they now were. They now made their way to it and rowed quietly across the stream; then they left it and waded through the water, which flowed knee deep at the foot of the walls.

Although Tours was still a walled town the habit of keeping sentry in time of peace had long since died out, and they had no fear, at that hour, of discovery. There was no moon, but the night was bright and clear, and they had no difficulty in finding that part of the wall which now formed the terrace of the convent.

They were provided with a rope knotted at every foot, and with a grapnel attached to one end. At the second attempt this caught on the parapet of the wall, and Ronald at once climbed it and stood on the terrace, where, a minute later, he was joined by Malcolm. The convent itself could not be seen, for a screen of trees at the foot of the wall shut it off from the view of people on the opposite bank of the river. They waited quietly until a sudden peal of the bells of the numerous churches announced that it was the hour. Then they moved towards the steps leading down into the garden. A minute later a figure was seen approaching. Malcolm fell back, and Ronald advanced towards it. As the countess approached she held out her arms, exclaiming:

"My boy, my boy!" and with a cry of "Mother!" Ronald sprang forward into her embrace.

For a short time not a word was spoken, and then the countess murmured:

"My God, I thank thee for this great happiness. And now, my son," she said, recovering herself, "tell me everything. First, have you news of your father?"

"Alas, no!" Ronald said. "Nothing has been heard of him since the fatal day when he was seized; but I am convinced that he is still alive, and since I have found you, surely I shall be able to find him."

"Who is that with you, Ronald?"

"That is Malcolm Anderson; it is to him I owe everything. He carried me off and took me away with him to Scotland the day my father was arrested. He has been my best friend ever since, and it is he who brought me here to you."

The countess advanced to Malcolm.

"My son has told me that we owe everything to you, my brave Malcolm!" she said, holding out her hand. "I guessed that it was to you that my husband had confided the care of the child when I learned that it had disappeared. I remember what confidence he had in your devotion, and how he confided everything to you."

"He was like a brother to me, madam," Malcolm replied; "and glad indeed am I that I have been able to befriend his son and to bring him back to you a gentleman who will be an honour even to his father's name and yours."

"And now let us sit down here," the countess said, taking a seat upon a bench. "It gets light very early, and you must not stay after two o'clock, and there is so much for me to hear."

For the next two hours Ronald sat holding his mother's hand, while he told her the story of his life. "And now, mother," he said, when he had concluded, "we have but an hour left, for it has just struck one, and we have not said a word yet about the principal thing of all. How are we to obtain your freedom? Cannot you arrange to escape with us? I do not, of course, mean tonight, for we have nothing prepared, and, moreover, I promised Jeanne that there should be no attempt at escape; but we can come again when everything is ready. We shall, of course, need a disguise for you, for there will be a hot pursuit when your escape is known. But we might manage to reach the coast and cross over to England, and so make our way north."

"No, my son," the countess said. "I have thought it over in every way since I knew you were here, and I am resolved to remain here. Were I to fly, the last hope that your father might be freed would be lost. My father would be more than ever incensed against him and me; and, moreover, although that is but a minor consideration, there would be no hope whatever of your ever recovering the rank and estate to which you are entitled. No, I am resolved to wait here, at any rate so long as my father lives. At his death doubtless there will be some change, for as heiress to his estates my existence must be in some way recognized, and my family may be enabled to obtain my release when his powerful opposition is removed; if not, it will be time to take the idea of flight into consideration; till then I remain here. Now that I have seen you, now that I know you as you are, for I can just make out your face by the light of the stars, I shall be as near contentment and happiness as I can be till I meet your father again. In the meantime your good friend here can advise you far better than I can as to what your course had better be. If you can obtain any high influence, use it for obtaining your father's release. If it be accompanied by a sentence of exile from France it matters not, so that he is freed. You can then return here, and I will gladly fly with you to join him in Scotland."

Malcolm now rose from his seat and left mother and son half an hour together. When two o'clock struck he returned to them.

"There is the signal," the countess said, rising, "and now we must part." She had already refused to accede to Ronald's entreaty that she would meet him there again.

"No, my son, we have been permitted to meet this once, but we must not tempt fortune again. Sooner or later something would be sure to occur which would lead to discovery, and bring ruin upon all our plans. It is hard to say no, and to refuse the chance of seeing you again now that we have come together, but I am fully resolved that I will not risk it."

"We will see you safe up the ladder, mother," Ronald said. "It is no easy matter to climb up a rope ladder swinging loosely."

"No, I discovered that in descending," the countess said; "but if you come with me you must take off your boots--the print of a man's footstep in the garden would ruin us all; and mind, not a word must be spoken when we have once left the terrace."

Taking off their boots they accompanied her through the garden. There was a last passionate embrace at the foot of the ladder, then the countess mounted it while they held it steady. Directly she entered the window she undid the fastening of the rope inside and let the ladder drop down to them. Five minutes later Ronald descended the rope into the river. Malcolm shifted the grapnel so that it caught only on the edge of the parapet and could be shaken off from below when the strain on the rope was removed, then he slid down to Ronald's side. A sharp jerk brought down the grapnel, and they returned along the edge of the river as they had come, crossed in the boat, and waited for morning.

They waited two days longer in Tours in order that they might receive, through Jeanne from the countess, a list of the noble families to which she was related, with notes as to those persons of whom she had seen most before her marriage, and who she believed would be most disposed to exert their influence on her behalf.

"Jeanne," Ronald said, "I am troubled that I do not know what I can do to show you how grateful I am. I should so like to give you some souvenir, but what can I do--you could not wear brooches, or earrings, or trinkets."

"That I could not, monsieur," Jeanne broke in with a smile; "and if I could I would not accept them from you. I have done what I have done because I pitied your mother and you, and I am content that if I have broken the rules I have done it with a good purpose."

"Well, Jeanne," Ronald said, "you may not be a lay sister all your life; you have taken no vows that will bind you for ever, and I have no doubt that the lady superior can absolve you from your engagements should you at any time wish to go back to the world; if so, and if I am still in France, I will come to dance at your wedding, and will promise you as pretty a necklace and earrings as are to be found in Touraine."

"Very well, that is a bargain," Jeanne said laughing; "and it is not impossible, young sir, that some day I may hold you to your promise, for only last market day I met my father, and he spoke more kindly to me than he used to, and even said that he missed me; and I hear that the miller has found someone who will put up with him for the sake of his money. I shouldn't be surprised if, when that comes off, father wants me home again; but I sha'n't go directly he asks me, you may be sure, but shall bargain that if there be again any question of a husband it will be for me to decide and not him."

The next day Ronald and his companion started for Paris. They were highly gratified with the success which had attended them, and Ronald felt his whole life brightened now that he had found the mother who had been so long lost to him. On arriving at Paris they found that Colonel Hume's regiment had returned to the capital. It was not expected that there would at present be any further fighting on the frontier, and two or three of the Scotch regiments had been brought back. Ronald at once called on Colonel Hume and related to him the success which had attended the first portion of his undertaking.

"I congratulate you indeed," Colonel Hume said. "I own that I thought your enterprise was a hopeless one, for it seemed to me impossible that you should be able to obtain an interview with a lady closely imprisoned in a convent. Why, Anderson, it is plain now that your talents have been lost, and that you ought to have been a diplomatist instead of wasting your time as a soldier. The way you carried out your plan was indeed admirable, and I shall really begin to think that Ronald will yet succeed; and now, my young friend, what do you mean to do next?"

"Would it be possible, sir, to ascertain where my father is confined?"

"I think not, my lad," the colonel said gravely. "In addition to the four or five prisons in Paris there are a score of others in different parts of France. The names of the prisoners in each are known only to the governors; to all others within the walls they exist as numbers only. The governors themselves are sworn to secrecy, and even if we could get at one or two of them, which would be difficult enough, we could hope for no more. Nor would it be much satisfaction to you merely to know in which prison your father is lying, for it is a very different matter to communicate with a prisoner in one of the royal fortresses to passing a message to a lady detained in a convent. I can see nothing for you but to follow the example of your mother and to practise patience, so conducting yourself as to gain friends and make a name and influence, so that at your grandfather's death we may bring as strong a pressure as possible to bear upon the king."

"How old is my grandfather?" Ronald asked.

"He is a man about sixty."

"Why, he may live twenty years yet!" Ronald exclaimed bitterly.

"Do not look at the worst side of the question," Colonel Hume replied with a smile. "But he may live some years," he went on more gravely, "and in the meantime you must think what you had better do. I will tell you as a great secret, that it has been finally resolved that an expedition shall sail this winter for Scotland, and fifteen thousand troops will assemble at Dunkirk under Marshal Saxe. Nothing could be more opportune. We are to form part of the expedition, with several other Scottish regiments. You are too young as yet for me to ask for a commission for you, but if you like I will enroll you as a gentleman volunteer; in this way you may have an opportunity of distinguishing yourself. I will introduce you to the Chevalier, and it may be that if he succeeds in gaining the crown of Scotland, if not of England, he will himself ask King Louis as a personal favour to release and restore to him Colonel Leslie of Glenlyon, who fought bravely with him in '15. If the expedition fails, and we get back alive to France, I will then obtain for you a commission in the regiment, and we can carry out our plan as we arranged. What do you say to that?"

"I thank you greatly, sir, and accept your offer most gratefully. I see that I am powerless to do anything for my father now, and your plan gives at least a prospect of success. In any case nothing will give me so much delight as to serve with the regiment he formerly commanded, and under so kind a friend as yourself."

"That is settled then," Colonel Hume said; "and now about outfit. A gentleman volunteer wears the uniform of the officers of the regiment, and indeed is one in all respects except that he draws no pay. My purse will be at your disposal. Do not show any false modesty, my lad, about accepting help from me. Your father would have shared his last penny with me had I needed it."

"I thank you heartily, colonel, for your offer, and should it be necessary I will avail myself of it, but at present I have ample funds. Malcolm carried off with me a bag with a hundred louis, and up to the day when I landed in France these had never been touched. I have eighty of them still remaining, which will provide my outfit and my maintenance for a long time to come."

"There is another advantage in your being a volunteer, rather than on the list of officers, Ronald; in that if it is necessary at any time, you can, after a word with me, lay aside your uniform and go about your affairs as long as you choose without question, which would be hard to do if you belonged regularly to the regiment."

At the end of a week Ronald had procured his uniform, and was presented by the colonel to the officers of the regiment as Ronald Leslie, the son of an old friend of his, who was joining the regiment as a gentleman volunteer. Malcolm joined only in the capacity of Ronald's servant. It was painful to the lad that his old friend and protector should assume such a relation towards him, but Malcolm laughed at his scruples.

"My dear Ronald," he said, "I was your father's servant, and yet his friend. Why should I not act in the same capacity to you? As to the duties, they are so light that, now I do not belong to the regiment, my only difficulty will be to kill time. There is nothing to do save to polish up your arms and your equipment. Your horse will be looked after by a trooper so long as you are with the regiment. I shall call you in the morning, get your cup of chocolate, and prepare your dinner when you do not dine abroad, carry your messages when you have any messages to send, and escort you when you go about any business in which it is possible that a second sword would be of use to you. As I have said, the only trouble will be to know what to do with myself when you do not want me."

It was now the end of August, and for the next four months Ronald worked hard at drill. He soon became a general favourite with the officers. The fact that his name was Leslie, and that he was accompanied by Malcolm, who was known to many of the old soldiers as being devoted to their former colonel and as having in some strange way disappeared from the regiment at the same time, gave ground to a general surmise that Leslie was the colonel's son.

Malcolm himself, when questioned, neither denied nor acknowledged the fact, but turned it off with a joke and a laugh. He was soon as much at home in his old regiment as if he formed a part in it, and when not required by Ronald passed the greater part of his time with his former comrades. As was natural, the opinion entertained by the men as to Leslie's identity was shared by the officers. The avoidance by Ronald of any allusion to his family, his declining when he first came among them to say to which branch of the Leslies he belonged, and the decided manner in which Colonel Hume, the first time the question was broached in his hearing in Ronald's absence, said that he begged no inquiries would be made on that score; all he could assure them was that Leslie's father was a gentleman of good family, and a personal friend of his own--put a stop to all further questioning, but strengthened the idea that had got abroad that the young volunteer was the son of Colonel Leslie.

Early in January the 2d Scottish Dragoons marched for Dunkirk, where twenty thousand men assembled, while a large number of men of war and transports were gathered in the port. One day, when Ronald was walking in the street with Malcolm at his heels, the latter stepped up to him and touched him.

"Do you see that officer in the uniform of a colonel of the Black Musketeers, in that group at the opposite corner; look at him well, for he is your father's greatest enemy, and would be yours if he knew who you are; that is the Duke de Chateaurouge."

Ronald gazed at the man who had exercised so evil an influence upon the fate of his parents. He was a tall dark man with a pointed moustache, and of from forty to forty-five years of age. His features were regular and handsome; but in his thin straight eyebrows, the curl of his lips, and a certain supercilious drooping of the eyelids, Ronald read the evil passions which rendered him so dangerous and implacable an enemy.

"So that is the duke!" Ronald said when he had passed on. "I did not know he was a soldier."

"He is an honorary colonel of the regiment, and only does duty when it is called on active service; but he served in it for some years as a young man, and had the reputation of being a good soldier, though I know that he was considered a harsh and unfeeling officer by the men who served under him. That is the man, Ronald, and if you could get six inches of your sword between his ribs it would go a good long way towards obtaining your father's release; but I warn you he is said to be one of the best swordsmen in France."

"I care not how good a swordsmen he is," Ronald said hotly, "if I do but get a fair chance."

"Don't do anything rash, Ronald; I have no fear about your swordsmanship, for I know in the last four months you have practised hard, and that Francois says that young as you are you could give a point to any officer in the regiment. But at present it were madness to quarrel with the duke; you have everything to lose and nothing to gain. If he killed you there would be an end of you and your plans; if you killed him you would have to fly the country, for a court favourite is not to be slain with as much impunity as a bourgeois, and equally would there be an end of all hope of obtaining your father's release.

"No, for the present you must be content to bide your time. Still it is as well for you to know your foe when you see him, and in the meantime go on frequenting the various schools of arms and learn every trick of the sword that is to be taught. Look!" he went on, as a group of mounted officers rode down the street; "that is Marshal Saxe, one of the best soldiers in France, if not the best, and just as wild and reckless in private life as he is calm and prudent as a general."

Ronald looked with some surprise at the great general. He had expected to see a dashing soldier. He saw a man who looked worn and bent with disease, and as if scarce strong enough to sit on his horse; but there was still a fire in his eye, and as he uttered a joke to an officer riding next to him and joined merrily in the laugh, it was evident that his spirit was untouched by the disease which had made a wreck of his body.

A few days later a messenger arrived with the news that the French fleet from Brest had sailed, and had met the English fleet which had gone off in pursuit of it, and the coast of Kent was in consequence unguarded. Orders were instantly given that the troops should embark on board the transports, and as fast as these were filled they set sail. The embarkation of the cavalry naturally took longer time than that of the infantry, and before the Scottish Dragoons had got their horses on board a portion of the fleet was already out of sight.

"Was there ever such luck!" Malcolm exclaimed, after assisting in getting the horses on board, a by no means easy task, as the vessel was rolling heavily at her mooring. "The wind is rising every moment, and blowing straight into the harbour; unless I mistake not, there will be no sailing tonight."

This was soon evident to all. Signals were made from ship to ship, fresh anchors were let down, and the topmast housed. By midnight it was blowing a tremendous gale, which continued for three days. Several of the transports dragged their anchors and were washed ashore, and messages arrived from different parts of the coast telling of the wreck of many of those which had sailed before the storm set in.

The portion of the fleet which had sailed had indeed been utterly dispersed by the gale. Many ships were lost, and the rest, shattered and dismantled, arrived at intervals at the various French ports. The blow was too heavy to be repaired. The English fleet had again returned to the coast, and were on the lookout to intercept the expedition, and as this was now reduced to a little more than half of its original strength no surprise was felt when the plan was abandoned altogether.

Marshal Saxe with a portion of the troops marched to join the army in Flanders, and the Scotch Dragoons were ordered to return to Paris for the present.

For a year Ronald remained with the regiment in Paris. He had during that time been introduced by Colonel Hume to several members of his mother's family. By some of these who had known her before her marriage he was kindly received; but all told him that it would be hopeless to make any efforts for the release of his father as long as the Marquis de Recambours remained alive and high in favour at court, and that any movement in that direction would be likely to do harm rather than good. Some of the others clearly intimated to him that they considered that the countess had, by making a secret marriage and defying her father's authority, forfeited all right to the assistance or sympathy of her mother's family.

Twice Ronald travelled to Tours and sent messages to his mother through Jeanne, and received answers from the countess. She had, however, refused to meet him again on the terrace, saying that in spite of the love she had for him, and her desire to see him again, she was firmly resolved not to run the risk of danger to him and the failure of all their hopes, by any rash step.

At the end of the summer campaign in Flanders Marshal Saxe returned to Paris, and Colonel Hume one day took Ronald and introduced him to him, having previously interested the marshal by relating his history to him. The marshal asked Ronald many questions, and was much pleased with his frank manner and bearing.

"You shall have any protection I can give you," the marshal said. "No man has loved adventures more than I, nor had a fairer share of them, and my sympathies are altogether with you; besides, I remember your father well, and many a carouse have we had together in Flanders. But I am a soldier, you know, and though the king is glad enough to employ our swords in fighting his enemies, we have but little influence at court. I promise you, however, that after the first great victory I win I will ask the release of your father as a personal favour from the king, on the ground that he was an old comrade of mine. I can only hope, for your sake, that the marquis, your grandfather, may have departed this world before that takes place, for he is one of the king's prime favourites, and even the request of a victorious general would go for little as opposed to his influence the other way. And now, if you like, I will give you a commission in Colonel Hume's regiment. You have served for a year as a volunteer now, and younger men than you have received commissions."

Ronald thanked the marshal most heartily for his kind promise, but said that at present he would rather remain as a volunteer, because it gave him greater freedom of action.

"Perhaps you are right," the marshal said. "But at any rate you had better abstain from attempting any steps such as Colonel Hume tells me you once thought of for obtaining the release of your father. Success will be all but impossible, and a failure would destroy altogether any hopes you may have of obtaining his release from the king."

It seemed that some of his mother's family with whom he had communicated must have desired to gain the favour of the favourite of the king by relating the circumstances to him, for a short time after Ronald's interview with the marshal the marquis came up to Colonel Hume when he was on duty in the king's antechamber, and, in the presence of a number of courtiers, said to him:

"So, Colonel Hume, I find that I have to thank you for harbouring in your regiment an imposter, who claims to be my grandson. I shall know, sir, how to repay the obligation."

"The gentleman in question is no imposter, marquis, as I have taken the pains to inform myself. And I am not aware of any reason why I should not admit the son of a Scottish gentleman into my regiment, even though he happen to be a grandson of yours. As to your threat, sir, as long as I do my duty to his majesty I fear the displeasure of no man."

Two nights later, as Ronald was returning from dining with Colonel Hume and some of his officers, he was suddenly attacked in a narrow street by six men. Malcolm was with him, for Colonel Hume had at once related to him the conversation he had had with the marquis, and had warned him to take the greatest precautions.

"He is perfectly capable of having you suddenly put out of his way by a stab in the back, Ronald. And if there were anywhere for you to go I should advise you to leave Paris at once; but nowhere in France would you be safe from him, and it would upset all your plans to return to Scotland at present. However, you cannot be too careful."

Ronald had related what had passed to Malcolm, who determined to watch more carefully than ever over his safety, and never left his side when he was outside the barracks.

The instant the six men rushed out from a lane, at whose entrance a lantern was dimly burning, Malcolm's sword was out, and before the assailants had time to strike a blow he had run the foremost through the body.

Ronald instantly recovered from his surprise and also drew. He was now nearly eighteen, and although he had not yet gained his full height he was a match for most men in strength, while his constant exercise in the school of arms had strengthened the muscle of his sword arm, until in strength as well as in skill he could hold his own against the best swordsman in the regiment. The men were for a moment checked by the fall of their leader; but then seeing that they had opposed to them only one man, and another whom they regarded as a lad, scarcely to be taken into consideration, they rushed upon them. They were quickly undeceived. Ronald parried the first blow aimed at him, and with his riposte stretched his opponent on the pavement, and then springing forward, after a few rapid thrusts and parries ran the next through the shoulder almost at the same moment that Malcolm stretched another opponent on the ground.

Terrified at the downfall of three of their number, while a fourth leaned against a door post disabled, the two remaining ruffians took to their heels and fled at the top of their speed, the whole affair having lasted scarce a minute.

"Tell your employer," Ronald said to the wounded man, "that I am not to be disposed of so easily as he imagined. I should be only giving you what you deserve if I were to pass my sword through your body; but I disdain to kill such pitiful assassins except in self defence."

The next morning Ronald communicated to Colonel Hume what had happened.

"It's just as well, my young friend, that you are going to leave Paris. I received orders half an hour ago for the regiment to march to the frontier at once. That is the marquis's doing, no doubt. He thought to get rid of you last night and to punish me this morning; but he has failed both ways. You have defeated his cutthroats; I shall be heartily glad to be at the front again, for I am sick of this idle life in Paris."

CHAPTER VIII: Hidden Foes.

"I am heartily glad to be out of Paris," Ronald said to Malcolm on their first halt after leaving the capital. "It is not pleasant to regard every man one meets after dark as a possible enemy, and although I escaped scot free from the gang who attacked us the other night, one cannot always expect such good fortune as that. It was a constant weight on one's mind, and I feel like a new man now that we are beyond the city walls."

"Nevertheless, Ronald, we must not omit any precautions. Your enemy has a long purse, and can reach right across France. That last affair is proof of his bitterness against you, and it would be rash indeed were we to act as if, having made one attempt and failed, he would abandon his plans altogether. He is clearly a man who nourishes a grudge for years, and his first failure is only likely to add to his vindictive feeling. I do not say that your danger is as great as it was in Paris, but that is simply because the opportunities of attacking you are fewer. I should advise you to be as careful as before, and to be on your guard against ambushes and surprises."

"Well, it may be so, Malcolm, and of course I will be careful; but till I have proof to the contrary I shall prefer to think that the marquis will trust to my being knocked on the head during the war, and will make no further move against me until the regiment returns to Paris."

"Think what you like, lad," Malcolm said, "so that you are cautious and guarded. I shall sleep with one eye open, I can tell you, till we are fairly beyond the frontier."

Two days later the regiment encamped outside the town of St. Quentin. They were usually quartered on the inhabitants; but the town was already filled with troops, and as the weather was fine Colonel Hume ordered his men to bivouac a short distance outside the walls. Ronald was seeing that his troop got their breakfast next morning, when a sergeant came up with two men with a horse.

"This is Monsieur Leslie," he said to them. "These men were asking for you, sir."

"What do you want with me?" Ronald said surprised.

"We heard, sir," one of the peasants said, "that you wanted to buy a horse. We have a fine animal here, and cheap."

"But I do not want to buy one," Ronald replied. "I am very well supplied with horses. What made you think I wanted one?"

"We asked one of the officers, sir, if anyone in the regiment would be likely to buy, and he said that Monsieur Leslie wanted one, he believed."

"No," Ronald said decidedly. "Whoever told you was mistaken. I have my full complement, and though your horse looks a nice animal I could not take him if you offered him to me for nothing. I don't think you will get anyone to buy him in the regiment. I believe that every officer has his full complement of chargers."

In the evening Ronald happened to mention to Malcolm the offer he had had in the morning.

"It was a nice looking beast," he said, "and I had half a mind to ask them what they would take to exchange him with my roan, but I did not want to dip further into my purse."

"I wish I had been beside you at the time," Malcolm said earnestly; "those two fellows wouldn't have gone out of the camp so easily."

"Why, what do you mean, Malcolm?"

"Mean!" Malcolm repeated in a vexed tone. "This is what comes of your being watchful and cautious, Ronald. Why, the matter is clear enough. The marquis has set men on your track, but of course they could do nothing until some of them knew you by sight, so two of them are sent into camp with this cock and bull story about a horse, and they come and have a good look at you and go quietly off. It is too provoking. Had I been there I would have given them in charge of a file of men at once. Then we would have asked every officer in the regiment if he had sent them to you, and when we found, as we certainly should have found, that none of them had done so, we should have marched the men off to Colonel Hume, and I am sure, when he heard the circumstances of the case, they would have been lashed up and flogged till he had got the truth of the matter out of them. My great hope has been that they could not very well attempt your life, because none of the men who might be engaged on the job would be likely to know your face, and they would therefore have no means of singling you out for attack; and now two of the ruffians will be able to follow you and watch their opportunity."

"Oh, nonsense, Malcolm, you are too suspicious altogether! I have no doubt the affair was just as they stated it to be. What was more natural?"

"Well, Ronald, you will meet all the other officers at supper in half an hour. Just ask if any of them sent two men wanting to sell a horse to you this morning; if any of them say that they did so, I will acknowledge I am wrong."

Accordingly Ronald, at supper, put the question, but none of the officers admitted they knew anything about the matter.

"You have two very good horses, Leslie; why should anyone suppose that you wanted another?" the colonel asked.

"I don't know," Ronald said. "I only know that two men did come up with a horse to me this morning, and said that one of the officers had told them that I wanted to buy one."

"It must have been one of the men," the colonel said carelessly, "though I don't know why anyone should suppose that you wanted another charger. Still, someone, knowing that you are the last joined officer, might think you had need for a second horse."

The subject dropped, and Malcolm shook his head ominously when Ronald acknowledged to him that his suspicions were so far right that none of the officers had sent the men to him. The next day, as the regiment was passing through a thick wood, and Ronald was riding with Captain Campbell behind his troop, which happened to be in the rear in the regiment, two shots were fired from among the trees. The first struck Ronald's horse in the neck, causing him to swerve sharply round, a movement which saved his rider's life, for the second shot, which was fired almost instantly after the first, grazed his body and passed between him and Captain Campbell.

"Are you hit, Leslie?" the latter exclaimed, for the sudden movement of his horse had almost unseated Ronald.

"Nothing serious, I think. The bullet has cut my coat and grazed my skin, I think, but nothing more."

The captain shouted orders to his men, and with a score of troopers dashed into the wood. The trees grew thickly and there was a dense undergrowth, and they had difficulty in making their way through them. For half an hour they continued their search without success, and then rejoined the regiment on its march.

"This is a curious affair," Colonel Hume said when Captain Campbell reported, at the next halt, that an attempt at assassination had taken place.

"It looks like a premeditated attempt upon one or other of you. You haven't been getting into any scrape, have you?" he asked with a smile; "kissing some peasant's wife or offering to run away with his daughter? But seriously this is a strange affair. Why should two men lie in wait for the regiment and fire at two of its officers? The men have been behaving well, as far as I have heard, on the line of march, and nothing has occurred which could explain such an outrage as this."

"It may be fancy on my part, colonel," Ronald said, "but I cannot help thinking that it is a sequence of that affair I told you about in Paris, just before we started. The first shot struck my horse and the second would certainly have killed me had it not been for the horse's sudden swerve, therefore it looks as if the shots were aimed at me. I have some reason, too, for supposing that I have been followed. If you remember my question last night at supper about the men who wanted to sell me a horse. Malcolm Anderson is convinced that the whole thing was only a ruse to enable them to become acquainted with my face. They wanted to be able to recognize me, and so got up this story in order to have me pointed out to them, and to have a talk with me. None of the officers did send them to me, as they said, and they could hardly have hit upon a better excuse for speaking to me."

"It certainly looks like it," Colonel Hume said gravely. "I would give a good deal if we had caught those two men in the wood. If we had I would have given them the choice of being hung at once or telling me what was their motive in firing at you and who paid them to do it. This is monstrous. If we could get but a shadow of proof against your enemies I would lay a formal complaint before the king. Marquis or no marquis, I am not going to have my officers assassinated with impunity. However, till we have something definite to go upon, we can do nothing, and until then, Leslie, you had best keep your suspicion to yourself. It were best to say nothing of what you think; in this country it is dangerous even to whisper against a king's favourite. Let it be supposed that this attack in the woods was only the work of some malicious scoundrels who must have fired out of pure hatred of the king's troops."

Captain Campbell and Ronald quite agreed with the view taken by the colonel, and answered all questions as to the affair, that they had not the least idea who were the men who fired on them, and that no one obtained as much as a glimpse of them.

With most of the officers of the regiment, indeed with all except one, Ronald was on excellent terms. The exception was a lieutenant named Crawford; he was first on the list of his company, and had, indeed, been twice passed over in consequence of his quarrelsome and domineering disposition. He was a man of seven or eight and twenty; he stood about the same height as Ronald and was of much the same figure, indeed the general resemblance between them had often been remarked.

His dislike to Ronald had arisen from the fact that previous to the latter joining the regiment Crawford had been considered the best swordsman among the officers, and Ronald's superiority, which had been proved over and over again in the fencing room, had annoyed him greatly. Knowing that he would have no chance whatever with Ronald in a duel, he had carefully abstained from open war, showing his dislike only by sneering remarks and sarcastic comments which frequently tried Ronald's patience to the utmost, and more than once called down a sharp rebuke from Colonel Hume or one or other of the majors. He did not lose the opportunity afforded by the shots fired in the wood, and was continually suggesting all sorts of motives which might have inspired the would be assassins.

Ronald, who was the reverse of quarrelsome by disposition, laughed good temperedly at the various suggestions; but one or two of the senior officers remonstrated sharply with Crawford as to the extent to which he carried his gibes.

"You are presuming too much on Leslie's good nature, Crawford," Captain Campbell said one day. "If he were not one of the best tempered young fellows going he would resent your constant attacks upon him; and you know well that, good swordsman as you are, you would have no chances whatever if he did so."

"I am quite capable of managing my own affairs," Crawford said sullenly, "and I do not want any advice from you or any other man."

"I am speaking to you as the captain of Leslie's troop," Captain Campbell said sharply, "and I do not mean to quarrel with you. You have had more quarrels than enough in the regiment already, and you know Colonel Hume said on the last occasion that your next quarrel should be your last in the regiment. I tell you frankly, that if you continue your course of annoyance to young Leslie I shall report the matter to the colonel. I have noticed that you have the good sense to abstain from your remarks when he is present."

Three days later the regiment joined the army before Namur.

That evening, having drunk more deeply than usual, Lieutenant Crawford, after the colonel had retired from the circle round the fire and to his tent, recommenced his provocation to Ronald, and pushed matters so far that the latter felt that he could no longer treat it as a jest.

"Mr. Crawford," he said, "I warn you that you are pushing your remarks too far. On many previous occasions you have chosen to make observations which I could, if I had chosen, have resented as insulting. I did not choose, for I hate brawling, and consider that for me, who have but lately joined the regiment, to be engaged in a quarrel with an officer senior to myself would be in the highest degree unbecoming; but I am sure that my fellow officers will bear me out in saying that I have shown fully as much patience as is becoming. I, therefore, have to tell you that I will no longer be your butt, and that I shall treat any further remark of the nature of those you have just made as a deliberate insult, and shall take measures accordingly."

A murmur of approval rose among the officers sitting round, and those sitting near Crawford endeavoured to quiet him. The wine which he had taken had, however, excited his quarrelsome instinct too far for either counsel or prudence to prevail.

"I shall say what I choose," he said, rising to his feet. "I am not going to be dictated to by anyone, much less a boy who has just joined the regiment, and who calls himself Leslie, though no one knows whether he has any right to the name."

"Very well, sir," Leslie said in a quiet tone, which was, however, heard distinctly throughout the circle, for at this last outburst on the part of Crawford a dead silence had fallen on the circle, for only one termination could follow such an insult. "Captain Campbell will, I hope, act for me?"

"Certainly," Captain Campbell said in a loud voice; "and will call upon any friend Lieutenant Crawford may name and make arrangements to settle this matter in the morning."

"Macleod, will you act for me?" Crawford said to a lieutenant sitting next to him.

"I will act," the young officer said coldly, "as your second in the matter; but all here will understand that I do solely because it is necessary that some one should do so, and that I disapprove absolutely and wholly of your conduct."

"Well, make what arrangements you like," Crawford said with an oath, and rising he left the circle and walked away.

When he had left there was an immediate discussion. Several of the officers were of opinion that the duel should not be allowed to proceed, but that Crawford's conduct should be reported to the colonel.

"I am entirely in your hands, gentlemen," Ronald said. "I have no desire whatever to fight. This affair has been forced upon me, and I have no alternative but to take it up. I am not boasting when I say that I am a far better swordsman than he, and I have no need to shrink from meeting him; but I have certainly no desire whatever to take his life. He has drunk more than he ought to do, and if this matter can be arranged, and he can be persuaded in the morning to express his regret for what he has said, I shall be very glad to accept his apology. If it can be settled in this way without either fighting or reporting his conduct to the colonel, which would probably result in his having to leave the regiment, I should be truly glad--What is that?" he broke off, as a loud cry rang through the air.

The whole party sprang to their feet, and snatching up their swords ran in the direction from which the cry had come. The tents were at some little distance, and just as they reached them they saw a man lying on the ground.

"Good heavens, it is Crawford!" Captain Campbell said, stooping over him. "See, he has been stabbed in the back. It is all over with him. Who can have done it?"

He questioned several of the soldiers, who had now gathered round, attracted like the officers by the cry. None of them had seen the act or had noticed anyone running away; but in so large a camp there were so many people about that an assassin could well have walked quietly away without attracting any attention.

The colonel was speedily on the spot, and instituted a rigid inquiry, but entirely without success. The attack had evidently been sudden and entirely unsuspected, for Crawford had not drawn his sword.

"It is singular," he said, as with the officers he walked slowly back to the fire. "Crawford was not a popular man, but I cannot guess at any reason for this murder. Strange that this should be the second attack made on my officers since we left Paris."

Captain Campbell now related what had taken place after he had left the circle.

"The matter should have been reported to me at once," he said; "although, as it has turned out, it would have made no difference. Perhaps, after all, it is best as it is, for a duel between two officers of the regiment would have done us no good, and the man was no credit to the regiment. But it is a very serious matter that we should be dogged by assassins. Leslie, come up with me to my tent. I am not going to blame you, lad," he said when they were together, "for you could not have acted otherwise than you have done. Indeed, I have myself noticed several times that Crawford's bearing towards you was the reverse of courteous. Have you any idea as to how he came by his death?"

"I, sir!" Ronald said in surprise. "No, I know no more than the others."

"It strikes me, Leslie, that this is only the sequel of that attack in the wood, and that your enemies have unwittingly done you a service. Crawford was very much your height and build, and might easily have been mistaken for you in the dark. I fancy that blow was meant for you."

"It is possible, sir," Ronald said after a pause. "I had not thought of it; but the likeness between him and myself has been frequently noticed. It is quite possible that that blow was meant for me."

"I have very little doubt of it, my lad. If any of these men were hanging about and saw you as they believed coming away from the circle alone, they may well have taken the opportunity. Let it be a lesson to you to be careful henceforth. It is unlikely that the attempt will be repeated at present. The men who did it will think that they have earned their money, and by this time are probably on the way to Paris to carry the news and claim their reward. So that, for a time at least, it is not probable that there will be any repetition of the attempt. After that you will have to be on your guard night and day.

"I wish to heaven we could obtain some clue that would enable me to take steps in the matter; but at present we have nothing but our suspicions, and I cannot go to the king and say three attempts have been made on the life of one of my officers, and that I suspect his grandfather, the Marquis de Recambours, has been the author of them."

When Malcolm heard the events of the evening his opinion was exactly the same as that of the colonel, and he expressed himself as convinced that Crawford had fallen by a blow intended for Ronald. He agreed that for a while there was no fear of a renewal of the attempt.

"The fellows will take the news straight to Paris that you have been put out of the way, and some time will elapse before the employers know that a mistake has been made. Then, as likely as not, they will decide to wait until the campaign is over."

The camp before Namur was a large and brilliant one. The king and dauphin had already arrived with the army. All the household troops were there, and a large contingent of the nobles of the court. The English army was known to be approaching, and was expected to fight a battle to relieve Namur, which the French were besieging vigorously. The French confidently hoped that in the approaching battle they would wipe our the reverse which had befallen them at Dettingen.

CHAPTER IX: Fontenoy.

A fortnight after the Scottish Dragoons joined the army the king was present at an inspection of their regiment. As the brilliant cortege passed along the line Ronald saw among the gaily dressed throng of officers riding behind the king and Marshal Saxe the Marquis de Recambours and the Duke de Chateaurouge side by side. Ronald with two other gentlemen volunteers were in their places in the rear of the regiment. It was drawn up in double line, and as the royal party rode along for the second time, Ronald saw that the two noblemen were looking scrutinizingly through the line of troopers at himself and his two companions.

That evening Colonel Hume on his return from a visit to Marshal Saxe told Ronald that the general had inquired after him, and had sent him word that if he won the battle he would not forget the promise he had made him. He had requested Colonel Hume to place Ronald at his disposal on the day of the battle.

"'I shall want active officers to carry my messages,' he said, 'and your young friend may have a greater opportunity of distinguishing himself than he would with the regiment. I should in that case find it all the easier to bring his business before the king.'

"The marshal is terribly ill," Colonel Hume said as he reported the conversation to Ronald, "so ill that he can only occasionally sit on his horse. Nothing but his indomitable courage sustains him. He is drawn about in a light carriage made of basketwork, and this serves him also for his bed."

On the 7th of May the enemy were known to be close at hand, and the French selected the position on which they would fight. The village of Fontenoy had already been occupied by a strong body of troops under Marshal Noailles, and the rest of the army now moved forward to the posts allotted to them. The English army were close at hand, and it was certain that the battle would be fought on the morrow. In the evening the king held a grand reception at which all the officers of rank were present. When Colonel Hume returned to his camp his officers were still sitting round the fire.

"Have you any news for us, sir?"

"No; I believe everything stands as was arranged. The king is in the highest spirits, though I must say his majesty did not choose reminiscences of a nature to encourage those who heard him. He remarked, for instance, that since the days of St. Louis the French had never gained a decisive success over the English, and a few minutes later he observed that the last time a king of France with his son had fought at the head of the French army was at the battle of Poictiers."

There was a general laugh.

"Certainly the king was not happy with his reminiscences," Major Munro remarked; "but I think this time the tables are going to be turned. In the first place we considerably outnumbered the enemy, even after leaving 15,000 men to continue the siege. In the second place, the position we have chosen is almost impregnable. The Scheldt covers our right, with the fortified bridge securing our communication, and the village of Antoin resting on the river. Along our front from Antoin to Fontenoy is a narrow and difficult valley. Our left is covered by the wood of Barre, where a strong redoubt has been constructed; and the whole of the position is fortified with breastworks and abattis as far as Fontenoy. Between that village and Barre the natural difficulties are so great that field works are unnecessary. I cannot believe myself that they will attack us in such a position, especially as nearly half their army are Dutch, who will count for little. The English are the only troops which we shall find formidable."

Before daybreak the camp was astir, and the troops took the positions assigned to them. Even now it was hardly believed that an attack would be made by the enemy so long as the French remained in their all but impregnable position; but presently the columns of the enemy were seen advancing. Ronald had ridden up to the litter on which Marshal Saxe was placed, and after saluting, had taken up his position with a number of other officers, in readiness to carry orders to different parts of the field.

At a short distance from the marshal the King of France with the dauphin and the brilliant cortege of nobles had taken up his post. From the position in which the marshal had caused himself to be placed a complete view of the enemy's approaching ranks was obtained. It could soon be seen that the Dutch troops, who on the English right were advancing to the attack, were moving against the villages of Antoin and Fontenoy. A strong force, headed, as was known afterwards, by General Ingoldsby, moved towards the wood of Barre; while a solid column of English and Hanoverians, 10,000 strong, marched forward to the attack across the broken ground between Fontenoy and the wood of Barre.

It was as yet but five o'clock in the morning when the cannon broke out into a roar on both sides. The Dutch, who were commanded by the Prince of Waldeck, soon hesitated, and in a short time fell back out of range of fire. On the English right General Ingoldsby penetrated some distance into the wood of Barre, and then fell back again as the Dutch had done. In an hour after the fighting had commenced the right and left of the allied army had ceased their attack. There remained only the centre, but this was advancing.

Under the command of the Duke of Cumberland the column crossed the ravine in front of Fontenoy. The ground was so broken that the troops were unable to deploy, but moved forward in a solid mass with a front of only forty men.

The French batteries from the right and left mowed them down in lines, but as steadily as if on parade the places were filled up, and unshaken and calm the great column moved forward. The cannon which they dragged along by hand opened against Fontenoy and the redoubts, and as, in spite of the hail of fire, they pressed steadily on, the French gunners were obliged to abandon their cannon and fly.

The regiment of French guards, officered almost entirely by the highest nobles, met the English guards, who composed the front lines of the column. A tremendous volley flashed along the English line, shattering the ranks of the French guard. There was a moment's fierce fighting, and then the English column swept from before it the remains of the French guard, and cleared the ravine which defended Fontenoy.

Ronald felt his heart beat with excitement and a feeling of pride and admiration as he saw the English advancing unmoved through the storm of fire. They advanced in the most perfect order. The sergeants calmly raised or depressed the soldiers' muskets to direct the fire; each vacant place was filled quietly and regularly without hesitation or hurry; and exclamations of surprise and admiration broke even from the French officers.

Regiment after regiment was brought up and hurled against the head of the column, but with no more effect than waves against a rock, each being dashed aside shattered and broken by the steady volleys and regular lines of bayonets. Ronald and other officers were sent off to bring up the cavalry, but in vain did these strive to break the serried column. One regiment after another charged down upon it, but the English, retaining their fire until they were within a few yards of their muzzles, received them with such tremendous volleys that they recoiled in disorder.

The French regiment of Vaisseaux next advanced to the attack, and fought with greater gallantry than any which had preceded it; but at last, when almost annihilated, its survivors fell back. And now it seemed as if this 10,000 men were to be victorious over the whole French army. Marshal Saxe begged the king to retire with the dauphin across the bridge of Calonne while he did what he could to retrieve the battle, but the king refused to leave the field. There was a hurried council held round Louis, and it was agreed to make a great effort by calling up the whole of the troops between Fontenoy and Antoin, as the positions they held were no longer threatened by the Dutch.

Had the latter now advanced nothing could have saved the French army from utter defeat; but they remained immovable at a distance from the field of battle. The English now won the crown of the position, had cut through the French centre, and were moving forward towards the bridge of Calonne, when the whole of the French artillery, which had, by the advice of the Duke of Richelieu, been brought up, opened fire on the English column. At the same moment the French regiments from Antoin fell upon it; while Marshal Saxe, who had, when the danger became imminent, mounted his horse, himself brought up the Irish Brigade, who, with a wild yell of hatred, flung itself furiously upon the flank of the English.

Attacked thus on all sides, mown down by a heavy fire of artillery, unsupported amid an army of foes, the column could do no more. Ten thousand men could not withstand fifty thousand. Their ranks were twice broken by the Irish, but twice their officers rallied them; until at last, when it became evident that no more could be done, the column fell slowly back in an order as perfect and regular as that in which it had advanced.

French historians have done ample justice to the extraordinary valour shown by the English troops on this occasion, a valour never surpassed in the long annals of the British army. Had they received the slightest assistance from their cowardly allies the victory must have been theirs. As it was, although unsuccessful, the glory and honour of the day rested with them, rather than with the victorious army of France. More than half the column had fallen in the desperate engagement, but the loss of the victors was even greater, and comprised many belonging to the noblest families of France.

Ronald had won the warm approval of Marshal Saxe for the manner in which he carried his orders across ground swept by a heavy fire, and brought up the regiments to within close quarters of the English; and after the battle was over Marshal Saxe presented to the king several of his staff who had most distinguished themselves, and calling up Ronald, who was standing near, for his horse had been shot under him as he rode by the side of the marshal with the Irish Brigade to the attack, the marshal said:

"Allow me to present to your majesty Ronald Leslie, a young Scottish gentleman of good family, who is a volunteer in the Scottish Dragoons, and has rendered great service today by the manner in which he has borne my orders through the thickest of the fire."

"I will bear you in mind, young gentleman," the king said graciously, "and I charge the marshal to bring your name before me on a future day."

His duty as aide de camp over, Ronald rejoined his regiment. They had lost nearly a third of their number in their charges upon the English column. Major Munro had been killed, the colonel severely wounded, and a number of officers had fallen. Ronald went about among the men assisting to bind up wounds, and supplying those who needed it with wine and other refreshments. Presently he was joined by Malcolm.

"Thank God you are safe, Ronald. I tell you, you have given me many a fright today as I watched you galloping along through the line of the English fire."

"Where were you, Malcolm? I did not see you."

"I had nothing to do," Malcolm said, "and I climbed a tree not fifty yards from the marshal's litter, and keeping the trunk in front of me to protect me from a stray bullet I had a good view of the whole proceedings. At one time I was on the point of slipping down and making a bolt for it, for I thought it was all over with us. How that column did fight! I have been in many a battle, but I never saw anything like it, it was grand; and if it hadn't been for the Irish Brigade, I think that they would have beaten the whole French army. But if you go into a battle again I sha'n't come to see you. I have done my share of fighting, and can take hard knocks as well as another; but I would not go through the anxiety I have suffered today about you on any condition. However, this has been a great day for you."

"You mean about the marshal presenting me to the king? Yes, that ought to help us."

"No, I didn't mean that, for I had not heard of it. I mean about that old rascal your grandfather, the Marquis de Recambours."

"What about him? I have not heard."

"No!" Malcolm exclaimed; "then I have good news for you. A ball from one of the English field pieces struck him full in the chest, and of course slew him instantly. He was not thirty yards from the tree when I saw him knocked over. He is quite dead, I can assure you, for when the others moved off I took the trouble to clamber down to assure myself. So now the greatest obstacle to the release of your father and mother is out of the way."

"Thank God for that!" Ronald said. "I have no reason for feeling one spark of regret at what has befallen him. He was the cruel persecutor of my parents, and did his best to get me removed. There is but one obstacle now to obtaining my father's release, and as he is neither a relation nor an old man I shall be able to deal with him myself."

"Yes, but you must be careful, Ronald; remember the decree against duelling. We must not make a false step now, when fortune is at last favouring us. There will be no more fighting, I fancy. The English will certainly not attack us again, and Tournay must fall, and I don't think that on our part there will be any desire whatever to go out of our way to seek another engagement with them. The king is sure to go back to Paris at once, where he will be received with enthusiasm. Marshal Saxe will probably follow as soon as Tournay has fallen. I should advise you, therefore, to get leave from the colonel to be absent from the regiment for a time, and we will make our way down to Tours and let your mother know the marquis is dead, and get her to write a memorial to the king requesting permission to leave the convent, and then when the marshall arrives in Paris we will get him to present it."

Ronald agreed to Malcolm's proposal, and the next morning, having obtained leave of absence from the colonel, he and Malcolm mounted and rode for Tours.

The message was duly conveyed to the countess by Jeanne, together with Ronald's earnest request that his mother would again meet him. She sent back by Jeanne the memorial he had asked her to write to the king, begging that she might be allowed to leave the convent; but she refused to agree to his wishes to meet her, bidding Jeanne say that now it seemed there was really a hope of her release shortly, she would less than ever risk any step which if discovered might prejudice their plans.

Although disappointed, Ronald could not deny that her decision was a wise one, and therefore contented himself by sending word that he had obtained one very powerful friend, and that he hoped that she would ere long receive good tidings. After a short stay at Tours, Ronald and Malcolm returned to Paris, where a series of brilliant fetes in honour of the victory of Fontenoy were in preparation. Tournay had surrendered a few days after the battle, the governor of that town having accepted a heavy bribe to open the gates, for the place could have resisted for months, and the allied army were ready to recommence hostilities in order to relieve it.

After its surrender they fell back and resumed a defensive attitude. The king therefore returned at once to Paris, and Marshal Saxe, handing over the command of the army to Marshal de Noailles, followed him by easy stages. Delighted above all things at a success gained over the English, who had for centuries been victorious in every battle in which England and France had met as enemies, the citizens of Paris organized a succession of brilliant fetes, which were responded to by entertainments of all kinds at Versailles. The Scottish Dragoons were still at the front; but Colonel Hume had been brought to Paris, as it would be some time ere he would be able again to take the command of the regiment. Ronald called at the house where the colonel lodged, upon the day after his return from Tours, and found that he had arrived upon the previous day. Ronald was at once shown up on sending in his name. The colonel was lying on the couch when he entered.

"How are you, colonel?"

"I am going on as well as possible, Ronald; they found the ball and got it out the day before I left the regiment, and I shall do well now. I have been carried on a litter all the way by eight of our troopers, and the good fellows were as gentle with me as if I had been a child, and I scarce felt a jar the whole distance. What I have got to do now is to lie quiet, and the doctor promises me that in six weeks' time I shall be fit to mount a horse again. Marshal Saxe sent yesterday evening to inquire after me, and I will send you to him to thank him for so sending, and to inquire on my part how he himself is going on. My message will be a good excuse for your presenting yourself."

Ronald found the antechamber of the marshal crowded with nobles and officers who had come to pay their respects to the victorious general, who was, next to the king himself, at that moment the most popular man in France. Hitherto, as a Protestant and a foreigner, Maurice of Saxony had been regarded by many with jealousy and dislike; but the victory which he had won for the French arms had for the first time obliterated every feeling save admiration and gratitude.

Presently the marshal came out from the inner room with the dauphin, who had called on the part of the king to inquire after his health. He was now able to walk, the excitement of the battle and the satisfaction of the victory having enabled him partially to shake off the disease which afflicted him. After the dauphin had left, the marshal made the tour of the apartment, exchanging a few words with all present.

"Ah! you are there, my young Leslie," he said familiarly when he came to Ronald. "Where have you been? I have not seen you since the day when you galloped about with my messages through the English fire as if you had a charmed life."

"Colonel Hume gave me leave, sir, to travel on private business. I am now the bearer of a message from him, thanking you for the kind inquiries as to his wound; he bids me say that he trusts that your own health is rapidly recovering."

"As you see, Leslie, Fontenoy has done wonders for me as well as for France; but wait here, I will speak with you again."

In half an hour most of the callers took their departure, then the marshal called Ronald into an inner room.

"Tomorrow," he said, "I am going to pay my respects to the king at Versailles. I will take you with me. Have you your mother's memorial? That is right. As her father was killed at Fontenoy there will, I hope, be the less difficulty over the matter; but we must not be too sanguine, for there will be a host of hungry competitors for the estates of the marquis, and all these will unite against you. However, I do not think the king will be able to refuse my first request, and when your mother is out we must put our heads together and see about getting your father's release."

Ronald expressed his deep gratitude at the marshal's kindness.

"Say nothing about it, my lad. Fortunately I want nothing for myself, and it is no use being a victorious general if one cannot utilize it in some way; so I am quite glad to have something to ask the king."

The next day Ronald presented himself at the hotel of Marshal Saxe and rode by the side of his carriage out to Versailles. The king, surrounded by a brilliant train of courtiers, received the marshal with the greatest warmth, and after talking to him for some time retired with him into his private closet. A few minutes later one of the royal pages came out into the audience chamber and said in a loud voice that the king desired the presence of Monsieur Ronald Leslie.

Greatly embarrassed at finding himself the centre of observation not unmingled with envy at the summons, Ronald followed the page into the presence of the king, who was alone with Marshal Saxe. Louis, who was in high good humour, gave Ronald his hand to kiss, saying:

"I told the marshal to recall your name to me, and he has done so now. He says that you have a boon to ask of me."

"Yes, sire," the marshal said; "and please consider graciously that it is I who ask it as well as he. Your majesty has always been gracious to me, and if you think me deserving of any mark of your favour after this success which your majesty and I have gained together, I would now crave that you grant it."

"It is granted before you name it, marshal," the king said. "I give you my royal word that whatever be your boon, provided that it be within the bounds of possibility, it is yours."

"Then, sire, I ask that an old comrade and fellow soldier of mine, who fought bravely for your majesty, but who fell under your majesty's displeasure many years ago on account of a marriage which he made contrary to your pleasure, may be released. He has now been over sixteen years in prison, and has therefore paid dearly for thwarting your will, and his wife has all this time been confined in a convent. They are the father and mother of this brave lad--Colonel Leslie, who commanded your majesty's regiment of Scotch Dragoons, and his wife, the Countess Amelie of Recambours. I ask your majesty, as my boon, that you will order this officer to be released and the lady to be allowed to leave the convent."

"Peste, marshal!" the king said good temperedly; "your request is one of which will get me into hot water with a score of people. From the day the marquis was killed at Fontenoy I have heard nothing but questions about his estates, and I believe that no small portion of them have been already promised."

"I say nothing about the estates," the marshal replied; "as to that, your majesty's sense of justice is too well known for it to be necessary for me to say a single word. The countess has estates of her own, which she inherited from her mother, but even as to these I say nothing. It is her liberty and that of her husband which I and this brave lad ask of your majesty."

"It is granted, marshal, and had your boon been a great one instead of a small one I would have granted it as freely;" and the king again held out his hand to Ronald, who bent on one knee to kiss it, tears of joy flowing down his cheeks and preventing the utterance of any audible thanks for the boon, which far surpassed his expectations; for the marshal had said nothing as to his intention of asking his father's freedom, which indeed he only decided to do upon seeing in how favourable a disposition he had found the king.

"You see, marshal," Louis went on, "marriages like this must be sternly discouraged, or all order in our kingdom would be done away with. Wilful girls and headstrong soldiers cannot be permitted to arrange their affairs without reference to the plans of their parents, and in this instance it happened that the father's plans had received our approval. The great estates of France cannot be handed over to the first comer, who may perhaps be utterly unworthy of them. I do not say that in the present case Colonel Leslie was in any way personally unworthy; but the disposal of the hands of the great heiresses of France is in the king's gift, and those who cross him are against his authority."

The king touched a bell and bade the page who entered to order his secretary to attend at once.

"Search the register of the state prisons," he said, "and tell me where Colonel Leslie, who was arrested by our orders sixteen years ago, is confined, and then make out an order to the governor of his prison for his release; also draw up an order upon the lady superior of--," and he paused.

"The convent of Our Lady at Tours," Ronald ventured to put in.

"Oh! you have discovered that, eh?" the king said with a smile; and then turned again to the secretary--"bidding her suffer the Countess Amelie de Recambours to leave the convent and to proceed where she will."

The secretary bowed and retired. Ronald, seeing that his own presence was no longer required, said a few words of deep gratitude to the king and retired to the audience room, where he remained until, ten minutes later, the door of the king's closet opened, and the king and Marshal Saxe again appeared. The audience lasted for another half hour, and then the marshal, accompanied by many of the nobles, made his way down to his carriage. Ronald again mounted, and as soon as the carriage had left the great courtyard of the palace, rode up alongside and poured out his gratitude to the marshal.

"It has been another Fontenoy," the marshal said smiling. "Here are the two orders, the one for Tours, the other for the governor of the royal castle at Blois. The king made light of it; but I know his manner so well that I could see he would rather that I had asked for a dukedom for you. It is not often that kings are thwarted, and he regards your parents as being rebels against his authority. However, he was bound by his promise, and there are the papers. Now, only one word, Leslie. Do not indulge in any hopes that you will see your father more than a shadow of the stalwart soldier that he was sixteen years ago. There are few men, indeed, whose constitution enable them to live through sixteen years' confinement in a state prison. Therefore prepare yourself to find him a mere wreck. I trust that freedom and your mother's care may do much for him, but don't expect too much at first. If you take my advice you will go first and fetch your mother, in order that she may be at hand to receive your father when he leaves the fortress. By the way, I thought it just as well not to produce your mother's memorial, as it seemed that we should be able to do without it, for it might have struck the king to ask how you obtained it, and he would probably have considered that your communication with your mother was a fresh act of defiance against his authority."

Malcolm was wild with joy when Ronald returned with the account of his interview with the king and its successful result, and had his not been a seasoned head, the number of bumpers which he drank that night in honour of Marshal Saxe would have rendered him unfit for travel in the morning. Ronald had, after acquainting him with the news, gone to Colonel Hume, whose pleasure at hearing that his former colonel and comrade was to regain his freedom was unbounded. Every preparation was made for an early start.

"Be sure you look well to the priming of your pistols before you put them in your holsters tomorrow," Malcolm said.

"Do you think it will be necessary?"

"I am sure of it, Ronald. News travels fast; and you may be sure that by this time the fact that the king has granted an order for the release of your father and mother is known to the Duke of Chateaurouge. If he did not hear it from the king himself, which he would be most likely to do, as Louis would probably lose no time in explaining to him that he had only gone against his wishes because under the circumstances it was impossible for him to refuse the marshal's request, the secretary who drew out the document would, no doubt, let the duke know of it. There are no secrets at court."

"But now that the orders for release have been granted," Ronald said, "the duke can have no motive in preventing them being delivered, for fresh ones could, of course, be obtained."

"In the first place, Ronald, the duke will be so furious at your success that he will stick at nothing to have his revenge; in the second place, he and the others, for there are many interested in preventing your mother from coming into her father's possessions, will consider that the gain of time goes for a good deal. You are the mover in the matter. Were you out of the way, and the documents destroyed, the matter might rest as it is for a long time. The marshal is busy from morning till night, and would be long before he missed you, and would naturally suppose that you had, after obtaining the release of your parents, retired with them to some country retreat, or even left the kingdom.

"This would give ample time for working upon Louis. Besides, the king might never inquire whether the prisoners had been released. Then the marshal might die or be sent away to the frontier. Therefore, as you see, time is everything. I tell you, Ronald, I consider the journey you are going to undertake tomorrow an affair of greater danger than going into a pitched battle. You will have to doubt everyone you meet on the road, the people at the inns you stop at--you may be attacked anywhere and everywhere. As to our travelling by the direct road, I look upon it as impossible. Our only chance is to throw them off the scent, and as they know our destination that will be no easy matter."

They were astir by daylight, and Malcolm soon brought the horses round to the door.

"It's a comfort to know," he said, "that the horses have passed the night in the barracks, and that therefore they have not been tampered with. Look well to the buckles of your girths, Ronald. See that everything is strong and in good order."

"That is not your own horse, Malcolm, is it?"

"No, it is one of the troopers'. It is one of the best in the regiment, and I persuaded the man to change with me for a week. No one is likely to notice the difference, as they are as nearly as possible the same colour. Your horse is good enough for anything; but if I could not keep up with you its speed would be useless. Now, I think, we can keep together if we have to ride for it.

"What have you got in that valise, Malcolm? One would think that you were going upon a campaign."

"I have got four bottles of good wine, and bread and meat enough to last us for two days. I do not mean, if I can help it, to enter a shop or stop at an inn till we arrive at Tours. We can make a shift to sleep for tonight in a wood. It would be safer a thousand times than an inn, for I will bet fifty to one that if we ventured to enter one we should find one or both of our horses lame on starting again."

"Oh come, Malcolm, that's too much! The Duke of Chateaurouge is not ubiquitous. He has not an army to scatter over all France."

"No, he has not," Malcolm agreed; "but from what I know of him I doubt not that he can lay his hands on a number of men who will stick at nothing to carry out his orders and earn his money. Paris swarms with discharged soldiers and ruffians of all kinds, and with plenty of gold to set the machine in motion there is no limit to the number of men who might be hired for any desperate deed."

As they were talking they were making their way towards one of the southern gates. They arrived there before it opened, and had to wait a few minutes. Several other passengers on horseback and foot were gathered there.

"I could bet a crown piece," Malcolm said, "that some one among this crowd is on the watch for us, and that before another half hour the Duke of Chateaurouge will know that we have started."

CHAPTER X: A Perilous Journey.

A number of peasants with market carts were waiting outside the gates, and for the first few miles of their ride the road was dotted with people making their way to the city. As they rode, Malcolm discussed the question of the best road to be taken. Ronald himself was still in favour of pushing straight forward, for he was not so convinced as his follower that a serious attempt would be made to interrupt their journey. He pointed out that the road, as far as Orleans at least, was one of the most frequented in France, and that in that city even the most reckless would hardly venture to assault them.

"I agree with you, Ronald, that the road offers less opportunities for ambushes than most others, for the country is flat and well cultivated; but after all a dozen men with muskets could lie in ambush in a cornfield as well as a wood, and the fact that people are going along the road counts for little one way or the other, for not one in fifty would venture to interfere if they saw a fray going on. But granting that so far as Orleans the country is open and cultivated, beyond that it is for the most part forest; but above all--although they may regard it as possible that we may be on our guard, and may travel by other roads--it is upon this direct line that they are sure to make the most preparations for us. Beyond that it can only be chance work. We may go by one road or by another. There may be one trap set on each road; but once past that and we are safe."

After riding for upwards of an hour they came, at the turn of the road, upon two carts. One had apparently broken down, and the other had stopped that those with it might give assistance in repairing it. One cart was turned across the road, and the other filled the rest of the space.

"Stop!" Malcolm exclaimed, checking his horse suddenly.

"What is it?" Ronald asked in surprise.

"Turn back!" Malcolm said sharply as he wheeled his horse round.

Ronald, without a word, did the same, and they galloped a hundred yards down the road.

"We were nearly caught there," Malcolm said.

"Why, how do you mean?"

"Never mind now, Ronald. Turn sharp to the right here, and make a detour through the fields. You will soon see whether I was right."

"It is a shame riding through this ripe corn," Ronald said, as without any further comment he leaped his horse over the bank and dashed off among the golden grain, which stretched far and wide on both sides of the road.

They had not gone fifty yards before they heard loud shouts, and as they came abreast of where the carts were standing several shots were fired, and ten or twelve men were seen running through the corn as if to cut them off. But although they heard the whiz of the bullets they were too far off to be in much danger, and the men on foot had no chance of cutting them off, a fact which they speedily perceived, as one by one they halted and fired. A few hundred yards farther the two horsemen came round into the road again and pursued their journey.

"Well, what do you think of that, Ronald?"

"It was an ambush, no doubt, Malcolm; but what on earth made you suspect it? I saw nothing suspicious. Merely two carts in the road, with three or four men doing something to one of the wheels."

"I am in a suspicious humour this morning, Ronald, and it is lucky I am. The sight of the two carts completely blocking the road brought me to a halt at once, and as I checked my horse I saw a movement among the bushes on the right of the road, and felt sure that it was an ambush. It was a well laid one, too, and had we ridden on we should have been riddled with bullets. No doubt there were men lying in the carts. They would have jumped up as we came up to them, and the fellows in the bushes would have taken us in the rear; between their two fires our chances would have been small indeed. No doubt they had a man on watch, and directly they saw us coming they got their carts across the road, and took up their positions. It was a well contrived scheme, and we have had a narrow escape."

"Thanks to your quickness and watchfulness, Malcolm, which has saved our lives. I admit that you are right and I was wrong, for I own that I did not share your apprehensions as to the dangers of our journey. Henceforth I will be as much on the lookout as you are, and will look with suspicion at every beggar woman that may pass."

"And you will be right to do so," Malcolm said seriously; "but for the present I think that we are safe. This, no doubt, was their main ambush, and they may reasonably have felt certain of success. However, we may be sure that they did not rely solely upon it. This, no doubt, is the unmounted portion of their gang. They were to try and put a stop to our journey at its outset; but mounted men will have ridden on ahead, especially as they couldn't have been sure that we should follow this road. We might have gone out by one of the other gates at the south side of the town, and they will have watched all the roads. Now I propose that we take the next lane which branches off to the right, and travel by byroads in future. Do not press your horse too fast. We have a long journey before us, and must always have something in hand in case it is necessary to press them to full speed."

Two miles further a road branched to the right. As they approached it Ronald was about to touch his horse's rein, when Malcolm said shortly, "Ride straight on."

Although surprised at this sudden change of plan, Ronald obeyed without question.

"What was that for?" he asked when he had passed the turning.

"Did you not see that man lying down by the heap of stones at the corner?"

"Yes, I saw him; but what of that?"

"I have no doubt he was on the lookout for us. Yes, I thought so," he went on, as he stood up in his stirrups and looked back; "there, do you see that horse's head in that little thicket, just this side of where the road separates? I expected as much. If we had turned off, in another two minutes that fellow would have been galloping along this road to take the news to those ahead, and they would have ridden to cut us off further along. I have no doubt we shall find someone on watch at every turning between this and Orleans."

"But this is a regular campaign, Malcolm."

"It is a campaign, Ronald. The ruffians and thieves of Paris form a sort of army. They have heads whom they implicitly obey, and those who have money enough to set this machine in motion can command the services of any number of men. Sharp fellows, too, many of them are, and when they received orders to arrest our journey to Tours at any cost, they would not omit a single precaution which could ensure success. Their former attack upon you, and its result, will have showed them that we are not children, and that the enterprise was one which demanded all their efforts."

"What is our next move now, Malcolm?"

"We will turn off before we get to the next road. They can see a long way across these level plains; so we will dismount and lead our horses. The corn is well nigh shoulder deep, and if we choose a spot where the ground lies rather low, neither that scoundrel behind nor the one at the next road is likely to see us."

Half a mile further there was a slight dip in the ground.

"This is a good spot," Malcolm said. "This depression extends far away on our right, and although it is very slight, and would not conceal us if the ground were bare, it will do so now, so let us take advantage of it."

So saying he dismounted, and leading his horse, turned into the cornfield. Ronald followed him, and for two miles they kept straight on through the corn; then they came upon a narrow road connecting two villages. They mounted and turned their horses' heads to the south.

"It is as well that none of the peasants saw us making through their corn," Ronald said, "or we should have had them upon us with stone and flail like a swarm of angry bees."

"It could not be helped," Malcolm replied, "and we could easily have ridden away from them. However, it is just as well that we have had no bother with them. Now we will quicken our pace. We are fairly between two of the main roads south, and if we can contrive to make our way by these village tracks we shall at any rate for some time be free from all risk of molestation."

"I should think we should be free altogether," Ronald said. "When they find we do not come along the road they will suppose we have been killed at the first ambush."

Malcolm shook his head.

"Do not build upon that, Ronald. No doubt as soon as we had passed, some of those fellows mounted the horses we saw in the carts, and rode off in accordance with an agreed plan to give notice that we had passed them safely, and were proceeding by that road. In the next place the fellow we saw on watch would most likely after a time mount and follow us, and when he got to the watcher at the next crossroad and found that we had not come along there would know that we must have turned off either to the right or left. One of them is doubtless before this on his way to the next party with the news, while the other has set to work to find out where we turned off, which will be easy enough to discover. Still, we have gained something, and may fairly reckon that if we ride briskly there is no fear of those who were posted along the road we have left cutting us off."

They rode all day at a steady pace, stopping occasionally for a short time to allow the horses a rest and a feed. The people in the quiet little villages looked in surprise at the young officer and his follower as they rode through their street or stopped for a quarter of an hour while the horses were fed, for even Malcolm agreed that such pauses were unattended by danger. It was rarely, indeed, that a stranger passed along these bypaths, and the peasants wondered among themselves what could induce them to travel by country byways instead of following the main roads.

As they left the rich plains of the Beauce, the country was less carefully cultivated. The fields of corn were no longer continuous, and presently they came to tracts of uncultivated land with patches of wood. They now left the little road they had been following, and rode straight across country, avoiding all villages. They crossed several hills, and late in the afternoon drew rein in a wide spreading forest. They were, Malcolm thought, quite as far south as Orleans, and by starting at daylight would arrive at Tours by midday.

"Here at least we are perfectly safe," he said; "when we approach Tours our perils will begin again. When once they find that we have given them the slip they are not likely to try to intercept us anywhere along the route till we near the town, for they will know that the chances are enormous against their doing so, and the parties along the various roads will push on so as to meet us somewhere near that city. The river can only be crossed at certain points, and they will feel sure we shall go by one or other of them."

"And I suppose we shall," Ronald said.

"No, Ronald; my idea is that we turn west and ride to Le Mans, then take a wide detour and enter Tours from the south side. It will take us a day longer, but that is of little consequence, and I think that we shall in that way entirely outwit them. The only precaution we shall have to take is to cross the main road on our right at some point remote from any town or village."

"I think that is a capital plan. I do not mind a share of fair fighting; but to be shot down suddenly in an ambush like that of this morning, I own I have little fancy for it."

Hobbling their horses, they turned them loose to pick up what they could in the forest, and then sat down to enjoy a good meal from the ample supply Malcolm had brought with him. When night fell they unstrapped their cloaks from their saddles and rolled themselves in them, and lay down to sleep. An hour later they were roughly awakened, each being seized by three men, who, before they could attempt to offer resistance, bound their arms to their sides, and then hurried them along through the forest.

"I have been a fool, Ronald," Malcolm said bitterly; "I ought to have kept watch."

"It was not your fault, Malcolm. One could never have guessed that they would have found us in this forest. Somebody must have followed us at a distance and marked us down, and brought the rest upon us; but even had you kept watch it would have been no good, for they would have shot us down before we could make any resistance."

"I wonder they didn't cut our throats at once," Malcolm said. "I don't know what they are troubling to make us prisoners for."

Presently they saw a light in the forest ahead of them, and soon arrived at a spot where a number of men were sitting round a fire.

"You had no trouble with them, Pierre, I suppose?"

"No, captain, they slept as soundly as moles. They have been speaking some strange language as we came along."

"Thank God!" Malcolm exclaimed fervently. "I think, after all, Ronald, we have only fallen in with a band of robbers, and not with our enemies."

"Unbind their hands," the captain of the band said, "but first take away their swords and pistols. Gentlemen, may I ask you to be seated; and then, perhaps, you will inform us what you, an officer in the Scotch dragoons, as I perceive by your uniform, are doing here in the forest?"

Ronald, to whom the question was principally addressed, replied frankly:

"We took to this forest, I fancy, for the same reason for which you use it, namely, for safety. We are on our way to Tours, and there are some people who have interest in preventing our arriving there. They made one attempt to stop us near Paris; fortunately that failed, or we should not be now enjoying your society; but as it was likely that another attempt would be made upon the road, we thought it better to leave it altogether and take to the forest for the night."

"What interest could anyone have in preventing an officer of the king from arriving at Tours?" the man asked doubtfully.

"It is rather a long story," Ronald said, "but if it is of interest to you I shall be happy to relate it; and I may mention that there are three bottles of good wine in the valise of one of the saddles, and a story is none the worse for such an accompaniment."

A laugh went round the circle at Ronald's coolness, and a man stepped forward with the two saddles which he had carried from the spot when the captives had been seized. The wine was taken out and opened.

"Yes," the captain of the band said, after tasting it, "the wine is good; now let us have your story."

Ronald gave them an outline of his history, told them how his father and mother had been for many years imprisoned for marrying contrary to the king's pleasure, and how he had at last obtained the royal order for their release, and how the enemies of his parents were now trying to prevent him from having those orders carried out. "There are the orders," Ronald said as he concluded, taking them from the inner pocket where he carried them. "You see they are addressed to the abbess of the convent of Our Lady at Tours, and to the governor of Blois."

"The story you tell us is a singular one," the captain replied, "and I doubt not its truth. What was the name of your father?"

"He was Colonel Leslie, and commanded the same regiment to which I belong."

"I remember him," one of the band said. "Our regiments were quartered together, nigh twenty years ago, at Flanders, and I was in Paris at the time when he was imprisoned. We were in the next barracks to the Scotchmen, and I remember what a stir it made. The regiment was very nigh mutinying."

"And I remember you too, though I cannot recall your name," Malcolm said, rising and looking hard at the speaker; "and if I mistake not we have cracked many a flask together, and made many a raid on the hen roosts of the Flemish farmers. My name is Malcolm Anderson."

"I remember you well," the other said, rising and giving him his hand. "Of course I met you scores of times, for the regiments were generally brigaded together."

"That confirms your story altogether, monsieur," the captain of the band said. "From this moment do not consider yourself a prisoner any longer. I may say that we had no expectation of booty in your case, and you were captured rather from curiosity than from any other reason. One of my men, this afternoon, happened to see you ride into the wood and then dismount and make preparations for passing the night there. He reported the matter to me. I know that gentlemen of your cloth--I may say of mine, for I was once an officer of his majesty, though I left the service somewhat hastily," and he smiled, "on account of an unfortunate deficiency in the funds of the regiment in which I happened, at the time, to be acting as paymaster--are seldom burdened with spare cash, but the incident seemed so strange that I determined to capture and question you. If you happen to have more cash on you than you care about carrying we shall be glad to purchase a few bottles of wine equal to that which you have given us. If not, I can assure you that I do not press the matter.".

"I am obliged to you for your courtesy," Ronald said; "and as at present I really happen to be somewhat flush of cash I am happy to contribute ten louis for the laudable purpose you mention."

So saying he took out his purse, counted out ten pieces, and handed them to the captain.

The action was received with a round of applause, for the robbers had not, from the first, anticipated obtaining any booty worth speaking of, and the turn affairs had taken had altogether driven any idea of gain from their minds.

"I thank you warmly, sir," the captain said, "and promise you that I will tomorrow despatch a messenger to Orleans, which is but ten miles away, and will lay out the money in liquor, with which we will, tomorrow night, drink your health and success in the enterprise. Nay, more, if you like, a dozen of my men shall accompany you on your road to Tours. They have, for various reasons, which I need not enter into, a marked objection to passing through towns, but as far as Blois they are at your service."

"I thank you for your offer," Ronald replied, "but will not accept it, as we intend to ride tomorrow morning to Le Mans, and then to enter Tours from the south side, by which we shall throw our enemies completely off the scent."

"But why do you not go to Blois first?" the man asked. "It is on your way to Tours."

"I wish my mother to be present at the release of my father. So long a confinement may well have broken him down. Now that I see how obstinately bent our enemies are upon our destruction I will take with me two or three stout fellows from Tours, to act as an escort."

"What day will you be leaving there?" the man asked.

"Today is Tuesday," Ronald said; "on Thursday we shall be at Tours, on Friday morning we shall leave."

"Very well," the man replied, "we will be on the road. It is no difference to us where we are, and as well there as here. I will have men scattered all along in the forest between Blois and Amboise, and if I find that there are any suspicious parties along the road we will catch them, and if you are attacked you will find that we are close at hand to help you. You are a generous fellow, and your story has interested me. We gentlemen of the woods are obliged to live, whatever the law says; but if we can do a good action to anybody it pleases us as well as others."

"I am greatly obliged to you," Ronald said, "and can promise you, anyhow, that your time shall be not altogether thrown away."

Soon afterwards the whole band lay down round the fire and were sound asleep. In the morning Malcolm saddled the two horses, and after a hearty adieu from the captain and his followers--all of whom were discharged soldiers who had been driven to take up this life from an inability to support themselves in any other way--they started for Le Mans, which town they reached late in the afternoon, without adventure.

Deeming it in the highest degree improbable that any watch would be set for them at a place so far from their line of travel, they put up for the night at the principal inn. In the morning they again started, and after riding for some distance to the south, made a wide sweep, and crossing the river, entered Tours from the south, late in the evening. They again put up at the principal inn, for although they doubted not that their arrival would be noticed by the emissaries of the enemy, they had no fear of molestation in a town like Tours. And on the following morning Ronald presented himself at the entrance to the convent.

"I wish to see the lady superior," he said to the lay sister at the wicket. "I am the bearer of a communication to her from the king."

He was left waiting for a few minutes outside the gate, then the wicket door opened, and the sister requested him to follow her. Not a soul was to be seen as he traversed the gloomy courts and passed through several corridors to the room where the abbess was waiting him. In silence he handed to her the king's order. The abbess opened and read it.

"His majesty's commands shall be obeyed," she said; "in an hour the countess will be in readiness to depart."

"A carriage shall be in waiting at the gate to receive her," Ronald said, bowing, and then, without another word, retired.

Malcolm was awaiting him outside, and they at once went to the officer of the royal post and engaged a carriage and post horses to take them to Blois.

The carriage was at the door at the appointed time, and a few minutes later the gate opened, and the countess, in travelling attire, issued out, and in a moment was clasped in her son's arms. He at once handed her into the carriage and took his place beside her. Malcolm closed the door and leapt up on the box, the postilion cracked his whip, and the carriage moved off.

"Can it be true, Ronald, or am I dreaming? It is but a week since you were here last, and the news of my release came upon me with such a surprise that, do you know, I fainted. Am I really free? Is it possible that I have seen the last of those hateful walls? It seems like a dream. Where are we going?"

"We are going to Blois."

"To a prison?" the countess exclaimed. "But no, there are no guards or escorts. Are we going, oh, Ronald, are we going to see my husband?"

"Yes, mother, we are going, not only to see him but to release him. I have the king's order in my pocket."

For some time the countess was unable to speak, her joy was too great for words. Then tears came to her relief, and she sobbed out exclamations of joy and gratitude. Ronald said nothing until she had somewhat recovered her calmness, and then he told her the manner in which Marshal Saxe had obtained the two orders of release.

"I will pray for him night and morning to the last day of my life," the countess said. "God is indeed good to me. I had hoped, from what you said, that my term of imprisonment was drawing to an end; but I had looked forward to a long struggle, to endless efforts and petitions before I could obtain your father's release, with, perhaps, failure in the end. Not for one moment did I dream that such happiness as this awaited me."

Ronald now thought it wise to repeat the warning which the marshal had given him.

"Mother, dear," he said "you must be prepared to find that a total change will have taken place in my father. His imprisonment has been a very different one to yours. You have had companions and a certain amount of freedom and comfort. You have had people to speak to, and have known what is going on in the world. He has been cut off altogether from mankind. He cannot even know whether you are alive, or whether you may not have yielded to the pressure that would be sure to be brought upon you, and acquiesced in a divorce being obtained. He has, doubtless, been kept in a narrow cell, deprived almost of the air and light of heaven. He will be greatly changed, mother. He will not be like you; for it does not seem to me that you have changed much from what you were. I could not see you much that night on the terrace; but now I see you I can hardly believe that you are my mother, so young do you look."

"I am nearly forty," the countess said smiling. "I was past twenty-one when I married. Had I not been of age they could have pronounced the marriage null and void. But you are right, Ronald, and I will prepare myself to find your father greatly changed. It cannot be otherwise after all he has gone through; but so that I have him again it is enough for me, no matter how great the change that may have taken place in him. But who are these men?" the countess exclaimed, as, a quarter of a mile outside the town, four men on horseback took up their places, two on each side of the carriage.

"Do not be alarmed, mother, they are our escort. Malcolm hired them at Le Mans. They are all old soldiers, and can be relied on in case of necessity."

"But what need can there be for them, Ronald? I have heard that bands of discharged soldiers and others make travelling insecure; but I had no idea that it was necessary to have an armed escort."

"Not absolutely necessary, mother, but a useful measure of precaution. We heard of them as we came through from Paris, and Malcolm and I agreed, that as you would have with you any jewels and valuables that you took to the convent, it would be just as well to be in a position to beat off any who might be disposed to trouble us. As you see, they have brought with them Malcolm's horse and mine, and we shall now mount. The less weight the horses have to draw the better. I will get in and have a talk from time to time where the road happens to be good; but, to tell you the truth, the jolting and shaking are neither pleasant nor good for talking."

"You are expecting to be attacked, Ronald," the countess said. "I am sure you would not be wanting to get out and leave me so soon after we have met did you not anticipate some danger."

"Frankly, mother, then, I do think it is probable that an attempt may be made to stop us, and that not by regular robbers, but by your enemies. They did their best to prevent me from reaching Tours, and will now most likely try to prevent our arriving at Blois. I will tell you all about it when we get there tonight. Here is the order for my father's release. Will you hide it in your dress? I had rather not have it about me. And, mother, if we should be attacked, do not be alarmed, for I have reason to believe that if we should be outnumbered and hard pressed, help will speedily be forthcoming."

"I am not in the least afraid for myself," the countess said; "but be careful, Ronald. Remember I have only just found you, and for my sake do not expose yourself unnecessarily."

"I will take care of myself, mother," he said. "You know I have always had to do so."

Malcolm had already mounted his horse, and Ronald was really glad when he took his place beside him a few yards ahead of the carriage. The art both of road making and carriage building was still in its infancy. When the weather was fine and the ground hard a fair rate of progress could be maintained; but in wet weather the vehicles often sank almost up to their axles in mud holes and quagmires, and the bumping and jolting were terrible.

"Now we take up our work of looking out for ambushes again, Malcolm."

"It will not be quite the same thing now," Malcolm said. "Before, two or three men with guns behind a wall might do the business, now they will have to make a regular attack. I have no doubt that we were watched from the time we entered the town, and that the news that we are travelling with the countess in a carriage, and with an escort of four armed men, has been carried on ahead already. It is by horsemen that we shall be attacked today if we are attacked at all, and they will probably fall upon us in the forest beyond Amboise. They will know that with a vehicle we must keep the road, and that as we cannot travel more than six miles an hour at the outside, we cannot attempt to escape by our speed."

"Do you think we had better wait at Amboise for the night and go on to Orleans tomorrow?"

"No, I think we had better push straight on, especially as we told our friends in the forest that we should come today, and I feel sure they will keep their promise to be on the lookout to aid us. If it were not for that I should have said let us stay at Tours for the present, for we may expect to be attacked by a force much superior to our own."

"Why, they would not have sent down more than six men to attack us two, Malcolm?"

"No, if they had been sure which road we should travel; but as they didn't know that, they may have had small parties at half a dozen spots, and these will now be united. Probably there may be a score of them. However, I rely on the robbers. The captain meant what he said, and you won the goodwill of all the men. If there are a dozen horsemen anywhere along the road they are sure to know of it, and will, I have no doubt, post themselves close at hand so as to be ready to join in the fray as soon as it commences."

Amboise was reached without adventure. Here the horses in the carriage were changed, and the party proceeded on their way. Four miles further they entered a great forest. Ronald now ordered two of the men to ride a few yards in front of the horses' heads. He and Malcolm rode on each side of the coach, the other two followed close behind. He ordered the driver, in case they were attacked, to jump off instantly and run to the horses' heads, and keep them quiet during the fray.

A vigilant lookout was kept. Suddenly, when they were in the thickest part of the wood, a number of mounted men dashed out from either side. In obedience to the orders Ronald had given, the men in front and behind at once closed in, so that there were three on either side of the carriage. The assailants fired their pistols as they dashed down, but the bullets flew harmlessly by, while the fire of the defenders, sitting quietly on their horses, was more accurate, two of the assailants falling dead, while another was severely wounded.

A moment later swords were drawn, and a furious combat ensued. Ronald had told his men to keep close to the carriage, so that they could not be attacked in the rear, keeping just far enough out on either side of him to be able to use their swords. For a short time the defenders of the coach maintained their position, the number of their assailants giving them but slight advantage, as they were unable to utilize their force.

Ronald ran the first man who attacked him through the body, and laid open the face of the next with a sweeping blow from left to right. The men they had hired fought stoutly; but they were being pressed together as the assailants urged forward their horses, when suddenly a volley of firearms was heard.

Several of the assailants fell dead, and with a loud shout a number of men rushed out from the wood and fell upon them in rear. The assailants turned to fly, and it was now the turn of the defenders of the coach to attack, which they did furiously.

In two or three minutes all was over. Five or six only of the assailants cut their way through the footmen who had attacked them in rear, while twelve lay dead or dying on the ground. Ronald's first impulse was to ride up to the carriage to assure his mother of his safety, his next to leap off his horse and grasp the hand of the chief of the robbers.

"You have kept your promise nobly," he said, "and arrived at the very nick of time. They were beginning to press us hotly; and though I fancy we should have rendered an account of a good many more, we must have been beaten in the end."

"I was farther behind than I intended to be," the man said; "but we were obliged to keep in hiding some little distance behind them. There were four parties of them. We kept them in sight all yesterday, and last night they assembled a mile or two away. I had men watching them all night, and this morning we followed them here, and saw them take up their position on both sides of the road. We crept up as closely as we dared without being observed, but you had for a couple of minutes to bear the brunt of it alone."

"I thank you most heartily," Ronald said. "My mother will thank you herself." So saying, he led them to the door of the carriage, which he opened.

"Mother, I told you that if we were attacked I relied upon help being near at hand. We owe our lives, for I have no doubt that yours as well as mine would have been taken, to this brave man and his followers."

"I thank you most sincerely, sir," the countess said. "At present I feel like one in a dream; for I have been so long out of the world that such a scene as this has well nigh bewildered me."

"I am only too glad to have been of service," the man said as he stood bareheaded. "I am not a good man, madame. I am one of those whom the necessities of the times have driven to earn their living as they can without much regard to the law; but I trust that I have not quite lost my instincts as a gentleman, and I am only too glad to have been able to be of some slight assistance to a persecuted lady; for your son, the other night, related to us something of the treatment which you have had to endure."

With a bow he now stepped back. His followers were engaged in searching the pockets of the fallen, and found in them a store of money which spoke well for the liberality of their employer, and well satisfied the robbers for the work they had undertaken. After a few words with her son the countess opened a small bag she carried with her, and taking from it a valuable diamond brooch, called the leader of the band up and presented it to him.

Ronald and his party then remounted their horses--the robbers had already overtaken and caught those of the fallen assailants--the driver mounted the box, and after a cordial farewell to their rescuers the party proceeded on their way to Blois.

CHAPTER XI: Free.

It was late at night before Blois was reached, and having alighted at the Aigle d'Or they engaged a private room.

"Even the Duke of Chateaurouge will be satisfied," Ronald said, "that his schemes have failed, and that no more can be done just at present. It will be a bitter blow to him when those scoundrels, on their return to Paris, report their utter failure, for he must have considered it impossible that we could escape from the toils he had laid for us. I only wish that we had clear evidence that he is the author of these attempts. If so, I would go straight with Marshal Saxe and lay an accusation against him before the king; but however certain we may feel about it, we have really nothing to connect him with the affair, and it would be madness to accuse a king's favourite unless one could prove absolutely the truth of what one says. However, I hope some day that I shall get even with him. It will not be my fault if I do not."

That night Ronald and his mother debated what would be the best way to proceed in the morning, and finally they agreed that Malcolm should present himself at the prison with the order of release, and that they should remain at the hotel, to which Malcolm should bring Colonel Leslie, after breaking to him the news that his wife and son were both awaiting him. The shock, in any case, of sudden liberty, would be a severe one, and the meeting with his attached comrade would act as a preparation for that with his wife.

Mother and son sat hand in hand after hearing the carriage drive off with Malcolm next morning. In the hours they had spent together they had come to know each other, and the relationship had become a real one. They had scarce been able to make out each other's features at their midnight meeting on the terrace, and at that meeting, rejoiced as they both were, there was still a feeling of strangeness between them. Now they knew each other as they were, and both were well satisfied. The countess was less strange to Ronald than he was to her. Malcolm had already described her to him as he knew her eighteen years before, and the reality agreed closely with the ideal that Ronald had pictured to himself, except that she was younger and brighter. For in thinking of her he had told himself over and over again that she would have grown much older, that her hair might have turned gray with grief and trouble, and her spirit been altogether broken.

She on her part had been able to form no idea as to what the infant she had last seen would have grown up, and was not even sure that he was in existence. She had hoped that if he had lived he would have grown up like his father, and although she now saw but slight resemblance between them, she was indeed well satisfied with her son.

He was not, she thought, as handsome as his father, but he bade fair to surpass him in strength and stature. She was delighted with his manly bearing; and when he laughed he reminded her of her husband, and she thought that she read in his gray eye and firm mouth a steadfastness and depth of character equal to his. They spoke but little now. Both were too anxious, Ronald for his mother's sake rather than his own. He was prepared to find this unknown father a man broken down by his years of captivity; but although his mother said that she too was prepared for great changes, he could not but think that the reality would be a sad shock to her. In little over an hour the carriage drove into the courtyard.

"Be brave, mother," Ronald said, as he felt the hand he held in his own tremble violently. "You must be calm for his sake."

Steps were heard approaching. The door opened, and Malcolm entered with a man leaning on his arm. The countess with a cry of joy sprang forward, and the next moment was clasped in her husband's arms.

"At last, my love, at last!" she said.

Ronald drew aside to the window to leave his father and mother to enjoy the first rapture of their meeting undisturbed, while Malcolm slipped quietly from the room again.

"Why, Amelie," Leslie said at last, holding her at arms' length that he might look the better at her, "you are scarce changed. It does not seem to me that you are five years older than when I saw you last, and yet Malcolm tells me that you too have been a prisoner. How much my love has cost you, dear! No, you are scarce changed, while I have become an old man--my hair is as white as snow, and I am so crippled with rheumatism I can scarce move my limbs."

"You are not so much changed, Angus. Your hair is white and your face is very pale; but you are not so much changed. If I have suffered for your love, dear, what have you suffered for mine! I have been a prisoner in a way, but I had a certain amount of freedom in my cage, while you--" And she stopped.

"Yes, it has been hard," he said; "but I kept up my spirits, Amelie. I never lost the hope that some day we should be reunited."

"And now, Angus, here is our boy, to whom we owe our liberty and the joy of this meeting. You may well be proud of such a son."

"I am proud," Leslie said as Ronald advanced, and he took him in his arms. "God bless you, my boy. You have performed well nigh a miracle. Malcolm has been telling me of you. Call him in again. It is right that he to whom you owe so much should share in our happiness."

Ronald at once fetched Malcolm, and until late at night they talked of all that had happened during so many years. Colonel Leslie had passed the first three years of his confinement in the Chatelet. "It was well it was no longer," he said; "for even I, hard as I was with years of soldiering, could not have stood that much longer. My cell there was below the level of the river. The walls were damp, and it was there I got the rheumatism which has crippled me ever since. Then they moved me to Blois, and there my cell was in one of the turrets, and the sun shone in through the window slit for half an hour a day; besides for an hour once a week I was allowed to take what they called exercise on the wall between my turret and the next. The governor was not a bad fellow, and did not try to pocket the best part of the money allowed for the keep of the prisoners. Fortunately I never lost hope. Had I done so I would have thrown myself over the parapet and ended it at once. I felt sure that you too were shut up, Amelie, and I pictured to myself how they would try to make you give me up; but I never thought they would succeed, dear. I knew you too well for that. Sometimes for months I lay as if paralysed by rheumatism, and I think I should have died if I had not known how my enemies would have rejoiced at the news of my death. So I held on stoutly, and I have got my reward."

But the hardships had told their tale. Although but the same age as Malcolm Anderson, Colonel Leslie looked fully ten years older. His long confinement had taken every tinge of colour out of his face, and left it almost ghastly in its whiteness. He could with difficulty lift his hands to his head, and he walked as stiffly as if his legs had been jointless. His voice only had not lost the cheery ring his wife remembered.

"No, Amelie," he said when she remarked this. "I kept my tongue in practice; it was the one member that was free. After I had been confined a few months it struck me that I was rapidly losing the power of speech, and I determined that if I could not talk for want of someone to answer me, I could at least sing, and having a good store of songs, Scottish and French, I sang for hours together, at first somewhat to the uneasiness of the prison authorities, who thought that I could not be so merry unless I had some communication from without, or was planning an escape; but at last they grew accustomed to it, and as my voice could not travel through the thick walls of my cells, it annoyed no one."

"And did you never think of escaping, father?"

"The first few years of my confinement I was always thinking of it, Ronald, but nothing ever came of my thought. I had no tools to burrow through a four foot wall, and if I could have done so I should have tried if it had only been to give me something to do, had it not been that I hoped some day to obtain my release, and that any attempt at escape would, if discovered, as it was almost certain to be, decrease my chances."

Not a word was said that evening as to their future plans, all their thoughts being in the past; but the next morning Colonel Leslie said at breakfast:

"And now what are we going to do next? How do we stand?"

"I know no more than you do, Angus. I do not know whether the king has gifted my mother's estate to others, as assuredly he has done my father's lands. If he has, I have been thinking that the best plan will be to ask the king's permission to leave the kingdom and return to your native Scotland."

"I am very fond of Scotland, Amelie; but I have also a fondness for living, and how I should live in Scotland I have not the most remote idea. My estate there was but a small one, and was forfeited thirty years ago; so unless I become a gaberlunzie and sit on the steps of St. Andrews asking for alms, I don't see how we should get porridge, to say nothing of anything else. No, Amelie, it seems to me that we must stop in France. For very shame they cannot let the daughter of the Marquis de Recambours starve, and they must at least restore you a corner of your parents estates, if it be but a farm. How are we off for funds at present?" he asked with a laugh. "I hope at least we have enough to pay our hotel bill."

"We have forty louis in cash, father; the remains of the hundred you committed to Malcolm with me."

"Is that so?" he exclaimed. "All I can say is that that money has lasted longer than any that ever passed through my fingers before."

"We have plenty of money," the countess said quietly. "I have all the jewels which came to me from my mother, and their sale will keep us for years, either in Scotland or France."

"That is good indeed," the colonel said cheerily.

"Yes; I took them all with me when I was sent to the convent, and have parted with none save the diamond necklet which I gave to the girl who brought Ronald and me together, as a parting keepsake, and a brooch with which I rewarded the men who aided us in the forest; but seriously, Angus, we must settle upon something."

"I quite agree with you, Amelie; but what is that something to be?"

"I should think, Angus, that the proper thing would be for me to write to the king thanking him for our release, asking his commands, and petitioning him that my mother's estates may be restored to me. I will also ask permission to retire to some southern town where there are waters which may do good to your rheumatism."

Colonel Leslie frowned.

"I suppose that is the right thing to do, Amelie; though, for my part, I cannot thank a sovereign whom I have served well after such treatment as I have received. I would rather beg my bread from door to door."

"No, I would not ask you, Angus, and of course you are differently placed; but I have my rights as a peeress of France; besides I have on my own account no complaint against the king. It was my father who shut me up in the convent, not the king."

"By the way, Amelie," her husband said, "you are not yet in mourning."

"Nor do I intend to be," she said firmly; "unless I have to go to court no thread of mourning do I put on. My father behaved like a tyrant to me, and I will not feign a grief at an event which has brought us happiness. Well, Ronald, what do you think had best be done? You and Malcolm have managed so well that we had best leave it for you to decide."

"I think what you propose, mother, is best. I think you had better travel down to some place near where your mother's estates lay, and then write your petition to the king. I will leave you there and return with it to Paris, and will there consult Colonel Hume and Marshal Saxe as to how it should be delivered to the king."

This plan was carried out. The party journeyed together to Poitiers, and there having seen his parents comfortably settled in a small house near the town, and remained with them a few days, Ronald with Malcolm returned to Paris, bearing with him his mother's memorial to the king.

Ronald was glad to find that Colonel Hume was now recovered from his wound. Marshal Saxe too was better; the latter at once took charge of the petition, and said that he would hand it to the king on the first opportunity. Ronald accompanied the marquis several times to Versailles, but the latter had no private audience with the king, and thought it better not to present the memorial in public. One day, however, he was called into the king's closet.

When he emerged with the king, Ronald thought from his expression of countenance that things had not gone well. On leaving the palace he mounted his horse--for he was now well enough to ride--and as he set out he called Ronald, who with other gentlemen had accompanied him to ride beside him.

"Things have not gone well," he said. "Your father's enemies have evidently been at work, and have been poisoning the king's mind. He read the memorial, and then said harshly, 'The Countess of Recambours has forfeited all rights to her mother's estates by marrying an alien. The lands of France are for the King of France's subjects, not for soldiers of fortune.' This touched me, and I said, 'Your majesty may recollect that I am an alien and a soldier of fortune, and methinks that in time of war the swords of our soldiers of fortune have done such things for France that they have earned some right to gratitude. In a hundred battles our Scottish troops have fought in the front ranks, and had it not been for the Irish Brigade we should not have had to write Fontenoy down among the list of French victories."

"You are bold, marshal," the king said angrily.

"I am bold, sire," I replied, "because I am in the right: and I humbly submit that a brave soldier like Colonel Leslie deserves better treatment than he has received at the hands of France."

The king rose at once.

"An answer to the petition will be sent to you tomorrow, marshal."

"I bowed, and without another word the king left his closet and entered the room of audience. However, lad, you must not look so downcast. We could perhaps expect no more the first time. Of course every man who has a hope, or who has a relation who has a hope, of obtaining the grant of your mother's estates is interested in exciting the king's displeasure against her; besides which there is, as you have told me, the Duc de Chateaurouge, who may be regarded as a personal enemy of your father, and who has the king's ear as much as anyone about him. However, we must have courage. I consider my personal honour is touched in the matter now, and I will not let the matter drop till justice is done."

At the appointed time Ronald again called at Marshal Saxe's hotel, and watched the gay crowd of officers and nobles who were gathered in his reception rooms. An hour later a royal attendant entered and handed a document to the marshal. The latter glanced at it and looked around. As soon as his eye fell upon Ronald he nodded to him.

"Here is the judgement," he said in a low tone, as he handed him the paper. "You see it is directed to the countess, to my care. I suppose you will start with it at once."

"Yes, marshal; the horses are saddled and we shall leave immediately."

"Don't hurry your horses," the marshal said with a slight smile; "from the king's manner I think that the contents are such that a few hours' delay in the delivery will cause the countess no pain. However, I do not anticipate anything very harsh. In the first place, although the king is swayed by favourites who work on his prejudices, his intention is always to be just; and in the second place, after granting the release of your parents as a boon to me he can scarcely annul the boon by any severe sentence. Will you tell the countess from me that I am wholly at her service, and that, should any opportunity offer, she may be sure that I will do what I can to incline the king favourably towards her. Lastly, Leslie, take care of yourself. The change in the king's manner shows that you have powerful enemies, and now that you have succeeded in obtaining your parents' freedom you have become dangerous. Remember the attack that was made upon you before, when there seemed but little chance that you would ever succeed in obtaining their release or in seriously threatening the interests of those who were looking forward to the reversion of the family estates. Their enmity now, when it only needs a change in the king's mood to do justice to your parents, will be far greater than before.

"Bid your father, too, to have a care for himself and your mother. Remember that violence is common enough, and there are few inquiries made. An attack upon a lonely house and the murder of those within it is naturally put down as the act of some party of discharged soldiers or other ruffians. Tell him therefore he had best get a few trusty men around him, and be on guard night and day against a treacherous attack. Those who stand in the way of powerful men in France seldom live long, so he cannot be too careful."

A quarter of an hour later Ronald was on horseback. He had already provided himself with a pass to leave the city after the usual hour of closing the gates, and he and Malcolm were soon in the open country. As they rode along Ronald repeated the warning that the marshal had given him.

"He is quite right, Ronald, and you cannot be too careful. We have against us, first, this vindictive Duc de Chateaurouge, who, no doubt, has poisoned the king's mind. In all France there is no one whom I would not rather have as a foe. He is powerful, unscrupulous, and vindictive; he would hesitate at nothing to carry out anything on which he had set his mind, and would think no more of obtaining the removal of one whom he considered to stand in his way than of crushing a worm. Even as a young man he had a villainous reputation, and was regarded as one of the most dangerous men about the court. To do him justice, he is brave and a fine swordsman, and for choice he would rather slay with his own hands those who offend him than by other means. Though he was but three-and-twenty at the time I first left France he had fought half a dozen duels and killed as many men, and several others who were known to have offended him died suddenly. Some were killed in street brawls, returning home at night, one or two were suspected of having been poisoned. Altogether the man was feared and hated in those days, although, of course, none spoke their suspicions openly.

"From what I have heard those suspicions have stuck to him ever since. He has not been engaged in many duels, because in the first place edicts against duelling are very strict, and in the second because his reputation as a swordsman is so great that few would risk their lives against him. Still all who stood in his way have somehow or other come to a sudden end. We must therefore be on our guard night and day. He is, of course, your most dangerous foe; but besides him must be numbered all those who hope to obtain your mother's estates. The heirs of the marquis doubtless feel perfectly safe from interference. There is no chance whatever of the king dispossessing them in favour of a foreigner, so we need not count them among your foes.

"It is just as well, Ronald, that we started tonight instead of waiting till tomorrow. The duke is pretty certain to learn that the king's answer will be sent this evening, and may possibly have made preparations for you on the road; but he will hardly expect that you will start before the morning. However, in order to be on the safe side I propose that we shall presently turn off from the main road and avoid all large towns on our way down to Poitiers."

"Do you think the danger is as great as that, Malcolm?"

"I do not think there is much danger, Ronald, just at present, though I do in the future."

Travelling by byways Ronald and Malcolm arrived at Poitiers without adventure.

"I have brought you the king's answer, mother," Ronald said as he alighted; "but before you open it I may tell you that it is unfavourable, though I am ignorant of the precise nature of its contents. But you must not be disappointed. Marshal Saxe bade me tell you that he considers his honour engaged in seeing you righted, and that whenever an opportunity occurs he will endeavour to move the king's mind in your favour. How is my father?"

"He suffers grievously from rheumatism, Ronald, and can scarce move from his couch."

As soon as they joined the colonel the countess opened the king's letter. It was brief. "The Countess Amelie de Recambours is hereby ordered to withdraw at once to her estate of La Grenouille and there to await the king's pleasure concerning her."

The king's signature was affixed.

"Well, that is not so very bad," the countess said. "At any rate my right to one of my mother's estates is recognized. La Grenouille is the smallest of them, and contains but three or four farms. Still that will suffice for our wants, and as it lies but twenty miles from Bordeaux the air will be warm and soft for you, Angus."

"Is there a chateau on it, mother?"

"Yes, there is a small chateau. I was there once as a girl. It has never been modernized, but is still a castle such as it was two hundred years ago."

"All the better," Ronald said; and he then gave Malcolm's reasons for their being on the watch against any sudden attack.

"He is quite right, Ronald," Colonel Leslie said. "The duke is capable of anything. However, we will be on our guard, and if, as your mother says, it is a fortified house, we need have no fear of any sudden attack."

"I would suggest, colonel, that I should ride to Tours," Malcolm said, "and hire two of the men who escorted madame's carriage. They have served in the wars and can be relied upon. They would not need high wages, for most of the discharged soldiers have trouble enough to keep body and soul together. With a couple of men of this kind, and two or three of the men on the estate, I think, colonel, you need fear no sudden attack."

The colonel approved of the suggestion, and a week later, Malcolm having returned with the two men, a carriage was hired to convey the colonel and his wife, and so they journeyed quietly down to La Grenouille. On arriving there they found that they were expected, the old steward in charge having received a letter from the royal chancellor, saying that he was to receive the countess as the owner of the estate.

The old man, who had known her mother well and remembered her visits as a child, received the countess with respectful joy. The chateau was, as Amelie had said, really a castle. It was surrounded by a moat filled with water, from which the walls rose abruptly, with no windows in the lower stories and only small loopholes in those above. Although the steward was ignorant when his mistress might be expected, he had already caused great fires to be lighted in all the rooms and had temporarily engaged two of the farmer's daughters to wait upon the countess, and three stout men as servitors.

"What are the revenues of the estate?" the countess asked the steward that evening. "My mother's other estates have not been restored to me as yet, and I have only this to depend upon, and I do not know what establishment I can afford to keep up."

"The revenue amounts to twelve thousand francs," he said. "There are three large farms and four small ones. Twelve thousand francs are not much, countess, for your mother's daughter; but they go a long way here, where one can live for next to nothing. We have a garden which will provide all the fruit and vegetables you require, and your poultry will cost you nothing. The vineyard attached to the chateau furnishes more than enough wine, and the cellars are well filled, for every year I have put aside a few barrels, so that in fact it will be only meat you have to buy."

"So that you think I can keep the two men I have brought with me and the servants you have engaged?"

"Easily, madam, and more if you wished it."

"Do you think five men will be sufficient?" the countess said. "I ask because I have powerful enemies, and in these lawless times an attack upon a lonely house might well be carried out."

"With the drawbridge drawn up, madam, five men could hold the chateau against a score, and the sound of the alarm bell would bring all the tenants and their men down to your assistance. I will answer for them all. There were great rejoicings last week when I sent round the news that you were expected. The memory of your mother, who once resided here for a year, is very dear to all of us, and there is not a man on the estate but would take up arms in your defence. The sound of the alarm bell would bring thirty stout fellows, at least, to your aid."

"Then we need not trouble on that score, Amelie," the colonel said cheerfully. "Malcolm will see to the drawbridge tomorrow; probably it has not been raised for years."

"I have already been examining it," Malcolm--who had just entered the room--said. "It only needs a little oil and a bolt or two. I will have it raised tonight. Things look better than I expected, colonel, and I shall be able to return to Paris without having any anxiety upon your score."

"But you are not thinking of going back, Ronald?" the countess asked anxiously. "If there is danger here for us, there must be surely danger for you in Paris. And I want you here with us."

"I will stop for a few days, mother, and then Malcolm and I will be off. As I have Marshal Saxe's protection I need fear no open enmity from anyone, and as I shall be with the regiment I shall be safe from the secret attacks; besides, my sword can guard my head."

"You have taught him to defend himself--eh, Malcolm?" Colonel Leslie said.

"I," Malcolm repeated--"I can use my sword in a melee, colonel, as you know, and hold my own against Dutchman or German when I meet them on the field; but Ronald is a different blade altogether. He was well taught in Glasgow, and has practised under the best maitres d'armes in Paris since, and I am proud to say that I do not think there are ten men in France against whom he could not hold his own."

"That is good, that is good, indeed," the colonel said, delighted. "Malcolm, I feel my obligations to you more and more every day. Truly I had never even hoped that if my son were ever to be restored to me, I should have such cause to be proud of him."

"But why do you think you had better return to Paris, Ronald?" his mother inquired.

"Because, mother, it will not do to let your enemies have entirely their own way now that you have been so far restored. Doubtless your family will be the more inclined to aid you with their influence, but there must be somebody to urge them to do so."

"Besides, Amelie," the colonel put in, "we must not cage the lad here at your apron strings. He has already won Saxe's regard and protection by his conduct in the field, and can now accept a commission in the old regiment. He has begun well, and may yet live to command it. No, no, my love. I should like to keep him here as much as you would, but in every way it is better that he should go out and take his place in the world. To you and me, after our long imprisonment, this place is life, freedom, and happiness, and we are together; but for him it is a dreary little country chateau, and he would soon long for a life among men."

And so, after three weeks' stay at the chateau, Ronald and Malcolm rode back to Paris, and the former received a week later a commission through Marshal Saxe in the Scottish Dragoons. That regiment had returned from the frontier, and Ronald at once took his place in its ranks, and was heartily received by all the officers, to whom he was formally introduced by Colonel Hume as the son of their former commanding officer.

A short time afterwards it became the turn of duty of the Scottish Dragoons to furnish guards for a week at Versailles, and Colonel Hume took down two troops for that purpose. That to which Ronald belonged was one of them. Ronald, knowing that for the present he was not in favour with the king, begged the colonel to put him on duty as often as possible, so that he might avoid the necessity of being present at the king's audiences with the other officers.

He was one day walking with the colonel and several other officers in the grounds at a distance from the palace, when they came, at the turn of the walk, upon the Duc de Chateaurouge and three other gentlemen of the court. The former stopped abruptly before Colonel Hume.

"I had the honour, Colonel Hume, to speak to you some time since of a volunteer in your regiment who chose to call himself the name of Leslie. I understand he is now an officer. I see by the lists in the courtyard that a Cornet Leslie is now on duty here. Where does he hide himself, for I have been seeking in vain to meet him?"

"Cornet Leslie is not one to balk any man's desire that way," Colonel Hume said gravely. "This is Cornet Leslie."

Ronald stepped forward and looked the duke calmly in the face.

"So this is the young cockerel," the duke said contemptuously. "A worthy son of a worthy father, I doubt not."

"At any rate, my lord duke," Ronald said quietly, "I do not rid myself of my foes by getting those I am afraid to meet as man to man thrown into prison, nor by setting midnight assassins upon them. Nor do I rely upon my skill as a swordsman to be a bully and a coward."

The duke started as if struck.

"I had made up my mind to kill you, young sir," he said, "sooner or later; but you have brought it on yourself now. Draw, sir!" And the duke drew his sword.

Colonel Hume and several others threw themselves before Ronald.

"Put up your sword, sir. Duelling is forbidden, and you know the consequence of drawing within the precincts of the palace."

"What care I for ordinances!" the duke said furiously. "Stand aside, gentlemen, lest I do you harm!"

"Harm or no harm," Colonel Hume said sternly, "my young friend shall not fight in the palace grounds. I protest against his being forced into a duel at all; but at any rate he shall not fight here."

The duke looked for a moment as if he was about to spring upon Colonel Hume, but he saw by their faces that his companions also were against him. For the consequences of drawing a sword within the precincts of a palace were so serious, that even the most powerful nobles shrank from braving them.

"Very well," he said at last, thrusting his sword back into its scabbard. "It is but ten minutes' walk to the boundary wall, I will let him live till then."

So saying he started off with rapid strides down the walk, followed at a slower pace by the rest.

CHAPTER XII: The End of the Quarrel.

"This is a serious business, Leslie," the colonel said in a low voice. "If it had been anyone but you I should have ordered him to the barracks at once under pain of arrest, and have laid the matter before the king, for it would have been nothing short of murder. But I can trust you to hold your own even against the Duke of Chateaurouge. And, in truth, after what has been said, I do not see that you can do other but meet him."

"I would not avoid it if I could," Ronald said. "His insults to me do not disturb me; but I have my father's wrongs to avenge."

"Forbes," the colonel said to one of the other officers, "do you go straight to the barracks, bid Leslie's man saddle his own horse and his master's instantly, and bring them round outside the wall of the park. If Leslie wounds or kills his man he will have to ride for it."

The officer at once hurried away.

"Ronald, I will tell you a piece of news I heard this morning. The young Chevalier left Paris secretly five days ago, and I have received certain private information this morning that he has gone to Nantes, and that he is on the point of sailing for Scotland on his own account. I am told that this plan of his is known to but five or six persons. If you get safely through this business mount and ride thither at all speed. They are more likely to pursue you towards the frontier or the northern ports, and will not think you have made for Nantes. If you get there before the prince has sailed, present yourself to him and join his expedition. The king will be furious at first, both at the loss of his favourite and the breaking of the edicts; but he must come round. The gentlemen here with the duke are all honourable men, and were, I could see, shocked at the insult which the duke passed on you. Therefore I can rely upon them to join me in representing the matter in its true light to the king. Before you return, the matter will have blown over, and it may be that the removal of your father's most powerful enemy may facilitate an arrangement. In any case, my dear boy, you can rely upon the marshal and myself to look after your interests."

They had now reached a wicket gate in the wall of the park. The duke was standing a few paces distant, having already removed his coat and turned up the shirt sleeve of the sword arm.

"You will act as second, marquis?" he said to one of the gentlemen.

The latter bowed coldly.

"I act as second to my friend Leslie," Colonel Hume said. "And I call upon you all, gentlemen, to bear witness in the future, that this encounter has been wantonly forced upon him by the Duc de Chateaurouge, and that Cornet Leslie, as a man of honour, has no alternative whatever but to accept the challenge forced upon him."

Ronald had by this time stripped to his shirt sleeves. The seconds took the two swords and compared their length. They were found to be as nearly as possible the same. They were then returned to their owners. A piece of even turf was selected, and a position chosen in which the light was equally favourable to both parties. Then both fell into position on guard, and as the rapiers crossed Colonel Hume said solemnly:

"May God defend the right!"

An instant later they were engaged in deadly conflict. It lasted but a few seconds. The duke, conscious of his own skill, and believing that he had but a lad to deal with, at once attacked eagerly, desirous of bringing the contest to a termination before there was any chance of interruption. He attacked, then, carelessly and eagerly, and made a furious lunge which he thought would terminate the encounter at once; but Ronald did not give way an inch, but parrying in carte, slipped his blade round that of the duke, feinted in tierce, and then rapidly disengaging, lunged in carte as before. The blade passed through the body of his adversary, and the lunge was given with such force that the pommel of his sword struck against the ribs. The duke fell an inert mass upon the ground as Ronald withdrew the rapier.

An exclamation of surprise and alarm broke from the three gentlemen who had accompanied the duke, while Colonel Hume said gravely:

"God has protected the right. Ah! here come the horses! Mount and ride, Leslie, and do not spare the spurs. I should advise you," he said, drawing him aside, "to take the northern route for a few miles, so as to throw them off the scent. When you get to Nantes search the inns till you find the Duke of Athole, he is an intimate friend of mine, and it was from him I learned in strict secrecy of the prince's intentions. Show him this ring, he knows it well, and tell him I sent you to join him; say nothing at first as to this business here. Your own name and my name will be enough. He will introduce you to Prince Charlie, who will be with him under a disguised name. May God bless you, my lad! We will do our best for you here."

At this moment Malcolm arrived with the two horses.

"Thank God you are safe, Ronald!" he exclaimed as Ronald leapt into his saddle, and with a word of thanks and adieu to the colonel dashed off at full speed.

Colonel Hume then rejoined the group gathered round the duke. The Scottish officers were looking very grave, the courtiers even more so. They had from the first recognized fully that the duel had been provoked by the duke, and had accompanied him reluctantly, for they regarded the approaching conflict as so unfair that it would excite a strong amount of feeling against all who had a hand in the matter. As to the edict against duelling, it had not concerned them greatly, as they felt sure that with the duke's influence the breach of the law would be passed over with only a show of displeasure on the part of the king, and an order to absent themselves for a short time from court. The contingency that this young Scottish officer, who had scarcely yet attained the age of manhood, should kill one of the best swordsmen in France had not occurred to them; but this had happened, and there could be no doubt that the king's anger, alike at the loss of his favourite and at the breach of the law, would fall heavily on all concerned, and that a prolonged exile from court was the least evil they could expect. Not a word had been spoken after they had, on stooping over the duke, found that death had been instantaneous, until Colonel Hume joined them.

"Well, gentlemen," he said; "this is a bad business, and means trouble for us all. His majesty will be vastly angry. However, the duke brought it upon himself, and is the only person to blame. His character is pretty well known, and it will be manifest that if he had made up his mind to fight no remonstrance on your part would have availed to induce him to abstain from doing so. At the same time the king will not, in the first burst of his anger, take that into consideration, and for awhile we shall no doubt all of us suffer from his displeasure; but I do not think that it will be lasting. The duke forced on the duel, and would have fought within the royal park had we not interfered, and we were in a way forced to be present. I propose that we return to the palace and give notice of what has occurred. Captain Forbes, as you were not present at the affair, and will not therefore be called upon to give any account of it, will you remain here until they send down to fetch the body?

"We will, if you please, gentlemen, walk slowly, for every mile that Leslie can put between him and Versailles is very important. The news will reach the king's ears very shortly after we have made it public. You and I, marquis, as the seconds in the affair, are sure to be sent for first. As, fortunately, we were both present at the quarrel we are both in a position to testify that the duke brought his fate upon himself, that there was no preventing the duel, and that had we refused to act he was in a frame of mind which would have driven him to fight without seconds if none had been forthcoming; lastly, we can testify that the combat was a fair one, and that the duke fell in consequence of the rashness of his attack and his contempt for his adversary, although in point of fact I can tell you that young Leslie is so good a swordsman that I am confident the result would in any case have been the same."

"I suppose there's nothing else for it," the marquis grumbled. "I must prepare myself for a prolonged visit to my country estates."

"And I shall no doubt be placed under arrest for some time," Colonel Hume said; "and the regiment will probably be packed off to the frontier again. However, these things don't make much difference in the long run. What I am most anxious about, marquis, is that his majesty should thoroughly comprehend that Leslie was not to blame, and that this affair was so forced upon him that it was impossible for him to avoid it. There is much more than the lad's own safety dependent on this."

"You may be sure, colonel, that I will do him justice."

At a slow pace the party proceeded until they neared the palace, when they quickened their steps. The marquis proceeded immediately to the apartments occupied by the duke, and told his domestics that their master had been killed in a duel, and directed them to obtain assistance and proceed at once to the spot where his body would be found. The colonel went to the king's surgeon, and told him of what had taken place.

"His death was instantaneous," he said; "the sword passed right through him, and I believe touched the heart. However, it will be as well that you should go and see the body, as the king will be sure to ask particulars as to the wound."

The rest of the party joined their acquaintances, and told them what had happened, and the news spread quickly through the palace. It created a great sensation. Breaches of the edict were not unfrequent; but the death of so powerful a noble, a chief favourite, too, of the king, took it altogether out of the ordinary category of such events. The more so since the duke's reputation as a swordsman and a duellist was so great that men could scarce believe that he had been killed by a young officer who had but just joined the regiment. It seemed like the story of David and Goliath over again. A quarter of an hour later a court official approached Colonel Hume and the Marquis de Vallecourt, who were standing together surrounded by a number of courtiers and officers.

"Monsieur le Marquis and Colonel Hume," he said, saluting them; "I regret to say that I am the bearer of the orders of his majesty that you shall deliver me your swords, and that you will then accompany me to the king's presence."

The two gentlemen handed over their swords to the official, and followed him to the king's presence. Louis was pacing angrily up and down his apartment.

"What is this I hear, gentlemen?" he exclaimed as they entered. "A breach of the edicts here at Versailles, almost in the boundaries of the park; and that the Duc de Chateaurouge, one of my most valued officers and friends has been killed; they tell me that you acted as seconds in the affair."

"They have told your majesty the truth," the marquis said; "but I think that, much as we regret what has happened, we could scarcely have acted otherwise than we did. The duke drew in the first place within the limits of the park, and would have fought out his quarrel there had we not, I may almost say forcibly, intervened. Then he strode away towards the boundary of the park, calling upon his antagonist to follow him; and had we not gone the encounter would have taken place without seconds or witnesses, and might then have been called a murder instead of a duel."

"You should have arrested him, sir," the king exclaimed, "for drawing in the park."

"Perhaps we should have done so, sire; but you must please to remember that the Duke of Chateaurouge was of a temper not to be crossed, and I believe that bloodshed would have taken place had we endeavoured to thwart him. He enjoyed your majesty's favour, and a forcible arrest, with perhaps the shedding of blood, in the royal demesne would have been a scandal as grave as that of this duel."

"How did it come about?" the king asked abruptly.

"The duke was walking with De Lisle, St. Aignan, and myself, when we suddenly came upon Colonel Hume with three of the officers of his regiment. The duke at once walked up to them and addressed Colonel Hume, and finding which of his companions was Monsieur Leslie, addressed him in terms of so insulting a nature that they showed that he had been waiting for the meeting to provoke a quarrel. The young officer replied perfectly calmly, but with what I must call admirable spirit and courage, which so infuriated the duke, that, as I have already had the honour of telling your majesty, he drew at once, and when we interfered he called upon him to proceed forthwith outside the park, and there settle the quarrel. We most reluctantly accompanied him, and determined to interfere at the first blood drawn; but the affair scarcely lasted for a second. The duke threw himself furiously and rashly upon the lad, for as your majesty is aware, he is but little more. The latter, standing firm, parried with admirable coolness, and in an instant ran the duke right through the body."

"But I have always heard," the king said, "that the duke was one of the best swordsmen in the army."

"Your majesty has heard correctly," Colonel Hume replied; "but young Leslie is one of the best swordsmen in France. The duke's passion and rashness led to the speedy termination of the duel; but had he fought with his accustomed coolness I believe that Leslie would have turned out his conqueror."

"But what was the cause of the quarrel? Why should the Duc de Chateaurouge fix a dispute, as you tell me he did, upon this officer of yours?"

"I believe, sire, that it was a long standing quarrel. The duke's words showed that he bore an enmity against the lad's father, and that it was on this account that he insulted the son."

"Leslie!" the king exclaimed, with a sudden recollection. "Is that the youth whom Marshal Saxe presented to me?"

"The same, sire; the lad who distinguished himself at Fontenoy, and whom the Marshal afterwards appointed to a commission in my regiment, in which he had served as a gentleman volunteer for nearly a year."

"These Leslies are always causing trouble," the king said angrily. "I have already given orders that he shall be arrested wherever he is found, and he shall be punished as he deserves."

"In punishing him," Colonel Hume said with grave deference, "I am sure that your majesty will not forget that this quarrel was forced upon him, and that, had he accepted the insults of the Duke of Chateaurouge, he would have been unworthy to remain an officer of your majesty."

"Silence, sir!" the king said angrily. "You will return immediately to Paris, under arrest, until my pleasure in your case is notified to you. I shall at once give orders that your troops here are replaced by those of a regiment whose officers will abstain from brawling and breaking the edicts in our very palace. Marquis, you will retire at once to your estates." The two gentlemen bowed and left the royal presence.

"Not worse than I expected," the marquis said, after the door had closed behind them. "Now he will send for St. Aignan and De Lisle, and will hear their account, and as it cannot but tally with ours the king must see that the duke brought his fate upon himself. Louis is not unjust when his temper cools down, and in a few weeks we shall meet again here."

"I expect to be on the frontier with my regiment before that," Colonel Hume replied; "but as I would rather be there than in Paris that will be no hardship."

Colonel Hume at once mounted and rode back to Paris and proceeded straight to the hotel of Marshal Saxe, to whom he communicated what had occurred.

"If Leslie gets safely away it will, perhaps, all turn out for the best," the marshal said. "As soon as the king's anger dies out I will begin to plead the cause of the boy's parents; and now that the influence of Chateaurouge the other way is withdrawn, I may hope for a more favourable hearing. As to the lad himself, we will make his peace in a few months. The king is brave himself, as he showed when under fire at Fontenoy, and he admires bravery in others, and when he has once got over the loss of Chateaurouge he will appreciate the skill and courage which the lad showed in an encounter with one of the most noted duellists in France. Now, too, that the duke has gone, some of the stories to his disadvantage, of which there are so many current, are likely to meet the king's ears. Hitherto no one has ventured to speak a word against so powerful a favourite; but the king's eyes will soon be open now, and he will become ashamed of so long having given his countenance to a man who is generally regarded as having not only killed half-a-dozen men in duels, but as having procured the removal, by unfair means, of a score of others. When he knows the truth the king is likely to do justice, not only to young Leslie, but to his parents. I only hope that they will not manage to overtake the lad before he reaches the frontier, for although I can rely on the king's justice when he is cool I would not answer for it just at present."

As Ronald rode off at full speed with Malcolm he related to him the whole circumstances of the quarrel and subsequent duel.

"It was well done, Ronald. I made sure that sooner or later you and the duke would get to blows, that is if he did not adopt other means to get you removed from his path; anyhow I am heartily glad it's over, and that the most dangerous enemy of your father and yourself is out of the way. And now we must hope that we sha'nt be overtaken before we get to the frontier. The danger is that orders for your arrest will be passed by signal."

"We are not going to the frontier, Malcolm; I am only riding this way to throw them off the scent. We are going to Nantes."

"Well, that's not a bad plan," Malcolm said. "They are not so likely to send orders there as to the northern ports. But it will not be easy to get a vessel to cross, for you see, now that we are at war with England, there is little communication. However, we shall no doubt be able to arrange with a smuggler to take us across."

"We are not going to England, Malcolm; we are going direct to Scotland. Colonel Hume has told me a secret: Prince Charles has gone down to Nantes and is going to cross at once to Scotland."

"What! Alone and without an army!" Malcolm exclaimed in astonishment.

"I suppose he despairs of getting assistance from Louis. Now that Fontenoy has put an end to danger on the frontier the King of France is no longer interested in raising trouble for George at home."

"But it is a mad scheme of the prince's," Malcolm said gravely. "If his father did not succeed in '15 how can he expect to succeed now?"

"The country has had all the longer time to get sick of the Hanoverians, and the gallantry of the enterprise will appeal to the people. Besides, Malcolm, I am not so sure that he will not do better coming alone than if he brought the fifteen thousand men he had at Dunkirk last year with him. Fifteen thousand men would not win him a kingdom, and many who would join him if he came alone would not do so if he came backed by an army of foreigners. It was the French, you will remember, who ruined his grandfather's cause in Ireland. Their arrogance and interference disgusted the Irish, and their troops never did any fighting to speak of. For myself, I would a thousand times rather follow Prince Charles fighting with an army of Scotsmen for the crown of Scotland than fight for him with a French army against Englishmen."

"Well, perhaps you are right, Ronald; it went against the grain at Fontenoy; for after all, as you said, we are closely akin in blood and language to the English, and although Scotland and France have always been allies it is very little good France has ever done us. She has always been glad enough to get our kings to make war on England whenever she wanted a diversion made, but she has never put herself out of the way to return the favour. It has been a one sided alliance all along. Scotland has for centuries been sending some of her best blood to fight as soldiers in France, but with a few exceptions no Frenchman has ever drawn his sword for Scotland.

"No, I am inclined to think you are right, Ronald, and especially after what we saw at Fontenoy I have no wish ever to draw sword again against the English, and am willing to be the best friends in the world with them if they will but let us Scots have our own king and go away peacefully. I don't want to force Prince Charles upon them if they will but let us have him for ourselves. If they won't, you know, it is they who are responsible for the quarrel, not us."

"That is one way of putting it, certainly," Ronald laughed. "I am afraid after having been one kingdom since King James went to London, they won't let us go our own way without making an effort to keep us; but here is a crossroad, we will strike off here and make for the west."

They avoided the towns on their routes, for although they felt certain that they were ahead of any messengers who might be sent out with orders for their arrest, they knew that they might be detained for some little time at Nantes, and were therefore anxious to leave no clue of their passage in that direction. On the evening of the third day after starting they approached their destination.

On the first morning after leaving Versailles they had halted in wood a short distance from Chartres, and Malcolm had ridden in alone and had purchased a suit of citizen's clothes for Ronald, as the latter's uniform as an officer of the Scotch Dragoons would at once have attracted notice. Henceforward, whenever they stopped, Malcolm had taken an opportunity to mention to the stable boy that he was accompanying his master, the son of an advocate of Paris, on a visit to some relatives in La Vendee. This story he repeated at the inn where they put up at Nantes.

The next morning Malcolm went round to all the inns in the town, but could hear nothing of the Duke of Athole, so he returned at noon with the news of his want of success.

"They may have hired a private lodging to avoid observation," Ronald said, "or, not improbably, may have taken another name. The best thing we can do is to go down to the river side, inquire what vessels are likely to leave port soon, and then, if we see anyone going off to them, to accost them. We may hear of them in that way."

Accordingly they made their way down to the river. There were several vessels lying in the stream, in readiness to sail when the wind served, and the mouth of the river was reported to be clear of any English cruisers. They made inquiries as to the destination of the vessels. All the large ones were sailing for Bordeaux or the Mediterranean ports of France.

"What is that little vessel lying apart from the rest?" Malcolm asked. "She looks a saucy little craft."

"That is the privateer La Doutelle, one of the fastest little vessels on the coast. She has brought in more than one English merchantman as a prize."

As they were speaking a boat was seen to leave her side and make for the shore. With a glance at Malcolm to break off his conversation with the sailor and follow him, Ronald strode along the bank towards the spot where the boat would land. Two gentlemen got out and advanced along the quay. As they passed Ronald said to Malcolm:

"I know one of those men's faces."

"Do you, Ronald? I cannot recall having seen them."

Ronald stood for a moment in thought.

"I know now!" he exclaimed. "And he is one of our men, sure enough."

"I think, sir," he said as he came up to them, "that I have had the honour of meeting you before."

A look of displeasure came across the gentleman's face.

"I think you are mistaken, sir," he said coldly. "You must take me for some one else. My name is Verbois--Monsieur Verbois of Le Mans."

"I have not the pleasure of knowing Monsieur Verbois," Ronald said with a slight smile; "but I hardly think, sir, that that is the name that you went by when I had the honour of meeting you in Glasgow more than two years ago?"

"In Glasgow!" the gentleman said, looking earnestly at Ronald. "In Glasgow! I do not remember you."

"I had the pleasure of doing you some slight service, nevertheless," Ronald said quietly, "when I brought you news that your enemies were upon you, and managed to detain them while you made your escape through the attic window."

"A thousand pardons!" the gentleman exclaimed, speaking in English. "How could I have forgotten you? But I saw you for such a short time, and two years have changed you greatly. This is the young gentleman, marquis, to whom I am indebted for my escape when I was so nearly captured at Glasgow, as you have heard me say. It was to his kindly warning in the first place, and to his courage in the second, that I owed my liberty. It is wonderful that you should remember me."

"Two years have not changed you as much as they have changed me," Ronald said; "besides, you were busy in destroying papers, while I had nothing to do but to watch you."

"That is so," the gentleman agreed. "At any rate I am heartily glad of the happy chance which has thrown us together, and has given me an opportunity of expressing to you the deep gratitude which I have felt for your warning and assistance. Had it not been for that, not only should I myself have been taken, but they would have got possession of those papers, which might have brought the heads of a score of the best blood of Scotland to the scaffold. I took a boat that was lying in readiness, and making down the river got on board a ship which was cruising there awaiting me, and got off. It has always been a matter of bitter regret to me that I never learned so much as the name of the brave young gentleman to whom I owed so much, or what had happened to him for his share in that night's work."

"My name is Ronald Leslie, sir. I am the son of Leslie of Glenlyon, who fought with the Chevalier in '15, and afterwards entered the service of the King of France, and was colonel of the 2nd Scorch Dragoons."

"Of course I knew him well," the gentleman said, "and with others endeavoured to obtain his pardon when he fell under the king's displeasure some fifteen years ago, although I regret to say without success. Believe me, if Prince Charles--" He stopped suddenly as his companion touched him.

"You would say, sir," Ronald said with a smile, "If Prince Charles succeeds in his present enterprise, and regains his throne, you will get him to exert his influence to obtain my father's release."

The two gentlemen gave an exclamation of astonishment.

"How do you know of any enterprise that is meditated?"

"I was told of it as a secret by a Scotch officer in Paris, and am the bearer of a message from him to the Duke of Athole, to ask him to allow me to join the prince."

"I am the duke," the other gentleman said.

"Since it is you, sir, I may tell you that the officer I spoke of is Colonel Hume, and that he bade me show you this ring, which he said you would know, as a token that my story was a correct one."

"Hume is my greatest friend," the duke exclaimed, "and his introduction would be sufficient, even if you had not already proved your devotion to the cause of the Stuarts. I will take you at once to the prince. But," he said, "before I do so, I must tell you that the enterprise upon which we are about to embark is a desperate one. The prince has but five companions with him, and we embark on board that little privateer lying in the stream. It is true that we shall be escorted by a man of war, which will convey the arms which Prince Charles has purchased for the enterprise; but not a man goes with us, and the prince is about to trust wholly to the loyalty of Scotland."

"I shall be ready to accompany him in any case, sir," Ronald said, "and I beg to introduce to you a faithful friend of my father and myself. His name is Malcolm Anderson. He fought for the Chevalier in '15, and accompanied my father in his flight to France, and served under him in the French service. Upon the occasion of my father's arrest he carried me to Scotland, and has been my faithful friend ever since."

So saying he called Malcolm up and presented him to the duke, and the party then proceeded to the lodging where Prince Charles was staying.

"I have the misfortune to be still ignorant of your name, sir," Ronald said to his acquaintance of Glasgow.

"What!" the gentleman said in surprise. "You do not know my name, after doing so much for me! I thought, as a matter of course, that when you were captured for aiding my escape you would have heard it, hence my remissness in not introducing myself. I am Colonel Macdonald. When you met me I was engaged in a tour through the Highland clans, sounding the chiefs and obtaining additions to the seven who had signed a declaration in favour of the prince three years before. The English government had obtained, through one of their spies about the person of the Chevalier, news of my mission, and had set a vigilant watch for me."

"But is it possible that there can be spies among those near the Chevalier!" Ronald exclaimed in astonishment.

"Aye, there are spies everywhere," Macdonald said bitterly. "All sorts of people come and go round the Chevalier and round Prince Charles. Every Scotch or Irish vagabond who has made his native country too hot to hold him, come to them and pretend that they are martyrs to their loyalty to the Stuarts; and the worst of it is their story is believed. They flatter and fawn, they say just what they are wanted to say, and have no opinion of their own, and the consequence is that the Chevalier looks upon these fellows as his friends, and often turns his back upon Scottish gentlemen who have risked and lost all in his service, but who are too honest to flatter him or to descend to the arts of courtiers. Look at the men who are here with the prince now."

"Macdonald! Macdonald!" the duke said warmly.

"Well, well," the other broke off impatiently; "no doubt it is better to hold one's tongue. But it is monstrous, that when there are a score, ay, a hundred of Scottish gentlemen of family, many of them officers with a high knowledge of war, who would gladly have accompanied him at the first whisper of his intentions, the prince should be starting on such a venture as this with yourself only, duke, as a representative of the Scottish nobles and chiefs, and six or eight mongrels--Irish, English, and Scotch--the sort of men who haunt the pot houses of Flanders, and spend their time in telling what they have suffered in the Stuart cause to any who will pay for their liquor."

"Not quite so bad as that, Macdonald," the duke said. "Still I admit that I could have wished that Prince Charles should have landed in Scotland surrounded by men with names known and honoured there, rather than by those he has selected to accompany him."

"But you are going, are you not, sir?" Ronald asked Colonel Macdonald.

"No, I do not accompany the prince; but I hope to follow shortly. As soon as the prince has sailed it is my mission to see all his friends and followers in France, and urge them to join him in Scotland; while we bring all the influence we have to bear upon Louis, to induce him to furnish arms and assistance for the expedition."

CHAPTER XIII: Prince Charles.

Upon arriving at the prince's lodgings Macdonald remained without, the Duke of Athole entering, accompanied only by Ronald.

"The prince is in disguise," he said, "and but one or two of us visit him here in order that no suspicion may be incited among the people of the house that he is anything beyond what he appears to be--a young student of the Scotch college at Paris."

They ascended the stairs to the upper story, and on the marquis knocking, a door was opened. The duke entered, followed by Ronald.

"Well, duke, what is the news?"

The question was asked by a young man, who was pacing restlessly up and down the room, of which he was, with the exception of his valet de chambre, an Italian named Michel, the person who had opened the door, the only occupant.

"Ah! whom have you here?"

"Allow me to present to your royal highness Lieutenant Leslie. He is the son of Leslie of Glenlyon, who fought by my side in your father's cause in '15, and has, like myself, been an exile ever since. This is the young gentleman who, two years since, saved Macdonald from arrest in Glasgow."

"Ah! I remember the adventure," the prince said courteously, "and right gallant action it was; but how did you hear that I was here, sir?"

"I was told by my good friend and commanding officer, Colonel Hume of the 2nd Scottish Dragoons, your royal highness."

"I revealed it to Hume before leaving Paris," the duke said, "he being a great friend of mine and as staunch as steel, and I knew that he could be trusted to keep a secret."

"It seems that in the last particular you were wrong," the prince remarked with a slight smile.

"Colonel Hume only revealed it to me, sir," Ronald said, anxious to save his friend from the suspicion of having betrayed a secret confided to him, "for very special reasons. I had the misfortune to kill in a duel the Duke of Chateaurouge, and as we fought just outside the park of Versailles, and the duke was a favourite of the king's, I had to ride for it; then Colonel Hume, knowing my devotion to the cause of your highness, whispered to me the secret of your intention, and gave me a message to his friend the Duke of Athole."

"Do you say that you have killed the Duke of Chateaurouge in a duel?" the duke exclaimed in astonishment. "Why, he has the reputation of being one of the best swordsmen in France, and has a most evil name as a dangerous and unscrupulous man. I met him constantly at court, and his arrogance and haughtiness were well nigh insufferable. And you have killed him?"

"I knew him well too," the prince said, "and his reputation. We do not doubt what you say, young gentleman," he added quickly, seeing a flush mount into Ronald's face; "but in truth it seems strange that such should have been the case."

"Colonel Hume did me the honour to be my second," Ronald said quietly, "and the Marquis de Vallecourt was second to the duke; some other officers of the Scottish regiment were present, as were two other French noblemen, De Lisle and St. Aignan."

"We doubt you not, sir," the duke said warmly. "You will understand that it cannot but seem strange that you at your age--for it seems to me that you cannot be more than nineteen--should have been able to stand for a moment against one of the best swordsmen in France, to say nothing of having slain him."

"Colonel Hume would scarcely have consented to act as my second had he thought that the contest was a wholly unequal one," Ronald said with a slight smile; "indeed I may say that he regarded it as almost certain that I should have the best of the fray."

"Why, you must be a very Paladin," the prince said admiringly; "but sit down and tell us all about it. Upon my word I am so sick of being cooped up for four days in this wretched den that I regard your coming as a godsend. Now tell me how it was that the Duc de Chateaurouge condescended to quarrel with a young officer in the Scottish Horse."

"It was a family quarrel, sir, which I had inherited from my father."

"Yes, yes, I remember now," the Duke of Athole broke in. "It is an old story now; but I heard all about it at the time, and did what I could, as did all Leslie's friends, to set the matter right, but in vain. Leslie of Glenlyon, prince, was colonel of the Scottish Dragoons, and as gallant and dashing a soldier as ever was in the service of the King of France, and as good looking a one too; and the result was, the daughter of the Marquis de Recambours, one of the richest heiresses in France, whom her father and the king destined as the bride of this Duke of Chateaurouge, who was then quite a young man, fell in love with Leslie, and a secret marriage took place between them. For three years no one suspected it; but the young lady's obstinacy in refusing to obey her father's orders caused her to be shut up in a convent. Somehow the truth came out. Leslie was arrested and thrown into the Bastille, and he has never been heard of since. What became of the child which was said to have been born no one ever heard; but it was generally supposed that it had been put out of the way. We in vain endeavoured to soften the king's anger against Leslie, but the influence of Recambours and Chateaurouge was too great for us. Hume told me some time since that Leslie's son had been carried off to Scotland by one of his troopers, and had returned, and was riding as a gentleman volunteer in his regiment; but we have had no further talk on the subject."

"You will be glad to hear, sir," Ronald said, "that my father and mother have within the last few weeks been released, and are now living on a small estate of my mother's in the south. They were ordered to retire there by the king."

"I am glad, indeed," the duke said cordially; "and how is your father?"

"He is sadly crippled by rheumatism, and can scarce walk," Ronald said, "and I fear that his health is altogether shaken with what he had to go through."

"How did you obtain their release, Leslie?" the prince asked.

"Marshal Saxe obtained it for me," Ronald answered. "Colonel Hume first introduced me to him, and as he too had known my father he promised that should he obtain a victory he would ask as a boon from the king the release of my father, and he did so after Fontenoy, where the Marquis de Recambours was killed, and the king thereby freed from his influence. The Duke of Chateaurouge, whose hostility against my father had always been bitter, was doubtless greatly irritated at his release, and took the first opportunity, on meeting me, of grossly insulting me. On my replying in terms in accordance with the insult, he drew, and would have fought me in the palace grounds had not Colonel Hume and his friends interfered; then we adjourned outside the park. The duke doubtless thought that he would kill me without difficulty, and so rushed in so carelessly that at the very first thrust I ran him through."

"And served him right," the prince said heartily. "Now since both your father's enemies are gone, it may be hoped that his troubles are over, and that your mother will recover the estates to which she is entitled. And now, duke, what is your news? When are we going to sail?"

"The Doutelle is already by this time on her way down the river, and it is proposed that we shall start this evening and board her there. The stores and arms are all safely on board the Elizabeth, and she is lying off Belleisle; so far as Mr. Walsh has heard, no suspicion has been excited as to their purpose or destination, so that we may hope in twenty-four hours to be fairly on board."

"That is the best news I have heard for months," the prince said; "thank goodness the time for action is at last at hand!"

"I have, I trust, your royal highness' permission to accompany you," Ronald said; "together with my follower, Anderson. He is the trooper who carried me over to Scotland as a child, and has been my faithful friend ever since."

"Certainly, Leslie. I shall be glad indeed to have a member of a family who have proved so faithful to my father's cause with me in the adventure upon which I am embarking."

Ronald with a few words of thanks bowed and took his leave, after receiving instructions from the duke to start shortly and to ride down the river towards Lorient.

"You can halt for a few hours on the road, and then ride on again; we shall overtake you before you reach the port. We shall all leave singly or in pairs, to avoid attracting any attention."

Ronald left, delighted with the kindness of the prince's manner. Prince Charles was indeed possessed of all the attributes which win men's hearts and devotion. In figure he was tall and well formed, and endowed both with strength and activity. He excelled in all manly exercises, and was an excellent walker, having applied himself ardently to field sports during his residence in Italy.

He was strikingly handsome, his face was of a perfect oval, his features high and noble, his complexion was fair, his eyes light blue, and, contrary to the custom of the time, when wigs were almost universally worn, he allowed his hair to fall in long ringlets on his neck. His manner was graceful, and although he always bore himself with a sort of royal dignity he had the peculiar talent of pleasing and attracting all with whom he came in contact, and had the art of adapting his conversation to the taste or station of those whom he addressed.

His education had been intrusted to Sir Thomas Sheridan, an Irish Roman Catholic, who had grossly neglected his duties, and who indeed has been more than suspected of acting as an agent in the pay of the British government. The weakness in the prince's character was that he was a bad judge of men, and inclined on all occasions to take the advice of designing knaves who flattered and paid deference to him, rather than that of the Scottish nobles who were risking their lives for his cause, but who at times gave their advice with a bluntness and warmth which were displeasing to him. It was this weakness which brought an enterprise, which at one time had the fairest prospect of success, to destruction and ruin.

On leaving the house Ronald was joined by Malcolm, and half an hour later they mounted their horses and rode for the mouth of the Loire. The whole party arrived on the following day at St. Nazaire, embarking separately on board the Doutelle, where Prince Charles, who had come down from Nantes in a fishing boat, was received by Mr. Walsh, the owner of the vessel. Ronald now saw gathered together the various persons who were to accompany Prince Charles on this adventurous expedition. These were Sheridan, the former tutor of the prince; Kelly, a non-juring clergyman, and Sullivan--both, like Sheridan, Irishmen; Strickland, a personage so unimportant that while some writers call him an Englishman, others assert that he was Irish; Aeneas Macdonald, a Scotchman; Sir John Macdonald, an officer in the Spanish service; the prince's valet, Michel; and the Duke of Athole, or, as he is more generally called, the Marquis of Tullibardine, the last named being the only man of high standing or reputation. Never did a prince start to fight for a kingdom with such a following.

The Doutelle weighed anchor as soon as the last of the party arrived on deck, and under easy sail proceeded to Belleisle. Here she lay for some days awaiting the arrival of the Elizabeth. Mr. Rutledge, a merchant at Nantes, had obtained an order from the French court that this man of war should proceed to cruise on the coast of Scotland, and had then arranged with the captain of the ship to take on board the arms that had been purchased by the prince with the proceeds of the sale of some of the family jewels.

These consisted of fifteen hundred muskets, eighteen hundred broadswords, twenty small field pieces, and some ammunition. The captain had also agreed that the Doutelle, which only mounted eighteen small guns, should sail in company with the Elizabeth to Scotland. As soon as the Elizabeth was seen the Doutelle spread her sails, and keeping a short distance from each other, the two vessels sailed north. So great was the necessity for prudence that the prince still maintained his disguise as a Scottish student, and, with the exception of Mr. Walsh, none of the officers and crew of the Doutelle were acquainted with his real rank, and the various members of his party treated him and each other as strangers.

Four days after leaving Belleisle a British man of war of fifty-eight guns hove in sight, and crowding on all sail rapidly came up. The Elizabeth at once prepared to engage her, signalling to the Doutelle to do the same. The prince urged Mr. Walsh to aid the Elizabeth, but the latter steadily refused.

He had undertaken, he said, to carry the prince to Scotland, and would do nothing to endanger the success of the enterprise. The two vessels were well matched, and he would not allow the Doutelle to engage in the affair. The prince continued to urge the point, until at last Mr. Walsh said "that unless he abstained from interference he should be forced to order him below."

The Doutelle, therefore, stood aloof from the engagement, which lasted for five or six hours, and sailed quietly on her course, in order to be beyond the risk of capture should the English ship prove victorious; neither of the vessels, however, obtained any decided advantage. Both were so crippled in the encounter that the Elizabeth returned to France, the Lion to Plymouth to refit. Thus the small supply of arms and artillery which the prince had with such great trouble got together was lost.

"Well, Ronald," Malcolm said that evening as they leant over the taffrail together, "I do think that such a mad headed expedition as this was never undertaken. An exiled prince, an outlawed duke, six adventurers, a valet, and our two selves. One could laugh if one was not almost ready to cry at the folly of invading a country like England in such a fashion."

"That is only one way of looking at it, Malcolm. We are not an army of invasion. The prince is simply travelling with a few personal followers to put himself at the head of an army. The affair depends, not upon us, but upon the country. If the clans turn out to support him as they did in '15 he will soon be at the head of some twenty thousand men. Not enough, I grant you, to conquer England, but enough for a nucleus round which the Lowland and English Jacobites can gather."

"Yes, it depends upon the ifs, Ronald. If all the Highland clans join, and if there are sufficient Jacobites in the Lowlands and England to make a large army, we may do. I have some hopes of the clans, but after what we saw of the apathy of the English Jacobites in '15 I have no shadow of faith in them. However, I fought for the Chevalier in '15, and I am ready to fight for Prince Charles now as long as there is any fighting to be done, and when that is over I shall be as ready to make for France as I was before."

Ronald laughed.

"You are certainly not enthusiastic about it, Malcolm."

"When one gets to my age, Ronald, common sense takes the place of enthusiasm, and I have seen enough of wars to know that for business a well appointed and well disciplined army is required. If Prince Charles does get what you call an army, but which I should call an armed mob, together, there will be the same dissensions, the same bickerings, the same want of plan that there was before; and unless something like a miracle happens it will end as the last did at Preston, in defeat and ruin. However, lad, here we are, and we will go through with it to the end. By the time we get back to France we must hope that King Louis will have got over the killing of his favourite. However, I tell you frankly that my hope is that when the Highland chiefs see that the prince has come without arms, without men, and without even promises of support by France, they will refuse to risk liberty and life and to bring ruin upon their people by joining in such a mad brained adventure."

"I hope not, Malcolm," Ronald said, as he looked at the prince as he was pacing up and down the deck with the Duke of Athole, talking rapidly, his face flushed with enthusiasm, his clustering hair blown backward by the wind. "He is a noble young prince. He is fighting for his own. He has justice and right on his side, and God grant that he may succeed!"

"Amen to that, Ronald, with all my heart! But so far as my experience goes, strength and discipline and generalship and resources go a great deal further than right in deciding the issue of a war."

Two days later another English man of war came in sight and gave chase to the Doutelle, but the latter was a fast sailer and soon left her pursuer behind, and without further adventure arrived among the Western Isles, and dropped anchor near the little islet of Erisca, between Barra and South Uist. As they approached the island an eagle sailed out from the rocky shore and hovered over the vessel, and the Duke of Athole pointed it out as a favourable augury to the prince.

Charles and his companions landed at Erisca and passed the night on shore. They found on inquiry that this cluster of islands belonged to Macdonald of Clanranald, a young chief who was known to be attached to the Jacobite cause. He was at present absent on the mainland, but his uncle and principal adviser, Macdonald of Boisdale, was in South Uist. The prince sent off one of his followers in a boat to summon him, and he came aboard the Doutelle the next morning; but when he heard from the prince that he had come alone and unattended he refused to have anything to do with the enterprise, which he asserted was rash to the point of insanity, and would bring ruin and destruction on all who took part in it.

The prince employed all his efforts to persuade the old chief, but in vain, and the latter returned to his isle in a boat, while the Doutelle pursued her voyage to the mainland and entered the Bay of Lochnanuagh, in Inverness shire, and immediately sent a messenger to Clanranald, who came on board shortly with Macdonald of Kinloch Moidart, and several other Macdonalds.

They received the prince with the greatest respect, but, like Macdonald of Boisdale, the two chiefs refused to take up arms in an enterprise which they believed to be absolutely hopeless. In vain Prince Charles argued and implored. The two chiefs remained firm, until the prince suddenly turned to a younger brother of Moidart, who stood listening to the conversation, and with his fingers clutching the hilt of his broadsword as he heard the young prince, whom he regarded as his future king, in vain imploring the assistance of his brother and kinsmen.

"Will you at least not assist me?" the prince exclaimed.

"I will, I will!" Ranald Macdonald exclaimed. "Though no other man in the Highlands shall draw a sword, I am ready to die for you."

The enthusiasm of the young man was catching, and throwing to the winds their own convictions and forebodings, the two Macdonalds declared that they also would join, and use every exertion to engage their countrymen. The clansmen who had come on board the ship without knowing the object of the visit were now told who the prince was, and they expressed their readiness to follow to the death. Two or three days later, on the 25th of July, Prince Charles landed and was conducted to Borodale, a farmhouse belonging to Clanranald.

Charles at once sent off letters to the Highland chiefs whom he knew to be favourable to the Stuart cause. Among these the principal were Cameron of Locheil, Sir Alexander Macdonald, and Macleod. Locheil immediately obeyed the summons, but being convinced of the madness of the enterprise he came, not to join the prince, but to dissuade him from embarking in it. On his way he called upon his brother, Cameron of Fassefern, who agreed with his opinion as to the hopelessness of success, and urged him to write to the prince instead of going to see him.

"I know you better than you know yourself," he said. "If the prince once sets eyes upon you, he will make you do whatever he pleases."

Locheil, however, persisted in going, convinced that the prince would, on his representation, abandon the design. For a long time he stood firm, until the prince exclaimed:

"I am resolved to put all to the hazard. In a few days I will erect the royal standard and proclaim to the people of Britain that Charles Stuart is come over to claim the crown of his ancestors or perish in the attempt. Locheil, who my father has often told me was our firmest friend, may stay at home and learn from the newspapers the fate of his prince."

Locheil's resolution melted at once at these words, and he said:

"Not so. I will share the fate of my prince whatsoever it be, and so shall every man over whom nature or fortune hath given me power."

The conversion of Locheil was the turning point of the enterprise. Upon the news of the prince's landing spreading, most of the other chiefs had agreed that if Locheil stood aloof they would not move; and had he remained firm not a man would have joined the prince's standard, and he would have been forced to abandon the enterprise. Sir Alexander Macdonald and Macleod, instead of going to see the prince, had gone off together, on the receipt of his letter, to the Isle of Skye, so as to avoid an interview. Clanranald was despatched by Prince Charles to see them, but they declined to join, urging with the truth that the promises which they had given to join in a rising were contingent upon the prince arriving at the head of a strong French force with arms and supplies. They therefore refused at present to move. Others, however, were not so cautious. Fired by the example of Locheil, and by their own traditions of loyalty to the Stuarts' cause, many of the lesser chiefs at once summoned their followers to the field. With the majority the absence of French troops had the exactly opposite effect that it had had with Sir Alexander Macdonald and Macleod. Had the prince landed with a French army they might have stood aloof and suffered him to fight out his quarrel unaided; but his arrival alone and unattended, trusting solely and wholly to the loyalty of the Scottish people, made an irresistible appeal to their generous feelings, and although there were probably but few who did not foresee that failure, ruin, and death would be the result of the enterprise, they embarked in the cause with as much ardour as if their success had been certain.

From Borodale, after disembarking the scanty treasure of four thousand louis d'or which he had brought with him and a few stands of arms from the Doutelle, Charles proceeded by water to Kinloch Moidart.

Mr. Walsh sailed in the Doutelle, after receiving the prince's warmest thanks, and a letter to his father in Rome begging him to grant Mr. Walsh an Irish earldom as a reward for the services he had rendered, a recommendation which was complied with.

The chiefs soon began to assemble at Moidart, and the house became the centre of a picturesque gathering.

Ronald had now put aside the remembrance of Malcolm's forebodings, and entered heart and soul into the enterprise. He had in Glasgow frequently seen Highlanders in their native dress, but he had not before witnessed any large gathering, and he was delighted with the aspect of the sturdy mountaineers in their picturesque garb.

The prince had at once laid aside the attire in which he had landed and had assumed Highland costume, and by the charm and geniality of his manner he completely won the hearts of all who came in contact with him. Among those who joined him at Moidart was Murray of Broughton, a man who was destined to exercise as destructive an influence on the prince's fortune as had Mr. Forster over that of his father. Murray had hurried from his seat in the south, having first had a large number of manifestoes for future distribution printed. He was at once appointed by Charles his secretary of state.

While the gathering at Moidart was daily growing, the English remained in ignorance of the storm which was preparing. It was not until the 30th of July that the fact that the prince had sailed from Nantes was known in London, and as late as the 8th of August, nearly three weeks after Charles first appeared on the coast, the fact of his landing was unknown to the authorities in Edinburgh.

On the 16th of August the English governor at Fort Augustus, alarmed at the vague reports which reached him, and the sudden news that bodies of armed Highlanders were hurrying west, sent a detachment of two companies under Captain Scott to reinforce the advance post of Fort William.

After marching twenty miles the troops entered the narrow ravine of Spean Bridge, when they were suddenly attacked by a party of Keppoch's clansmen who were on their way to join the prince when they saw the English troops on their march. They were joined by some of Locheil's clansmen, and so heavy a fire was kept up from the heights that the English, after having five or six men killed and many more wounded, among them their commanding officer, were forced to lay down their arms.

They were treated with great humanity by their captors, and the wounded were well cared for. The news of this success reached the prince on the day before that fixed for the raising of his standard, the 19th of August, and added to the enthusiasm which prevailed among the little force gathered in Glenfinnan, where the ceremony took place. The glen lay about halfway between Borodale and Fort William, both being about fifteen miles distant. The gathering consisted principally of the Camerons of Locheil, some six hundred strong, and they brought with them two English companies captured on the 16th, disarmed and prisoners.

The Duke of Athole performed the ceremony of unfurling the banner. He was the heir to the dukedom of Athole, but had been exiled for taking part in the rising of '15 and the dukedom bestowed by the English government upon his brother; thus among the English he was still spoken of as the Marquis of Tullibardine, while at the French court and among the followers of the Stuarts he was regarded as the rightful Duke of Athole.

The unfurling of the standard was greeted with loud shouts, and the clansmen threw their bonnets high in the air. The duke then read the manifesto of the Chevalier, and the commission of regency granted by him to Prince Charles. After this the prince himself made an inspiring speech, and declared that at the head of his faithful Highlanders he was resolved to conquer or to perish.

Among the spectators of the ceremony was Captain Swetenham, an English officer taken prisoner a few days before while on his way to assume the command of Fort William. He had been treated with great courtesy and kindness by the prince, who, after the ceremony, dismissed him with the words, "You may now return to your general; tell him what you have seen, and add that I am about to give him battle."

Soon after the conclusion of the ceremony Keppoch marched in with three hundred of his clan, and some smaller parties also arrived. The next morning the force marched to Locheil's house at Auchnacarrie, where the prince was joined by the Macdonalds of Glencoe, a hundred and fifty strong, two hundred Stuarts of Appin under their chief, and by the younger Glengarry with two hundred more, so that the force had now swelled to sixteen hundred men.

"We begin to look like an army," Ronald said to Malcolm.

"Well, yes," the latter replied drily, "we are rather stronger than one regiment and not quite so strong as two; still, if things go on like this we shall ere very long have mounted up to the strength of a brigade; but even a brigade, Ronald, does nor go very far towards the conquest of a kingdom, especially when only about one man in three has got a musket, and so far there are neither cavalry nor artillery. Still, you know, these things may come."

Ronald laughed gaily at his companion's want of faith. He himself had now caught the enthusiasm which pervaded all around. It was true that as yet the prince's adherents were but a handful, but it was not to be expected that an army would spring from the ground. Promises of assistance had come from all quarters, and if the army was a small one the English army in Scotland was but little larger, and if a first success could be achieved, all Scotland might be expected to rise, and the news would surely influence the Jacobites of England to declare for the prince.

Sir John Cope, the English officer commanding the English forces in Scotland, at the first rumour of troubles had ordered his troops to assemble at Stirling. He had with him two regiments of dragoons, Gardiner's and Hamilton's, both young regiments, and the whole force at his disposal, exclusive of troops in garrison, did not exceed three thousand men. With these he proposed to march at once to the west, and crush the rebellion before it gained strength. The English government approved of his proposal, and sent him a proclamation offering a reward of thirty thousand pounds to any person who should seize and secure the pretended Prince of Wales.

On the day of the raising of the standard Cope set out from Edinburgh for Stirling and the next day commenced his march at the head of fifteen hundred infantry, leaving the dragoons behind him, as these could be of but little service among the mountains, where they would have found it next to impossible to obtain forage for their horses. He took with him a large quantity of baggage, a drove of black cattle for food, and a thousand stand of arms to distribute among the volunteers who he expected would join him. As, however, none of these came in, he sent back seven hundred muskets to Crieff.

The first object of the march was Fort Augustus, which he intended to make his central post. As he advanced he was met by Captain Swetenham, who informed him of the raising of the standard and the gathering he had witnessed. As, however, only Locheil's clansmen had arrived before Swetenham left, Cope considered his force ample for the purpose, and continued his march. In order to reach Fort Augustus, however, he had to pass over Corry Arrack, a lofty and precipitous mountain which was ascended by a military road with fifteen zigzags, known to the country as the devil's staircase.

Prince Charles, who had received early news of the advance from Stirling, had recognized the importance of the position, and having burned and destroyed all baggage that would impede his progress, made a forced march and reached Corry Arrack on the 27th, before Sir John Cope had commenced his ascent. As Sir John saw that the formidable position was in the hands of the enemy he felt that it would be in vain to endeavour to force it. Each zigzag would have to be carried in turn, and the enterprise would be a desperate one. Success would be of no great advantage, as the Highlanders, lightly clad and active, would make off and defy pursuit; defeat would be disastrous. He, therefore, called a council of war and asked his officers to decide whether it would be best to remain at Dalwhinnie at the foot of the mountain, to return to Sterling, or to march to Inverness, where they would be joined by the well affected clans. He himself strongly urged the last course, believing that the prince would not venture to descend into the Lowlands while he remained in his rear. The council of war adopted his opinion. No officer advocated remaining inactive at Dalwhinnie, one only supported the alternative of the retreat to Stirling, the rest agreed upon an advance to Inverness.

When it was found that Cope's army had moved away without fighting, the exultation of the Highlanders was great. Most of the chiefs wished to follow at once and give battle, urging that it would be hazardous to advance south and leave the enemy to cut off their retreat; but the prince himself saw the supreme importance of a descent into the Lowlands, and that plan of action was decided upon.

CHAPTER XIV: Prestonpans.

Advancing in high spirits through the mountains of Badenoch, Prince Charles with his army came down into the vale of Athole, and visited, with Tullibardine, the castle of Blair Athole, the noble property of which the marquis had so long been deprived, owing to his constancy to the cause of the Stuarts, but which would again be his own were this great enterprise successful.

From Blair Athole the little army moved on to Perth. Here they were joined by powerful friends, of whom the principal were the young Duke of Perth, Lord Nairn, and Lord George Murray, the younger brother of the Marquis of Tullibardine. Lord George Murray was but ten years of age when the events of 1715 had taken place, but four years later he came over with the marquis with a handful of Spaniards and was wounded at the battle of Glenshiels. The influence of the family obtained his pardon on the plea of his extreme youth, but he remained at heart a Jacobite, and, going to the Continent, entered the service of Sardinia, then a portion of the possessions of the Duke of Savoy. For many years he served abroad, and acquired a considerable reputation as an excellent officer and a most gallant soldier.

He had, indeed, a natural genius for military operations, and had he not been thwarted at every turn by the jealousy of Murray of Broughton, it is by no means improbable that he would have brought the enterprise to a successful termination and seated the Stuarts upon the throne of England. The accession of such an officer was of the highest value to the prince.

Hitherto the army had consisted merely of wild clansmen, full of valour and devotion but wholly undisciplined; while among those who accompanied him, or who had joined him in Scotland, there was not a single officer of any experience in war or any military capacity whatever. Lord George Murray and the Duke of Perth were at once named generals in the prince's army; but the command in reality remained entirely in the hands of Murray, for Lord Perth, though an estimable young nobleman possessed of considerable ability, had no military experience and was of a quiet and retiring disposition.

Lord George Murray at once set about raising the tenantry of his brother the Hanoverian Duke of Athole, who was absent in England, and as these had always remained attached to the Stuart cause, and still regarded the Marquis of Tullibardine as their rightful head, they willingly took up arms upon Lord George Murray's bidding. Lord George decided at once that it would be useless to attempt to drill the Highlanders into regular soldiers, but that they must be allowed to use their national style of fighting and trust to their desperate charge with broadsword and target to break the enemy's ranks.

Unfortunately dissensions commenced among the leaders from the very first. Secretary Murray, who desired to be all powerful with the prince, saw that he should not succeed in gaining any influence over so firm and energetic a character as Lord George Murray, while it would be easy for him to sway the young Duke of Perth, and he was not long in poisoning the ear of the latter against his companion in arms by representing to him that Lord George treated him as a mere cipher, although of equal rank in the army. The secretary's purpose was even more easily carried out with Prince Charles. The latter was no judge of character, and fell readily under the influence of the wily and unscrupulous Murray, who flattered his weaknesses and assumed an air of deference to his opinions. Lord George Murray, on the other hand, was but too prone to give offence. He was haughty and overbearing in manner, expressed his opinions with a directness and bluntness which were very displeasing to the prince, and, conscious of his own military genius and experience, put aside with open contempt the suggestions of those who were in truth ignorant of military matters. Loyal, straightforward, and upright, he scorned to descend to the arts of the courtier, and while devoting his whole time to his military work, suffered his enemies to obtain the entire command of the ear of the prince.

Ronald was introduced to him as soon as he joined at Perth, and finding that young Leslie had had some military experience, Lord George at once appointed him one of his aides de camp, and soon took a warm liking to the active and energetic young officer, whose whole soul was in his work, and who cared nothing for the courtly gatherings around the person of the prince.

Malcolm rode as Ronald's orderly, and during the few days of their stay in Perth, Ronald was at work from morning till night riding through the country with messages from Lord George, and in the intervals of such duty in trying to inculcate some idea of discipline into the wild Highland levies. At this time Charles was using all his efforts to persuade Lord Lovat, one of the most powerful of the northern noblemen, to join him, offering him his patent as Duke of Fraser and the lord lieutenancy of the northern counties.

Lovat, however, an utterly unscrupulous man, refused openly to join, although he sent repeatedly assurances of his devotion. Throughout the struggle he continued to act a double part, trying to keep friends with both parties, but declaring for the prince at the moment when his fortunes were at their highest. The result was that while he afforded the prince but little real assistance, his conduct cost him his head.

Sir John Cope, finding that his march to Inverness had failed to draw the prince after him, and had left the Lowlands and the capital open to the insurgents, directed his march to Aberdeen, and sent to Edinburgh for transports to bring down his army to cover that city. But Prince Charles determined to forestall him, and on the 11th of September commenced his march south. The age and infirmities of the Marquis of Tullibardine prevented his accompanying Prince Charles during active operations.

It was impossible for the army to march direct against Edinburgh, as the magistrates of that town had taken the precaution to withdraw every ship and boat from the northern side of the Forth, and the prince was consequently obliged to make a detour and to cross the river at the fords eight miles above Stirling, and then marching rapidly towards Edinburgh, arrived on the evening of the 16th within three miles of that town.

So long as the coming of the prince was doubtful the citizens of Edinburgh had declared their willingness to defend the town to the last. Volunteer regiments had been formed and guns placed on the walls; but when the volunteers were ordered to march out with Hamilton's regiment of dragoons, to oppose the advance of the insurgents, the men quitted their ranks and stole away to their houses, leaving the dragoons to march out alone. The latter, however, showed no greater courage than that of their citizen allies, when on the following day they came in contact with a party of mounted gentlemen from the prince's army, who fired their pistols at their pickets. These rode off in haste, their panic was communicated to the main body, whose officers in vain endeavoured to check them, and the whole regiment galloped away in wild confusion, and passing close under the walls of Edinburgh continued their flight, without halting, to Preston. There they halted for the night; but one of the troopers happening in the dark to fall into a disused well, his shouts for assistance caused an alarm that they were attacked, and mounting their horses the regiment continued their flight to Dunbar, where they joined General Cope's army, which had just landed there.

This disgraceful panic added to the terror of the citizens of Edinburgh, and when, late in the afternoon, a summons to surrender came in from Prince Charles, the council could arrive at no decision, but sent a deputation to the prince asking for delay, hoping thereby that Cope's army would arrive in time to save them. But the prince was also well aware of the importance of time, and that night he sent forward Lochiel with five hundred Camerons to lie in ambush near the Netherbow Gate. They took with them a barrel of powder to blow it in if necessary; but in the morning the gate was opened to admit a carriage, and the Highlanders at once rushed in and overpowered the guard, and sending parties through the streets they secured these also without disturbance or bloodshed, and when the citizens awoke in the morning they found, to their surprise, that Prince Charles was master of the city.

The Jacobite portion of the population turned out with delight to greet the prince, while the rest thought it politic to imitate their enthusiasm. The Highlanders behaved with perfect order and discipline, and although the town had, as it were, been taken by storm, no single article of property was touched. An hour later Prince Charles, at the head of his troops, entered the royal palace of Holyrod, being met by a crowd of enthusiastic supporters from the city, who received him with royal shouts and tears of joy.

In the evening a grand ball was held in the palace, in spite of the fact that it was within range of the guns of Edinburgh Castle, which still held out. But one day was spent in Edinburgh. This was occupied in serving out about a thousand muskets found in the magazines to the Highlanders, and in obtaining tents, shoes, and cooking vessels, which the town was ordered to supply. They were joined during the day by many gentlemen, and on the night of the 19th the army, two thousand five hundred strong, of whom only fifty were mounted, moved out to the village of Duddingston. There the prince that evening called a council of war, and proposed to march next morning to meet the enemy halfway, and declared that he would himself lead his troops and charge in the first ranks.

The chiefs, however, exclaimed against this, urging that if any accident happened to him ruin must fall upon the whole, whether they gained or lost the battle; and upon the prince persisting they declared that they would return home and make the best terms they could for themselves. He was therefore obliged to give way, declaring, however, that he would lead the second line. The next morning the army commenced its march. They had with them only one cannon, so old that it was quite useless, and it was only taken forward as an encouragement to the Highlanders, who had the greatest respect for artillery.

Sir John Cope, who had received intelligence of all that had happened at Edinburgh, had also moved forward on the 19th, and on the 20th the two armies came in sight of each other. The Highlanders, after passing the bridge of Musselburgh, left the road, and turning to the right took up their position on the brow of Carberry Hill, and there waited the attack. The English forces were marching forward with high spirit, and believed that the Highlanders would not even wait their assault. Cope had with him two thousand two hundred men, including the six hundred runaway dragoons. The numbers, therefore, were nearly equal; but as the English were well armed, disciplined, and equipped, while only about half the Highlanders had muskets, and as they had, moreover, six pieces of artillery against the one unserviceable gun of Prince Charles, they had every reason to consider the victory to be certain.

On seeing the Highland array Cope drew up his troops in order of battle--his infantry in the centre, with a regiment of dragoons and three pieces of artillery on each flank. His right was covered by a park wall and by the village of Preston. On his left stood Seaton House, and in his rear lay the sea, with the villages of Prestonpans and Cockenzie. Their front was covered by a deep and difficult morass.

It was now about three o'clock in the afternoon, and the Highlanders, seeing that the English did not advance against them, clamoured to be led to the attack. Prince Charles was himself eager to fight, but his generals persuaded him to abstain from attacking the English in such a formidable position. The Highlanders, however, fearing that the English would again avoid a battle, were not satisfied until Lord Nairn with five hundred men was detached to the westward to prevent the English from marching off towards Edinburgh.

During the night the two armies lay upon the ground. Cope retired to sleep at Cockenzie, the prince lay down in the middle of his soldiers. Before doing so, however, he held a council, and determined to attack next morning in spite of the difficulty of the morass. But in the course of the night Anderson of Whitburg, a gentleman well acquainted with the country, bethought himself of a path from the height towards their right by the farm of Ruigan Head, which in a great measure avoided the morass. This important fact he imparted to Lord George Murray, who at once awoke the prince.

Locheil and some other chiefs were sent for, and it was determined to undertake the enterprise at once. An aide de camp was sent to recall Lord Nairn and his detachment, and under the guidance of Anderson the troops made their way across the morass. This was not, however, accomplished without great difficulty, as in some places they sank knee deep. The march was unopposed, and covered by the darkness they made their way across to firm ground just as the day was breaking dull and foggy. As they did so, however, the dragoon outposts heard the sound of their march, and firing their pistols galloped off to give the alarm. Sir John Cope lost no time facing his troops about, and forming them in order of battle. He was undisturbed while doing so, for the Highlanders were similarly occupied.

As the sun rose the mist cleared away, and the two armies stood face to face. The Macdonalds had been granted the post of honour on the Highland right, the line being completed by the Camerons and Stuarts, Prince Charles with the second line being close behind. The Highlanders uncovered their heads, uttered a short prayer, and then as the pipers blew the signal they rushed forward, each clan in a separate mass, and raising their war cry, the Camerons and Stuarts rushed straight at the cannon on the left.

These guns were served, not by Royal Artillerymen, but by some seamen brought by Cope from the fleet. They, panic struck by the wild rush of the Highlanders, deserted their guns and fled in all directions. Colonel Gardiner called upon his dragoons to follow him, and with his officers led them to the charge. But the Stuarts and Camerons, pouring in a volley from their muskets, charged them with their broadswords, and the dragoons, panic stricken, turned their horses and galloped off.

The Macdonalds on the right had similarly captured three guns, and charging with similar fury upon Hamilton's regiment of dragoons, drove them off the field; Macgregor's company, who, for want of other weapons were armed with scythes, doing terrible execution among the horses and their riders. The English infantry, deserted by their cavalry, and with their guns lost, still stood firm, and poured a heavy fire into the Highlanders; but these, as soon as they had defeated the cavalry, faced round and charged with fury upon both flanks of the infantry. Their onslaught was irresistible. The heavy masses of the clans broke right through the long line of the English infantry, and drove the latter backward in utter confusion. But the retreat was impeded by the inclosure and park wall of Preston, and the Highlanders pressing on, the greater portion of the English infantry were killed or taken prisoners.

A hundred and seventy of the infantry alone succeeded in making their escape, four hundred were killed, and the rest captured. Colonel Gardiner and many of his officers were killed fighting bravely, but the loss of the dragoons was small. Only thirty of the Highlanders were killed, and seventy wounded. The battle lasted but six minutes, and the moment it had terminated Prince Charles exerted himself to the utmost to obtain mercy for the vanquished.

He treated the prisoners with the greatest kindness and consideration, and the wounded were relieved without any distinction of friend or foe. The dragoons fled to Edinburgh, and dashed up the hill to the castle; but the governor refused to admit them, and threatened to open his guns upon them as cowards who had deserted their colours. Later on in the day the greater portion were rallied by Sir John Cope and the Earls of Loudon and Home; but being seized with a fresh panic they galloped on again at full speed as far as Coldstream, and the next morning continued their flight in a state of disgraceful disorder as far as Berwick. The contents of the treasure chest, consisting of two thousand five hundred pounds, with the standards and other trophies, were brought to Prince Charles. The rest of the spoil was divided among the Highlanders, of whom a great number immediately set off towards their homes to place the articles they had gathered in safety.

So greatly was the Highland army weakened by the number of men who thus left the ranks that the prince was unable to carry out his wish for an instant advance into England. His advisers, indeed, were opposed to this measure, urging that in a short time his force would be swelled by thousands from all parts of Scotland; but unquestionably his own view was the correct one, and had he marched south he would probably have met with no resistance whatever on his march to London. There were but few troops in England. A requisition had been sent to the Dutch by King George for the six thousand auxiliaries they were bound to furnish, and a resolution was taken to recall ten English regiments home from Flanders.

Marshal Wade was directed to collect as many troops as he could at Newcastle, and the militia of several counties was called out; but the people in no degree responded to the efforts of the government. They looked on coldly, not indeed apparently favouring the rebellion, but as little disposed to take part against it. The state of public feeling was described at the time by a member of the administration, Henry Fox, in a private letter.

"England, Wade says, and I believe, is for the first comer, and if you can tell me whether these six thousand Dutch and the ten battalions of England, or five thousand French or Spaniards, will be here first, you know our fate. The French are not come, God be thanked; but had five thousand landed in any part of this island a week ago, I verily believe the entire conquest would not have cost a battle."

The prince indeed was doing his best to obtain assistance from France, conscious how much his final success depended upon French succour.

King Louis for a time appeared favourable. The prince's brother, Henry of York, had arrived from Rome, and the king proposed to place him at the head of the Irish regiments in the king's service and several others to enable him to effect a landing in England; but with his usual insincerity the French king continued to raise difficulties and cause delays until it was too late, and he thus lost for ever the chance of placing the family who had always been warm friends of France, and who would in the event of success have been his natural friends and allies, on the throne of England.

In the meantime Prince Charles had taken up his abode in Edinburgh, where he was joined by most of the gentry of Scotland. He was proclaimed king in almost every town of the Tweed, and was master of all Scotland, save some districts beyond Inverness, the Highland forts, and the castles of Edinburgh and Stirling.. Prince Charles behaved with the greatest moderation. He forbade all public rejoicing for victory, saying that he could not rejoice over the loss which his father's misguided subjects had sustained. He abstained from any attempt to capture Edinburgh Castle, or even to cut off its supplies, because the general of the castle threatened that unless he were allowed to obtain provisions he would fire upon the city and lay it in ruins, and he even refused to interfere with a Scotch minister who continued from his pulpit to pray for King George.

In one respect he carried his generosity so far as to excite discontent among his followers. It was proposed to send one of the prisoners taken at Preston to London with a demand for the exchange of prisoners taken or to be taken in the war, and with the declaration that if this were refused, and if the prince's friends who fell into the enemy's hands were put to death as rebels, the prince would be compelled to treat his captives in the same way. It was evident that this step would be of great utility, as many of the prince's adherents hesitated to take up arms, not from fear of death in battle, but of execution if taken prisoners.

The prince, however, steadily refused, saying, "It is beneath me to make empty threats, and I will never put such as this into execution. I cannot in cold blood take away lives which I have saved in the heat of action."

Six weeks after the victory the prince's army mustered nearly six thousand men; but Macleod, Macdonald, and Lovat, who could have brought a further force of four thousand men, still held aloof. Had these three powerful chiefs joined at once after the battle of Prestonpans, Prince Charles could have marched to London, and would probably have succeeded in placing his father on the throne, without having occasion to strike another blow; but they came not, and the delay caused during the fruitless negotiations enabled the English troops to be brought over from Flanders, while Prince Charles on his side only received a few small consignments of arms and money from France.

But in the meantime Edinburgh was as gay as if the Stuart cause had been already won. Receptions and balls followed each other in close succession, and Prince Charles won the hearts of all alike by his courtesy and kindness, and by the care which he showed for the comfort of his troops.

At the commencement of the campaign Lord George Murray had but one aide de camp besides Ronald. This was an officer known as the Chevalier de Johnstone, who afterwards wrote a history of the campaign. After the battle of Prestonpans he received a captain's commission, and immediately raised a company, with which he joined the Duke of Perth's regiment. Two other gentlemen of family were then appointed aides de camp, and this afforded some relief to Ronald, whose duties had been extremely heavy.

A week after the battle Lord George said to Ronald:

"As there is now no chance of a movement at present, and I know that you care nothing for the court festivities here, I propose sending you with the officers who are riding into Glasgow tomorrow, with the orders of the council that the city shall pay a subsidy of five thousand pounds towards the necessities of the state. The citizens are Hanoverians to a man, and may think themselves well off that no heavier charge is levied upon them. Do you take an account of what warlike stores there are in the magazines there, and see that all muskets and ammunition are packed up and forwarded."

The next morning Ronald started at daybreak with several other mounted gentlemen and an escort of a hundred of Clanranald's men, under the command of the eldest son of that chief, for Glasgow, and late the same evening entered that city. They were received with acclamation by a part of the population; but the larger portion of the citizens gazed at them from their doorways as they passed in sullen hostility. They marched direct to the barracks lately occupied by the English troops, the gentlemen taking the quarters occupied by the officers. A notification was at once sent to the provost to assemble the city council at nine o'clock in the morning, to hear a communication from the royal council.

As soon as Malcolm had put up Ronald's horse and his own in the stables, and seen to their comfort, he and Ronald sallied out. It was now dark, but they wrapped themselves up in their cloaks so as not to be noticed, as in the hostile state of the town they might have been insulted and a quarrel forced upon them, had they been recognized as two of the new arrivals. The night, however, was dark, and they passed without recognition through the ill lighted streets to the house of Andrew Anderson. They rang at the bell. A minute later the grille was opened, and a voice, which they recognized as that of Elspeth, asked who was there, and what was their business.

"We come to arrest one Elspeth Dow, as one who troubles the state and is a traitor to his majesty."

There was an exclamation from within and the door suddenly opened.

"I know your voice, bairn. The Lord be praised that you have come back home again!" and she was about to run forward, when she checked herself. "Is it yourself, Ronald?"

"It is no one else, Elspeth," he replied, giving the old woman a hearty kiss.

"And such a man as you have grown!" she exclaimed in surprise. For the two years had added several inches to Ronald's stature, and he now stood over six feet in height.

"And have you no welcome for me, Elspeth?" Malcolm asked, coming forward.

"The Lord preserve us!" Elspeth exclaimed. "Why, it's my boy Malcolm!"

"Turned up again like a bad penny, you see, Elspeth."

"What is it, Elspeth?" Andrew's voice called from above. "Who are these men you are talking to, and what do they want at this time of night?"

"They want some supper, Andrew," Malcolm called back, "and that badly."

In a moment Andrew ran down and clasped his brother's hand. In the darkness he did not notice Malcolm's companion, and after the first greeting with his brother led the way up stairs.

"It is my brother Malcolm," he said to his wife as he entered the room.

Ronald followed Malcolm forward. As the light fell on his face Andrew started, and, as Ronald smiled, ran forward and clasped him in his arms.

"It is Ronald, wife! Ah, my boy, have you come back to us again?"

Mrs. Anderson received Ronald with motherly kindness.

"We had heard of your escape before your letter came to us from Paris. Our city constables brought back the news of how you had jumped overboard, and had been pulled into a boat and disappeared. And finely they were laughed at when they told their tale. Then came your letter saying that it was Malcolm who had met you with the boat, and how you had sailed away and been wrecked on the coast of France; but since then we have heard nothing."

"I wrote twice," Ronald said; "but owing to the war there have been no regular communications, and I suppose my letters got lost."

"And I suppose you have both come over to have a hand in this mad enterprise?"

"I don't know whether it is mad or not, Andrew; but we have certainly come over to have a hand in it," Malcolm said. "And now, before we have a regular talk, let me tell you that we are famishing. I know your supper is long since over, but doubtless Elspeth has still something to eat in her cupboard. Oh, here she comes!"

Elspeth soon placed a joint of cold meat upon the table, and Ronald and Malcolm set to at once to satisfy their hunger. Then a jar of whiskey and glasses were set upon the table, and pipes lighted, and Ronald began a detailed narration of all that had taken place since they had last met.

"Had my father and mother known that I was coming to Scotland, and should have an opportunity of seeing you both, they would have sent you their warmest thanks and gratitude for your kindness to me," he concluded. "For over and over again have I heard them say how deeply they felt indebted to you for your care of me during so many years, and how they wished that they could see you and thank you in person."

"What we did was done, in the first place, for my brother Malcolm, and afterwards for love of you, Ronald; and right glad I am to hear that you obtained the freedom of your parents and a commission as an officer in the service of the King of France. I would be glad that you had come over here on any other errand than that which brings you. Things have gone on well with you so far; but how will they end? I hear that the Jacobites of England are not stirring, and you do not think that with a few thousand Highland clansmen you are going to conquer the English army that beat the French at Dettingen, and well nigh overcame them at Fontenoy. Ah, lad, it will prove a sore day for Scotland when Charles Stuart set foot on our soil!"

"We won't talk about that now, Andrew," Malcolm said good temperedly. "The matter has got to be fought out with the sword, and if our tongues were to wag all night they could make no difference one way or another. So let us not touch upon politics. But I must say, that as far as Ronald and I are concerned, we did not embark on this expedition because we had at the moment any great intention of turning Hanoverian George off his throne; but simply because Ronald had made France too hot to hold him, and this was the simplest way that presented itself of getting out of the country. As long as there are blows to be struck we shall do our best. When there is no more fighting to be done, either because King James is seated on his throne in London, or because the clans are scattered and broken, we shall make for France again, where by that time I hope the king will have got over the breach of his edict and the killing of his favourite, and where Ronald's father and mother will be longing for his presence."

"Eh, but it's awful, sirs," Elspeth, who as an old and favourite servant had remained in the room after laying the supper and listened to the conversation, put in, "to think that a young gallant like our Ronald should have slain a man! He who ought not yet to have done with his learning, to be going about into wars and battles, and to have stood up against a great French noble and slain him. Eh, but it's awful to think of!"

"It would be much more awful, Elspeth, if the French noble had killed me, at least from the light in which I look at it."

"That's true enough," Elspeth said. "And if he wanted to kill you, and it does seem from what you say that he did want, of course I cannot blame you for killing him; but to us quiet bodies here in Glasgow it seems an awful affair; though, after you got in a broil here and drew on the city watch, I ought not to be surprised at anything."

"And now we must go," Ronald said, rising. "It is well nigh midnight, and time for all decent people to be in bed."

CHAPTER XV: A Mission.

The next morning early Ronald proceeded to take an inventory of the arms and ammunition left behind by the troops when they had marched to join Sir John Cope at Stirling. Having done this he saw that they were all packed up in readiness to be sent off the next day under the escort, who were also to convey the money which the city was required to pay. For the provost and council, knowing that it was useless to resist the order, and perhaps anxious in the present doubtful state of affairs to stand well with Prince Charles, had arranged that the money should be forthcoming of the following morning. After his work was over Ronald again spent the evening at Andrew Anderson's.

The next morning he returned to Edinburgh with the arms and escort. It was late when he arrived; but as he knew that Lord George Murray would be at work in his tent, he repaired there at once.

"We have brought back the money and arms, Lord George. I have handed over the arms and ammunition at the magazine tent, and those in charge of the money have gone into the town with a part of the escort to give it over to the treasurer."

"How many arms did you get?"

"Two hundred and twenty-three muskets and eighty pistols, fourteen kegs of gunpowder, and well nigh a ton of lead."

"That is more than I had expected. And now, Leslie, I have an important mission for you. The prince this morning asked me whom I could recommend, as a sure and careful person likely to do the business well, to go down into Lancashire to visit the leading Jacobites there, and urge them to take up arms. I said that I knew of none who would be more likely to succeed than yourself. Your residence of two years in France has rubbed off any Scotch dialect you may have had, and at any rate you could pass for a northern Englishman. In the next place, your youth would enable you to pass unsuspected where an older man might be questioned. The prince agreed at once, and took shame to himself that he had not before given promotion to one who was his companion on his voyage to Scotland, the more so as he had made Johnstone a captain. Your claims are far greater than his, and moreover you have served as an officer in the French army. But, in truth, the fault is in some degree your own, for you spend all your time in carrying out your duties, and do not show yourself at any of the levees or festivities. And you know, with princes, as with other people, out of sight is out of mind. However, the prince at once took steps to repair the omission, and has signed your commission as captain. Here it is. You will understand, of course, that it is for past services, and that you are perfectly free to decline this mission to the south if you would rather not undertake it. It is unquestionably a dangerous one."

"I will undertake it readily, sir," Ronald said, "and I thank you sincerely for bringing my name before the prince, and the prince himself for his kindness in granting me his commission, which so far I have done but little to win. I shall be able, I trust, to carry out this mission to his satisfaction; and although I am ignorant of the country I shall have the advantage of taking with me my brave follower, Malcolm Anderson, who for years was in the habit of going with droves of cattle down into Lancashire, and will not only know the country but have acquaintances there, and being known as a drover would pass without suspicion of his being engaged with politics."

"That will do well," Lord George said. "I will get the list of persons on whom you should call prepared tomorrow. You had best go to Sir Thomas Sheridan and Francis Strickland, who came over with you, and get them to present you to Secretary Murray and recommend you to him. If he hears that your mission is of my recommendation he will do all he can to set the prince against you. Everything that I do is wrong in his eyes, and I do believe that he would ruin the cause in order to injure me, did he see no other way to accomplish that end. Therefore, if he mentions my name, as he is like to do, knowing that you have been my aide de camp, be sure that you say nought in my favour, or it will ruin you with him. You will, of course, attend the prince's levee tomorrow, and had best make preparation to start at nightfall."

The next day, accordingly, Ronald called upon Sir Thomas Sheridan and Strickland, and telling them that the prince had determined to send him on a mission into Lancashire, asked them to present him to Secretary Murray, from whom he would receive orders for his guidance and instruction as to the persons whom he was to visit. The two gentlemen proceeded with him to the house in which Secretary Murray had taken up his abode, and introduced him, with much warmth, as a fellow passenger on board the Doutelle.

"You have been serving since as Lord Murray's aide de camp?"

"Yes, sir, the prince recommended me to him at Perth, and I have since had the honour to carry his orders."

"Captain Leslie, for so the prince has granted him a commission," Sir Thomas said, "has served two years in the French army, and was present at Dettingen and Fontenoy. He mentioned to me on the voyage that he had the honour of being presented by Marshal Saxe to the King of France, and that he received his commission from the marshal, to whom he had acted as aide de camp at Fontenoy."

"You have begun well, indeed, young sir," Murray said, "to have received at your age, for I judge that you are not yet twenty, commissions in the French army and ours."

Ronald bowed.

"He has another claim upon all you Scottish gentlemen," Sir Thomas said, "for Colonel Macdonald told us, when he introduced him to us at Nantes, that it was through his interference and aid alone that he escaped safely from Glasgow, and that all his papers, with the names of the king's friends in Scotland, did not fall into George's hands. He was taken prisoner for his share in that affair, but escaped from the ship in the Thames, and succeeded in crossing to France. So you see, young as he is, he has rendered good service to the cause."

The expression of the secretary's face, which had before been cold and distant, changed at once. He had been aware that Ronald had been chosen for this business on the recommendation of Lord George Murray, and his jealousy of that nobleman had at once set him against Ronald, of whose antecedents he was entirely ignorant; but what he now heard entirely altered the case, and disposed him most favourably towards him, especially as his own name would have been one of the most prominent in the list, he having been in constant communication with Colonel Macdonald during the stay of the latter in Scotland.

"I had no idea it was to you that we are all so indebted," he said warmly. "I heard from Colonel Macdonald, after his return from France, that he owed his escape entirely to the quickness and bravery of a young gentleman of whose name he was ignorant, but who, he feared, would suffer for his interference on his behalf, and prayed me and all other loyal gentlemen of Scotland to befriend you should they ever discover your name, for that we assuredly owed it to you that we escaped imprisonment, if not worse. I am truly glad to meet you and thank you in person. And so you are going on this mission?"

"I have undertaken to do my best, sir. Fortunately I have a faithful follower who fought beside my father in '15, followed him to France and fought by his side in the Scottish Dragoons for fifteen years, and who has since been my best friend. He worked for years, when I was a child, as a drover of cattle from the Highlands into England. He knows Cumberland and Lancashire well, and would be known at every wayside inn. He will accompany me, and I shall pass as his nephew, therefore no suspicion will be likely to light upon me."

"And you set out tonight?"

"Yes, sir, if my orders and letters are ready."

"There will not be many letters," the secretary said. "It would not do for you to have documents upon you which might betray you and our friends there should you be arrested. I will give you a list of the gentlemen on whom you have to call, which you had best learn by heart and destroy before you cross the frontier. You shall have one paper only, and that written so small that it can be carried in a quill. This you can show to one after the other. If you find you are in danger of arrest you can destroy or swallow it. I will give them to you at the prince's levee this afternoon, and will send to your tent a purse of gold for your expenses."

"I shall need but little for that, sir," Ronald said smiling.

"For your expenses, no," the secretary said; "but one never can say what money may be required for. You may have to buy fresh horses, you may want it to bribe someone to conceal you. Money is always useful, my young friend. By the way, what family of Leslies do you belong to? I heard that one of your name had accompanied the prince, but no more."

"My father was Leslie of Glenlyon."

"Indeed!" the secretary exclaimed. "Of course, I know the name well. The lands were confiscated; but we shall soon set that right, and I will see that they are added to when the time comes to reward the king's friends and punish his foes."

Ronald now took his leave and returned to Malcolm, who was making preparation for the enterprise. He had already purchased two suits of clothes, such as would be worn by Lowland drovers, and was in high spirits, being more elated than was Ronald himself at the latter's promotion. In the course of the day he bought two rough ponies, as being more suitable for the position they were to assume than the horses with which they had been furnished at Perth. Ronald attended the levee, and thanked the prince for the favour which he bestowed upon him.

"You are a young gentleman after my own heart," Prince Charles said, "and I promised myself on shipboard that we should be great friends; but I have been so busy since I landed, and you have been so occupied in my service, that I have seen but little of you. On your return I hope that I shall be able to have you near my person. I am half jealous of you, for while you are younger than I am you have seen good service and taken part in great battles, but hitherto I have led a life almost of idleness."

Ronald bowed deeply at the prince's gracious speech. On his return to his tent he found a messenger from the secretary with a purse which, on counting its contents, they found to amount to a hundred guineas.

They started immediately, and travelled twenty miles before stopping for the night at a small wayside inn.

"This seems like old times to me," Malcolm said as, after eating supper, they sat by a turf fire, "except that on my way down I had the herd to look after. There is no fear of our being questioned or suspected till we reach the border, for there is not an English soldier between the Forth and the Tweed; nor is it likely that we shall meet with any difficulty whatever till we get to Carlisle. Cope's forces, or what remain of them, are at Newcastle, and it will be there that the English will gather, and the western road is likely to be open until, at any rate, Prince Charles moves south. George's troops have plenty to think about without interfering with the Lowlands drovers. At the same time, after we have once crossed the Tweed, we may as well leave the high road. I know every bypath over the fells."

On the third day after starting they crossed the border and were among the hills of Cumberland. They found that among the villages great apprehension existed. The tales of the rapine and destruction wrought in the old times by the Scottish forays had been handed down from father to son, and nothing less than the destruction of their homes and the loss of their flocks and herds was looked for. Malcolm was welcomed warmly at the little village inn where they put up for the night.

"Why, it's well nigh three years since I saw you last," the host said, "and before that it was seldom two months without our seeing you. What have you been doing with yourself?"

"I have been gathering the herds in the Highlands," Malcolm said, "while others have driven them down for sale; but at present my occupation is gone. The Highlanders are swarming like angry bees whose hive has been disturbed, and even if we could collect a herd it would not be safe to drive it south; it would be seized and despatched to Edinburgh for the use of the clans there."

"Is it true that there are fifty thousand of them, and that they have sworn to kill every English man, woman, and child?"

"No, they are not so strong as that," Malcolm said. "From what I hear I should say they were not more than half; and I do not think there is any occasion for peaceful people to be afraid, for they say that the prince has treated all the prisoners who fell into his hands in the kindest manner, and that he said that the English are his father's subjects as well as the Scots, and that he will see that harm is done to no man."

"I am right glad to hear it," the innkeeper said. "I don't know that I am much afraid myself; but my wife and daughter are in a terrible fright, and wanted me to quit the house and go south till it is all over."

"There is no occasion for that, man," Malcolm said; "you will have no reason for fear were the whole of the clans to march through your village, unless you took it into your head to stand at the door and shout, 'God bless King George.'"

"I care not a fig about King George or King James," the man said. "It's nought to me who is king at London, and as far as I know that's the way with all here. Let them fight it out together, and leave us hard working folks to ourselves."

"I don't suppose either James or George would care for that," Malcolm said laughing; "but from what I have heard of Prince Charles I should say that there is nothing in the world that he would like better than to stand with broadsword or dagger against the Duke of Cumberland, and so settle the dispute."

"That would be the most sensible thing to my mind," the innkeeper said; "but what brings you here, Anderson, since you have no herd with you?"

"I am just getting out of it all," Malcolm said. "I have had my share of hard knocks, and want no more of them. I don't want to quarrel with Highlanders or Lowlanders, and as trade is at a standstill at present, and there's nothing for me to do in the Highlands, I thought I would come south till it was all over. There is money to collect and things to look after, and I have to notify to our regular customers that the herds will come down again as soon as the tempest is over; and between ourselves," he said in a lower voice, "I wanted to get my nephew out of harm's way. He has a hankering to join the prince's army, and I don't want to let him get his brains knocked out in a quarrel which isn't his, so I have brought him along with me."

"He is a good looking young fellow, I can see, and a strong one. I don't wonder that he wanted to mount the white cockade; lads are always wanting to run their heads into danger. You have had your share of it, as you say; still you are wise to keep the lad out of it. I don't hold with soldiering, or fighting in quarrels that don't concern you.

Malcolm and Ronald travelled through Cumberland and Westmoreland, calling upon many of the gentlemen to whom the latter had been charged to deliver Prince Charles's messages. They could not, however, flatter themselves that their mission was a success, for from few of those on whom they called did they receive assurances that they were prepared to take action; all the gentlemen professed affection for the Stuarts, but deprecated a descent into England unless the prince were accompanied by a strong body of French troops.

The rising of '15 had been disastrous for the Jacobites of the North of England, and though all declared that they were ready again to take up arms and risk all for the cause of the Stuarts, if the prince was at the head of a force which rendered success probable, they were unanimously of opinion that it would be nothing short of madness to rise until at any rate the prince had marched into England at the head of a strong army.

The principal personage upon whom they called was Mr. Ratcliff, a brother of the Earl of Derwentwater, who had been executed after the rising of '15. That gentleman assured them that he himself was ready to join the prince as soon as he came south, but that he wished the prince to know that in his opinion no large number of English would join.

"The memory of '15 is still too fresh," he said; "while the Stuarts have been absent so long that, although there are great numbers who would prefer them to the Hanoverians, I do not believe that men have the cause sufficiently at heart to risk life and property for it. Many will give their good wishes, but few will draw their swords. That is what I wish you to say to Prince Charles. Among gentlemen like myself the feeling of respect and loyalty to his father's house is as strong as ever, and we shall join him, however desperate, in our opinion, the chances of success may be; but he will see that the common people will stand aloof, and leave the battle to be fought out by the clansmen on our side and George's troops on the other."

Some weeks were passed in traversing the country to and fro, for the desired interviews were often only obtained after considerable loss of time. They could not ride up as two Highland drovers to a gentleman's house, and had to wait their chances of meeting those they wished to see on the high road, or of sending notes requesting an interview, couched in such terms that while they would be understood by those to whom they were addressed they would compromise no one if they fell into other hands. There was indeed the greatest necessity for caution, for the authorities in all the towns and villages had received orders from the government to be on the lookout for emissaries from the north, and they were frequently exposed to sharp examination and questioning. Indeed it was only Malcolm's familiarity with the country, and the fact that he had so many acquaintances ready to testify that he was, as he said, a Scotch drover, in the habit for many years of journeying down from the north with cattle, that enabled them to escape arrest.

After much thought they had decided upon a place of concealment for the quill containing Ronald's credentials, which would, they thought, defy the strictest scrutiny. A hole had been bored from the back into the heel of Ronald's boot deep enough to contain the quill, and after this was inserted in the hiding place the hole was filled up with cobbler's wax, so that it would need a close examination indeed to discover its existence. Thus, although they were several times closely searched, no document of a suspicious nature was found upon them.

Their money was the greatest trouble, as the mere fact of so large a sum being carried by two drovers would in itself have given rise to suspicions, although had they been on their return towards Scotland the possession of such an amount would have been easily explained as the proceeds of the sale of the cattle they had brought down. They had therefore left the greater part of it with a butcher in Carlisle, with whom Malcolm had often had dealings, retaining only ten pounds for their necessary expenses.

The day after they reached Manchester four constables came to the little inn where they were stopping and told them that they were to accompany them before the magistrates.

"I should like to know what offence we are charged with," Malcolm said angrily. "Things have come to a pretty pass, indeed, when quiet drovers are to be hauled before magistrates without rhyme or reason."

"You will hear the charge quickly enough when you are before their worships," the constable said; "but that is no affair of mine--my orders are simply to take you there."

"Well, of course we must go," Malcolm said grumblingly; "but here we have been well nigh twenty years travelling to and fro between England and Scotland, as my host here can testify, without such a thing happening before. I suppose somebody has been robbed on the highway, and so you sharp sighted gentlemen clap hands on the first people you come across."

Three magistrates were sitting when Ronald and Malcolm were brought into the courthouse. They were first asked the usual questions as to their names and business, and then one of the magistrates said:

"Your story is a very plausible one; but it happens that I have here before me the reports, sent in from a score of different places, for in times like these it is needful to know what kinds of persons are travelling through the country, and two men answering to your description are reported to have visited almost every one of these places. It is stated in nearly every report that you are drovers ordinarily engaged in bringing down herds of Highland cattle, and it is added that in every case this account was verified by persons who have previously known you. All this would seem natural enough, but you seem to have journeyed hither and thither without any fixed object. Sometimes you have stopped for two days at little villages, where you could have had no business, and, in short, you seem for upwards of a month to have been engaged in wandering to and fro in such a way as is wholly incompatible with the affairs upon which you say you were engaged."

"But you will observe, sir," Malcolm said quietly, "that I have not said I am engaged upon any affairs whatever. I am not come to England on business, but solely to escape from the troubles which have put a stop to my trade in the Highlands, and as for fifteen years I was engaged in journeying backwards and forwards, and had many friends and acquaintances, I came down partly, as I have said, to avoid being mixed up in the trouble, partly to call upon old acquaintances, and partly to introduce to them my nephew, who is new to the work, and will shortly be engaged in bringing down cattle here. I thought the present was a good opportunity to show him all the roads and halting places in order that he might the better carry out the business."

"Your story has been well got up," one of the magistrates said, "though I doubt whether there be a single word of truth in it. However, you will be at present searched, and detained until we get to the bottom of the matter. This is not a time when men can travel to and fro through the country without exciting a suspicion that they are engaged upon other than lawful business. At present I tell you that in our eyes your conduct appears to be extremely suspicious."

The prisoners were then taken to a cell and searched with the utmost rigour. Their clothes were examined with scrupulous care, many of the seams being cut open and the linings slit, to see if any documents were concealed there. Their shoes were also carefully examined; but the mud had dried over the opening where the quill was concealed, and the officials failed to discover it. Even their sticks were carefully examined to see if they contained any hollow place; but at last, convinced that had they been the bearers of any documents these must have been discovered, the officials permitted them to resume their clothes, and then paying no heed to the angry complaints of Malcolm at the state to which the garments had been reduced, they left the prisoners to themselves.

"Be careful what you say," Malcolm whispered to Ronald. "Many of these places have cracks or peepholes, so that the prisoners can be watched and their conversation overheard."

Having said this Malcolm indulged in a long and violent tirade on the hardship of peaceful men being arrested and maltreated in this way, and at the gross stupidity of magistrates in taking an honest drover known to half the countryside for a Jacobite spy. Ronald replied in similar strains, and any listeners there might have been would certainly have gained nothing from the conversation they overheard.

"I should not be surprised," Malcolm said in low tones when night had come and all was quiet, "if some of our friends outside try to help us. The news will speedily spread that two men of the appearance of drovers have been taken on suspicion of being emissaries from Scotland, and it will cause no little uneasiness among all those on whom we have called. They cannot tell whether any papers have been found upon us, nor what we may reveal to save ourselves, so they will have a strong interest in getting us free if possible."

"If we do get free, Malcolm, the sooner we return to Scotland the better. We have seen almost all those whom we are charged to call upon, and we are certainly in a position to assure the prince that he need hope for no rising in his favour here before he comes, and that it is very doubtful that any numbers will join him if he marches south."

The next morning they were removed from the cell in which they had been placed to the city jail, and on the following day were again brought before the magistrates.

"You say that you have been calling on people who know you," one of the magistrates began; "and as I told you the other day we know that you have been wandering about the country in a strange way, I now requite that you shall tell us the names of all the persons with whom you have had communication."

The question was addressed to Malcolm as the oldest of the prisoners. Ronald looked round the court, which was crowded with people, and thought that in several places he could detect an expression of anxiety rather than curiosity.

"It will be a long story," Malcolm said in a drawling voice, "and I would not say for sure but that I may forget one or two, seeing that I have spoken with so many. We came across the hills, and the first person we spoke to was Master Fenwick, who keeps the Collie Dog at Appleswade. I don't know whether your worship knows the village. I greeted him as usual, and asked him how the wife and children had been faring since I saw him last. He said they were doing brawly, save that the eldest boy had twisted his ankle sorely among the fells."

"We don't want to hear all this nonsense," the magistrate said angrily. "We want a list of persons, not what you said to them."

"It will be a hard task," Malcolm said simply; "but I will do the best I can, your worship, and I can do no more. Let me think, there was Joseph Repton and Nat Somner--at least I think it was Nat, but I won't be sure to his Christian name--and John Dykes, and a chap they called Pitman, but I don't know his right name."

"Who were all these people?" the magistrate asked.

"Joe Repton, he is a wheelwright by trade, and Nat Somner he keeps the village shop. I think the others are both labouring men. Anyhow they were all sitting at the tap of the Collie Dog when I went in."

"But what have we to do with these fellows?" the magistrate exclaimed angrily.

"I don't know no more than a child," Malcolm said; "but your worship ordered me to tell you just the names of the persons I met, and I am doing so to the best of my ability."

"Take care, prisoner," the magistrate said sternly; "you are trifling with the court. You know what I want you to tell me. You have been to these villages," and he read out some fifteen names. "What did you go there for, and whom did you see?"

"That is just what I was trying to tell your worship in regular order, but directly I begin you stop me. I have been going through this district for fifteen years, and I am known in pretty well every village in Cumberland, Westmoreland, and Lancashire. Having been away for three years, and my trade being stopped by the war, as your worship well knows, I have been going round having a crack with the people I know. Such as were butchers I promised some fine animals next time I came south; such as were innkeepers I stayed a night with and talked of old times. If your worship will have patience with me I can tell you all the names and what I said to each of them, and what they said to me, and all about it."

"I don't want to know about these things. I am asking you whether you have not been calling on some of the gentry."

"Indeed, now," Malcolm said with an air of astonishment, "and this is the first time that I have heard a word about the gentry since I came into the court. Well, let me think now, I did meet Squire Ringwood, and he stopped his horse and said to me: 'Is that you, Malcolm Anderson, you rascal;' and I said, 'It's me, sure enough, squire;' and he said, 'You rascal, that last score of beasts I bought of you--'"

"Silence!" shouted the magistrate as a titter ran through the court. "All this fooling will do you no good, I can tell you. We believe that you are a traitor to the king and an emissary of the Pretender. If you make a clean breast of it, and tell me the names of those with whom you have been having dealings, there may be a hope of mercy for you; but if not, we shall get at the truth other ways, and then your meanness of condition will not save you from punishment."

"Your worship must do as you like," Malcolm said doggedly. "I have done my best to answer your questions, and you jump down my throat as soon as I open my mouth. What should a man of my condition have to do with kings or pretenders? They have ruined my trade between them, and I care not whether King George or King James get the best of it, so that they do but make an end of it as soon as possible, and let me bring down my herds again. There's half a dozen butchers in the town who know me, and can speak for me. I have sold thousands of beasts to Master Tregold; but if this is the treatment an honest man meets with I ain't likely to sell them any more, for as soon as I am let free and get the money the constables have taken from me I am off to Glasgow and if I ever come south of the border again, may I be hung and quartered."

Finding that nothing was to be made out of the prisoners, the magistrate ordered them to be taken back to jail.

CHAPTER XVI: The March to Derby.

Two days later when the jailer brought in breakfast to their cell he dropped on the table by the side of the loaf a tiny ball of paper, and then without a word went out and locked the back door. Malcolm put his finger to his lips as Ronald was about to utter an exclamation of joy.

"One's appetite is not as good here as it was when we were tramping the hills, Ronald; but one looks forward to one's meals; they form a break in the time."

So saying, he took up one of the lumps of bread and began to ear, securing at the same time the pellet of paper. "We can't be too careful," he said in a whisper. "It is quite possible that they may be able to overhear us."

"I don't see how," Ronald replied in the same tone; "I see no crack or crevice through which sound could pass."

"You may not see one," Malcolm said, "but it may exist for all that. One of the boards of the ceiling may be as thin as paper, and anyone listening through could hear every word we say when we speak in our natural voices. The magistrates evidently believe that they have made a valuable capture, and would give anything to prove that their suspicions are correct. Now, I will go and stand at that grated opening and look at this paper, if they are watching us they will see nothing then."

The little piece of paper when unfolded contained but a few words: "Keep up your courage. You have friends without working for you. Destroy this."

Malcolm at once again rolled up the pellet, put it into his mouth and swallowed it, and then whispered to Ronald what he had just read.

"I thought," he whispered, "that we should soon get a message of some sort. The news of our arrest will have set the hearts of a score of people quaking, and they would do anything now to get us out from this prison. They have already, you see, succeeded in bribing our warder."

At his evening visit the warder passed into Ronald's hand a small parcel, and then, as before, went out without speaking.

"I am confirmed in the belief that we can be overheard," Malcolm said. "Had the man not been afraid of listeners he would have spoken to us. Now let us see what he has brought us this time."

The parcel contained a small file, a saw made of watch spring, and a tiny phial of oil.

"So far so good," Malcolm said quietly. "Our way through these bars is clear enough now. But that is only the beginning of our difficulties. This window looks into the prison yard, and there is a drop of some forty feet to begin with. However, I have no doubt our friends will send us the means of overcoming these difficulties in due course. All we have to concern ourselves about now is the sawing through of these bars."

As soon as it was dark they began the work, relieving each other in turns. The oil prevented much sound being made, but to deaden it still further they wrapped a handkerchief over the file. The bars had been but a short time in position and the iron was new and strong. It was consequently some hours before they completed their work. When they had done, the grating was left in the position it before occupied, the cuts being concealed from any but close observation by kneading up small pieces of bread and pressing them into them, and then rubbing the edges with iron filings.

"That will do for tonight," Malcolm said. "No one is likely to pay us a visit; but if they did, they would not notice the bars unless they went up and shook them. Tomorrow morning we can put a finishing touch to the work."

As soon as it was daylight they were upon their feet.

"It does very well as it is," Malcolm said, examining the grating. "It is good enough to pass, and we need not trouble further about it. Now collect every grain of those iron filings. No, don't do that on any account," he broke in, as Ronald was preparing to blow some of it from the lower stonework through the opening. "Were you to do that, it would be quite possible that one of the prisoners walking in the yard might see it, and would as likely as not report the circumstance to one of the warders in order to curry favour and perhaps obtain a remission of his sentence. Scrape it inside and pour every atom down the crevices in the floor. That done, we are safe unless anyone touches the grating."

They watched their warder attentively when he next came into the cell, but this time he had no message for them. "We must not be impatient," Malcolm said; "our friends have a good many arrangements to make, for they will have to provide for our getting away when we are once out; besides, they will probably have to bribe other warders, and that kind of thing can't be done in a hurry."

It was not for another two days that the warder made any fresh sign. Then, as on the first occasion, he placed a pellet of paper on the table with their bread.

"This is a good deal larger than the last," Ronald whispered.

It was not until some little time after they had finished their meal that Ronald moved to the grating and unrolled the little ball of paper; it contained only the words:

"You will receive a rope this evening. With this lower yourselves from your window into the courtyard. Start when you hear the church bells strike midnight, cross the court and stand against the wall near the right hand corner of the opposite side. The third window on the second floor will be opened, and a rope lowered to you. Attach yourselves to this, and you will be pulled up from above."

After reading the note Ronald passed it on to Malcolm, who, as before, swallowed it, but had this time to tear it into several pieces before doing so. The warder was later bringing their supper than usual that evening, and it was dark when he came in. As he entered the room he let the lamp fall which he carried.

"Confound the thing!" he said roughly. "Here, take hold of this bread, and let me feel for the lamp. I can't be bothered with going down to get another light. You can eat your supper in the dark just as well, I have no doubt."

As he handed Ronald the bread he also pushed into his hand the end of the rope, and while he pretended to search for the lamp he turned round and round rapidly, and so unwound the rope, which was twisted many times round his body. As soon as this was done he picked up the lamp, and with a rough "Goodnight," left them.

"It is just as I suspected," Malcolm said in Ronald's ear. "There is a peephole somewhere, otherwise there could be no occasion for him to have dropped the lamp. It is well that we have always been on our guard."

They ate their bread in silence, and then after a short talk on the stupidity of the English in taking two drovers for messengers of Prince Charles, they lay down on their rough pallets to pass with what patience they could the long hours before midnight, for it was late in October, and it was little after five o'clock when the warder visited them. They felt but slight anxiety as to the success of the enterprise, for they had no doubt that every detail had been carefully arranged by their friends without, although certainly it seemed a strange method of escape that after lowering themselves from a third floor window they should afterwards be hauled up into a second. At last, after what seemed almost an endless watch, they heard the church clocks strike twelve, and simultaneously rose to their feet. Not a word was spoken, for although it was improbable in the extreme that any watcher would be listening at that hour of the night, it was well to take every precaution. The grating was lifted out and laid down on one of the couches so that all noise should be avoided. The rope was then strongly fastened to the stump of one of the iron bars.

"Now, Malcolm, I will give you a leg up; I am younger and more active than you are, so you had better go first."

Without debating the question, Malcolm put his foot on Ronald's hand, and in a moment was seated in the opening of the window. Grasping the rope he let himself quietly out, and lowered himself to the ground, reaching it so noiselessly that Ronald, who was listening, did nor hear a sound. After waiting a minute, however, he sprang up on to the sill, and feeling that the rope was slack, was soon by Malcolm's side below. Then both removed their shoes and hung them round their necks, and walking noiselessly across the court they took up their post under the window indicated in the note. In less than a minute the end of a rope was dropped upon their heads.

"You go first this time, Ronald," Malcolm said, and fastened it beneath Ronald's arms. Then he gave a pull at the rope to show that they were ready. The rope tightened, and Ronald found himself swinging in the air. He kept himself from scraping against the walls by his hands and feet, and was especially careful as he passed the window on the first floor. In a minute he was pulled into the room on the second floor by the men who had hoisted him up. A low "Hush!" warned him that there was still a necessity for silence. The rope was lowered again, and Ronald lent his aid to hoist Malcolm up to the window. As soon as he was in, it was as slowly and carefully closed.

"You are mighty heavy, both of you," a voice whispered. "I should not have thought it would have been such hard work to lift a man up this height. Now, follow us, and be sure you make no noise."

Two flights of stairs were descended, and then they stood before a small but heavy door; some bolts were drawn and a key turned in the lock, this being done so noiselessly that Ronald was sure they must have been carefully oiled. The two men passed through with them, locking the door behind them.

"Thank God we are out!" Malcolm said fervently. "I have been in a watch house more than once in my young days, but I can't say I like it better as I grow older." They walked for some minutes, and then their guides opened a door and they entered a small house.

"Stir up those peats, Jack," one of the men said, "and blow them a bit, while I feel for a candle."

In a minute or two a light was obtained.

"That's very neatly done, I think, gentlemen," laughed the man addressed as Jack, and who they now saw was the warder who had attended upon them. "We had rare trouble in hitting upon that plan. The cell you were in opened upon a corridor, the doors to which are always locked by the chief constable himself; and even if we could have got at his key, and opened one of them, we should have been no nearer escape, for two of the warders sleep in the lodge, and there would be no getting out without waking them, and they could not be got at. They are both of them married men, with families, and that sort of man does not care about running risks, unless he happens to be tired of his wife and wanting a change. Nat here and I have no incumbrances, and weren't sorry of a chance to shift. Anyhow, there was no way, as far as we could see, of passing you out through that part of the prison, and at last the idea struck us of getting you out the way we did. That wing of the jail is only used for debtors, and they are nothing like so strict on that side as they are on the other. Some of the warders sleep there, so there was no difficulty in getting hold of the key for an hour and having a duplicate made. Till yesterday all the cells were full, and we had to wait till a man, whose time was just up, moved out. After that it was clear sailing."

"Well, we are immensely obliged to you," Ronald said.

"Oh, you needn't be obliged to us," the warder replied; "we are well paid for the job, and have a promise of good berths if Prince Charles gets the best of it. Anyhow, we shall both make for London, where we have acquaintances. Now we are going to dress up; there's no time to be lost talking. There is a light cart waiting for us and horses for you half a mile outside the town."

He opened a cupboard and took our two long smock frocks, which he and his companion put on.

"Now, gentlemen, will you put on these two suits of soldiers' clothes. I think they will about fit you."

Ronald and Malcolm were soon attired as dragoons.

"There's a regiment of them here," the man said, "so there was no difficulty in buying a cast off suit and getting these made from it. As to the helmets, I guess there will be a stir about them in the morning. We got hold of a soldier today and told him we wanted a couple of helmets for a lark, and he said, for a bottle of brandy he would drop them out of a barrack window at ten o'clock tonight; and he kept his word. Two of them will be surprised in the morning when they find that their helmets have disappeared; as to the swords and belts, I don't know that they are quite right; they were bought at an old shop, and I believe they are yeomanry swords, but I expect they are neat enough. I was to give you this letter to take with you; it is, as you see, directed to General Wade at Newcastle, and purports to come from the colonel of your regiment here, so that if by any chance you are questioned on the way, that will serve as a reason for your journeying north. Here is a purse of twenty guineas; I think that's about all."

"But are we not to see those who have done us such service," Ronald asked, "in order that we may thank them in person?"

"I don't know who it is any more than the man in the moon," the warder replied. "It was a woman dressed as a serving wench, though I doubt it was only a disguise, who came to me. She met me in the street and asked me if I should like to earn fifty pounds. I said I had no objection, and then after a good deal of beating about the bush it came out that what was wanted was that I should aid in your escape. I didn't see my way to working it alone, and I told her so. She said she was authorized to offer the same sum to another, so I said I would talk it over with Nat. He agreed to stand in, and between us we thought about the arrangements; but I never got to know any more about her. It was nothing to me whom the money came from, as long as it was all right. We have had half down, and are to have the other half when we get to the cart with you. And now if you are ready we will be starting. The further we get away from here before morning the better."

They made their way quietly along the streets. The town was in total darkness, and they did not meet a single person abroad, and in a quarter of an hour they were in the open country. Another ten minutes and they came upon the cart and horses. Three men were standing beside them, and the impatient stamp of a horse's hoof showed that the horses were tied up closely. A lantern was held up as the party came up.

"All safe?"

"All safe," Ronald replied. "Thanks, many thanks to you for our freedom."

The man holding the lantern was masked, so they could not see his face. He first turned to the two warders, and placed a bag of money in their hand.

"You have done your work well," he said; "the cart will take you thirty miles on your road, and then drop you. I wish you a safe journey. You had best hide your money in your boots, unless you wish it to fall into the hands of highwaymen. The London road is infested with them."

With a word of farewell to Ronald and Malcolm, the two warders climbed into the cart, one of them mounted beside them and took the reins, and in another minute the cart drove away in the darkness. As soon as it had started the man with the lantern removed his mask.

"Mr. Ratcliff!" Ronald exclaimed in surprise.

"Yes, it is myself. There are half a dozen of us engaged in the matter. As soon as we heard of your arrest we determined to get you out. I was only afraid you would have been taken up to London before we could get all our plans arranged, for I knew they had sent up for instructions. It was well that we were ready to act tonight, for orders were received this afternoon that you should be sent up under an escort tomorrow. You puzzled them rarely at your examination, and they could make nothing of you. Our greatest fear was that you might betray yourselves in the prison when you fancied you were alone, for we learned from the men who have just left us that you were placed in a special cell where all that you said could be overheard, and your movements to some extent watched through a tiny hole in the wall communicating with the cell next to it. It widens out on that side so that a man can get his ear or his eye to the hole, which is high up upon the wall, and but a quarter of an inch across, so that it could scarcely be observed unless by one who knew of its existence. The warder said that they could hear plainly enough through this hole, but could see very little. However, they do not seem to have gathered much that way."

"We were on guard, sir; my friend Malcolm thought it possible that there might be some such contrivance."

"And now, my young friend," Mr. Ratcliff said, "you had best mount at once; follow this road for half a mile, and then take the broad road to the left; you cannot mistake it. It goes straight to Penrith. You have got the letter to General Wade?"

"Yes, sir, and the money; we are indeed in every way greatly indebted to you."

"Say nothing about it," Mr. Ratcliff said. "I am risking my life as well as my fortune in the cause of Prince Charles, and this money is on his service. I hear he is already on the march south. Repeat to him when you join him what I have already told you, namely, that I and other gentlemen will assuredly join him; but that I am convinced there will be no general rising in his favour unless a French army arrive to his assistance. The delay which has taken place has, in my opinion, entirely destroyed his chances, unless he receives foreign assistance. Wade has ten thousand men at Newcastle, the Duke of Cumberland has gathered eight thousand in the Midlands, and there is a third army forming to cover London. Already many of the best regiments have returned from Holland, and each day adds to their number. Do all you can to dissuade him from advancing until French aid arrives; but tell him also that if he comes with but half a dozen followers, Charles Ratcliff will join him and share his fate, whatever it be."

With a hearty shake of the hand he leapt on his horse, and, followed by his servant, galloped off in one direction, while Ronald and Malcolm set out in the other.

"This is a grand disguise," Ronald said. "We might ride straight into Wade's camp at Newcastle without being suspected."

"I have no doubt we could," Malcolm agreed. "Still, it will be wiser to keep away from the neighbourhood of any English troops. Awkward questions might be asked, and although the letter you have for the general may do very well to impress any officers of militia or newly raised troops we may meet on the road, and would certainly pass us as two orderlies conveying despatches, it would be just as well not to have to appear before the general himself. Our swords and belts would probably be noticed at once by any cavalry officers. I know nothing about the English army, and do not know how much the yeomanry swords and belts may differ from those of the line. However, it is certain the less observation we attract from the soldiers the better; but as to civilians we can ride straight on through towns and villages with light hearts."

"We may as well breathe our horses a bit, Malcolm, now there is no occasion for haste, and we can jog along at our own pace. There is no probability of pursuit, for when they find that we and the warders are missing and see the rope from our window they will be sure that we shall have started early and are far away by the time they find out we are gone."

Accordingly they travelled quietly north, boldly riding through small towns and villages, putting up at little inns, and chatting freely with the villagers who came in to talk over the news, for the north was all excitement. Orders had been issued for all the militia to turn out, but there was little response, for although few had any desire to risk their lives in the cause of the Stuarts, fewer still had any intention of fighting for the Hanoverians.

When they arrived within a few miles of Newcastle they left the main road and struck across country, their object being to come down upon the road running north from Carlisle, for they thought it likely that parties of General Wade's troops would be scattered far over the country north of Newcastle. At a farm house they succeeded in buying some civilian clothes, giving out that they were deserters, and as they were willing to pay well, the farmer, who had no goodwill towards the Hanoverians, had no difficulty in parting with two of his best suits.

They were now in a country perfectly well known to Malcolm, and travelling by byways across the hills they crossed the Cheviots a few miles south of Carter Fell, and then rode down the wild valleys to Castletown and thence to Canobie of the Esk. As they entered the little town they found the wildest excitement prevailing. An officer with two orderlies had just ridden in to say that quarters were to be prepared for Prince Charles, and a quantity of bullocks and meal got in readiness for the use of the army, which would arrive late that evening. Ronald soon found the officer who had brought the order and recognized him as one of Lord Perth's aides de camp. He did not know Ronald in his present dress, but greeted him heartily as soon as he discovered who he was.

"How is it the troops are coming this way?" Ronald asked.

"They are marching through Liddesdale from Kelso. We halted there for two days, and orders were sent forward to Wooler to prepare quarters. This was to throw Wade off the scent and induce him to march north from Newcastle to oppose us on that road, while, as you see, we have turned west and shall cross into Cumberland and make a dash at Carlisle."

A few hours later the prince arrived with his army, and as soon as he entered the quarters prepared for him Ronald proceeded there and made his report.

"I could wish it had been better, Captain Leslie," the prince said; "but the die is cast now, and I cannot think that our friends in the north, who proved so loyal to our cause in '15, will hang back when we are among them. When they see that Charles Ratcliff and other gentlemen whom you have visited range themselves under our banner I believe the common people will join us also. Now give me a full account of your mission."

Ronald gave the list of the gentry he had visited, and described his arrest and imprisonment in Manchester and the manner in which Mr. Ratcliff had contrived his escape.

"You have done all that is possible, sir," the prince said, "and at an early opportunity I will show you I appreciate your services."

On the next day, the 8th of November, the corps crossed the border; on the 9th they were joined by another column, which had marched from Edinburgh by the western road, and the united force marched to Carlisle and sat down before it. The walls of the city were old and in bad condition, the garrison was ill prepared for a siege. It consisted of a company of invalids in the castle, under the command of Colonel Durand, and a considerable body of Cumberland Militia. The walls, however, old as they were, could for some time have resisted the battery of four pounder guns which formed the prince's sole artillery.

The mayor returned no answer to the prince's summons and orders were issued to begin to throw up trench works, but scarcely had the operations begun when news arrived that Marshal Wade was marching from Newcastle to relieve the city. The siege was at once abandoned, and the prince marched out with the army to Brampton and took up a favourable position there to give battle. The news proved incorrect, and the Duke of Perth with several regiments were sent back to resume the siege.

On the 13th the duke began to raise a battery on the east side of the town, but after a few shots had been fired from the walls the courage of the besieged failed them. The white flag was hung out, and the town and castle surrendered on the condition that the soldiers and militia might march away, leaving their arms and horses behind and engaging not to serve again for a year. On the 17th the prince made a triumphal entry into the place, but was received with but little show of warmth on the part of the inhabitants.

A halt was made at Carlisle and a council was held to determine upon the next step to be taken. The news which had been received from Scotland was very unfavourable. Lord Strathallan, who had been appointed by the prince as commander in chief, and directed to raise as many troops as possible, had collected between two and three thousand men at Perth, and Lord Lewis Gordon had raised three battalions in Aberdeenshire; but on the other hand a considerable force had been collected at Inverness for King George. The towns of Glasgow, Paisley, and Dumfries had turned out their militia for the house of Hanover. The officers of the crown had re-entered Edinburgh and two regiments of cavalry had been sent forward by Marshal Wade to their support.

While even Scotland was thus wavering it seemed almost madness for the little army to advance into England. The greater portion of the Highlanders had from the first objected strongly to leave their country, and upwards of a thousand had deserted and gone home on the march down from Edinburgh. They had started less than six thousand strong, and after leaving a garrison of two hundred men in Carlisle, but four thousand five hundred were available for the advance south, while Wade, with his ten thousand men, would be in their rear and two English armies of nearly equal strength be waiting to receive them. At the council the opinions of the leaders were almost unanimous against an advance, but upon Lord George Murray saying that if Prince Charles decided upon advancing the army would follow him, he determined upon pressing forward.

The army began its advance on the 20th of November, and halted a day at Penrith, upon the news that Marshal Wade was moving to attack them; but the English general had not made any move, and the Scotch again pushed on through Shap, Kendal, and Lancaster, to Preston. During the march Prince Charles marched with his troops clad in Highland garb, and with his target thrown across his shoulder. He seldom stopped for dinner, but ate his food as he walked, chatting gaily with the Highlanders, and by his cheerfulness and example kept up their spirits. The strictest discipline was enforced, and everything required by the troops was paid for. At Preston the prince on his entry was cheered by the mob, and a few men enlisted.

From Preston the army marched to Wigan, and thence to Manchester. The road was thronged with people, who expressed the warmest wishes for the prince's success; but when asked to enlist, they all hung back, saying they knew nothing about fighting. Still the feeling in favour of the prince's cause became stronger as he advanced south, and at Manchester he was received with the acclamations of the inhabitants, the ringing of the bells, and an illumination of the city in the evening. The people mounted white cockades, and the next day about two hundred men enlisted and were enrolled under the name of the Manchester Regiment, the command of which was given to Mr. Francis Townley, a Roman Catholic belonging to an old Lancashire family, who, with Mr. Ratcliff and a few other gentlemen, had joined the army on the advance.

The leaders, however, of the prince's army were bitterly disappointed at the general apathy of the people. Lancashire had in '15 been the stronghold of the Jacobites, and the mere accession of two or three hundred men was evident that nothing like a popular rising was to be looked for, and they had but themselves to rely upon in the struggle against the whole strength of England. Marshal Wade was in full march behind them. The Duke of Cumberland lay at Lichfield in their front with a force of eight thousand veteran troops; while a third army, of which the Royal Guards were the nucleus, was being formed at Finchley. Large bodies of militia had been raised in several districts. Liverpool had declared against them; Chester was in the hands of the Earl of Cholmondeley; the bridges of the Mersey had been broken down; difficulties and dangers multiplied on all sides.

Prince Charles, ever sanguine, was confident that he should be joined by large numbers as he advanced south; but his officers were now thoroughly alarmed, and the leaders in a body remonstrated with Lord George Murray against any further advance. He advised them, however, to offer no further opposition to the prince's wishes until they came to Derby, promising that, unless by that time they were joined by the Jacobites in considerable numbers, he would himself, as general, propose and insist upon a retreat. Ronald utilized the short halt at Manchester to obtain new uniforms for himself and Malcolm, which he was glad to exchange for the farmer's garb, which had been the occasion of a good deal of joking and mirth among his fellow officers on the downward march.

On the first of December, Prince Charles, at the head of one division, forded the Mersey near Stockport, where the water was waist deep. The other division, with the baggage and artillery, crossed lower down, at Cheadle, on a hastily constructed bridge, and the two columns joined that evening at Macclesfield. Here Lord George Murray succeeded in misleading the Duke of Cumberland as to his intentions by a dexterous manoeuvre. Advancing with a portion of his force he dislodged and drove before him the Duke of Kingston and a small party of English horse posted at Congleton, and pursued them some distance along the road towards Newcastle under Tyne.

The Duke of Cumberland, supposing that the prince's army were on their march either to give him battle or to make their way into Wales, where the Jacobite party were extremely strong, pushed forward with his main body to Stone. Lord George Murray, however, having gained his object, turned sharp off to the left, and after a long march arrived at Ashborne, where the prince, with the other division of the army, had marched direct. The next afternoon they arrived at Derby, having thus altogether evaded the Duke of Cumberland, and being nearly three days' march nearer London than was his army.

The prince that night was in high spirits at the fact that he was now within a hundred and thirty miles of London, and that neither Wade's nor Cumberland's forces interposed between him and the capital. But his delight was by no means shared by his followers, and early next morning he was waited upon by Lord George Murray and all the commanders of battalions and squadrons, and a council being held, they laid before the prince their earnest and unanimous opinion that an immediate retreat to Scotland was necessary.

They had marched, they said, so far on the promise either of an English rising or a French descent upon England. Neither had yet occurred. Their five thousand fighting men were insufficient to give battle to even one of the three armies that surrounded them--scarcely adequate, indeed, to take possession of London were there no army at Finchley to protect it. Even did they gain London, how could they hold it against the united armies of Wade and Cumberland? Defeat so far from home would mean destruction, and not a man would ever regain Scotland.

In vain the prince replied to their arguments, in vain expostulated, and even implored them to yield to his wishes. After several hours of stormy debate the council broke up without having arrived at any decision. The prince at one time thought of calling upon the soldiers to follow him without regard to their officers; for the Highlanders, reluctant as they had been to march into England, were now burning for a fight, and were longing for nothing so much as to meet one or other of the hostile armies opposed to them. The prince's private advisers, however, Sheridan and Secretary Murray, urged him to yield to the opinion of his officers, since they were sure that the clansmen would never fight well if they knew that their chiefs were unanimously opposed to their giving battle. Accordingly the prince, heartbroken at the destruction of his hopes, agreed to yield to the wishes of his officers, and at a council in the evening gave his formal consent to a retreat.

CHAPTER XVII: A Baffled Plot.

Utterly disheartened and dispirited the army commenced its march north. The prince himself was even more disappointed than his soldiers, and showed by his manner how bitterly he resented the decision at which his officers had arrived. It had seemed to him that success was within his grasp, and that he had but to march to London to overthrow the Hanoverian dynasty. And it is by no means improbable that his instincts were more correct than the calculations of his advisers. The news of his rapid march south had sent a thrill through the country; and although so far the number of those who had joined him was exceedingly small, at that moment numbers of gentlemen in Wales and other parts of the country were arming their tenants, and preparing to take the field.

There was no hostile force between himself and London, for the force at Finchley was not yet organized, and could have offered no effectual opposition. A panic reigned in the metropolis, and the king was preparing to take ship and leave the country. Had the little army marched forward there is small doubt that James would have been proclaimed king in London. But it may be doubted whether Prince Charles could have maintained the advantage he had gained. Two armies, both superior to his own, were pressing on his rear, and would have arrived in London but a few days after himself; and although the Londoners might have accepted him, they would hardly have risen in arms to aid him against Cumberland's army. Had this halted at a distance, the reinforcements which might have joined the prince would have been more than counterbalanced by the regiments of English and Hanoverian troops which the king could have sent over, and although the strife might have been lengthened the result would in all probability have been the same.

Prince Charles had no ability in governing. His notions of the absolute power of kings were as strong as those of his ancestors, and, surrounded as he was by hotheaded Highlanders, he would speedily have caused discontent and disgust even among those most favourably inclined by hereditary tradition to the cause of the Stuarts. But of all this he was ignorant, and in the retreat from Derby he saw the destruction of his hopes.

Hitherto he had marched on foot with the Highlanders, chatting gaily as he went. Now he rode in rear of the column, and scarce exchanged a word with even his most intimate advisers. The Highlanders no longer preserved the discipline which had characterized their southward march. Villages were plundered and in some cases burned, and in retaliation the peasantry killed or took prisoners stragglers and those left behind. Even at Manchester, where the reception of the army had been so warm a few days before, its passage was opposed by a violent mob, and the prince was so offended at the conduct of the townspeople that he imposed a fine of five thousand pounds upon the city.

The next morning the march was continued. The Highlanders laid hands on every horse they could find, and so all pressed on at the top of their speed for the border. The Duke of Cumberland, who had fallen back in all haste for the protection of London, was close to Coventry when he heard that the Scotch had retreated northward. With all his cavalry, and a thousand foot whom he mounted on horses supplied by the neighbouring gentry, he set out in pursuit. At Preston he was joined by another body of horse, sent across the country from the army of Marshal Wade; but it was not until he entered Westmoreland that he came up with the rear guard of the insurgents, which was commanded by Lord George Murray.

Defeating some local volunteers who molested him, Lord George learned from the prisoners that the duke with four thousand men was close at hand, and he sent on the news to the prince, who despatched two regiments, the Stuarts of Appin and the Macphersons of Cluny, to reinforce him. It was nearly dark when by the light of the moon Lord George saw the English infantry, who had now dismounted, advancing. He at once charged them at the head of the Macphersons and Stuarts, and in a few minutes the English were completely defeated, their commander, Colonel Honeywood, being left severely wounded on the field, with a hundred killed or disabled men, while the loss of the Scotch was but twelve.

It was with great difficulty that the Highlanders could be recalled from the pursuit, and Lord George himself sent an urgent message to the prince begging for a further reinforcement, in order that he might maintain his ground and defeat the whole force of the duke. As usual his wishes were disregarded, and he was ordered to fall back and join the main body at Penrith. The check, however, was so effective that the duke made no further attempt to harass the retreat of the Highlanders.

Passing through Carlisle, some men of a Lowland regiment, and Colonel Twonley with his regiment raised at Manchester, were left there as a garrison, so that the road should be kept open for another and, as the prince hoped, not far distant invasion. The step was, however, a cruel one, for the Duke of Cumberland at once laid siege to the place, battered a breach in its ancient wall, and the garrison were forced to surrender. Many of them were afterwards executed and imprisoned, and ruin fell upon all.

Charles with his army marched north to Glasgow, where they remained eight days, requisitioning supplies from the town. During their stay Ronald and Malcolm put up at the house of Andrew Anderson.

"What think you of the chances now, Malcolm?" Andrew asked his brother, after hearing what had taken place since he had last seen him.

"I think no better and no worse of it than I did before, brother. They have had more success than I looked for. I did not think they would ever have got as far south as Derby. Who would have thought that a few thousand Highlanders could have marched half through England? But I see no prospect of success. The prince is badly advised. He has but one really good soldier with him, and he is set against him by the intrigues and spite of Secretary Murray and his friends, and partly, it may be, by Lord George's own frankness of speech. He has at his back but half the Highlands, for the other portion stand aloof from him. In the Lowlands he has found scarce an adherent, and but a handful in England. The Highlanders are brave; but it is surely beyond human expectation that five or six thousand Highlanders can vanquish a kingdom with a brave and well trained army with abundant artillery. Ronald and I mean to fight it out to the end; but I do not think the end will be very far off."

"I am sorry for the young prince," Andrew said. "He is a fine fellow, certainly--handsome and brave and courteous, and assuredly clement. For three times his life has been attempted, and each time he has released those who did it without punishment. I could not but think, as I saw him ride down the street today, that it was sad that so fine a young man should be doomed either to the block or to a lifelong imprisonment, and that for fighting for what he has been doubtless taught to consider his right. There are many here who are bitter against him; but I am not one of them, and I am sorry for him, sorry for all these brave gentlemen and clansmen, for I fear that there will be a terrible vengeance for all that has been done. They have frightened the English king and his ministers too sorely to be ever forgiven, and we shall have sad times in Scotland when this is all over."

Two evenings later Ronald noticed that Andrew, who had been absent for some time, and had only returned just in time for supper, looked worried and abstracted, and replied almost at random to any questions put to him.

"It is of no use," he said suddenly when his wife had left the room after the conclusion of the meal. "I am a loyal subject of King George, and I wish him every success in battle, and am confident that he will crush out this rebellion without difficulty, but I cannot go as far as some. I cannot stand by and see murder done on a poor lad who, whatever his faults, is merciful and generous to his enemies. Malcolm, I will tell you all I know, only bidding you keep secret as to how you got the news, for it would cost me my life were it known that the matter had leaked out through me."

"This evening five of the council, knowing that I am a staunch king's man, took me aside after the meeting was over, and told me that there was a plan on foot to put an end to all the trouble by the carrying off or slaying of Prince Charles. I was about to protest against it, when I saw that by so doing I should, in the first place, do no good; in the second, be looked upon as a Jacobite; and in the third, be unable to learn the details of what they were proposing. So I said that doubtless it was a good thing to lay by the heels the author of all these troubles, and that the life of one man was as nought in the balance compared to the prosperity of the whole country. Whereupon they revealed to me their plan, asking me for a subscription of a hundred pounds to carry it out, and saying truly that I should get back the money and great honour from the king when he learned I had done him such service. After some bargaining I agreed for fifty pounds."

"But what is the plot, Andrew?" Malcolm said anxiously.

"It is just this. The prince, as you know, goes about with scant attendance, and though there are guards in front of his house, there are but two or three beside himself who sleep there. There is a back entrance to which no attention is paid, and it will be easy for those who know the house to enter by that door, to make their way silently to his chamber, and either to kill or carry him off. I threw my voice in against killing, pointing out that the king would rather have him alive than dead, so that he might be tried and executed in due form. This was also their opinion, for they had already hired a vessel which is lying in the stream. The plan is to seize and gag him and tie his arms. There will be no difficulty in getting him along through the streets. There are few folks abroad after ten o'clock, and should they meet anyone he will conclude that it is but a drunken Highlander being carried home. You see, Malcolm, there is not only honour to be gained from the king, but the thirty thousand pounds offered for the prince's person. I pretended to fall in with the plan, and gave them the fifty pounds which they lacked for the hire of the vessel, the captain refusing to let them have it save for money paid down. Now, Malcolm, I have told you and Ronald all I know about the matter, and it is for you to see how a stop may be put to it."

"The scoundrels!" Malcolm said. "Their loyalty to the king is but a veil to hide their covetousness for the reward. When is it to take place, and how many men are likely to be engaged in it?"

"Six trusty men of the city watch and their five selves. I said I would subscribe the money, but would have no active share in the business. They might have all the honour, I would be content with my share of the reward offered. Two of them with four of the guards will enter the house and carry off the prince. The rest will wait outside and follow closely on the way down to the port ready to give aid if the others should meet with any obstruction. The whole will embark and sail to London with him."

"And when is this plot to be carried out?" Malcolm asked.

"Tomorrow at midnight. Tide will be high half an hour later; they will drop down the river as soon as it turns, and will be well out to sea by the morning. And now I have told you all, I will only ask you to act so that as little trouble as possible may arise. Do not bring my name into the matter if you can avoid doing so; but in any case I would rather run the risk of the ruin and death which would alight upon me when this rebellion is over than have such a foul deed of treachery carried out. There is not a Scotchman but to this day curses the name of the traitor Menteith, who betrayed Wallace. My name is a humble one, but I would not have it go down to all ages as that of a man who betrayed Charles Stuart for English gold."

"Make yourself easy, brother; Ronald and I will see to that. When once treachery is known it is easy to defeat, and Ronald and I will see that your name does not appear in the matter."

"Thank God that is off my mind!" Andrew said. "And I will off to bed, or Janet will wonder what I am talking about so long. I will leave you two to settle how you can best manage the affair, which you can do without my help, for matters of this kind are far more in your way than in mine."

"This is a villainous business, Ronald," Malcolm said when they were alone; "and yet I am not surprised. Thirty thousand pounds would not tempt a Highlander who has naught in the world save the plaid in which he stands up; but these money grubbing citizens of Glasgow would sell their souls for gain. And now what do you think had best be done in the matter, so that the plot may be put a stop to, and that without suspicion falling upon Andrew? It would be easy to have a dozen men hiding in the yard behind the house and cut down the fellows as they enter."

"I do not think that would do, Malcolm; it would cause a tumult, and the fact could not be hidden. And besides, you know what these Highlanders are; they already loathe and despise the citizens of Glasgow, and did they know that there had been a plot on foot to capture and slay the prince, nothing could prevent their laying the town in ashes."

"That is true enough. What do you propose then, Ronald?"

"I think it best that if there should be any fighting it should be on board the ship, but possibly we may avoid even that. I should say that with eight or ten men we can easily seize the vessel, and then when the boat comes alongside capture the fellows as they step on to the deck without trouble, and leave it to the prince to settle what is to be done with them."

"That is certainly the best plan, Ronald. I will get together tomorrow half a dozen trusty lads who will ask no questions as to what I want them to do, and will be silent about the matter afterwards. We must get from Andrew tomorrow morning the name of the vessel, and see where she is lying in the stream, and where the boat will be waiting for the prince."

The next night Ronald and Malcolm with six men made their way one by one through the streets so as not to attract the attention of the watch, and assembled near the strand. Not until the clock struck twelve did they approach the stairs at the foot of which the boat was lying. There were two men in it.

"You are earlier than we expected," one said as they descended the steps. "The captain said a quarter past twelve."

"Yes, we are a little early," Malcolm replied as he stepped into the boat; "we are ready earlier than we expected."

A moment later Malcolm suddenly seized one of the sailors by the throat and dragged him down to the bottom of the boat, a handkerchief was stuffed into his mouth, and his hands and feet tied. The other was at the same time similarly secured.

So suddenly and unexpected had been the attack that the sailors had had no time to cry out or to offer any resistance, and their capture was effected without the slightest sound being heard. The oars were at once got out and the boat was rowed out towards the vessel lying out in the middle of the stream with a light burning at her peak. As they approached the side the captain appeared at the gangway.

"All is well, I hope?" he asked.

"Could not be better," Malcolm replied as he seized the rope and mounted the gangway, the others closely following him. As he sprang upon the deck he presented a pistol at the captain's head.

"Speak a word and you die," he said sternly.

Taken by surprise, the captain offered no resistance, but suffered himself to be bound. Two or three sailors on deck were similarly seized and secured, the hatchway was fastened to prevent the rest of the crew from coming on deck, and the ship being thus in their possession two of the men at once took their places in the boat and rowed back to the stairs.

A quarter of an hour later those on board heard a murmur of voices on shore, and two or three minutes later the splash of oars as the boat rowed back to the ship. Ronald put on the captain's cap and stood at the gangway with a lantern.

"All right, I hope?" he asked as the boat came alongside.

"All right, captain! You can get up your anchor as soon as you like."

Two men mounted on to the deck, and then four others carried up a figure and were followed by the rest. As the last one touched the deck Ronald lifted the lantern above his head, and, to the astonishment of the newcomers, they saw themselves confronted by eight armed men.

The six men of the watch, furious at the prospect of losing the reward upon which they had reckoned, drew their swords and rushed forward; but they were struck down with handspikes and swords, for Ronald had impressed upon his men the importance of not using their pistols, save in the last extremity. In two minutes the fight was over. The five citizens had taken little part in it, save as the recipients of blows; for Malcolm, furious at their treachery, had bade the men make no distinction between them and the watch, and had himself dealt them one or two heavy blows with his handspike after he had seen that the guard was overpowered.

The whole of them were then bound, and warned that their throats would be cut if they made the least noise. The prince was released from his bonds, and he was at once conducted by Malcolm and Ronald to the cabin, where a light was burning.

The prince was so much bewildered by the events that had occurred that he did not yet understand the state of the case. He had been awoke by a gag being roughly forced into his mouth, while at the same moment his hands were tightly bound. Then he was lifted from his bed, some clothes were thrown on to him, a man took his place on either side, and, thrusting their arms into his, threatened him with instant death if he did not come along with them without resistance. Then he had been hurried down stairs and along the streets, two men keeping a little ahead and others following behind. He had been forced into a boat and rowed up to a ship, and on reaching the deck a desperate combat had suddenly commenced all round him. Then the gag had been removed and the bonds cut. Bewildered and amazed he gazed at the two men who had accompanied him to the cabin.

"Why, Captain Leslie!" he exclaimed. "Is it you? What means all this scene through which I have passed?"

"It means, your royal highness," Ronald said respectfully, "that I and my friend Malcolm obtained information of a plot on the part of some of the citizens to carry you off and sell you to the English. We could have stopped it by attacking them as they entered the house to seize you; but had we done so an alarm must have been raised, and we feared that the Highlanders, when they knew of the treachery that had been attempted against you, might have fallen upon the citizens, and that a terrible uproar would have taken place. Therefore we carried out another plan. We first of all obtained possession of the ship in which you were to have been taken away, and then overcame your captors as they brought you on board. All this has been done without any alarm having been given, and it now rests with you to determine what shall be done with these wretches."

"You have done well, indeed, Captain Leslie, and I thank you and your friend not only for the great service you have rendered me, but for the manner in which you have done it. I ought to have foreseen this. Did not the Lowlanders sell King Charles to the English? I might have expected that some at least would be tempted by the reward offered me. As for punishment for these men, they are beneath me. And, moreover, if I can trust my eyes and my ears, the knocks which you gave them will be punishment enough even did I wish to punish them, which I do not. I could not do so without the story of the attempt being known, and in that case there would be no keeping my Highlanders within bounds. As it is they are continually reproaching me with what they call my mistaken clemency, and there would be no restraining them did they know of this. No, we had best leave them to themselves. We will order the captain to put to sea with them at once, and tell him he had best not return to Glasgow until I have left it. They will have time to reflect there at leisure, and as, doubtless, they have each of them given reasons at home for an absence of some duration there will be no anxiety respecting them. And now, gentlemen, will you fetch in those who have aided in my rescue. I would thank every one of them for the service they have rendered, and impress upon them my urgent desire that they should say nothing to anyone of this night's work."

While the prince was speaking to the men, Malcolm went out, and having unbound the captain, ordered him to deliver up the sum which he had received for the conveyance of the prince and his captors to England.

The captain did as he was ordered.

"How much is there here?" Malcolm asked.

"Three hundred pounds."

Malcolm counted out fifty of it and placed them in his pocket, saying to Ronald:

"There is no reason Andrew should be a loser by the transaction. That will leave two hundred and fifty, which I will divide among our men when we get ashore."

Malcolm then gave the prince's orders to the captain; that he must, immediately they left the ship, get up his anchor as before intended, and make out to sea; and that under pain of being tried and executed for his share in this treacherous business, he was not to return to Glasgow with his eleven passengers for the space of a week.

The prince and his rescuers then entered the boats and rowed to shore, and the prince regained his apartment without anyone in the house being aware that he had been absent from it. The next day the prince sent for Ronald and Malcolm, and in a private interview again expressed to them his gratitude for his rescue from the hands of his enemies.

"I have none but empty honour to bestow now," he said; "but believe me, if I ever mount the throne of England you shall see that Charles Edward Stuart is not ungrateful."

The incident was kept a close secret, only two or three of the prince's most intimate advisers ever informed of it. These were unanimous in urging that an absolute silence should be maintained on the subject, for the fact that the attempt would have certainly been crowned with success had it not been for the measures Ronald had taken, might encourage others to attempt a repetition of it.

Having rested his army by a stay of eight days at Glasgow, Prince Charles set out on the 3rd of January, 1746, for Stirling, where he was joined by Lords John Drummond, Lewis Gordon, and Strathallan, the first named of whom had brought some battering guns and engineers from France. Their following raised the force to nearly nine thousand men--the largest army that Charles mustered during the course of the campaign. The siege of Stirling was at once commenced; but the castle was strong and well defended, and the siege made but little progress.

In the meantime the Duke of Cumberland had been recalled with the greater part of his force to guard the southern coasts of England, which were threatened by an invasion by a French force now assembled at Dunkirk, and which, had it sailed before the Highlanders commenced their retreat from Derby, might have altogether altered the situation of affairs. The command of the English army in the north was handed by the duke to General Hawley, a man after his own heart, violent in temper, brutal and cruel in conduct.

He collected at Edinburgh an army of nearly the same strength as that of Prince Charles, and with these he matched out as far as Falkirk to raise the siege of Stirling, and, as he confidently boasted, to drive the rebels before him. Prince Charles, leaving a few hundred men to continue the siege, matched out to Bannockburn. The English did not move out from Falkirk, and the prince, after waiting for a day, determined to take the initiative.

Hawley himself was stopping at Callendar House at some distance from his army and General Huske remained in command of the camp. To occupy his attention the prince despatched Lord John Drummond, with all the cavalry, by the straight road by Stirling to Falkirk, which ran north of the English camp. They displayed, as they marched, the royal standard and other colours, which had the desired effect of impressing Huske with the idea that the prince with all his army was moving that way. In the meantime Charles with his main force had crossed the river Carron to the south and was only separated from the English by Falkirk Muir, a rugged and rigid upland covered with heath.

Just as the English were about to take their dinner some country people brought in the news of the approach of the Highlanders. Huske at once got his men under arms, but he had no authority, in the absence of Hawley, to set them in motion. Messengers, however, were sent off on horseback at once to Callendar House, and the general presently galloped up in breathless haste, and putting himself at the head of his three regiments of dragoons, started for Falkirk Muir, which he hoped to gain before the Highlanders could take possession of it. He ordered the infantry to follow as fast as possible. A storm of wind and rain beat in the face of the soldiers, and before they could gain the crest of the muir the Highlanders had obtained possession. The English then halted and drew up on somewhat lower ground.

Between them was a ravine which formed but a small depression opposite the centre of the English line, but deepened towards the plain on their right. The English artillery, in the hurry of their advance, had stuck fast in a morass, but as the Highlanders had brought no guns with them the forces were equal in this respect. Lord John Drummond had from a distance been watching the movements of the English, and as soon as he saw that they had taken the alarm and were advancing against the prince, he made a detour, and, riding round the English, joined the Highland infantry. The prince's army was divided into two lines: its right was commanded by Lord George Murray, the left by Lord John Drummond; the prince, as at Preston, took up his station in the centre of the second line on a conspicuous mound, still known by the name of Charlie's Hill.

The English infantry were also drawn up in two lines, with the Argyle militia and the Glasgow regiment in reserve behind the second line. The cavalry were in front under Colonel Ligonier, who, at the death of Colonel Gardiner, had succeeded to the command of his regiment. General Hawley commanded the centre and General Huske the right.

The battle commenced by a charge of Ligonier with his cavalry upon the Highland right. Here the Macdonald clansmen were posted, and these, at Lord George Murray's order, reserved their fire until the dragoons were within ten yards, and then poured in a scathing volley, under which numbers of the horsemen went down. The two dragoon regiments, which had fled so shamefully at Preston and Coltbridge, turned and galloped at once from the field; but Cobham's regiment fought well, and when compelled to retreat rallied behind the right of the line.

Lord George Murray endeavoured to get the victorious Macdonalds into line again; but these were beyond control and rushing forward fell upon the flank of Hawley's two lines of foot, which were at the same moment furiously assailed in front; the Highlanders, after pouring in their fire, dropped their muskets and charged broadsword in hand.

The English, nearly blinded by the wind and rain, were unable to withstand this combined assault. General Hawley, who at least possessed the virtue of courage, rode hither and thither in their front, trying to encourage them, but in vain, the whole centre gave way and fled in confusion. On the right, however, the English were defending themselves successfully. The three regiments placed there, on the edge of the ravine, maintained so steady a fire that the Highlanders were unable to cross it, and Cobham's dragoons charged down upon the scattered and victorious Highlanders in the centre and effectually checked their pursuit. Prince Charles, seeing the danger, put himself at the head of the second line and advanced against the three English regiments who still stood firm.

Unable to withstand so overwhelming a force these fell back from the ground they had held, but did so in steady order, their drums beating, and covering, in their retreat, the mingled mass of fugitives. Had the Highlanders, at this critical moment, flung themselves with their whole force upon these regiments the English army would have been wholly destroyed; but night was already setting in, and the Scottish leaders were ignorant how complete was their victory, and feared an ambuscade. Lord John Drummond, a general officer in the French service, especially opposed the pursuit, saying, "These men behaved admirably at Fontenoy; surely this must be a feint."

The Highlanders remained stationary on the field until some detachments, sent forward by the prince, brought back word that the English had already retreated from Falkirk. They left behind them on the field four hundred dead or dying, with a large portion of officers, and a hundred prisoners; all their artillery, ammunition, and baggage fell into the hands of the Highlanders, whose total loss was only about a hundred. The English, on their retreat, burned to the ground the royal palace at Linlithgow.

CHAPTER XVIII: Culloden.

The victory of Falkirk brought but little advantage to Prince Charles, and dissensions arose among the officers; Lord George Murray being furious with Lord John Drummond for preventing the complete destruction of the English army, while Lord John Drummond severely criticised Lord George for the confusion which had taken place among his troops after their success.

Great numbers of the Highlanders, who had spent the night after the battle in plundering the English camp and stripping the slain, made off with their booty to the mountains, and the number of desertions was increased by the withdrawal of the greater part of Glengarry's clansmen. On the day after the battle the musket of one of the Clanranald clansmen went off by accident and killed the son of Glengarry. His clansmen loudly demanded life for life, and Clanranald having reluctantly consented to surrender his follower, the poor fellow was immediately led out and shot; but even this savage act of vengeance was insufficient to satisfy the Glengarry men, the greater part of whom at once left the army and returned to their homes.

After the battle the siege of Stirling was renewed; but owing to the gross incompetence of a French engineer, who had come over with Lord Drummond, the batteries were so badly placed that their fire was easily silenced by that of the castle guns. The prince, in spite of the advice of Lord George Murray and the other competent authorities, and listening only to his favourite councillors, Secretary Murray and Sir Thomas Sheridan, continued the siege, although on the 30th of January the Duke of Cumberland arrived in Edinburgh and took the command of the army.

Never had Scotland a more bitter enemy. Relentless and savage as General Hawley had been, his deeds were more than rivalled by those of the Duke of Cumberland, who was justly branded by contemporary historians with the name of "the butcher." He was, however, an able general, of great activity and high personal courage.

After halting but one night in Edinburgh he set out at the head of his army to meet the enemy; but these did not repeat their tactics at Falkirk. Disgusted at the conduct of the prince in slighting their advice and listening only to his unworthy counsellors, Lord George Murray with all the principal military leaders held a consultation, and presented a memorial to the prince. In this they stated that, seeing the great numbers of Highlanders who had gone home, they were of opinion that another battle could not be fought with a chance of success, and therefore recommended that the army should at once retire to the Highlands, where a sufficient number of men could be kept together to defy the efforts of the enemy at such a season of the year, and that in the spring ten thousand Highlanders could be got together to go wheresoever the prince might lead them. Prince Charles was struck with grief and dismay at this decision, but as all the military leaders had signed it he was forced to give way.

The army at once blew up its magazines, spiked its guns, and marched for the north in two divisions with much confusion and loss of order. The Duke of Cumberland pursued, but was unable to come up to them, and halted at Perth.

Ronald, who had, from the time he returned to the army, again taken up his former appointment of aide de camp to Lord George Murray, had during this time tried his best to reconcile the differences which were constantly breaking out between that general, the prince, and the clique who surrounded him. It was a difficult task, for Lord George's impetuosity and outspoken brusqueness, and his unconcealed contempt for Secretary Murray and Sheridan, reopened the breach as fast as it was closed.

Since the day when he had saved the prince from being carried off at Glasgow the latter had shown a marked partiality for Ronald's society, and the latter had therefore many opportunities of intervening to prevent open quarrels from breaking out. The prince himself was frequently greatly depressed in spirits, and the light hearted gaiety which had distinguished him on the first landing was now fitful and short lived. His disappointment at the failure of a campaign in which he had won every battle was deep and bitter. He had relied upon the aid of France, but no aid had come. He had been grossly misinformed as to the willingness of the Jacobites of England to take up arms in his favour; and although a portion of the Highlanders of Scotland had warmly embraced his cause, yet many on whom he had relied stood aloof or were in arms against him, while in the Lowlands he had found but few adherents.

So far from gaining ground, he was losing it. Numbers of the Highlanders had gone off to their homes. The retreat from Derby had completely chilled the enthusiasm of his adherents, while the waverers and time servers had been induced thereby to declare against him. The Duke of Cumberland's army steadily increased, and even had the advice of the Highland chiefs been followed and the army dispersed to reassemble in the spring, the chances of success would have been no more favourable than at present, for now that the first surprise and panic were past England would put forth her whole strength, and would by the spring have an army assembled in Scotland against which the Highland clans, even if unanimous, could not hope to cope.

Ronald was perfectly alive to the hopelessness of final success. He had seen the British infantry at Dettingen and Fontenoy, and felt sure that although the wild Highland rush had at first proved irresistible, this could nor continue, and that discipline and training must eventually triumph over mere valour. When he and Malcolm talked the matter over together they agreed that there could be but one issue to the struggle, and that ruin and disaster must fall upon all who had taken part in the enterprise.

"I feel thankful indeed," Ronald said one day, "that I am here only as a private gentleman risking my own life. I do not know what my feelings would be, if, like these Highland chiefs, I had brought all my kinsmen and followers with me into the field. The thought of the ruin and misery which would fall upon them would be dreadful. I fear that the vengeance which will be taken after this is over will be far greater and more widespread than that which followed '15. All say that the Duke of Cumberland is brutal and pitiless, and the fact that we were nearly successful will naturally add to the severity with which the English government will treat us if we fall into their power. Had the enterprise been defeated at its commencement they could have afforded to be lenient. As it is, I fear that they will determine to teach the Highlands such a lesson as will ensure their never again venturing to rise in arms against the house of Hanover."

"And I don't know that they are altogether to be blamed," Malcolm said. "I am not so young as I was, Ronald, and I see now that I was wrong in teaching you to be a Jacobite. It is all very well for men like Tullibardine, who knew the Stuarts on the throne, to fight to put them back again; but to your generation, Ronald, the Stuarts are after all only a tradition, and it is a sort of generous madness for you to risk your life to set them again on the throne of England. It cannot matter a brass pin to you whether James or George rules at St. James's. It is not, as in the case of the Royalists in England in Charles's time or of the Covenanters of Scotland, that a great principle is involved--a principle for which men may well risk their lives and all they hold dear. It is a question of persons only, and although I may hold that by right of descent Charles Edward is Prince of Wales and rightful heir to the throne of England, that is no reason why I should risk my life to place him there; and after all it seems to me that if the majority in these islands determine that they will be ruled by the house of Hanover instead of the house of Stuart they have some right to make their own choice."

"You argue like a philosopher, Malcolm," Ronald said laughing, "and do not remind me in the slightest degree of the Malcolm who used to chat with me in Glasgow."

"You are right there, lad. You see I was brought up a Jacobite, and I have been a soldier all my life, accustomed to charge when I was told to charge and to kill those I was told to kill; but I own that since I have been out now I have got to look at matters differently. The sight of all these poor Highland bodies blindly following their chiefs and risking life and all for a cause in which they have no shadow of interest has made me think. A soldier is a soldier, and if he were to sit down to argue about the justice of every cause in which he is ordered to fight there would be an end to all discipline. But these poor fellows are not soldiers, and so I say to myself, What concern have they in this matter? Their chiefs would gain honours and rewards, patents of high nobility, and additions to their estates if the Stuarts conquered, but their followers would gain nothing whatever. No, lad, if we get over this scrape I have done with fighting; and I hope that no Stuart will ever again succeed in getting Scotland to take up his cause. I shall go on fighting for Prince Charles as long as there is a man left with him; but after that there is an end of it as far as I am concerned, and I hope as far as Scotland is concerned."

"I hope so too, Malcolm. When Scotland is herself divided, Ireland passive, and all England hostile, success is hopeless. The Stuarts will never get such another chance again as they had on the day when we turned our backs on London at Derby, and I hope that they will not again make the attempt, especially as it is manifest now that France has only used them as tools against England, and has no idea of giving them any effectual aid."

Charles on approaching Inverness found it toughly fortified and held by Lord Loudon with a force of two thousand men. The prince halted ten miles from the town at Moy Castle, where he was entertained by Lady M'Intosh, whose husband was serving with Lord Loudon, but who had raised the clan for Prince Charles. The prince had but a few personal attendants with him, the army having been halted at some distance from the castle.

One evening Ronald had ridden over to Moy Castle with some despatches from Lord George Murray to the prince, and had remained there to dine with him. It was late before he mounted his horse. He was, as usual, accompanied by Malcolm. They had ridden but a short distance through the wood which surrounded the castle when a shot was fired, and almost immediately afterwards four or five men came running through the trees.

"What is the matter?" Malcolm shouted.

"The English army are upon us!" one of the M'Intoshes--for they were clansmen who had been sleeping in the wood--answered.

"They must intend to seize the prince," Ronald said, "and will already have sent round a body of horse to cut off his retreat. Scatter through the wood, men, and do each of you raise the war cry of one of the clans as if the whole army were here. This may cause a delay and enable the prince to ride off. Malcolm, do you ride back with all speed to the castle and warn the prince of Loudon's approach."

The Highlanders at once obeyed Ronald's orders, and in a minute or two the war cries of half a dozen of the principal clans in Prince Charles's army rang through the woods, while at the same time the Highlanders discharged their muskets. Ronald also shouted orders, as to a large body of men.

The English, who had made sure of effecting a successful surprise, hesitated as they heard the war cries of the clans ringing through the woods, and believing that the whole of Prince Charles's army were at hand and they were about to be attacked in overwhelming numbers, they retreated hastily to Inverness. No sooner had Ronald discovered that they had fallen back than he rode off to inform the prince that the danger was over.

He found Prince Charles mounted, with Lady M'Intosh on horseback by his side, and the retainers in the castle gathered round, broadsword in hand, in readiness to cut their way through any body of the enemy's horse who might intercept their retreat. Charles laughed heartily when he heard of the strategy which Ronald had employed to arrest the advance of the enemy, and thanked him for again having saved him from falling into the hands of the enemy.

The English made their retreat to Inverness in such confusion and dismay that the affair became known in history as the "rout of Moy."

The next morning, the 17th of February, the prince called up his army, and the next day advanced against Inverness. Lord Loudon did not await his coming. The panic of his soldiers two days before showed him that no reliance could be placed upon them, and embarking with them in boats he crossed the Moray Frith to Cromarty, where the troops shortly afterwards disbanded upon hearing that the Earl of Cromarty was marching against them with some Highland regiments.

The town of Inverness was occupied at once, and the citadel surrendered in a few days. The army, now in a barren and mountainous region, were deprived of all resources. Many ships with supplies were sent off from France, but few of them reached their destination; several being captured by British cruisers, and others compelled to go back to French ports.

The supply of money in the treasury was reduced to the lowest ebb, and Charles was obliged to pay his troops in meal, and even this was frequently deficient, and the men suffered severely from hunger. Many deserted, and others scattered over the country in search of subsistence.

In the meantime the Duke of Cumberland's army was receiving powerful reinforcements. In February Prince Frederick of Hesse Cassel, with five thousand of his troops, who had been hired by the British government, landed at Leith. These troops were placed in garrison in all the towns in the south of Scotland, thus enabling the Duke of Cumberland to draw together the whole of the English forces for his advance into the Highlands.

On the 8th of April he set out from Aberdeen with eight thousand foot and nine hundred horse. He marched along the coast accompanied by the fleet, which landed supplies as needed. At the Spey, Lord John Drummond had prepared to defend the fords, and some works had been thrown up to protect them; but the English cannon were brought up in such numbers that Lord John, considering the position untenable, retired to Inverness, while the English army forded the Spey, and on the 14th entered Nairn, where some skirmishing took place between their advance guard and the Highland rear.

Prince Charles and his principal officers rested that night at Culloden House and the troops lay upon the adjacent moor. On the morning of the 15th they drew up in order of battle. The English, however, rested for the day at Nairn, and there celebrated the Duke of Cumberland's birthday with much feasting, abundant supplies being landed from the fleet.

The Highlanders, on the other hand, fasted, only one biscuit per man being issued during the day. Consequently many straggled away to Inverness and other places in search of food. Lord Cromarty, with the regiments under his command, were absent, so that barely five thousand men were mustered in the ranks. At a council of war Lord George Murray suggested that a night surprise should be made on the duke's camp at Nairn, and as this was the prince's own plan it was unanimously agreed to.

Before, however, the straggling troops could be collected it was eight o'clock at night. Nairn was twelve miles distant, and the men, weakened by privation and hunger, marched so slowly across the marshy ground that it was two o'clock in the morning before the head of the columns arrived within four miles of the British camp, while the rear was still far away, and many had dropped out of the ranks from fatigue.

It was now too late to hope that a surprise could be effected before daylight, and the army retraced its steps to Culloden Moor. Worn out and exhausted as they were, and wholly without supplies of provisions, Lord George Murray and the other military officers felt that the troops could not hope to contend successfully against a vastly superior army, fresh, well fed, and supported by a strong force of artillery, on the open ground, and he proposed that the army should retire beyond the river Bairn, and take up a position there on broken ground inaccessible to cavalry.

The prince, however, supported by Sir Thomas Sheridan and his other evil advisers, overruled the opinion of the military leaders, and decided to fight on level ground. The Highlanders were now drawn up in order of battle in two lines. On the right were the Athole brigade, the Camerons, the Stuarts, and some other clans under Lord George Murray; on the left the Macdonald regiments under Lord John Drummond. This arrangement, unfortunately, caused great discontent among the Macdonalds, just as their being given the post of honour at Falkirk had given umbrage to the other clans.

At eleven o'clock the English army was seen approaching. It was formed in three lines, with cavalry on each wing, and two pieces of cannon between every two regiments of the first line. The battle began with an artillery duel, but in this the advantage was all on the side of the English, the number of their pieces and the skill of their gunners being greatly superior.

Prince Charles rode along the front line to animate his men, and as he did so several of his escort were killed by the English cannonade. A storm of snow and hail had set in, blowing full in the face of the Highlanders. At length Lord George Murray, finding that he was suffering heavily from the enemy's artillery fire, while his own guns inflicted but little damage upon them, sent to Prince Charles for permission to charge.

On receiving it he placed himself at the head of his men, and with the whole of the right wing and centre charged the enemy. They were received with a tremendous musketry fire, while the English artillery swept the ranks with grape; but so furious was their onslaught that they broke through Munro and Burrel's regiments in the first line and captured two pieces of cannon. But behind were the second line drawn up three deep, with the front rank kneeling, and these, reserving their fire until the Highlanders were close at hand, opened a rolling fire so sustained and heavy that the Highlanders were thrown into complete disorder.

Before they could recover themselves they were charged by horse and foot on both flanks, and driven together till they became a confused mass. In vain did their chiefs attempt to rally them. Exhausted and weakened in body, swept by the continuous fire of the English, they could do no more, and at last broke and fled. In the meantime the Macdonalds on the left remained inactive. In vain Lord John Drummond and the Duke of Perth called upon them to charge, in vain their chief, Keppoch, rushed forward with a few of his clansmen and died in front of them. Nothing would induce them to fight, and when the right and centre were defeated they fell back in good order, and, joining the remnants of the second line, retired from the field unbroken.

Charles, from the heights on which he stood with a squadron of horse, could scarce believe the evidence of his eyes when he saw the hitherto victorious Highlanders broken and defeated, and would have ridden down himself to share their fate had not O'Sullivan and Sheridan seized his horse by the bridle and forced him from the field. Being pressed by the English, the retreating force broke into two divisions. The smaller retreated to Inverness, where they next day laid down their arms to the Duke of Cumberland; the other, still preserving some sort of order, marched by way of Ruthven to Badenoch.

Fourteen colours, two thousand three hundred muskets, and all their cannon fell into the hands of the English. The loss of the victors in killed and wounded amounted to three hundred and ten men, that of the Highlanders to a thousand. No quarter was given to the stragglers and fugitives who fell into the hands of the English. Their wounded were left on the ground till the following day without care or food, and the greater portion of them were then put to death in cold blood, with a cruelty such as never before or since disgraced an English army.

Some were beaten to death by the soldiers with the stocks of their muskets, some were dragged out from the thicket or caverns to which they had crawled and shot, while one farm building, in which some twenty wounded men had taken refuge, was deliberately set on fire and burned with them to the ground. In any case such conduct as this would have inflicted eternal discredit upon those who perpetrated it; but it was all the more unjustifiable and abominable after the extreme clemency and kindness with which Prince Charles had, throughout the campaign, treated all prisoners who fell into his hands.

Ronald had ridden close beside Lord George Murray as he led the Highlanders to the charge; but he had, as they approached the first English line, received a ball in the shoulder, while almost at the same instant Malcolm's horse was shot under him. Ronald reeled in the saddle, and would have fallen had not Malcolm extricated himself from his fallen horse and run up to him.

"Where are you hit, lad?" he asked in extreme anxiety.

"In the shoulder, Malcolm. Help me off my horse, and do you take it and go on with the troops."

"I shall do nothing of the kind," Malcolm said. "One man will make no difference to them, and I am going to look after you."

So saying he sprang up behind Ronald, and placing one arm round him to support him, took the reins in the other and rode to the rear. He halted on rising ground, and for a short time watched the conflict.

"The battle is lost," he said at last. "Lord George's troops are in utter confusion. The Macdonalds show no signs of moving, though I can see their officers are urging them to charge. Now, Ronald, the first thing is to get you out of this, and beyond the reach of pursuit."

So saying he turned the horse and rode away from the field of battle.

"Does your shoulder hurt much?" he asked after they had gone a short distance.

"It does hurt abominably," Ronald said faintly, for he was feeling almost sick from the agony he was suffering from the motion of the horse.

"I am a fool," Malcolm said, "not to have seen to it before we started. I can't do much now; but at least I can fasten it so as to hurt you as little as possible."

He took off his scarf, and, telling Ronald to place his arm in the position which was most comfortable to him, he bound it tightly against his body.

"That is better, is it not?" he asked as he again set the horse in motion.

"Much better, Malcolm. I feel that I can go on now, whereas before I could not have gone much further if all Cumberland's cavalry had been close behind. How far are you thinking of going? I don't think my horse can carry double much further. Poor beast, he has had as short rations as his master, and was on the move all last night."

"No. But we shall not have to make a very long journey. The English marched twelve miles before they attacked us, and I do not think they are likely to closely pursue far tonight; besides, I have no intention of riding now that there is no fear of immediate pursuit. I think that in another two miles we shall be safe from any fear of the English cavalry overtaking us, for we shall then reach a forest. Once in that we shall be safe from pursuit, and shall soon be in the heart of the hills."

On reaching the forest Malcolm dismounted, and leading the horse turned off from the road. Following a little trodden path they were soon in the heart of the forest, and after keeping on for two hours, and crossing several hills, he stopped by the side of a stream.

"We are perfectly safe here," he said, "and can sleep as securely as if we were in a palace."

The saddle was taken off and the horse turned loose to graze. Malcolm then removed Ronald's coat and shirt, bathed the wound for some time with water, cut some pieces of wood to act as splints, and tearing some strips off his sash bound these tightly.

"The ball has regularly smashed the bone, Ronald, and we must be careful to keep the shoulder in its proper position or you will never look square again."

"That does not seem very important to me just at present, Malcolm."

"No. Just at present the most important question is that of getting something to eat. We have had nothing today and not much yesterday, and now that we are no longer in danger of pursuit one begins to feel one is hungry. You stay here while I go and forage. There ought to be a village somewhere among the hills nor far away."

"Do you know the country, Malcolm?"

"I never came by this path, lad; but I have travelled pretty well all over the Highlands, and, just as you found to be the case in Lancashire, there are few villages I do not know. I will first pull you a couch of this dead bracken, and then be off; an hour's sleep will do you almost as much good as a meal."

Ronald lay down on the soft couch Malcolm prepared for him, and before he had been alone for a minute he was fast asleep.

The sun was setting when he awoke. Malcolm stood beside him.

"Here is supper, lad. Not a very grand one, but there's enough of it, which is more than has been the case for some weeks."

So saying he laid down by Ronald's side a large loaf of black bread, a cheese made of sheep's milk, and a bottle of spirits.

"The village is five miles away, which is farther than I expected. However, I came back quicker than I went, for I had had a bowl of milk and as much bread as I could eat. I found the place in a state of wild excitement, for two or three of the men had just come in from the battlefield, and brought the news with them. They are all for the Stuarts there, and you would be well entertained, but there is sure to be a search high and low, and you would not be safe in any village. However, a lad has promised to be here in the morning, and he will guide us to a lonely hut in the heart of the hills, used by the shepherds in summer. You will be perfectly safe there."

"It is about three miles from the village, he said. So I can go down two or three times a week and get food, and learn how things are going on. The Highlanders may rally again and make another fight of it; but I hardly expect they will. They are not like regular troops, whose home is naturally with their colours, and who, after the first rout, try to rejoin their regiments. There is no discipline among these Highlanders. Each man does as he likes, and their first impulse after a battle is to make for their homes--if it is a victory, to carry home their spoil; if they are defeated, for rest and shelter. At any rate, whether they gather again or not, you will have to keep perfectly quiet for a time. When your shoulder is perfectly healed we can act according to circumstances, and make for the army if there be an army, or for the seacoast if there is not."

Although he had eaten but a short time before, Malcolm was quite ready for another meal, and sitting down beside Ronald he joined him in his assault upon the black bread and cheese. Then he collected some more of the bracken, mixed himself a strong horn of whiskey and water, and a much weaker one for Ronald, after which the two lay down and were fast asleep.

They were awake at sunrise, and shortly afterwards the lad whom Malcolm had engaged to act as guide made his appearance. The horse was saddled, Ronald mounted, and they started at once for their destination among the hills. They followed the path which Malcolm had taken the afternoon before for some three miles, and then struck off to the left. Half an hour took them out of the forest, and they journeyed for an hour along the bare hillsides, until, lying in a sheltered hollow, they saw the hut which was their destination.

"They are not likely to find us here," Malcolm said cheerfully, "even were they to scour the mountains. They might ride within fifty yards of this hollow without suspecting its existence. Where are we to get water?" he asked the lad in Gaelic.

"A quarter of a mile away over that brow is the head of a stream," the lad replied. "You cannot well miss it."

"That is all right," Malcolm said. "I don't mind carrying up provisions or a bottle of spirits now and then; but to drag all the water we want three miles would be serious."

The door of the hut was only fastened by a latch, and they entered without ceremony. It consisted of but a single room. There were two or three rough wooden stools, and a heap of bracken in one corner. Nor a large amount of furniture, but, in the opinion of a Highlander, amply sufficient.

"We shall do here capitally," Malcolm said. "Now, what do you think about the horse, Ronald?"

"Of course he might be useful if we were obliged to move suddenly; but we have no food to give him, and if we let him shift for himself he will wander about, and might easily be seen by anyone crossing these hills. A horse is always a prize, and it might bring troops out into our neighbourhood who would otherwise not have a thought about coming in this direction."

"I quite agree with you, Ronald. The lad had better take him down to the village, and give him to the head man there. He can sell him, or keep him, or get rid of him as he likes. At any rate he will be off our hands."

CHAPTER XIX: Fugitives.

For three weeks Ronald and Malcolm remained in hiding in the hut among the hills. Every two or three days Malcolm went down to the village and brought back food. He learned that the remains of the army at Ruthven had entirely dispersed, the prince himself seeing the hopelessness of any longer continuing the struggle. Terrible tales of slaughter and devastation by Cumberland's troops circulated through the hills. The duke had fixed his headquarters at Fort Augustus, and thence his troops ravaged the whole country of the clans lately in insurrection. Villages were burned, cattle slaughtered, women subjected to the grossest insult and ill treatment, and often wantonly slain, and the fugitives among the mountains hunted like wild beasts, and slain as pitilessly whenever overtaken.

Ronald's arm was healing fast. Youth and a good constitution, and the care and attention of Malcolm, aided perhaps by the pure mountain air, did wonders for him. The splints had proved efficacious, and although they had not yet been taken off, Malcolm was confident that the injury would be completely repaired. One morning Malcolm had left but half an hour for the village when he returned.

"The enemy are in the village," he said. "I can see clouds of smoke rising in that direction. We had better be off at once. They will be scouring all the hills here, as they have done elsewhere, and we had better get out of the neighbourhood."

There was no packing to be done, and taking with them what remained of the food Malcolm had last brought, they started on their way. They made first for the spring from which they had drawn their water, and then followed the little stream on its way down the hill, as it flowed in the opposite direction to the village. An hour's walking took them into the forest.

"Before we go further let us have a consultation," Malcolm said. "We are safe now from pursuit, and had better settle upon what course we intend to adopt. Shall we make for Glasgow, and lie hid there until things blow over a little; or make for the isles, and stay there until we get a chance of being taken off by some French ship? That is what they say the prince has done; and indeed as there would be no chance of his getting a ship on the east coast, and all the Lowlands are against them, he is certain to have made for the isles. The Clanranalds and most of the other islemen are loyal to him, and would receive and shelter him. Skye is hostile, but elsewhere he will be safe, and would move from island to island or get across to the mainland by night if the pursuit became too hot. What do you say, Ronald?"

"I would not try Glasgow unless as a last resource, Malcolm; you are known to many there, and as I was there as one of the prince's officers on two occasions I might easily be recognized. You may be sure that there is a very strict lookout for fugitives, and every stranger who enters a town will be closely examined. After some time, when Prince Charles and the principal chiefs and the leaders will either have escaped across the water or been hunted down, things will calm down; but at present we must not try to pass through the Lowlands."

"At any rate we cannot try to do so till your shoulder is completely healed, and you can use your arm naturally; but I do not think that we had better try and cross to the isles just at present. If Prince Charles is there, or is believed by the English to be there, the search will be so keen that every stranger would be hunted down; and although the Highlanders might risk imprisonment and death for the prince himself, they could not be expected to run the same risk for anyone else. If the prince escapes it will be because the whole population are with him, and every man, woman, and child is trying to throw the pursuers off the scent. No, I think we should be safer in Edinburgh itself than in the isles. We will make a shift to live as we can for a month or so; by that time I hope you will be able to use one arm as well as the other, and we will then boldly go down into the Lowlands in our old characters as two drovers."

"That will be the best plan, no doubt," Ronald agreed; "the difficulty will be the getting over the next month."

"We shall manage that," Malcolm said; "fortunately you have still got some money left."

"Yes, I have over fifty pounds; it was lucky I was able to draw it, as we returned north, from the man I left it with at Carlisle."

"Yes, and you wanted to give it back to the treasury," Malcolm said, "and would have done it if I had not almost quarrelled with you about it, saying that it had been given you for a certain purpose, that you had carried out that purpose, and had, therefore, a right to it, and that you would be only looked upon as a fool if you offered to pay it back. However, there it is now, and lucky it is you have got it. However hard the times, however great the danger, a man will hardly starve in Scotland with fifty pounds in his pocket; so now we will turn our faces west, and make for the head of one of the lochs; there are plenty of fish to be had for catching, and with them and a little oatmeal and a bottle or two of whiskey we can live like lords."

They walked for some hours, and stopped for the night in the hut of a shepherd, who received them hospitably, but could give them but little food, his scanty supplies being almost exhausted, for, as he told them, "the hills are full of fugitives, and those who come all cry for meal; as for meat, there is no want of it. Men won't starve as long as there are sheep and cattle to be had for lifting them, and at present there are more of these than usual in the hills, for they have all been driven up from the villages lest they should fall into the hands of the troopers; but meal is scarce, for men dare not go down to the villages to buy, and we only get it when the women bring it up as they have a chance."

In the morning the shepherd gave them directions as to the way they should take, and a few hours later they came down upon the head of one of the many deep inlets on the western coast. A small fishing boat stood on the shore, but they dared not descend into this, but made their way to the point where, as the shepherd had told them, a stream which flowed from a mountain tarn some miles inland made its way down into the sea.

The banks were thickly wooded for some two miles from its outlet; beyond that was a moorland covered with heather. They determined to encamp near the upper edge of the wood, and at once set to with their swords to cut down branches and construct a hut. This was completed before dusk, and Malcolm then started for the village on the seashore. Ronald besought him to be most careful.

"There is likely," he said, "to be a party of soldiers in every village round the coast, for they will know that all the chiefs and officers would be making for the sea. The clansmen have only to remain in the hills until this persecution dies out, and then go quietly home again; but for the leaders the only hope is escape by sea."

"I will be careful, lad," Malcolm said. "I shall not enter the village, but will hang about in its outskirts until I come across someone, and with plenty of money in my pocket it is hard if I cannot manage to get a bag of meal and a net, even if the place is full of English soldiers."

Three hours later Malcolm returned laden with a sack containing forty pounds of meal, a jar with two gallons of whiskey, and a net.

"There," he said as he entered; "we can do for a month now, if needs be. There is a party of militia in the village, and I hear the whole coast is closely watched, and there are a number of English cruisers among the islands."

"How did you get the things?"

"I waited till a woman came down with a bundle of faggots, and told her what I wanted. She said at first it was impossible; but when I said I was prepared to pay well she altered her tone, and said she would send her husband out to me. He soon came, and after some bargaining he agreed to bring me out the things I wanted for three pounds, and here they are. I see you have got a fire alight, so we will make some cakes at once. I have brought a griddle and two horns with me."

The next morning they set to work to fish. The net was stretched across the lower end of a pool, and they then stripped and waded in, splashing and throwing stones as they went. It was just up to their necks in the deepest parts, shallowing to two feet below. When they reached the net they found two fine salmon caught there, and carrying these ashore they split one and placed it above the fire. The net was then removed, and in half an hour they were sitting down to a breakfast of grilled salmon and hot oatmeal cakes, which Ronald thought the most delicious repast he had ever tasted.

For three weeks they remained at this spot. They were not always alone, being sometimes joined for a day or two by other fugitives, who, like themselves, were wandering near the sea coast seeking escape. These seldom stayed long, for it was felt unsafe to keep in parties of more than two or three at the utmost. Some of the fugitives were in wretched condition, having been wandering among the moors and forests for weeks, and as the fishing was very successful, Ronald and Malcolm were able to give them at parting a good supply of smoked salmon, and a portion of meal, of which Malcolm from time to time brought a fresh supply up from the village.

The people there knew little of what was passing in the outer world; but from the conversation of the soldiers they were sure that Prince Charles had so far escaped capture, and an opinion began to prevail that he had succeeded in making his escape by sea, in spite of the vigilance of the English cruisers.

By the end of the three weeks even Malcolm admitted that Ronald's wound was completely cured. Two large blue scars showed where the bullet had passed through, and beneath this could be felt a lump where the broken bone had knitted together, and this would in time become as strong as the rest of the shoulder. Malcolm's splints had done their duty, and the eye could detect no difference between the level or width of the two shoulders. Ronald could move his arm freely in all directions, and, except that he could not at present venture to put any strain upon the arm, he might be considered as perfectly cured. They determined, therefore, to continue their way. In the first place, however, it was necessary to procure other clothes, for Ronald was still in uniform, and although Malcolm's attire was not wholly military, it yet differed materially from that of a countryman.

"We shall have to get other clothes when we get south," Malcolm said; "for a Highlander's dress would be looked upon with as much suspicion in Glasgow as would that uniform of yours. But until we get down to the Lowlands the native garb will be the best."

Accordingly he paid another visit to the village, and with the utmost difficulty persuaded the man he had before dealt with to bring him two suits of clothes, such as were worn by the fishermen there. In these, although Malcolm's small stock of Gaelic would betray them at once for other than they seemed to the first clansman who might address them, they could pass muster with any body of English troops they might meet by the way.

Before starting they caught and smoked as many salmon as they could carry, as the fishermen of the coast were in the habit of exchanging fish for sheep with their inland neighbours. They cut each a short pole, and slung some fish at each end, and then placing it on their shoulder, started on their way. They kept along the hillside until they struck the track--for it could scarcely be called a road--leading from the village into the interior, and then boldly followed this; for the difficulty of travelling across the hilly and broken country was so great that they preferred to run the slight extra risk of keeping to the road, feeling certain that for the first day's march at least their appearance and the fish they carried would answer for themselves with any body of troops they might meet.

Of this, however, they did not think there was much chance. The authorities would have long since learned the futility of hunting the fugitives among the hills, and would be confining their efforts to the sea coast. They were now at a considerable distance from the scene of the bloody persecutions of Cumberland and Hawley, and although in other parts of Scotland severe measures might be adopted against known adherents of the Stuarts, it was among the Highland clans only that savage and wholesale massacres were being carried into effect.

Occasionally in the course of the day's walk they met with clansmen passing along the road. These generally passed with a brief word of greeting in Gaelic. One or two who stopped to speak recognized at once by Malcolm's accent that the wayfarers were not what they pretended to be; but they asked no questions, and with a significant smile and an expression of good wishes went on their way.

At the village where they stopped, after a long day's journey, the same line of conduct was observed towards them. The inhabitants guessed at once that they were in disguise; but the edicts against those who assisted fugitive insurgents were so severe that none made any open sign of their recognition. They paid for their night's lodging and food with a portion of their fish, which they were indeed glad to get rid of.

The next day they resumed their journey, and towards sunset arrived at a village where they saw a party of English cavalry, who had apparently but just arrived. The men were cleaning their horses, and an officer was sitting on a bench in front of the principal house in the village; for he had already made a close inspection of every house in the village, and the angry faces of the women and the sullen looks of a few men there were about showed how they resented the disturbance of their households.

It was too late to retreat, and Malcolm and Ronald walked boldly to the public house in the centre of the village. The officer at once rose and walked across to him.

"Who are you?" he asked; "and where do you come from?"

Malcolm shook his head and said in Gaelic:

"I do not understand English."

"What fools these people are!" the officer exclaimed. "Ho, within there!"

The landlady came to the door.

"Do you speak English?"

"I speak a little," the woman said.

"Just ask these men who they are and where they come from."

The woman asked the question in Gaelic, and Malcolm replied:

"We are, as you see, fishermen, and we come from Huish."

As he spoke there was a slight change in the woman's face; but it passed away, and she translated Malcolm's answer to the officer.

"But that is forty miles away," the officer said. "What do they do with their fish at this distance from their home?"

The question being put in Gaelic by the woman, Malcolm replied that owing to the boats being seized by the soldiers, and trade being at a standstill, they could no longer make a living at home, and were therefore on their way to Glasgow to ship as sailors. They were carrying their fish with them to pay for their food and lodging on the way.

The story was probable enough, and the officer's suspicion was allayed.

"They are fine looking fellows, both of them," he said to himself as he returned to his bench. "Father and son, I suppose. The young one would make a strapping soldier. Like enough he was at Culloden. However, thank goodness, I have no grounds for suspecting or detaining them. I am sick of this brutal business of fugitive hunting. We are officers and not butchers, and this slaying of brave men who have met us fairly in battle is a disgrace to the British name."

Ronald and Malcolm followed the woman into the house.

"I am ready to buy some of your fish," she said in a loud tone of voice in Gaelic, "for there will be many to feed this evening; as my house is full of soldiers I cannot take you in, but if you like you can sleep in that shed over there. I can cook one of your fish for you, and let you have some black bread; but that is all I can do. Now, how much do you want for the fish?"

Malcolm named a low price, and the woman took three or four of the largest. For these she offered him the price he had asked. He glanced round, and seeing that they were not overlooked, he shook his head.

"We don't want money," he said. "We are well provided. Many thanks for keeping our secret."

The woman nodded, and without another word the two went out and sat down on a stone bench outside until the landlady brought out a platter with a fish and some black bread. This they ate where they sat. Malcolm then went in to get some tobacco, and returned with his pipe alight, and sat with Ronald watching with apparent interest the operations of the soldiers until night closed in. Then they retired to the shed the landlady had pointed out, and found that a large bundle of freshly gathered rushes had been shaken out to form a bed. Carrying in their poles with their now diminished load of fish, they closed the door and threw themselves down upon the rushes.

"That has passed off well," Malcolm said. "Tomorrow we will only go a mile or so out of the village, and stop in the first wood we come to, and go on at night. Thirty miles will take us close down to Dumbarton, and there we must manage to get some fresh clothes."

"We shall be able to leave our poles behind us," Ronald said, "and that will be a comfort. Although my load of fish was not nearly as heavy as yours, still carrying it on one shoulder was no joke, and I shall be heartily glad to get rid of it."

"I shall not be sorry myself, Malcolm said; "but there will be no occasion to waste the fish. We shall be up and away long before the soldiers are stirring, and we may as well hand them over as a present to the landlady."

This was done, and at an early hour in the morning they were upon the road again. After an hour's walking they stopped in a wood till evening and then continued on their way until they reached Dumbarton, where they threw themselves down beside some boats drawn up upon the shore, and slept till the morning.

They then boldly entered the town, and as their garb was similar to that of the men who brought down the fish caught at the villages on the coast, no attention whatever was paid to them. They had no difficulty in purchasing the clothes they required, and carrying them out of the town they changed in the first retired spot they reached, and, as two Lowland drovers, tramped on to Glasgow. With their bonnets pulled well down over their eyes they entered the town. They had little fear of discovery, for none would be likely to recognize in Ronald the gaily dressed young officer of Prince Charles.

As to Malcolm, he felt safe from molestation. He was, of course, known to many drovers and others, but they would not concern themselves with what he had been doing since they last saw him, and even had they noticed him when he was there with Ronald, would not denounce an old comrade. He went, therefore, boldly to the little inn where he had been in the habit of staying when in the city.

"Ah, Malcolm, is that you, man?" the landlord said as he entered. "I didna think o' seeing you again. I thought it likely ye were laying stiff and stark somewhere out on the muirs. Eh, man, you are a foolish fellow to be mixing yourself up in the affairs of ithers."

"I have done with it now, Jock, for good and all," Malcolm said, "and am going back to my old trade again."

"I think you are a fule to come back here so soon. There's mony a one marked ye as ye rode in behind that young officer of the prince's, and if they denounce you now they would soon clap you in between four walls."

"Hoots, man!" Malcolm laughed; "who would trouble themselves about a body like me!"

"There are bleudy doings up i' the Highlands," the landlord said gravely, "if a' they say is true."

"It is true, Jock, more shame to them, but they wouldn't do in Glasgow what they are doing there. They are hunting down the clansmen like wild beasts; but here in the Lowlands they will not trouble themselves to ask who was for King George and who was against him, except among those who have got estates they can confiscate."

"May be no," the landlord replied. "Still, Malcolm, if you will take my advice you won't show yourself much in the streets, nor your friend either," he added significantly. "You may be safe, but the citizens are smarting yet over the requisitions that were made upon them, and your friend had best keep in his room as long as ye stay here."

Malcolm nodded.

"He will be careful, Jock, never fear. We shall be off again as soon as we get a chance. I will leave him here while I go down the town and find whether there is a herd starting for England. If there is we will go with it; if not, I shall try and get a passage by sea."

Malcolm could not hear of any drove of cattle going south. The troubles had, for the time, entirely put a stop to the trade. After it was dark he went to Andrew's. His brother's face expressed both pleasure and dismay at seeing him.

"Right glad I am to see you have got safely through it all, Malcolm, but you must be mad to show yourself here again at present. But how is the boy? We have troubled sorely over him. I trust that he too has come safely through it?"

"Safe and sound, Andrew, save that he had a bullet through his shoulder at Culloden; but he is tight enough again now."

"And what have you been doing ever since?"

"Curing his shoulder and fishing;" Malcolm briefly related their adventures since Culloden.

"And is he with you here in Glasgow, Malcolm? Surely you are not mad enough to bring him here where he is known to scores of people as one of the rebel officers!"

"He is here, sure enough," Malcolm said, "and safer than he has been for some time. It is nearly two months since Culloden, and people are beginning to think of other things, except in the Highlands, where those fiends Cumberland and Hawley are burning and slaying. Ronald is dressed like a drover, and no one is likely to recognize him. However, he will remain within doors. And now, brother, I want you to take us a passage in the next vessel sailing for London. If I go to a shipper he may ask questions, and like enough it may be necessary to get passes signed before we can go on board."

"Certainly it is," Andrew said. "A strict lookout is kept to prevent the rebel leaders from escaping, and no captain of a ship is permitted to take a passenger unless he is provided with a pass, signed by a magistrate, saying that he is a peaceable and well known person."

"But just at present we are both peaceable persons, Andrew, and we can certainly claim to be well known citizens."

"It is no joking matter, Malcolm, I can tell you," Andrew said irritably; "but of course I will see what I can do. And now I will put on my bonnet and come with you and have a chat with Ronald. It will not do to bring him here tonight, but we must arrange for him to come and see Janet before he sails. I shall not tell her anything about it till he is ready to start, for you know she is very particular, and I am afraid I shall have to say what is not quite true to get the order. I can sign it myself, but it must have the signature of the provost too."

So saying he took his cap and accompanied Malcolm to the lodging.

"Stay here a moment, Andrew," Malcolm said when he arrived within a few yards of the little inn. "I will see that there is no one drinking within. It wouldna look well to see a decent bailie of the city going into a liquor shop after dark. It will be best for me to fetch him out here, for I doubt there's any room where you could talk without fear of being overheard."

Ronald, who was sitting with his cap pulled down over his eyes as if asleep, in a corner of the room, where three or four drovers were smoking and talking, was called out by Malcolm.

"I am right glad to see you again," Andrew Anderson said heartily. "Janet and I have passed an ill time since the battle was fought. Elspeth has kept up our hopes all along. She said she was sure that you were alive, quite downright sure; and though neither Janet nor I have much faith in superstitions, the old woman's assertions that she should assuredly know it if you were dead did somehow keep up our spirits. Besides, I had faith in Malcolm's knowledge of the country, and knew you were both famous for getting into scrapes and out of them, so I thought that if neither bullet nor sabre had stretched you on the moor of Culloden you would manage to win your way out of the trouble somehow. However, I think you are pretty safe here. The bloody doings of Cumberland have shocked every Scotchman, and even those who were strongest against the Stuarts now cry shame, and so strong is the feeling that were the prince to appear now with a handful of followers I believe the whole country would rise in his favour. So deep is the wrath and grief at the red slaughter among the Highlands there would not be many Scotchmen found who would betray a fellow Scot into the hands of these butchers. I will make inquiry tomorrow as to what ships are sailing, and will get you a passage in the first. There may be some difficulty about the permit; but if I can't get over it we must smuggle you on board as sailors. However, I don't think the provost will ask me any questions when I lay the permit before him for his signature. He is heart and soul for the king, but, like us all, he is sick at heart at the news from the North, and would, I think, shut an eye if he saw a Jacobite making his escape. And now, lad, I must be going back, for the hour is getting late and Janet does not know why I am away. Come to us tomorrow evening as soon as the shop closes. Janet and Elspeth will be delighted to see you, and we will have a long talk over all that you have gone through."

On the following evening Ronald and Malcolm presented themselves at Andrew's and were received with delight by Elspeth and Mrs. Anderson. The latter had, while the rebellion appeared to have a chance of success, been its bitter opponent, and had spoken often and wrathfully against her husband's brother and Ronald embarking in such an enterprise; but with its overthrow all her enmity had expired, and she would have been ready to give assistance not only to them, but to any other fugitive trying to escape.

"I have good news for you," Andrew said, when the first greetings were over. "A vessel sails in the morning, and I have taken passages for you in it; and what is more, have brought your permits. I went to the provost and said to him, 'Provost, I want you to sign these permits for two friends of mine who are wanting to go up to London.'

"'Who are they?' said he.

"'They are just two drover bodies,' I said. He looked at me hard.

"'One question, Andrew. I know how you feel just at present. You are a loyal man like myself, but we all feel the same. I will sign your permit for any save one. Give me your word that neither of these men is Charles Stuart. I care not who they may be beside, but as a loyal subject of King George I cannot aid his arch enemy to escape.'

"'I give you my word, provost,' I said. 'One is--'

"'I don't want to know who they are,' he interrupted. 'I had rather not know. It is enough for me that you give me your word that neither of them is Charles Stuart,' and he took the pen and signed the permit. 'Between ourselves,' he went on, 'I shall be glad to hear that the misguided young man is safe across the water, but as Provost of Glasgow I could lend him no help to go.'

"'They say he has got safe away already,' I said.

"'I think not, Andrew; the coast has been too closely watched for that. The young man is hiding somewhere among the isles, among the Clanranalds or Macdonalds. I fear they will have him yet. I dread every day to get the news; but I hope beyond all things, that if they do lay hands on him it will be through the treachery of no Scot.'

"'I hope not, provost,' I said. 'They haven't got over throwing it in our teeth that we sold King Charles to Cromwell.' So we just shook hands and said goodbye, and here is the permit."

They spent a long evening talking over the past.

"I wonder if I shall ever see you again, Ronald!" Mrs. Anderson said, with tears in her eyes, as they rose to say goodbye.

"You need nor fear about that, Janet, woman," her husband said. "Ronald and Malcolm aye fall on their legs, and we shall see them back again like two bad pennies. Besides," he went on more seriously, "there will be an end of these savage doings in the north before long. Loyal men in Scotland are crying out everywhere against them, and the feeling in England will be just as strong when the truth is known there, and you will see that before long there will be a general pardon granted to all except the leaders. Fortunately Ronald and Malcolm are not likely to be in the list of exceptions, and before a year is up they will be able to come back if they will without fear of being tapped on the shoulder by a king's officer."

"I shall come back again if I can, you may be sure," Ronald said. "Of course I do not know yet what my father and mother's plans may be; but for myself I shall always look upon Scotland as my home, and come back to it as soon as I have an opportunity."

"You do not intend to stay in the French army?"

"Certainly not. After the treatment my father has received I have no inclination to serve France. The chief reason why Scotchmen have entered her service has been that they were driven from home, and that they looked to France for aid to place the Stuarts on the throne again. Now that the time has come, France has done nothing to aid, and has seen the Stuart cause go down without striking a blow to assist it. I consider that cause is lost for ever, and shall never again draw my sword against the House of Hanover. Nor have I had any reason for loving France. After living in a free country like Scotland, who could wish to live in a country where one man's will is all powerful--where the people are still no better than serfs--where the nobles treat the law as made only for them--where, as in my father's case, a man may not even marry according to his own will without incurring the risk of a life's imprisonment? No, I have had enough of France; and if ever I get the opportunity I shall return to Scotland to live."

The next morning early Ronald and Malcolm embarked on board a ship. Their permits were closely scrutinized before the vessel started, and a thorough search was made before she was allowed to sail. When the officers were satisfied that no fugitives were concealed on board they returned to shore, and the vessel started on her voyage for London.

CHAPTER XX: Happy Days.

On arriving in London, after ten days' voyage, Ronald and Malcolm obtained garments of the ordinary cut. The one attired himself as an English gentleman, the other in a garb suitable to a confidential attendant or steward, and after a stay of two or three days they made their way by coach down to Southampton.

Here they remained for a week, and then effected a bargain with the captain of a fishing lugger to set them on shore in France. As the two countries were at war this could only be done by landing them at night at some quiet spot on the French coast. The lugger cruised about a couple of days, and then, choosing a quiet night when there was a mist on the water, she ran in as closely as she dared, then the boat was lowered, and Malcolm and Ronald were rowed to shore and landed a few miles south of Boulogne.

When it was light they made their way to a village; here but few questions were asked them, for many refugees from Scotland and England were crossing to France. As they had been well provided with funds by Andrew they posted to Paris, and on arriving there put up at the inn where they had stopped on the occasion of their first visit.

"We must be careful," Malcolm said, "how we stir out until we know how things stand. The first thing to do is to find out whether the regiment is still in Paris."

This they were not long in doing, as their host was able to inform them at once that it had left the capital several months before, and on comparing dates they found that its departure had followed within a day or two that of their own flight from Paris.

"It was no doubt meant as a punishment," Ronald said, "on Colonel Hume for acting as my second in that affair with the duke. I hope that no further ill befell him."

His mind was set easy on this score by the news that Colonel Hume had accompanied his regiment. On asking after Marshal Saxe they learned that he was away on the frontier, where he had been carrying on the war with great success, Antwerp, Mons, Namur, and Charleroi all having been captured.

The king was in person with the army. This being the case Ronald saw that it was of no use remaining in Paris, as he was without friend or protector there, and he dared not rejoin his regiment until he learned whether the king's anger was as hot as ever. He therefore started at once with Malcolm and travelled down to La Grenouille.

It was a joyful meeting between him and his parents, who were in the greatest anxiety respecting him, for although he had written several times, communication was uncertain owing to the war, the only chance of sending letters being by such French vessels as arrived at Scottish ports after running the gauntlet with English cruisers. Some of these had been captured on the way back, and only two of Ronald's letters had arrived safely. The last of these had been written a few days after the battle of Falkirk, and Ronald had then stated that he no longer had any hope of the final success of the expedition. They had received the news of the defeat at Culloden, and had since passed nearly three months of painful suspense, relieved only by the arrival of Ronald himself. He found his mother looking well and happy; his father had somewhat recovered from his rheumatism, and looked a younger man by some years than when he saw him last.

"He will recover fast now," the countess said; "but he has worried about you night and day, Ronald. I hope that you will stay with us for a time. We have seen so little of you yet."

Ronald learned that a few days after his flight an officer had appeared at the chateau with the royal order for his arrest, and it was from him that his parents had first learned the news of his duel with the Duke of Chateaurouge and its result.

"I could hardly believe my ears, Ronald," his father said; "to think that my son, scarce a man yet, should have killed in fair fight one of the first duellists in France. It seemed almost incredible. Malcolm told me that you were a first rate swordsman, but this seemed extraordinary indeed. The officer remained here for three days, and then, convinced that you had not made in this direction, left us. A day or two afterwards we received the letter you wrote us from Nantes, saying that you were starting for Scotland with the prince. I grumbled sorely over my rheumatism, I can tell you, which prevented my drawing my sword once more for the Stuarts; but it was no use my thinking of it."

"No, indeed," the countess said; "and I can tell you, Ronald, that had he been ever so well I should not have let him go. After being separated from one's husband for sixteen years one is not going to let him run off to figure as a knight errant at his pleasure."

"Your friend Colonel Hume wrote to us," the colonel said with a smile at his wife's word, "giving us details of the duel, and speaking of your conduct in the highest terms. He said that at present the king was furious; but that he hoped in time he would get over it. Colonel Hume had seen Marshal Saxe, who had promised on the first opportunity to speak to the king, and to open his eyes to the character of his late favourite, and to tell him of the attempts which the duke had made to prevent the royal orders for our release being carried out, and to remove you by assassination. Two months ago he wrote again to us from Antwerp, which had just fallen, saying that Marshal Saxe had bid him tell us that the king was in a much more favourable disposition, and that he had taken the opportunity when his majesty was in a good humour to tell him the whole circumstances of your journey with the orders for our release, and that in consequence the king had made other inquiries respecting the late duke, and had acknowledged that he had been greatly deceived as to his character. At the same time, as your name had been by the king's order removed from the list of officers of the Scottish Dragoons immediately after the duel, he recommended that should you return to France you should not put yourself in the king's way or appear at all in public for the present.

"'The marshal,' Colonel Hume wrote, 'has made your affair a personal matter, and he, as is his habit in war, will persevere until he succeeds. His reputation and influence are higher than ever, and are daily rising; be assured that when the campaign is over, and he reaps all the honours to which he is entitled, he will push your claim as before.'"

In the first week in October the suspense from which they had suffered as to the fate of Prince Charles was relieved by the news that on the 29th of September he had safely landed at the little port of Roscoff near Morlaix. He made his way to Paris, and Ronald, accompanied by Malcolm, took horse at once and rode there to pay his respects to the prince, and congratulate him on his escape. The prince received him with great warmth and cordiality, and from his own lips Ronald learned the story of his adventures.

He had, eight days after Culloden, embarked for the cluster of islets to which the common name of Long Island is applied. After wandering from place to place and suffering greatly from hunger, he gained South Uist, where his wants were relieved by Clanranald. The English, suspecting or learning that he was there, landed two thousand men on the island, and commenced an active search for him. He must have been detected had not Flora Macdonald--stepdaughter of a captain in a militia regiment which formed part of the troops who had landed--upon being appealed to by Lady Clanranald, nobly undertaken to save him.

She obtained from her stepfather a passport to proceed to Skye with a manservant and a maid. Charles was dressed in female clothes, and passed as Betty Bourk, while a faithful Highlander, Neil M'Eachan, acted as her servant. They started at night in an open boat, and disembarked in Skye. Skye was ever a hostile country, as its chief, Sir Alexander Macdonald, who had at first wavered, was now a warm supporter of the Hanoverians, and was with the Duke of Cumberland. Nevertheless Flora appealed to his wife, Lady Margaret, a daughter of the Earl of Eglinton, and informed her that her attendant was Prince Charles in disguise. Lady Margaret nobly responded to her appeal. Her own house was full of militia officers, and she intrusted Charles to the charge of Macdonald of Kingsburgh, her husband's kinsman and factor, who took the party to his house.

The next day Charles took leave of Flora Macdonald with warm expressions of gratitude, and passed over to the Isle of Rasay, in the disguise of a male servant. Thence he made his way to the mainland, where on landing he was compelled to lie in concealment for two days cooped up within a line of sentries. After many dangers he took refuge in a mountain cave inhabited by seven robbers, who treated him with the greatest kindness, and supplied his wants for the three weeks he remained with them. After many other adventures he joined his faithful adherents Cluny and Locheil, who were in hiding in a retreat on the side of Mount Benalder, and here he lived in comparative comfort until he heard that two French vessels under the direction of Colonel Warren of Dillon's regiment had anchored in Lochnanuagh.

Travelling by night he made his way to that place, and embarked on the 20th of September, attended by Locheil, Colonel Roy Stuart, and about a hundred other fugitives who had learned of the arrival of the French vessels. It was almost precisely the spot at which he had disembarked fourteen months before. A fog concealed the vessel as she passed through the British fleet lying to intercept her, and they reached Roscoff after a nine days' voyage.

Such was the tale which Prince Charles told to Ronald. He had after Culloden entirely recovered his high spirits, and had borne all his fatigues and hardships with the greatest cheerfulness and good humour, making light of hunger, fatigue, and danger. Ronald only remained two days in Paris, and then returned home.

In October the campaign of Flanders ended with the complete defeat of Prince Charles of Lorraine at Rancaux, and Marshal Saxe returned to Paris, where he was received with enthusiasm by the population. The royal residence of Chambord was granted him for life, and he was proclaimed marshal general of the king's armies. A fortnight later Colonel Leslie received a letter from him, saying that he had received his majesty's command that he with the countess and his son should present themselves in Paris, and that he was happy to say that the king's disposition was most favourable. They set off at once. On their arrival there they called upon Marshal Saxe, who greeted the colonel as an old friend, and refused to listen to the warm expression of gratitude of Leslie and the countess.

"Say nothing about it, madam," he exclaimed. "Your son won my heart, and I was only too glad to be of service to him and my old comrade here. What is the use of a man winning victories if he cannot lend a helping hand to his friends!"

The next day they went down to Versailles, where Marshal Saxe presented them to the king in a private audience. Louis received them graciously.

"I fear, countess, that you and your husband have been treated with some harshness; but our royal ear was deceived by one in whom we had confidence. Your husband and yourself were wrong in marrying without the consent and against the will of your father, and such marriages cannot be permitted; but at the request of Marshal Saxe, who has done so much for France that I cannot refuse anything he asks, I have now consented to pardon and overlook the past, and have ordered my chancellor to prepare an order reinstating you in all the possessions and estates of the countess, your mother. I hope that I shall often see you together with your husband and son, both of whom have done good service as soldiers of France, at my court; and now that I see you," he said with a gracious smile, "I cannot but feel how great a loss our court has suffered by your long absence from it."

Upon leaving the king's private chamber and entering the great audience hall Colonel Hume came up and grasped the hand of his old friend, and was introduced by him to his wife; while many of the courtiers, who were either connections or friends of the family of the countess, also gathered round them, for the news that she was restored to royal favour had spread quickly. The countess knew how small was the real value of such advances, but she felt that it was best for her husband and son's sake to receive them amicably. For a few weeks they remained in Paris, taking part in the brilliant fetes which celebrated the success of the French arms, and they then retired to the handsome chateau which was now the property of the countess.

Here they lived quietly for two years, making occasional visits to Paris. At the end of that time Ronald received a letter from Andrew Anderson, to whom he had written several times since his return to France. He told him that he had just heard that Glenlyon and the rest of the property which had been confiscated after the rising of 1715 was for sale. It had been bestowed upon a neighbouring chief, who had been active in the Hanoverian cause. He was now dead without leaving issue, and his wife, an English lady, was anxious to dispose of the property and return to England.

"I do not know whether your father is disposed to buy back his estates," Andrew wrote, "but I hear that a general amnesty will very shortly be issued to all who took part in the insurrection, saving only certain notorious persons. The public are sick of bloodshed. There have been upwards of eighty trials and executions, besides the hundreds who were slaughtered in the Highlands. Besides this, thousands have been transported. But public opinion is now so strong, and persons of all shades of politics are so disgusted with the brutal ferocity which has been shown, that it is certain government will ere long be compelled to pass an act of amnesty. In the meantime, if it should be your father's wish to purchase the property, I can buy it in my name. The priced asked is very low. The income arising from it is stated to be about four hundred a year, and four thousand pounds will be accepted for it. I understand that as the late owner took no part in the insurrection, and joined the Duke of Cumberland when he came north, the property is in good condition and the clansmen have escaped the harrying which befell all those who sided with Charles Stuart."

Ronald at once laid the letter before his father, who, after reading it through, passed it, without a word, to the countess.

"You would like to return to Scotland?" she asked quietly, when she read it. "Do not hesitate to tell me, dear, if you would. It is no matter to me whether we live there or here, so long as I have you and Ronald with me."

Colonel Leslie was silent.

"For Ronald's sake," she went on, "perhaps it would be better so. You are both of opinion that the cause of the Stuarts is lost for ever, and he is determined that he will never again take part in any rising. He does not care again to enter the French army, nor, indeed, is there any reason why Scotchmen should do so, now that they no longer look for the aid of the King of France to set the Stuarts on the English throne. I myself have no ties here. My fifteen years of seclusion have separated me altogether from my family, and although they are willing enough to be civil now, I cannot forget that all those years they did nothing towards procuring our liberty. The king has so far given way that he has restored me my mother's estates, but it was only because he could not refuse Marshal Saxe, and he does not like French lands to be held by strangers; therefore I feel sure, that were I to ask his permission to sell my estates and to retire with you to Scotland he would at once grant my request."

"No, Amelie, it would not be fair to accept your generous offer."

"But it would be no sacrifice," she urged. "I have little reason to love France, and I can assure you I should be just as happy in your country as in my own."

"But it would be exile," the colonel said.

"No more exile than you and Ronald are suffering here. Besides, I suppose we should get as many comforts in Scotland as here in France. Of course our estates here will fetch a sum many times larger than that which would purchase Glenlyon, and we need not live all our time among the mountains you tell me of, but can go sometimes to Edinburgh or even to London. Even if you did not wish it, I should say it would be far better to do so for Ronald's sake. You have lived so long in France that you may have become a Frenchman; but it is not so with Ronald."

It was not until two or three days later that the discussion came to an end and the countess had her way. Colonel Leslie had resisted stoutly, but his heart beat at the thought of returning to the home of his youth and ending his days among the clansmen who had followed him and his fathers before him. Ronald had taken no part whatever in the debate, but his mother read in his eyes the delight which the thought of returning to Scotland occasioned him. As soon as this was settled they went to Paris, and as the countess had foreseen, the king was pleased at once to give his consent to her disposing of her lands on his approval of the purchaser.

No difficulty was experienced on this score, as a noble whose lands adjoined her own offered at once to purchase them. As soon as this was arranged instructions were sent to Andrew to purchase not only the Glenlyon property, but the other estates of its late owner.

In due time a letter was received from Andrew saying that he had arranged for the purchase of the whole for the sum of thirteen thousand pounds, and the money was at once sent over through a Dutch banking house. Very shortly afterwards, at the end of 1747, the act of general amnesty was passed, and as Ronald's name was not among those excluded from its benefits they at once prepared to return to Scotland. The journey was facilitated by the fact that shortly after the passing of the act, peace was concluded between England and France.

Accompanied by Malcolm, Colonel Leslie, the countess, and Ronald sailed for Scotland. The colonel and his wife remained in Edinburgh while Ronald and Malcolm went to Glasgow, where Andrew had in readiness all the papers transferring the estates purchased in his name to Colonel Leslie, who shortly afterwards journeyed north with his wife and son and took possession of his ancestral home amid the enthusiastic delight of the clansmen, who had never ceased to regret the absence of him whom they considered as their rightful chief.

There is little more to tell. Colonel Leslie lived but a few years after returning home, and Ronald then succeeded him as Leslie of Glenlyon. He had before this married the daughter of a neighbouring gentleman, and passed his time between Glenlyon and Edinburgh, varied by an occasional visit to London.

The countess never regretted her native land, but, happy in the affection of her son and daughter in law and their children, lived happily with them until nearly the end of the century. Malcolm remained the faithful and trusty friend of the family; and his brother and his wife were occasionally persuaded to pay a visit to Glenlyon, where their kindness to Ronald as a child was never forgotten. Happily the rising of '45 was the last effort on behalf of the Stuarts. Scotland accepted the decision as final, and the union between the two countries became close and complete. Henceforth Scotchmen went no longer to fight in the armies of France, but took service in that of their own country, and more than one of Ronald's grandsons fought stoutly in Spain under Wellington.

The End.

www.ingramcontent.com/pod-product-compliance
Lightning Source LLC
LaVergne TN
LVHW081352090125
800893LV00008B/298